The World's Best Short Stories

Anthology & Criticism

Volume VI

Horror and Science Fiction

The World's Best Series

The World's Best Short Stories

I. *Short Story Masters: Early 19th Century*
II. *Short Story Masters: Late 19th & Early 20th Centuries*
III. *Famous Stories*
IV. *Fables and Tales*
V. *Mystery and Detection*
VI. *Horror and Science Fiction*

Forthcoming:
VII. *Characters*
VIII. *Places*
IX. *Cultures*
X. *Research and Reference: Criticism and Indexes*

The World's Best Poetry

Foundation Volumes I-X

Supplements:
I. *Twentieth Century English and American Verse, 1900-1929*
II. *Twentieth Century English and American Verse, 1930-1950*
III. *Critical Companion*
IV. *Minority Poetry of America*
V. *Twentieth Century Women Poets*
VI. *Twentieth Century African and Latin American Verse*
VII. *Twentieth Century Asian Verse*

CoreFiche: *World's Best Drama*

Microfiche with companion reference

The World's Best Short Stories

Anthology & Criticism

Volume VI

Horror and Science Fiction

Stories by Bloch, Campbell, Etchison, Jacobs, M.R. James, Le Fanu, Leiber, Lovecraft, Stevenson, Tieck; & Asimov, Bradbury, Clarke, Philip K. Dick, Lem, Niven, Pollack, Mary Shelley, Cordwainer Smith, Sturgeon, Verne, Wells

With Critical Appreciations by
Thomas F. Monteleone and Laurence M. Janifer

Prepared by
The Editorial Board

Roth Publishing, Inc.
Great Neck, New York

ISBN 0-89609-312-3
ISBN for 10 Volume Set 0-89609-400-6
Library of Congress Catalog Card Number 89-60440

Manufactured in the U.S.A.

Contents

Horror

Science Fiction

Preface

The World's Best Short Stories is designed to give both the serious student and the general reader a large selection and broad range of stories from around the world. Its ten volumes organize the stories into seven reader-friendly groupings:

Short Story Masters (Volumes I and II)
Famous Stories (Volume III)
Fables and Tales (Volume IV)
Mystery and Detection (Volume V)
Horror and Science Fiction (Volume VI)
Characters (Volume VII)
Places (Volume VIII)
Cultures (Volume IX)

Volume X is a research and reference guide and includes a cumulative index to all the volumes.

The arrangement of the stories suggests the multiple approaches for using these volumes. *Short Story Masters* focuses on the author; it contains stories that demonstrate the development of the short story as a conscious art form. *Famous Stories* is the volume to go to for well-known stories by authors who may or may not themselves be well-known. *Fables and Tales* includes fairy tales and other short non-realistic literature, as well as tales that are ancestors of the short story form. Volumes V and VI contain genre fiction; they act as a kind of counterpart to *Short Story Masters.* Whereas *Masters* places the short story in the tradition of an evolving art, these genre-centered volumes put it at the disposal of the general reader and the popular imagination. *Mystery and Detection* makes the case for a genre that has been continuously popular and critically treated since Poe, while *Horror and Science Fiction* looks at two different styles of fantastic literature—one finding its elements in the supernatural, the other in the superscientific.

The later volumes contain stories that are remarkable for a salient feature. The stories in *Characters* are portrait studies: their primary function is to examine the character of the hero or heroine. *Places* compiles stories that evoke a setting in a way that is memorable and important to the being of the story. Finally, *Cultures* uses ethnicity as its backdrop. It carries stories that are informed by their cultural setting.

The organization, variety, and breadth of **The World's Best Short Stories** makes it a unique anthology collection that can be used for study or read for pleasure.

Introduction

This and the preceding volume of **The World's Best Short Stories** focus on genre fiction. This volume contains Horror and Science Fiction, genres that introduce *super*natural or *supra*natural elements, respectively, to stories that in other ways seem realistic enough. Its companion, Volume V, contains stories of Mystery and Detection, stories that are firmly grounded in the realistic tradition of literature but of a type: there is a problem that needs to be solved; sometimes a detective is required.

These four types—mystery, detection, horror, and science fiction—are not intended to stand in for all of genre literature. There are many genres not covered in these volumes, including adventure, the western, romance, historical romance, and fantasy, as well as emerging ones, like steampunk, splatterpunk, and cyberpunk. Another two books could have been devoted to these types. We have chosen not to represent them as genres (though individual stories appear elsewhere in this short story series) for several reasons, not the least of which is space. Additionally, the paucity of short stories in some genres, like historical romance and fantasy, ruled them out. Other genres simply do not have the variety, tradition, and acceptance that mystery, detective, horror, and science fiction have.

The four genres represented in Volumes V and VI, then, are strong genres with an equally strong contribution from the short story form. They have been written about by scholars and argued over by fans. Even then, the issue so often comes back to first principles. What is a genre?

An Historical Definition of Genre

The American Heritage Dictionary defines a genre as "a category of literature marked by a distinctive style, form, or content." This definition falls short, for genre literature is also, always, popular literature, read by a general readership that may not even be consciously aware of the genre as a concept.

Like the short story itself, the genre was an invention of the early nineteenth century, and was produced to meet some of the same needs. An increasingly literate populace had made the mass production and distribution of periodicals a viable venture for entrepreneurs. Throughout the better part of the 1800's, these periodicals provided entertainment for the growing middle classes. Toward the end of the century, when magazines such as *The Strand* (which published the Sherlock Holmes stories) and *Graham's* lowered their prices to make themselves accessible to an even wider readership, there was fierce competition to acquire the stories of proven and popular authors, like H.G. Wells or W.W. Jacobs, to help sell the magazines. In the days before copyright, editors would ask for stories based on previously published material or require stories similar in tone and subject matter to that of the popular authors of the day. Publishing historian Sam Moscowitz tells of brief manias for cannibal plant stories or helpful-insect tales that proliferated in the magazines at the turn of the century. Some of these stories edged on the plagiaristic (like the "sequel" one author wrote to *The War of the Worlds*), but mostly it was the tone, not the subject matter, that was copied.

Certain authors were celebrated for their talents, and magazines capitalized on their fame. Stories were trumpeted as being a "scientific romance in the style of Mr. Verne," or "a mystery in the manner of Mr. Arthur Conan Doyle." This was only one step away from assigning a genre label.

By the 1930's, it was feasible for a publisher to devote an entire magazine to one genre. These magazines, printed on a cheap woodpulp paper (thus the name "pulps"), gave rise to some of the greatest writers the genres have known. H.P. Lovecraft and Robert

Bloch saw their early stories published in *Weird Tales,* while the legendary John W. Campbell guided the early careers of such giants as Isaac Asimov and Theodore Sturgeon in *Astounding*, and *Black Mask* started its own school of detective fiction by publishing the work of Dashiell Hammett.

The pulps died out in the 1950's, to be replaced by digest-sized magazines like *Ellery Queen's Mystery Magazine* and *The Magazine of Fantasy and Science Fiction* (occasionally joined by larger-sized efforts like the horror-themed *Twilight Zone* magazine). But by that time, the genres had become firmly entrenched in the mass culture. Presses specializing in specific genres (most importantly Arkham House, the training ground for Ramsey Campbell, and the Mysterious Press) produced works geared toward a growing group of fans.

While the four genres represented here have been treated by critics and academicians as "serious" literature, they are foremost popular literature. That's the basic ingredient: a genre tale must entertain. Whether it does so by frightening us or infusing us with a sense of wonder is irrelevent—the impulse to amuse the reader is paramount (although there are some writers, like Philip K. Dick and Ross Macdonald, who have additional things on their agendas), and that is how a genre tale must be judged. While the style, form, and content of the stories in these two volumes vary greatly, all of them can be said to do one thing, and do it well. Every one of them entertains.

Horror

Critical Appreciation

Since I've avoided the angst of a grown-up-people's job for most of my life by being a fiction writer, I thought it might be fitting to liven up this introduction by telling you a story or two.

The first story is about me when I was just a little kid. I guess I was maybe five years old, but I could have been six.

Listen:

Down the block from our house there was a very large manse, which had been a summer home for wealthy people in the previous century, and was at the time the home of the mother of a '50's movie star named Dorothy Lamour. Not that we lived in a posh neighborhood—rather, this old place kind of stood out on our block like the hood ornament on a '38 Lasalle. Anyway, part of the property which held the house was an acre or so of trees and undergrowth we kids called "The Woods," and the whole bunch of us used to play in its honeysuckle and poison-ivied shadows for endless hours. The leading edge of this woods, where it touched the shoulder of the street was a strip of verge and mud-fossils of tire tread-marks and scraps of roadside debris. Like most kids I loved picking through the debris to find pieces of magic: fountain pens, liquor bottle "miniatures," the occasional "pinup" magazine or calendar page, and even broken or discarded toys.

So there I was one day walking along the edge of The Woods, and I found this discarded comic book that hadn't yet been beaten by the rain and fused into a hard, unreadable slab. I can't remember the title because I know I hadn't learned how to read at the time, but it was probably one of the old EC comics like *Tales from the Crypt* or *Vault of Horror* or something like that.

It doesn't matter, really, because I'll never forget the cover (and if I really wanted to do some research I could get a real comics freak to check out the title for me). The cover was an illustration of this guy in a barber's chair. The guy had this look of abject terror on his face as he looked at a barber looming over him with a wickedly gleaming straight razor. All you could see of the barber was the back of his head—a bald guy with a little tonsured monk's fringe around the back and over the ears. Just this little tableaux looked scary enough, but the worst part for me was an added detail: the mirror behind the guy in the chair.

Because when you looked in the mirror you could see the barber's face, only it wasn't really a face...*it was a skull!*

Yeah, a skull. Which for me was a very scary thing. It was, I think the first time, I had been made to realize that there was a skeleton underneath our skins, that everybody, even *me,* had a grim, scary *skull* under our faces. Ray Bradbury wrote a story called "Skeleton" which deals with the same self-realization, and I've often wondered if the story had its origins in a similar moment of childhood *satori* for Ray.

So picture the scene. A five-year-old Tommy, standing by the side of the road, staring at this lurid EC comics cover and being unable to move, unable to stop *staring* at the damned thing. Something was happening to me as I remained motionless and transfixed. Something that changed me, and made me a mutant, a dreamer. It was that very instant when I became hooked forever on things outré, bizarre, and all the stuff which lurched and shambled off the known paths of knowledge and imagination.

I mean, I was *scared* by this tawdry comic, truly shaken to the five-year-old marrow in my bones, but I was also attracted to it. I brought the comic home and hid it in my room, knowing instinctively that my mother would trash it if she ever saw. I wasn't so sure about my father because he loved to talk about things like ghosts and flying saucers and listening to creepy shows like *Inner Sanctum* and *Lights Out* on the radio. I sensed a kindred spirit in my father, although I wasn't certain enough to trust him at that early age.

So the comic stayed hidden and I would pull it out at night and look at the interior panels with a flashlight after I was supposed to be asleep. I couldn't read the stories very well, if at all, but the drawings were horrific enough—I have vivid memories of skeletal corpses clawing their way out of the ground (an overly familiar *shtick* in the old EC books) to exact revenge on those who killed them. Those panels surged with power, like lightning in a bottle, and I felt it tingle through me as I flipped through the pages. It was the first time I'd been made aware of mortality, of the finality and the corruption of death. I realized that I too would one day die, and the essential truth of it lay on my five-year-old psyche like an anvil.

But therein lies the reason for my fascination with the literature of the darkly fantastic and the horrific—a morbid curiosity and interest in Death. The Final Door, the Dark Passage, the Grim Reaper. Whatever you want to call it, it is the common denominator of our lives; the single intrigue which no one can ultimately ignore. If this essay has any theme at all, it turns upon this simple observation. We like to read horror stories because they allow us to vicariously explore what awaits us all. Maybe we have some unspoken, unconscious hope that by stepping through the looking glass of fiction to walk for awhile upon the grim landscape of death, it may shake loose some of its mystery and power to terrify us.

Stephen King addresses this issue in his marvelous examination of why we like to be scared, *Danse Macabre.* He offers the notion of the "shape beneath the sheet," which refers to our need to lift the edge of the sheet which conceals what *just might be* a body, or even a monster, laid out on a covered slab. It is the door left ajar leading into darkness; it is the black mouth of an open cave; the heavy rag of night which hangs just beyond the glow of a campfire; the oddly configured shape which lurks in the shadowed corner of a room and simply *refuses* to resolve itself into anything familiar.

But there's more to it than that. I don't think it's enough to simply have an interest in death. Sure, that might be enough to attract at least once, but what is it that makes us keep staggering back for more? For us to be drawn to the tale of horror or the supernatural over and over, there must be more. There must be an enduring appeal which gets us hooked, makes us keep reading the stuff.

But that's not to say I know what it is...

I can only offer a few guesses and reveal what works on me, and hope that maybe we're talking about some of the same things.

When written well, horror and suspense literature evokes an emotional response from its readers. This can range from a mild sensation of *unease* across the spectrum to abject *repulsion.* We're talking simple scared-of-the-dark and funny-noises-at-night all the way to mind-numbing nihilist rejection. We're talking about a literature which has the ability to involve us on a visceral, as well as psychological level. We're talking about a literature that possesses an innate *power* to hammer out a flamenco dance on our imaginations and fire up a blowtorch under our phobias.

I don't know about you, but any writing that can do that to me is writing that's going to get my respect and attention.

The other reason I like a good horror story is strong characterization. Unlike mysteries which are heavy on plot, or science fiction which relies on startling premises or clever ideas, the tale of horror leans more in the direction of psychologically intriguing characters. From its earliest beginnings, as written by Le Fanu, Poe, Bierce, de Maupassant, and the rest of the classic writers, the tale of horror always centered around the tormented psyche of a solitary character.

And I think that pretty much sums it up without a lot of scholarly ramadoola. We like horror stories because they make us *feel* things, and because they're usually about fascinating people—people like us. There's probably a third reason why we like this kind of literature, but it concerns reasons more nebulous and therefore targetable by the skeptics and the more literally-minded among you. But, since I'm in a good mood today, I'll offer it up to you—along with a story to illustrate my point (Remember, I promised you a story or two... well, here's no. 2).

I was 14 years old, just starting my freshman year at a Jesuit high school. It was a very traditional place, on a campus that rivalled the scope and beauty of lots of small colleges.

The main building housed a huge library defined by vaulted alcoves, polished mahogany wainscotting, 10 foot leaded windows, long reading tables with greenglass shades, and endless shelves of books. During the first week at the school, they put all the freshman through "orientation," wherein they get you familiar with all the *shticks* at the school. One of the orientation exercises was to spend a few hours wandering around the library, getting familiar with everything. It was an interesting way to get us freshman involved with the process of discovery and learning.

So, here I was, 14 years old, wearing my sport coat and tie, meandering among the alcoves and stacks and carrels, reading this spine and that, pulling down titles that sounded interesting, learning the locations of various categories of reference materials. One of the orientation assignments included checking out a book to read for a report, and I was eager to find something that would be a kick to read.

And here's the weird part: I'm surrounded by thousands of old books, no dust jackets on most of them, no pictures or lurid covers to catch my adolescent eye—just a lot of cloth bindings and goldstamped spines looking very classical—and I paused as my gaze settles, most randomly it seemed, upon a title called *The Complete Stories of Edgar Allan Poe.* Now, believe it or not, I'd never heard of Poe. Nobody'd ever recommended him to me and other than the comics and piles of science fiction and mystery paperbacks that littered my room, we didn't have many books in our house. The name "Poe" meant nothing to the *tabula rasa* that was my puerile mind.

And yet, I reached out and pulled the book from its niche...as though drawn to it by some arcane force.

I can still remember the mental jolt as I read down the table of contents. You know what I'm talking about: "The Black Cat," "The Pit and the Pendulum," "The Murders in the Rue Morgue," "The Facts in the Case of M. Valdemar," "The Tell-Tale Heart," and on and on. The story titles seemed to glow like barbed neon signs, leaping off the page to hook themselves in my imagination. I can remember thinking something like *this dude sounds pretty weird—my kind of stuff...*

And so I checked out the book, and spent the next few nights reading into the middle of the night, lost in the dark fantasies of a brilliant, but tormented soul. It was a simple and pure joy that I haven't experienced very often in life. I'd *discovered* Poe. In the same serendipitous way of all great discoveries, and it was like his work was *mine,* and nobody else knew about him. I can remember turning my friends onto Poe and mentioning to my freshman English instructor that I happened onto this book of great short stories by a guy name Poe and asking him if he'd ever heard of the writer.

"Slightly," said my teacher with a smile.

So what's the point of this personal, although highly fascinating, aside? Simply this: it's hard for me to accept that I pulled down that book of Poe stories totally by *accident.* I mean, out of tens of thousands of books I could have stumbled upon, I just *happened* to have selected a collection of what may be the most seminal and influential group of tales in the history of literature, and surely in the history of darkly imaginative (horror, suspense, etc.) fiction...?

Yeah, sure.

Somehow, I just can't buy it. And that's my other reason why I think we like to read this horror stuff—we are *drawn* to it by means beyond our power to understand. Some of us are mutants, you see. We want to read this stuff and a small percentage of our lot are compelled to actually *write* it. And as such beings who carry the gene for Darkness, we have an unconscious sensory power which helps us locate the good stuff and savor it the way one might sip a fine vintage in a cool cellar.

(Not very scholarly, I know, but hey, if they wanted Northrop Frye, they shouldn't have asked me to introduce this section.)

And speaking of jobs, part of mine was to introduce the stories in this volume by means of saying a few words about each one. I'm going to do that in the paragraphs that follow, but first I've got to confess that as steeped in this literature of the horrific as I am, there were actually a few stories in here that I'd not only never read, but had never even *heard* of. Just for fun, you might want to try to guess which ones they might be.

Okay, let's go.

"The Bride of the Grave" by Johann Ludwig Tieck is an interesting piece if for no other reason than its age. Definitely one of the older horror tales I've ever read. "Bride..." is also interesting because it plays around with several of our strongest emotions—love, fear, and good old lust. As I said earlier, horror literature is concerned with eliciting an emotional response from its audience, and Tieck's story, despite the overwrought prose and the predictable ending, succeeds at least on that level.

"The White Cat of Drumgunnoil" by Joseph Sheridan Le Fanu is one of those "harbinger of death" stories which has become a cliche for serious readers of the horror genre—a fact which robs this tale of its implicit power and sense of overwhelming dread. I can remember (surprise!) an EC comic story about a deckhand on a passenger liner who has the ability to predict the impending death of those around him by seeing the doomed person's skull shining briefly through the flesh of his face. The climax occurs when he looks in the mirror one morning and (gee, wow!) sees his own skull a-shining through, and in what is supposed to be a real double-whammy, the reader discovers in the final panel that the sailor is a crewman on the (yawn) Titanic (!). At the time it was written, "The White Cat..." was not a cliche; rather, it was probably the progenitor of all of this "type" of story.

And what can I say about "The Strange Case of Dr. Jekyll and Mr. Hyde" that hasn't been harped over *ad infinitum* (I told you I went to a Jesuit high school, didn't I?)? Probably not much, but that won't keep me from offering up a few choice observations. The first of which is a little-known fact about the original manuscript of this novella: when Stevenson first completed it, he decided it was such a malevolent piece of writing that the world would be better off without it, and in a fit of raging, self-censoring morality, he tossed it into the fire. Afterwards, the author could not get the story out of his mind, and realized the only solution was to *rewrite* it, which he did. This may be one of those apocryphal stories, but even if it is, I like it a lot. And I like the novella even more. "Jekyll and Hyde" is a masterful example of how characterization remains essential to the successful horror story. It is a remarkably modern, incisive, and realistic examination of the mind of a solitary character who acquires a unique perspective on both his own nature and the world at large.

M.R. James is best known as perhaps the finest practitioner of the traditional English ghost/supernatural story. His "Casting the Runes" is a great example of how an impeccable prose style can enliven even the most transparent and predictable horror tale. I think the charm of "...Runes" is how James reveals, almost from the very beginning, the identity of the villain and the nature of the evil which gives the story its dramatic tension—and still maintains the reader's interest.

The classic themes examined in the "The Monkey's Paw" by W.W. Jacobs may seem painfully obvious to modern readers, but friends, you have to realize this story is what you call a real *classic*. This one emphasizes everything I said about eliciting an emotional response from the reader. The scene which unfolds after the second wish is an unforgettable blend of love and apprehension and, ultimately, pure dread. That the story lurches forward on a pair of didactic hind-legs, offering us axiomatic lessons which seem tired and shopworn, does not diminish the raw emotional power of parents grieving for a lost child and the desperation they feel.

"The Outsider" by H. P. Lovecraft is another one you can call a *classic* and get no arguments. Its prose is a modern version of Poe's; its imagery full of neo-Victorian excess; and its final climactic scene one of those in-your-face revelations that lingers in your thoughts for a long, long time.

Fritz Leiber is probably *the* premiere fantasist of the twentieth century. His story, "The Girl with the Hungry Eyes," is considered to be the prototype for all the other "dangerous and seductive" female stories ever written. This story has directly influenced other writers' attempts to plumb the dark pool of mystery that is the essence of *female-ness*—from Harlan Ellison's "Nedra at *f*:5.6" to my own novel of the lamia, *Lyrica.* Leiber showed us all how to do it.

And speaking of serial killers (we weren't? Well let's start now...), Jack the Ripper has to be the archetype for all the others. There is a mystique surrounding the butcher of Whitechapel that transcends all the rest of the mass murderers. I have no idea how many books and stories have been written about Jack, but I'd bet it's an impressive number. Robert Bloch has long been fascinated with the Ripper Mythos, and he's contributed to its corpus with several striking tales, the most famous of which is "Yours Truly, Jack the Ripper." The story turns on several elements, one of which is the time when it was written. If read as a contemporary tale, the dates do not hold up, but it is so clever and so smoothly executed that it doesn't matter when you reach the final line.

But enough of the classic stuff. Two of the most successful horror writers working today—that is, in the '90's—are Ramsey Campbell and Dennis Etchison. Most anthologies of modern dark fantasy contain work by these two writers. Campbell's "The Chimney" is a tightly focused character study written in the first person, reminiscent of Lovecraft, but with a sharper edge and a more urban setting. Campbell's trademark of a gradually escalating sense of complete and utter terror can be found as the driving force in this early story about the horrors of childhood.

Dennis Etchison's "The Dead Line" has perhaps the most chilling, most arresting, opening line to a short story I've ever read. If you can't resist that kind of hype, go ahead and flip to the beginning of the story and check it out for yourself. (It's okay—I'll wait...) If you surrended to the compulsion to read more than that single sentence, I don't blame you. Etchison's tale is a perfect representative of the contemporary horror story. Gone are the traditional symbols and images—the vampires and werewolves and ghosts and other boogeymen—to be replaced by far more modern dreadnaughts of technology, biology, and the inner space of the human psyche.

And there you have it, friends, a quick but trenchant assessment of the contents of this anthology. I've avoided passing critical judgement on, or real, academic analysis of, the assembled stories because reading is such a personal, subjective experience. It would be better for all concerned if each one of you just flipped the page and got started. There are plenty of shapes beneath plenty of sheets. We just need a few of you to get close enough to maybe grab the leading edge of the nearest shroud, and lift it up just a little bit so we can see, and then...

—Thomas F. Monteleone

The Bride of the Grave

Johann Ludwig Tieck

Johann Ludwig Tieck (1773-1853) was born in Berlin. At an early age, Tieck was very interested in theater and politics. When he was 18, he was hired by Freidrich Rambach as a ghost writer, providing the endings for horror novels. In 1792, he entered the University of Halle before transferring to Gottingen. Three years later, Tieck began contributing sketches and tales to Freidrich Nicolai's *Ostrich Feathers.* His first novel, *The History of Mr. William Lovell,* was published over a period of time from 1795-96. In 1796, his translation of *The Tempest* cemented his reputation as a Shakespeare scholar. His *Folk Fairy Tales,* published in 1797 under the pen-name "Peter Leberecht," acted as an inspiration for the German Romantic movement. In 1798, the year he married Amalie Alberti, Tieck began to suffer from severe rheumatoid arthritis. He began a translation of *Don Quixote* the following year. At the turn of the century, Tieck began wandering Germany in search of steady employment, finally settling in Ziebingen as the guest of Wilhelm von Burgsdorff. While there he began *The Book About Shakespeare,* a massive project that was never finished, as was a translation of *Das Nibelungenlied.* Tieck travelled throughout Europe and England from 1811-1817, during which he collected his short stories in *The Phantasus* (1812-16). In 1819 he was appointed the Dramaturg of the Dresden Theater. Tieck began to experiment with the novella form, the most notable example of which is *The Uprising in the Cevennes Mountains* (1826). In 1837, his wife died, followed by his daughter four years later. He petitioned Fredrick William VI of Prussia for a position at the Berlin Theater, and was appointed Dramaturg in 1843. After the death of his son in 1851, Tieck lived the rest of his life alone, although he frequently met with younger authors and composers like Richard Wagner.

Tieck's reputation as the father of the German Romantics makes "The Bride of the Grave" a notable, as well as chilling, example of a genuine gothic tale.

"WILT THOU for ever sleep? Wilt thou never more awake, my beloved, but henceforth repose for ever from thy short pilgrimage on earth? O yet once again return! and bring back with thee the vivifying dawn of hope to one whose existence hath, since thy departure, been obscured by the dunnest shades. What! dumb? for ever dumb? Thy friend lamenteth, and thou heedest him not? He sheds bitter, scalding tears, and thou reposest unregarding his affliction? He is in despair, and thou no longer openest thy arms to him as an asylum from his grief? Say then, doth the paly shroud become thee better than the bridal veil? Is the chamber of the grave a warmer bed than the couch of love? Is the spectre death more welcome to thy arms than thy enamored consort? Oh! return, my beloved, return once again to this anxious disconsolate bosom." Such were the lamentations which Walter poured forth for his Brunhilda, the partner of his youthful, passionate love: thus did he bewail over her grave at the midnight hour, what time the spirit that presides in the troublous atmosphere, sends his legions of monsters through mid-air; so that their shadows, as they flit beneath the moon and across the earth, dart as wild, agitating thoughts that chase each other o'er the sinner's bosom:—thus did he lament under the tall linden trees by her grave, while his head reclined on the cold stone.

Walter was a powerful lord in Burgundy, who, in his earliest youth, had been smitten with the charms of the fair Brunhilda, a beauty far surpassing in loveliness all her rivals; for her tresses, dark as the raven face of night, streaming over her shoulders, set off to the utmost advantage the beaming lustre of her slender form, and the rich dye of a cheek whose tint was deep and brilliant as that of the western heaven: her eyes did not resemble those burning orbs whose pale glow gems the vault of night, and whose immeasurable distance fills the soul with deep thoughts of eternity, but rather as the sober beams which cheer this nether world, and which, while they enlighten, kindle the sons of earth to joy and love. Brunhilda became the wife of Walter, and both being equally enamored and devoted, they abandoned themselves to the enjoyment of a passion that rendered them reckless of aught besides, while it lulled them in a fascinating dream. Their sole apprehension was lest aught should awaken them from a delirium which they prayed might continue for ever. Yet how vain is the wish that would arrest the decrees of destiny! as well might it seek to divert the circling planets from their eternal course. Short was the duration of this frenzied passion; not that it gradually decayed and subsided into apathy, but death snatched away his blooming victim, and left Walter to a widowed couch. Impetuous, however, as was his first burst of grief, he was not inconsolable, for ere long another bride became the partner of the youthful nobleman.

Swanhilda also was beautiful: although nature had formed her charms on a very different model from those of Brunhilda. Her golden locks waved bright as the beams of morn: only when excited by some emotion of her soul did a rosy hue tinge the lily paleness of her cheek: her limbs were proportioned in the nicest symmetry, yet did they not possess that luxuriant fullness of animal life: her eye beamed eloquently, but it was with the milder radiance of a star, tranquillizing to tenderness rather than exciting to warmth. Thus formed, it was not possible that she should steep him in his former delirium, although she rendered happy his waking hours—tranquil and serious, yet cheerful, studying in all things her husband's pleasure, she restored order and comfort in his family, where her presence shed a general influence all around. Her mild benevolence tended to restrain the fiery, impetuous disposition of Walter: while at the same time her prudence recalled him in some degree from his vain, turbulent wishes, and his aspirings after unattainable enjoyments, to the duties and pleasures of actual life. Swanhilda bore her husband two children, a son and a daughter; the latter was mild and patient as her mother, well contented with her solitary sports, and even in these recreations displayed the serious turn of her character. The boy possessed his father's fiery, restless disposition, tempered, however, with the solidity of his mother. Attached by his offspring more tenderly towards their mother, Walter now lived for several years very happily: his thoughts would frequently, indeed, recur to Brunhilda, but without their former violence, merely as we dwell upon the memory of a friend of our earlier days, borne from us on the rapid current of time to a region where we know that he is happy.

But clouds dissolve into air, flowers fade, the sands of the hour-glass run imperceptibly away, and even so, do human feelings dissolve, fade, and pass away, and with them too, human happiness. Walter's inconstant breast again sighed for the ecstatic dreams of those days which he had spent with his equally romantic, enamored Brunhilda—again did she present herself to his ardent fancy in all the glow of her bridal charms, and he began to draw a parallel between the past and the present; nor did imagination, as it is wont, fail to array the former in her brightest hues, while it proportionably obscured the latter; so that he pictured to himself, the one much more rich in enjoyment, and the other, much less so than they really were. This change in her husband did not escape Swanhilda; whereupon, redoubling her attentions towards him, and her cares towards their children, she expected, by this means, to re-unite the knot that was slackened; yet the more she endeavored to regain his affections, the colder did he grow,—the more intolerable did her caresses seem, and the more continually did the image of Brunhilda haunt his thoughts. The children, whose endearments were now become indispensable to him, alone stood between the parents as genii eager to affect a reconciliation; and, beloved by them both, formed a uniting link between them. Yet, as evil can be plucked from the heart of man, only ere its root has yet struck deep, its fangs being afterwards too firm to be eradicated; so was Walter's diseased fancy too far affected to have its disorder stopped, for, in a short time, it completely tyrannized over him. Frequently of a night, instead of retiring to his consort's chamber, he repaired to Brunhilda's grave, where he murmured forth his discontent, saying: "Wilt thou sleep for ever?"

One night as he was reclining on the turf, indulging in his wonted sorrow, a sorcerer from the neighboring mountains, entered into this field of death for the purpose of gathering, for his mystic spells, such herbs as grow only from the earth wherein the dead repose, and which, as if the last production of mortality, are gifted with a powerful and supernatural influence. The sorcerer perceived the mourner, and approached the spot where he was lying.

"Wherefore, fond wretch, dost thou grieve thus, for what is now a hideous mass of mortality—mere bones, and nerves, and veins? Nations have fallen unlamented; even worlds themselves, long ere this globe of ours was created, have mouldered into nothing; nor hath any one wept over them; why then should'st thou indulge this vain affliction for a child of the dust—a being as frail as thyself, and like thee the creature but of a moment?"

Walter raised himself up:—"Let yon worlds that shine in the firmament," replied he, "lament for each other as they perish. It is true, that I who am myself clay, lament for my fellow-clay: yet is this clay impregnated with a fire,—with an essence, that none of the elements of creation possess—with love: and the divine passion, I felt for her who now sleepeth beneath sod." "Will thy complaints awaken her: or could they do so, would she not soon upbraid thee for having disturbed that repose in which she is now hushed?"

"Avaunt, cold-hearted being: thou knowest not what is love. Oh! that my tears could wash away the earthy covering that conceals her from these eyes;—that my groan of anguish could rouse her from her slumber of death!—No, she would not again seek her earthy couch."

"Insensate that thou art, and couldst thou endure to gaze without shuddering on one disgorged from the jaws of the grave? Art thou too thyself the same from whom she parted; or hath time passed o'er thy brow and left no traces there? Would not thy love rather be converted into hate and disgust?"

"Say rather that the stars would leave you firmament, that the sun will henceforth refuse to shed his beams through the heavens. Oh! that she stood once more before me;—that once again she reposed on this bosom!—how quickly should we then forget that death or time had ever stepped between us."

"Delusion! mere delusion of the brain, from heated blood, like to that which arises from the fumes of wine. It is not my wish to tempt thee;—to restore to thee thy dead; else wouldst thou soon feel that I have spoken truth."

"How! restore her to me," exclaimed Walter casting himself at the sorcerer's feet. "Oh! if thou art indeed able to effect that, grant it to my earnest supplication; if one throb of human feeling vibrates in thy bosom, let thy tears prevail with thee: restore to me my beloved; so shalt thou hereafter bless the deed, and see that it was a good work."

"A good work! a blessed deed!"—returned the sorcerer with a smile of scorn; "for me there exists nor good nor evil; since my will is always the same. Ye alone know evil, who will that which ye would not. It is indeed in my power to restore her to thee: yet, bethink thee well, whether it will prove thy weal. Consider too, how deep the abyss between life and death; across this, my power can build a bridge, but it can never fill up the frightful chasm."

Walter would have spoken, and have sought to prevail on this powerful being by fresh entreaties, but the latter prevented him, saying: "Peace! bethink thee well! and return hither to me tomorrow at midnight. Yet once more do I warn thee, 'Wake not the dead.'"

Having uttered these words, the mysterious being disappeared. Intoxicated with fresh hope, Walter found no sleep on his couch; for fancy, prodigal of her richest stores, expanded before him the glittering web of futurity; and his eye, moistened, with the dew of rapture, glanced from one vision of happiness to another. During the next day he wandered through the woods, lest wonted objects by recalling the memory of later and less happier times, might disturb the blissful idea, that he should again behold her—again fold her in his arms, gaze on her beaming brow by day, repose on her bosom at night: and, as this sole idea filled his imagination, how was it possible that the least doubt should arise; or that the warning of the mysterious old man should recur to his thoughts.

No sooner did the midnight hour approach, than he hastened before the gravefield where the sorcerer was already standing by that of Brunhilda. "Hast thou maturely considered?" enquired he.

"Oh! restore to me the object of my ardent passion," exclaimed Walter with impetuous eagerness. "Delay not thy generous action, lest I die even this night, consumed with disappointed desire; and behold her face no more."

"Well then," answered the old man, "return hither again tomorrow at the same hour. But once more do I give thee this friendly warning, 'Wake not the dead.'"

All in the despair of impatience, Walter would have prostrated himself at his feet, and supplicated him to fulfill at once a desire now increased to agony; but the sorcerer had already disappeared. Pouring forth his lamentations more wildly and impetuously than ever, he lay upon the grave of his adored one, until the grey dawn streaked the east. During the day, which seemed to him longer than any he had ever experienced, he wandered to and fro, restless and impatient, seemingly without any object, and deeply buried in his own reflections, inquest as the murderer who meditates his first deed of blood: and the stars of evening found him once more at the appointed spot. At midnight the sorcerer was there also.

"Hast thou yet maturely deliberated?" enquired he, "as on the preceding night?"

"Oh what should I deliberate?" returned Walter impatiently. "I need not to deliberate: what I demand of thee, is that what thou hast promised me—that which will prove my bliss. Or dost thou but mock me? if so, hence from my sight, lest I be tempted to lay my hand on thee."

"Once more do I warn thee," answered the old man with undisturbed composure, "'Wake not the dead'—let her rest."

"Aye, but not in the cold grave: she shall rather rest on this bosom which burns with eagerness to clasp her."

"Reflect, thou mayst not quit her until death, even though aversion and horror should seize thy heart. There would then remain only one horrible means."

"Dotard!" cried Walter, interrupting him, "how may I hate that which I love with such intensity of passion? how should I abhor that for which my every drop of blood is boiling?"

"Then be it even as thou wishest," answered the sorcerer; "step back."

The old man now drew a circle round the grave, all the while muttering words of enchantment. Immediately the storm began to howl among the tops of the trees; owls flapped their wings, and uttered their low voice of omen; the stars hid their mild, beaming aspect, that they might not behold so unholy and impious a spectacle; the stone then rolled from the grave with a hollow sound, leaving a free passage for the inhabitant of that dreadful tenement. The sorcerer scattered into the yawning earth, roots and herbs of most magic power, and of most penetrating odor, so that the worms crawling forth from the earth congregated together, and raised themselves in a fiery column over the grave: while rushing wind burst from the earth, scattering the mold before it, until at length the coffin lay uncovered. The moonbeams fell on it, and the lid burst open with a tremendous sound. Upon this the sorcerer poured upon it some blood from out of a human skull, exclaiming at the same time: "Drink, sleeper, of this warm stream, that thy heart may again beat within thy bosom." And, after a short pause, shedding on her some other mystic liquid, he cried aloud with the voice of one inspired: "Yes, thy heart beats once more with the flood of life: thine eye is again opened to sight. Arise, therefore, from the tomb."

As an island suddenly springs forth from the dark waves of the ocean, raised upwards from the deep by the force of subterraneous fires, so did Brunhilda start from her earthy couch, borne forward by some invisible power. Taking her by the hand, the sorcerer lead her towards Walter, who stood at some little distance, rooted to the ground with amazement.

"Receive again," said he, "the object of thy passionate sighs: mayest thou never more require my aid; should that, however, happen, so wilt thou find me, during the full of the moon, upon the mountains in that spot and where the three roads meet."

Instantly did Walter recognize in the form that stood before him, her whom he so ardently loved; and a sudden glow shot through his frame at finding her thus restored to him: yet the night-frost had chilled his limbs and palsied his tongue. For a while he gazed upon her without either motion or speech, and during this pause, all was again become hushed and serene; and the stars shone brightly in the clear heavens.

"Walter! " exclaimed the figure; and at once thc well-known sound, thrilling to his heart, broke the spell by which he was bound.

"Is it reality? Is it truth?" cried he, "or a cheating delusion?"

"No, it is no imposture: I am really living:—conduct me quickly to thy castle in the mountains."

Walter looked around: the old man had disappeared, but he perceived close by his side, a coal-black steed of fiery eye, ready equipped to conduct him thence; and on his back lay all proper attire for Brunhilda, who lost no time in arraying herself. This being done, she cried; "Haste, let us away ere the dawn breaks, for my eye is yet too weak to endure the light of day." Fully recovered from his stupor, Walter leaped into his saddle, and catching up, with a mingled feeling of delight and awe, the beloved being thus mysteriously restored from the power of the grave, he spurred on across the wild, towards the mountains, as furiously as if pursued by the shadows of the dead, hastening to recover from him their sister.

The castle to which Walter conducted his Brunhilda, was situated on a rock between other rocks rising up above it. Here they arrived, unseen by any save one aged domestic, on whom Walter imposed secrecy by the severest threats.

"Here will we tarry," said Brunhilda, "until I can endure the light, and until thou canst look upon me without trembling: as if struck with a cold chill." They accordingly continued to make that place their abode: yet no one knew that Bnunhilda existed, save only that aged attendant, who provided their meals. During seven entire days they had no light except that of tapers; during the next seven, the light was admitted through the lofty casements only while the rising or setting-sun faintly illumined the mountain-tops, the valley being still enveloped in shade.

Seldom did Walter quit Brunhilda's side: a nameless spell seemed to attach him to her; even the shudder which he felt in her presence, and which would not permit him to touch her, was not unmixed with pleasure, like that thrilling awful emotion felt when strains of sacred music float under the vault of some temple; he rather sought, therefore, than avoided this feeling. Often too as he had indulged in calling to mind the beauties of Brunhilda, she had never appeared so fair, so fascinating, so admirable when depicted by his imagination, as when now beheld in reality. Never till now had her voice sounded with such tones of sweetness; never before did her language possess such eloquence as it now did, when she conversed with him on the subject of the past. And this was the magic fairy-land towards which her words constantly conducted him. Ever did she dwell upon the days of their first love, those hours of delight which they had participated together when the one derived all enjoyment from the other: and so rapturous, so enchanting, so full of life did she recall to his imagination that blissful season, that he even doubted whether he had ever experienced with her so much felicity, or had been so truly happy. And, while she thus vividly portrayed their hours of past delight, she delineated in still more glowing, more enchanting colors, those hours of approaching bliss which now awaited them, richer in enjoyment than any preceding ones. In this manner did she charm her attentive auditor with enrapturing hopes for the future, and lull him into dreams of more than mortal ecstacy; so that while he listened to her siren strain, he entirely forgot how little blissful was the latter period of their union, when he had often sighed at her imperiousness, and at her harshness both to himself and all his household. Yet even had he recalled this to mind would it have disturbed him in his present delirious trance? Had she not now left behind in the grave all the frailty of mortality? Was not her whole being refined and purified by that long sleep in which neither passion nor sin had approached her even in dreams? How different now was the subject of her discourse! Only when speaking of her affection for him, did she betray anything of earthly feeling: at other times, she uniformly dwelt upon themes relating to the invisible and future world; when in descanting and declaring the mysteries of eternity, a stream of prophetic eloquence would burst from her lips.

In this manner had twice seven days elapsed, and, for the first time, Walter beheld the being now dearer to him than ever, in the full light of day. Every trace of the grave had disappeared from her countenance; a roseate tinge like the ruddy streaks of dawn again beamed on her pallid cheek; the faint, mouldering taint of the grave was changed into a delightful violet scent; the only sign of earth that never disappeared. He no longer felt either apprehension or awe, as he gazed upon her in the sunny light of day: it was not until now, that he seemed to have recovered her completely; and, glowing with all his former passion towards her, he would have pressed her to his bosom, but she gently repulsed him, saying:—"Not yet—spare your caresses until the moon has again filled her horn."

Spite of his impatience, Walter was obliged to await the lapse of another period of seven days: but, on the night when the moon was arrived at the full, he hastened to Brunhilda, whom he found more lovely than she had ever appeared before. Fearing no obstacles to his transports, he embraced her with all the fervor of a deeply enamored and successful lover. Brunhilda, however, still refused to yield to his passion. "What!" exclaimed she, "is it fitting that I who have been purified by death from the frailty of mortality, should become thy concubine, while a mere daughter of the earth bears the title of thy wife: never shall it be. No, it must be within the walls of thy palace, within that chamber where I once reigned as queen, that thou obtainest the end of thy wishes,—and of mine also," added she, imprinting a glowing kiss on the lips, and immediately disappeared.

Heated with passion, and determined to sacrifice everything to the accomplishment of his desires, Walter hastily quitted the apartment, and shortly after the castle itself. He travelled over mountain and across heath, with the rapidity of a storm, so that the turf was flung up by his horse's hoofs; nor once stopped until he arrived home.

Here, however, neither the affectionate caresses of Swanhilda, or those of his children could touch his heart, or induce him to restrain his furious desires. Alas! is the impetuous torrent to be checked in its devastating course by the beauteous flowers over which it rushes, when they exclaim:—"Destroyer, commiserate our helpless innocence and beauty, nor lay us waste?"—the stream sweeps over them unregarding, and a single moment annihilates the pride of a whole summer.

Shortly afterwards, did Walter begin to hint to Swanhilda, that they were ill-suited to each other; that he was anxious to taste that wild, tumultous life, so well according with the spirit of his sex, while she, on the contrary, was satisfied with the monotonous circle of household enjoyments:—that he was eager for whatever promised novelty, while she felt most attached to what was familiarized to her by habit: and lastly, that her cold disposition, bordering upon indifference, but ill assorted with his ardent temperament: it was therefore more prudent that they should seek apart from each other, that happiness which they could not find together. A sigh, and a brief acquiescence in his wishes was all the reply that Swanhilda made: and, on the following morning, upon his presenting her with a paper of separation, informing her that she was at liberty to return home to her father, she received it most submissively: yet, ere she departed, she gave him the following warning: "Too well do I conjecture to whom I am indebted for this our separation. Often have I seen thee at Brunhilda's grave, and beheld thee there even on that night when the face of the heavens was suddenly enveloped in a veil of clouds. Hast thou rashly dared to tear aside the awful veil that separates the mortality that dreams, from that which dreameth not? Oh! then woe to thee, thou wretched man, for thou hast attached to thyself that which will prove thy destruction." She ceased: nor did Walter attempt any reply, for the similar admonition uttered by the sorcerer flashed upon his mind, all obscured as it was by passion, just as the lightning glares momentarily through the gloom of night without dispersing the obscurity.

Swanhilda then departed, in order to pronounce to her children, a bitter farewell, for they, according to national custom, belonged to the father; and, having bathed them in her tears, and consecrated them with the holy water of maternal love, she quitted her husband's residence, and departed to the home of her father's.

Thus was the kind and benevolent Swanhilda, driven an exile from those halls, where she had presided with such grace;—from halls which were now newly decorated to receive another mistress. The day at length arrived, on which Walter, for the second time, conducted Brunhilda home, as a newly-made bride. And he caused it to be reported among his domestics, that his new consort had gained his affections by her extraordinary likeness to Brunhilda, their former mistress. How ineffably happy did he deem himself, as he conducted his beloved once more into the chamber which had often witnessed their former joys, and which was now newly gilded and adorned in a most costly style: among the other decorations were figures of angels scattering roses, which served to support the purple draperies, whose ample folds o'ershadowed the nuptial couch. With what impatience did he await the hour that was to put him in possession of those beauties, for which he had already paid so high a price, but, whose enjoyment was to cost him most dearly yet! Unfortunate Walter! revelling in bliss, thou beholdest not the abyss that yawns beneath thy feet, intoxicated with the luscious perfume of the flower thou hast plucked, thou little deemest how deadly is the venom with which it is fraught, although, for a short season, its potent fragrance bestows new energy on all thy feelings.

Happy, however, as Walter now was, his household were far from being equally so. The strange resemblance between their new lady and the deceased Brunhilda, filled them with a secret dismay,—an undefinable horror; for there was not a single difference of feature, of tone, of voice, or of gesture. To add too to these mysterious circumstances, her female attendants discovered a particular mark on her back, exactly like one which Brunhilda had. A report was now soon circulated, that their lady was no other than Brunhilda herself, who had been recalled to life by the power of necromancy. How truly horrible was the idea of living under the same roof with one who had been an inhabitant of the tomb, and of being obliged to attend upon her, and acknowledge her as mistress! There was also in Brunhilda, much to increase this aversion, and favor their superstition: no ornaments of gold ever decked her person; all that others were wont to wear of this metal, she had formed of silver: no richly colored and sparkling jewels glittered upon her;

pearls alone, lent their pale lustre to adorn her bosom. Most carefully did she always avoid the cheerful light of the sun, and was wont to spend the brightest days in the most retired and gloomy apartments: only during the twilight of the commencing, or declining day did she ever walk abroad, but her favorite hour was, when the phantom light of the moon bestowed on all objects a shadowy appearance, and a somber hue; always too at the crowing of the cock, an involuntary shudder was observed to seize her limbs. Imperious as before her death, she quickly imposed her iron yoke on every one around her, while she seemed even far more terrible than ever, since a dread of some supernatural power attached to her, appalled all who approached her. A malignant withering glance seemed to shoot from her eye on the unhappy object of her wrath, as if it would annihilate its victim. In short, those halls which in the time of Swanhilda were the residence of cheerfulness and mirth, now resembled an extensive desert tomb. With fear imprinted on their pale countenances, the domestics glided through the apartments of the castle; and, in this abode of terror, the crowing of the cock caused the living to tremble, as if they were the spirits of the departed; for the sound always reminded them of their mysterious mistress. There was no one but who shuddered at meeting her in a lonely place, in the dusk of evening, or by the light of the moon, a circumstance that was deemed to be ominous of some evil: so great was the apprehension of her female attendants, they pined in continual disquietude, and, by degrees, all quitted her. In the course of time even others of the domestics fled, for an insupportable horror had seized them.

The art of the sorcerer had indeed bestowed upon Brunhilda an artificial life, and due nourishment had continued to support the restored body; yet, this body was not able of itself to keep up the genial glow of vitality, and to nourish the flame whence springs all the affections and passions, whether of love or hate; for death had for ever destroyed and withered it: all that Brunhilda now possessed was a chilled existence, colder than that of the snake. It was nevertheless necessary that she should love, and return with equal ardor the warm caresses of her spell-enthralled husband, to whose passion alone she was indebted for her renewed existence. It was necessary that a magic draught should animate the dull current in her veins, and awaken her to the glow of life and the flame of love—a potion of abomination—one not even to be named without a curse—human blood, imbibed whilst yet warm, from the veins of youth. This was the hellish drink for which she thirsted: possessing no sympathy with the purer feelings of humanity; deriving no enjoyment from aught that interests in life, and occupies its varied hours; her existence was a mere blank, unless when in the arms of her paramour husband, and therefore was it that she craved incessantly after the horrible draught. It was even with the utmost effort that she could forbear sucking even the blood of Walter himself, as he reclined beside her. Whenever she beheld some innocent child, whose lovely face denoted the exuberance of infantine health and vigor, she would entice it by soothing words and fond caresses into her most secret apartment, where, lulling it to sleep in her arms, she would suck from its bosom the warm, purple tide of life. Nor were youths of either sex safe from her horrid attack: having first breathed upon her unhappy victim, who never failed immediately to sink into a lengthened sleep, she would then in a similar manner drain his veins of the vital juice. Thus children, youths, and maidens quickly faded away, as flowers gnawn by the cankering worm: the fullness of their limbs disappeared; a sallow line succeeded to the rosy freshness of their cheeks, the liquid lustre of the eye was deadened, even as the sparkling stream when arrested by the touch of frost; and their locks became thin and grey, as if already ravaged by the storm of life. Parents beheld with horror this desolating pestilence, devouring their offspring; nor could simple or charm, potion or amulet avail aught against it. The grave swallowed up one after the other; or did the miserable victim survive, he became cadaverous and wrinkled even in the very morn of existence. Parents observed with horror, this devastating pestilence snatch away their offspring—a pestilence which, nor herb however potent, nor charm, nor holy taper, nor exorcism could avert. They either beheld their children sink one after the other into the grave, or their youthful forms withered by the unholy, vampire embrace of Brunhilda assume the decrepitude of sudden age.

At length strange surmises and reports began to prevail; it was whispered that Brunhilda herself was the cause of all these horrors; although no one could pretend to tell in what manner she destroyed her victims, since no marks of violence were discernable. Yet when young children confessed that she had frequently lulled them asleep in her arms, and elder ones said that a sudden slumber had come upon them whenever she began to converse with them, suspicion became converted into certainty, and those whose offspring had hitherto escaped unharmed, quitted their hearths and home—all their little possessions—the dwellings of their fathers and the inheritance of their children, in order to rescue from so horrible a fate those who were dearer to their simple affections than aught else the world could give.

Thus daily did the castle assume a more desolate appearance; daily did its environs become more deserted; none but a few aged decrepid old women and grey-headed menials were to be seen remaining of the once numerous retinue. Such will in the latter days of the earth, be the last generation of mortals, when child-bearing shall have ceased, when youth shall no more be seen, nor any arise to replace those who shall await their fate in silence.

Walter alone noticed not, or heeded not, the desolation around him; he apprehended not death, lapped as he was in a glowing elysium of love. Far more happy than formerly did he now seem in the possession of Brunhilda. All those caprices and frowns which had been wont to overcloud their former union had now entirely disappeared. She even seemed to dote on him with a warmth of passion that she had never exhibited even during the happy season of bridal love; for the flame of that youthful blood, of which she drained the veins of others, rioted in her own. At night, as soon as he closed his eyes, she would breathe on him till he sank into delicious dreams, from which he awoke only to experience more rapturous enjoyments. By day she would continually discourse with him on the bliss experienced by happy spirits beyond the grave, assuring him that, as his affection had recalled her from the tomb, they were now irrevocably united. Thus fascinated by a continual spell, it was not possible that he should perceive what was taking place around him. Brunhilda, however, foresaw with savage grief that the source of her youthful ardor was daily decreasing, for, in a short time, there remained nothing gifted with youth, save Walter and his children, and these latter she resolved should be her next victims.

On her first return to the castle, she had felt an aversion towards the off-spring of another, and therefore abandoned them entirely to the attendants appointed by Swanhilda. Now, however, she began to pay considerable attention to them, and caused them to be frequently admitted into her presence. The aged nurses were filled with dread at perceiving these marks of regard from her towards their young charges, yet dared they not to oppose the will of their terrible and imperious mistress. Soon did Brunhilda gain the affection of the children, who were too unsuspecting of guile to apprehend any danger from her; on the contrary, her caresses won them completely to her. Instead of ever checking their mirthful gambols, she would rather instruct them in new sports; often too did she recite to them tales of such strange and wild interest as to exceed all the stories of their nurses. Were they wearied either with play or with listening to her narratives, she would take them on her knees and lull them to slumber.

Then did visions of the most surpassing magnificence attend their dreams: they would fancy themselves in some garden where flowers of every hue rose in rows one above the other, from the humble violet to the tall sun-flower, forming a party-colored broidery of every hue, sloping upwards towards the golden clouds, where little angels, whose wings sparkled with azure and gold, descended to bring them delicious cates, or splendid jewels; or sung to them soothing melodious hymns. So delightful did these dreams in short time become to the children, that they longed for nothing so eagerly as to slumber on Brunhilda's lap, for never did they else enjoy such visions of heavenly forms. Thus were they most anxious for that which was to prove their destruction:—yet do we not all aspire after that which conducts us to the grave—after the enjoyment of life? These innocents stretched out their arms to approaching death, because it assumed the mask of pleasure; for, while they were lapped in these ecstatic slumbers, Brunhilda sucked the life-stream from their bosoms. On waking, indeed, they felt themselves faint and exhausted, yet did no pain, nor any mark betray the cause. Shortly, however, did their strength entirely fail, even as the summer brook is gradually dried up; their sports became less and less noisy; their loud, frolicsome laughter was converted into a faint smile; the full tones of their voices died away into a mere whisper. Their attendants were filled with horror and despair; too well did they conjecture the horrible truth, yet dared not to impart their suspicions to Walter, who was so devotedly attached to his horrible partner. Death had already smote his prey: the children were but the mere shadows of their former selves, and even this shadow quickly disappeared.

The anguished father deeply bemoaned their loss, for, notwithstanding his apparent neglect, he was strongly attached to them, nor until he had experienced their loss, was he aware that his love was so great. His affliction could not fail to excite the displeasure of Brunhilda: "Why dost thou lament so fondly," said she, "for these little ones? What satisfaction could such unformed beings yield to thee, unless thou wert still attached to their mother? Thy heart then is still hers? Or dost thou now regret her and them because thou art satiated with my fondness, and weary of my endearments? Had these young ones grown up, would they not have attached thee, thy spirit and thy affections more closely to this earth of clay—to this dust, and have alienated thee from that sphere to which I, who have already passed the grave, endeavor to raise thee? Say is thy spirit so heavy, or thy love so weak, or thy faith so hollow, that the hope of being mine for ever is unable to touch thee?" Thus did Brunhilda express her indignation at her consort's grief, and forbade him her presence. The fear of offending her beyond forgiveness, and his anxiety to appease her soon dried up his tears; and he again abandoned himself to his fatal passion, until approaching destruction, at length awakened him from his delusion.

Neither maiden, nor youth, was any longer to be seen, either within the dreary walls of the castle, or the adjoining territory:—all had disappeared; for those whom the grave had not swallowed up, had fled from the region of death. Who, therefore, now remained to quench the horrible thirst of the female vampire, save Walter himself? and his death she dared to contemplate unmoved; for that divine sentiment that unites two beings in one joy and one sorrow was unknown to her bosom. Was he in his tomb, so was she free to search out other victims, and glut herself with destruction, until she herself should, at the last day, be consumed with the earth itself, such is the fatal law, to which the dead are subject, when awoke by the arts of necromancy from the sleep of the grave.

She now began to fix her blood-thirsty lips on Walter's breast, when cast into a profound sleep by the odor of her violet breath, he reclined beside her quite unconscious of his impending fate: yet soon did his vital powers begin to decay; and many a grey hair peeped through his raven locks. With his strength, his passion also declined; and he now frequently left her in order to pass the whole day in the sports of the chase, hoping thereby, to regain his wonted vigor. As he was reposing one day in a wood beneath the shade of an oak, he perceived, on the summit of a tree, a bird of strange appearance, and quite unknown to him; but, before he could take aim at it with his bow, it flew away into the clouds; at the same time, letting fall a rose-colored root which dropped at Walter's feet, who immediately took it up, and, although he was well acquainted with almost every plant, he could not remember to have seen any at all resembling this. Its delightfully odoriferous scent induced him to try its flavor, but ten times more bitter than wormwood, it was even as gall in his mouth; upon which, impatient of the disappointment, he flung it away with violence. Had he, however, been aware of its miraculous quality, and that it acted as a counter charm against the opiate perfume of Brunhilda's breath, he would have blessed it in spite of its bitterness: thus do mortals often blindly cast away in displeasure, the unsavory remedy that would otherwise work their weal.

When Walter returned home in the evening, and laid him down to repose as usual by Brunhilda's side, the magic power of her breath produced no effect upon him; and for the first time during many months did he close his eyes in a natural slumber. Yet hardly had he fallen asleep, ere a pungent smarting pain disturbed him from his dreams; and, opening his eyes, he discerned, by the gloomy rays of a lamp, that glimmered in the apartment, what for some moments transfixed him quite aghast, for it was Brunhilda, drawing with her lips, the warm blood from his bosom. The wild cry of horror which at length escaped him, terrified Brunhilda, whose mouth was besmeared with the warm blood. "Monster! " exclaimed he, springing from the couch, "is it thus that you love me?"

"Aye, even as the dead love," replied she, with a malignant coldness.

"Creature of blood!" continued Walter, "the delusion which has so long blinded me is at an end: thou art the fiend who hast destroyed my children—who hast murdered the offspring of my vassals." Raising herself upwards and, at the same time, casting on him a glance that froze him to the spot with dread, she replied. "It is not I who have murdered them;—I was obliged to pamper myself with warm youthful blood, in order that I might satisfy thy furious desires—thou art the murderer!"—These dreadful words summoned, before Walter's terrified conscience, the threatening shades of all those who had thus perished; while despair choked his voice. "Why," continued she, in a tone that increased his horror, "why dost thou make mouths at me like a puppet? Thou who hadst the courage to love the dead—to take into thy bed, one who had been sleeping in the grave, the bed-fellow of the worm—who hast clasped in thy lustful arms, the corruption of the tomb—dost thou, unhallowed as thou art now raise this hideous cry for the sacrifice of a few lives?—They are but leaves swept from their branches by a storm.—Come, chase these idiot fancies, and taste the bliss thou hast so dearly purchased." So saying, she extended her arms towards him; but this motion served only to increase his terror, and exclaiming: "Accursed Being,"—he rushed out of the apartment.

All the horrors of a guilty, upbraiding conscience became his companions, now that he was awakened from the delirium of his unholy pleasures. Frequently did he curse his own obstinate blindness, for having given no heed to the hints and admonitions of his children's nurses, but treating them as vile calumnies. But his sorrow was now too late, for, although repentance may gain pardon for the sinner, it cannot alter the immutable decrees of fate—it cannot recall the murdered from the tomb. No sooner did the first break of dawn appear, than he set out for his lonely castle in the mountains, determined no longer to abide under the same roof with so terrific a being; yet vain was his flight, for, on waking the following morning, he perceived himself in Brunhilda's arms, and quite entangled in her long raven tresses, which seemed to involve him and bind him in the fetters of his fate; the powerful fascination of her breath held him still more captivated, so that, forgetting all that had passed, he returned her caresses, until awakening as if from a dream he recoiled in unmixed horror from her embrace. During the day he wandered through the solitary wilds of the mountains, as a culprit seeking an asylum from his pursuers; and, at night, retired to the shelter of a cave; fearing less to couch himself within such a dreary place, than to expose himself to the horror of again meeting Brunhilda; but alas! it was in vain that he endeavored to flee her. Again, when he awoke, he found her the partner of his miserable bed. Nay, had he sought the center of the earth as his hiding place; had he even imbedded himself beneath rocks, or formed his chamber in the recesses of the ocean, still had he found her his constant companion; for, by calling her again into existence, he had rendered himself inseparably hers; so fatal were the links that united them.

Struggling with the madness that was beginning to seize him, and brooding incessantly on the ghastly visions that presented themselves to his horror-stricken mind, he lay motionless in the gloomiest recesses of the woods, even from the rise of sun till the shades of eve. But, no sooner was the light of day extinguished in the west, and the woods buried in impenetrable darkness, than the apprehension of resigning himself to sleep drove him forth among the mountains. The storm played wildly with the fantastic clouds, and with the rattling leaves, as they were caught up into the air, as if some dread spirit was sporting with these images of transitoriness and decay: it roared among the summits of the oaks as if uttering a voice of fury, while its hollow sound rebounding among the distant hills, seemed as the moans of a departing sinner, or as the faint cry of some wretch expiring under the murderer's hand: the owl too, uttered its ghastly cry as if foreboding the wreck of nature. Walter's hair flew disorderly in the wind, like black snakes wreathing around his temples and shoulders; while each sense was awake to catch fresh horror. In the clouds he seemed to behold the forms of the murdered; in the howling wind to hear their laments and groans; in the chilling blast itself he felt the dire kiss of Brunhilda; in the cry of the screeching bird he heard her voice; in the mouldering leaves he scented the charnel-bed out of which he had awakened her. "Murderer of thy own offspring," exclaimed he in a voice making night, and the conflict of the clement still more hideous, "paramour of a blood-thirsty vampire, reveller with the corruption of the tomb!" while in his despair he rent the wild locks from his head. Just then the full moon darted from beneath the bursting clouds; and the sight recalled to his remembrance the advice of the sorcerer, when he trembled at the first apparition of Brunhilda rising from her sleep of death;—namely, to seek him, at the season of the full moon, in the mountains, where three roads met. Scarcely had this gleam of hope broke in on his bewildered mind, than he flew to the appointed spot.

On his arrival, Walter found the old man seated there upon a stone, as calmly as though it had been a bright sunny day, and completely regardless of the uproar around. "Art thou come then?" exclaimed he to the breathless wretch, who, flinging himself at his feet, cried in a tone of anguish:—"Oh save me—succor me—rescue me from the monster that scattereth death and desolation around her."

"I am acquainted with all," returned the sorcerer, "thou now perceivest how wholesome was the advice—'Wake not the dead.'"

"And wherefore a mysterious warning? why didst thou not rather disclose to me, at once, all the horrors that awaited my sacrilegious profanation of the grave?"

"Wert thou able to listen to any other voice than that of thy impetuous passions? Did not thy eager impatience shut my mouth at the very moment I would have cautioned thee?"

"True, true:—thy reproof is just: but what does it avail now;—I need the promptest aid."

"Well," replied the old man, "there remains even yet a means of rescuing thyself, but it is fraught with horror, and demands all thy resolution."

"Utter it then, utter it; for what can be more appalling, more hideous than the misery I now endure?"

"Know then," continued the sorcerer, "that only on the night of the new moon, does she sleep the sleep of mortals; and then all the supernatural power which she inherits from the grave totally fails her. 'Tis then that thou must murder her."

"How! murder her!" echoed Walter.

"Aye," returned the old man calmly, "pierce her bosom with a sharpened dagger, which I will furnish thee with; at the same time renounce her memory for ever, swearing never to think of her intentionally, and that, if thou dost involuntarily, thou wilt repeat the curse."

"Most horrible! yet what can be more horrible than she herself is?—I'll do it."

"Keep then this resolution until the next new moon."

"What, must I wait until then?" cried Walter, "alas ere then, either her savage thirst for blood will have forced me into the night of the tomb, or horror will have driven me into the night of madness."

"Nay," replied the sorcerer, "that I can prevent"; and, so saying, he conducted him to a cavern further among the mountains. "Abide here twice seven days," said he; "so long can I protect thee against her deadly caresses. Here wilt thou find all due provision for thy wants; but take heed that nothing tempt thee to quit this place. Farewell, when the moon renews itself, then do I repair hither again." So saying, the sorcerer drew a magic circle around the cave, and then immediately disappeared.

Twice seven days did Walter continue in this solitude, where his companions were his own terrifying thoughts, and his bitter repentance. The present was all desolation and dread; the future presented the image of a horrible deed, which he must perforce commit; while the past was empoisoned by the memory of his guilt. Did he think on his former happy union with Brunhilda, her horrible image presented itself to his imagination with her lips defiled with dropping blood: or, did he call to mind the peaceful days he had passed with Swanhilda, he beheld her sorrowful spirit, with the shadows of her murdered children. Such were the horrors that attended him by day: those of night were still more dreadful, for then he beheld Brunhilda herself, who, wandering round the magic circle which she could not pass, called upon his name, till the cavern re-echoed the horrible sound. "Walter, my beloved," cried she, "wherefore dost thou avoid me? art thou not mine? for ever mine—mine here, and mine hereafter? And dost thou seek to murder me?—ah! commit not a deed which hurls us both to perdition—thyself as well as me." In this manner did the horrible visitant torment him each night, and, even when she departed, robbed him of all repose.

The night of the new moon at length arrived, dark as the deed it was doomed to bring forth. The sorcerer entered the cavern; "Come," said he to Walter, "let us depart hence, the hour is now arrived": and he forthwith conducted him in silence from the cave, to a coal-black steed, the sight of which recalled to Walter's remembrance the fatal night. He then related to the old man Brunhilda's nocturnal visits, and anxiously enquired whether her apprehensions of eternal perdition would be fulfilled or not. "Mortal eye," exclaimed the sorcerer, "may not pierce the dark secrets of another world, or penetrate the deep abyss that separates earth from heaven." Walter hesitated to mount the steed. "Be resolute," exclaimed his companion, "but this once is it granted to thee to make the trial, and, should thou fail now, nought can rescue thee from her power."

"What can be more horrible than she herself?—I am determined": and he leaped on the horse, the sorcerer mounting also behind him.

Carried with a rapidity equal to that of the storm that sweeps across the plain, they in brief space arrived at Walter's castle. All the doors flew open at the bidding of his companion, and they speedily reached Brunhilda's chamber, and stood beside her couch. Reclining in a tranquil slumber; she reposed in all her native loveliness, every trace of horror had disappeared from her countenance; she looked so pure, meek and innocent that all the sweet hours of their endearments rushed to Walter's memory, like interceding angels pleading in her behalf. His unnerved hand could not take the dagger which the sorcerer presented to him. "The blow must be struck even now": said the latter, "shouldst thou delay but an hour, she will lie at day-break on thy bosom sucking the warm life-drops from thy heart."

"Horrible! most horrible!" faltered the trembling Walter, and turning away his face, he thrust the dagger into her bosom, exclaiming—"I curse thee for ever!"—and the cold blood gushed upon his hand. Opening her eyes once more, she cast a look of ghastly horror on her husband, and, in a hollow dying accent said—"Thou too art doomed to perdition."

"Lay now thy hand upon her corse," said the sorcerer, "and swear the oath."—Walter did as commanded, saying—"Never will I think of her with love, never recall her to mind intentionally, and, should her image recur to my mind involuntarily, so will I exclaim to it: be thou accursed."

"Thou hast now done every thing," returned the sorcerer; "—restore her therefore to the earth, from which thou did'st so foolishly recall her; and be sure to recollect thy oath: for, shouldst thou forget it but once, she would return, and thou wouldst be inevitably lost. Adieu—we see each other no more." Having uttered these words he quitted the apartment, and Walter also fled from this abode of horror, having first given directions that the corse should be speedily interred.

Again did the terrific Brunhilda repose within her grave; but her image continually haunted Walter's imagination, so that his existence was one continued martyrdom, in which he continually struggled, to dismiss from his recollection the hideous phantoms of the past; yet, the stronger his effort to banish them, so much the more frequently and the more vividly did they return; as the night-wanderer, who is enticed by a fire-wisp into quagmire or bog, sinks the deeper into his damp grave the more he struggles to escape. His imagination seemed incapable of admitting any other image than that of Brunhilda: now he fancied he beheld her expiring, the blood streaming from her beautiful bosom: at others he saw the lovely bride of his youth, who reproached him with having disturbed the slumbers of the tomb: and to both he was compelled to utter the dreadful words, "I curse thee for ever." The terrible imprecation was constantly passing his lips; yet was he in incessant terror lest he should forget it, or dream of her without being able to repeat it, and then, on awaking, find himself in her arms. Else would he recall her expiring words, and, appalled at their terrific import, imagine that the doom of his perdition was irrecoverably passed. Whence should he fly from himself? or how erase from his brain these images and forms of horror? In the din of combat, in the tumult of war and its incessant pour of victory to defeat; from the cry of anguish to the exultation of victory—in these he hoped to find at least the relief of distraction: but here too he was disappointed. The giant fang of apprehension now seized him who had never before known fear; each drop of blood that sprayed upon him seemed the cold blood that had gushed from Brunhilda's wound; each dying wretch that fell beside him looked like her, when expiring, she exclaimed:—"Thou too art doomed to perdition"; so that the aspect of death seemed more full of dread to him than aught beside, and this unconquerable terror compelled him to abandon the battlefield. At length, after many a weary and fruitless wandering, he returned to his castle. Here all was deserted and silent, as if the sword, or a still more deadly pestilence had laid every thing waste: for the few inhabitants that still remained, and even those servants who had once shewn themselves the most attached, now fled from him, as though he had been branded with the mark of Cain. With horror he perceived that, by uniting himself as he had done with the dead, he had cut himself off from the living, who refused to hold any intercourse with him. Often, when he stood on the battlements of his castle, and looked down upon desolate fields, he compared their present solitude with the lively activity they were wont to exhibit, under the strict but benevolent discipline of Swanhilda. He now felt that she alone could reconcile him to life, but durst he hope that one, whom he had so deeply agrieved, could pardon him, and receive him again? Impatience at length got the better of fear; he sought Swanhilda, and, with the deepest contrition, acknowledged his complicated guilt; embracing her knees he beseeched her to pardon him, and to return to his desolate castle, in order that it might again become the abode of contentment and peace. The pale form which she beheld at her feet, the shadow of the lately blooming youth, touched Swanhilda. "The folly," said she gently "though it has caused me much sorrow, has never excited my resentment or my anger. But say, where are my children?" To this dreadful interrogation the agonized father could for a while frame no reply: at length he was obliged to confess the dreadful truth. "Then we are sundered for ever," returned Swanhilda; nor could all his tears or supplications prevail upon her to revoke the sentence she had given.

Stripped of his last earthly hope, bereft of his last consolation, and thereby rendered as poor as mortal can possibly be on this side of the grave, Walter returned homewards; when, as he was riding through the forest in the neighborhood of his castle, absorbed in his gloomy meditations, the sudden sound of a horn roused him from his reverie. Shortly after he saw appear a female figure clad in black, and mounted on a steed of the same color: her attire was like that of a huntress, but, instead of a falcon, she bore a raven in her hand; and she was attended by a gay troop of cavaliers and dames. The first salutations being passed, he found that she was proceeding the same road as himself; and, when she found that Walter's castle was close at hand, she requested that he would lodge her for that night, the evening being far advanced. Most willingly did he comply with this request, since the appearance of the beautiful stranger had struck him greatly; so wonderfully did she resemble Swanhilda, except that her locks were brown, and her eye dark and full of fire. With a sumptuous banquet did he entertain his guests, whose mirth and songs enlivened the lately silent halls. Three days did this revelry continue, and so exhilarating did it prove to Walter, that he seemed to have forgotten his sorrows and his fears; nor could he prevail upon himself to dismiss his visitors, dreading lest, on their departure, the castle would seem a hundred times more desolate than before, and his grief be proportionably increased. At his earnest request, the stranger consented to stay seven days, and again another seven days. Without being requested, she took upon herself the superintendance of the household, which she regulated as discreetly and cheerfully as Swanhilda had been wont to do, so that the castle, which had so lately been the abode of melancholy and horror, became the residence of pleasure and festivity, and Walter's grief disappeared altogether in the midst of so much gaiety. Daily did his attachment to the fair unknown increase; he even made her his confidant; and, one evening as they were walking together apart from any of her train, he related to her his melancholy and frightful history. "My dear friend," returned she, as soon as he had finished his tale, "it ill beseems man of thy discretion to afflict thyself, on account of all this. Thou hast awakened the dead from the sleep of the grave, and afterwards found,—what might have been anticipated, that the dead possess no sympathy with life. What then? thou wilt not commit this error a second time. Thou hast however murdered the being whom thou had'st thus recalled again to existence—but it was only in appearance, for thou couldst not deprive that of life, which properly had none. Thou hast, too, lost a wife and two children: but, at thy years, such a loss is most easily repaired. There are beauties who will gladly share thy couch, and make thee again a father. But thou dread'st the reckoning of hereafter:—go, open the graves and ask the sleepers there whether that hereafter disturbs them." In such manner would she frequently exhort and cheer him, so that, in a short time, his melancholy entirely disappeared. He now ventured to declare to the unknown the passion with which she had inspired him, nor did she refuse him her hand. Within seven days afterwards the nuptials were celebrated, and the very foundations of the castle seemed to rock from the wild tumultuous uproar of unrestrained riot. The wine streamed in abundance; the goblets circled incessantly: intemperance reached its utmost bounds, while shouts of laughter, almost resembling madness, burst from the numerous train belonging to the unknown. At length Walter, heated with wine and love, conducted his bride into the nuptial chamber: but, oh! horror! scarcely had he clasped her in his arms, ere she transfomned herself into a monstrous serpent, which entwining him in its horrid folds, crushed him to death. Flames crackled on every side of the apartment; in a few minutes after, the whole castle was enveloped in a blaze that consumed it entirely: while, as the walls fell in with a tremendous crash, a voice exclaimed aloud—"Wake not the dead!"

The White Cat of Drumgunnoil

Joseph Sheridan Le Fanu

Joseph Sheridan Le Fanu (1814-1873) was born in Dublin, Ireland. Le Fanu's father was the minister of the Royal Hibernian Military School, and the family lived on the school's campus. In 1823, his father accepted a post in Abingdon, but did not move to his new parish until 1826. This delay caused hostility among the residents, especially during the Tithe Wars. In 1832, Le Fanu entered Trinity College, University of Dublin to study law. He graduated with honors in 1837, and published his first story in *The Dublin University Magazine* a year later. While admitted to the Irish bar in 1839, Le Fanu never practiced law. In 1840, he purchased two newspapers, *The Dublin Statesman* (which he closed down six years later) and *The Dublin Warder.* In 1843, he married Susanna Bennett. Le Fanu's first novel, *The Cock and Anchor: A Chronicle of Old Dublin City,* was published two years later. In 1851, his first collection of stories was published, *Ghost Stories and Tales of Mystery.* After his wife's death in 1858, Le Fanu became reclusive, writing prolifically for the English market. In 1861, he bought two other periodicals, including *The Dublin University Magazine.* In 1873, he died at home of a heart attack. Among Le Fanu's most famous novels and collections are *Uncle Silas* (1864), *The House by the Churchyard* (1864), *Wylder's Hand* (1864), *Guy Deverell* (1866), *All in the Dark* (1866), *The Tenants of Malory* (1867), *A Lost Name* (1868), *Checkmate* (1871), *In a Glass Darkly* (1872), and *Willing to Die* (1873).

"The White Cat of Drumgunnoil" is one of the last stories Le Fanu wrote about his native Ireland. The rural flavor and the nature of its grotesque revenant show why Le Fanu was considered by M.R. James to be the finest writer of horror stories.

THERE IS A famous story of a white cat, with which we all become acquainted in the nursery. I am going to tell a story of a white cat very different from the amiable and enchanted princess who took that disguise for a season. The white cat of which I speak was a more sinister animal.

The traveller from Limerick towards Dublin, after passing the hills of Killaloe upon the left, as Keeper Mountain rises high in view, finds himself gradually hemmed in, up the right, by a range of lower hills. An undulating plain that dips gradually to a lower level than that of the road interposes, and some scattered hedgerows relieve its somewhat wild and melancholy character.

One of the few human habitations that send up their films of turf-smoke from that lonely plain, is the loosely thatched, earth-built dwelling of a "strong farmer," as the more prosperous of the tenant-farming classes are termed in Munster. It stands in a clump of trees near the edge of a wandering stream, about half-way between the mountains and the Dublin road, and had been for generations tenanted by people named Donovan.

In a distant place, desirous of studying some Irish records which had fallen into my hands, and inquiring for a teacher capable of instructing me in the Irish language, a Mr. Donovan, dreamy, harmless, and learned, was recommended to me for the purpose.

I found that he had been educated as a Sizar in Trinity College, Dublin. He now supported himself by teaching, and the special direction of my studies, I suppose, flattered his national partialities, for he unbosomed himself of much of his long-reserved thoughts, and recollections about his country and his early days. It was he who told me this story, and I mean to repeat it, as nearly as I can, in his own words.

I have myself seen the old farmhouse, with its orchard of huge moss-grown apple trees. I have looked round on the peculiar landscape; the roofless, ivied tower, that two hundred years before had afforded a refuge from raid and rapparee, and which still occupies its old place in the angle of the haggard; the bush-grown "liss," that scarcely a hundred and fifty steps away records the labors of a bygone race; the dark and towering outline of old Keeper in the background; and the lonely range of furze and heath-clad hills that form a nearer barrier, with many a line of grey rock and clump of dwarf oak or birch. The pervading sense of loneliness made it a scene not unsuited for a wild and unearthly story. And I could quite fancy how, seen in the grey of a wintry morning, shrouded far and wide in snow, or in the melancholy glory of an autumnal sunset, or in the chill splendor of a moonlight night, it might have helped to tone a dreamy mind like honest Dan Donovan's to superstition and a proneness to the illusion of fancy. It is certain, however, that I never anywhere met with a more simple-minded creature, or one on whose good faith I could more entirely rely.

When I was a boy, said he, living at home at Drumgunniol, I used to take my Goldsmith's *Roman History* in my hand and go down to my favorite seat, the flat stone, sheltered by a hawthorn tree beside the little lough, a large and deep pool, such as I have heard called a tarn in England. It lay in the gentle hollow of a field that is overhung towards the north by the old orchard, and being a deserted place was favorable to my studious quietude.

One day reading here, as usual, I wearied at last, and began to look about me, thinking of the heroic scenes I had just been reading of. I was as wide awake as I am at this moment, and I saw a woman appear at the corner of the orchard and walk down the slope. She wore a long, light grey dress, so long that it seemed to sweep the grass behind her, and so singular was her appearance in a part of the world where female attire is so inflexibly fixed by custom, that I could not take my eyes off her. Her course lay diagonally from corner to corner of the field, which was a large one, and she pursued it without swerving.

When she came near I could see that her feet were bare, and that she seemed to be looking steadfastly upon some remote object for guidance. Her route would have crossed me—had the tarn not interposed—about ten or twelve yards below the point at which I was sitting. But instead of arresting her course at the margin of the lough, as I had expected, she went on without seeming conscious of its existence, and I saw her, as plainly as I see you, sir, walk across the surface of the water, and pass, without seeming to see me, at about the distance I had calculated.

I was ready to faint from sheer terror. I was only thirteen years old then, and I remember every particular as if it had happened this hour.

The figure passed through the gap at the far corner of the field, and there I lost sight of it. I had hardly strength to walk home, and was so nervous, and ultimately so ill, that for three weeks I was confined to the house, and could not bear to be alone for a moment. I never entered that field again such was the horror with which from that moment every object in it was clothed. Even at this distance of time I should not like to pass through it.

This apparition I connected with a mysterious event; and, also, with a singular liability, that has for nearly eighty years distinguished, or rather afflicted, our family. It is no fancy. Everybody in that part of the country knows all about it. Everybody connected what I had seen with it.

I will tell it all to you as well as I can.

When I was about fourteen years old—that is about a year after the sight I had seen in the lough field—we were one night expecting my father home from the fair of Killoloe. My mother sat up to welcome him home, and I was with her, for I liked nothing better than such a vigil. My brothers and sisters, and the farm servants, except the men who were driving home the cattle from the fair, were asleep in their beds. My mother and I were sitting in the chimney corner chatting together, and watching my father's supper, which was kept hot over the fire. We knew that he would return before the men who were driving home the cattle, for he was riding, and told us that he would only wait to see them fairly on the road, and then push homeward.

At length we heard his voice and the knocking of his loaded whip at the door, and my mother let him in. I don't think I ever saw my father drunk, which is more than most men of my age, from the same part of the country, could say of theirs. But he could drink his glass of whiskey as well as another, and he usually came home from fair or market a little merry and mellow, and with a jolly flush in his cheeks.

Tonight he looked sunken, pale, and sad. He entered with the saddle and bridle in his hand, and he dropped them against the wall, near the door, and put his arms round his wife's neck, and kissed her kindly.

"Welcome home, Meehal," said she, kissing him heartily.

"God bless you, mavourneen," he answered.

And hugging her again, he turned to me, who was plucking him by the hand, jealous of his notice. I was little, and light of my age, and he lifted me up in his arms, and kissed me, and my arms being about his neck, he said to my mother:

"Draw the bolt, acuishla."

She did so, and setting me down very dejectedly, he walked to the fire and sat down on a stool, and stretched his feet toward the glowing turf, leaning with his hands on his knees.

"Rouse up, Mick, darlin'," said my mother, who was growing anxious, "and tell me how did the cattle sell, and did everything go lucky at the fair, or is there anything wrong with the landlord, or what in the world is it that ails you, Mick, jewel?"

"Nothin', Molly. The cows sould well, thank God, and there's nothin' fell out between me an' the landlord, an' everything's the same way. There's no fault to find anywhere."

"Well, then, Mickey, since so it is, turn round to your hot supper, and ate it, and tell us is there anything new."

"I got my supper, Molly, on the way, and I can't ate a bit," he answered.

"Got your supper on the way, an' you knowin' 'twas waiting for you at home, an' your wife sittin' up an' all! " cried my mother, reproachfully.

"You're takin' a wrong meanin' out of what I say," said my father. "There's something happened that leaves me that I can't eat a mouthful, and I'll not be dark with you, Molly, for, maybe, it ain't very long I have to be here, an' I'll tell you what it was. It's what I've seen, the white cat."

"The Lord between us and harm!" exclaimed my mother, in a moment as pale and as chap-fallen as my father; and then, trying to rally, with a laugh, she said: "Ha! 'tis only funnin' me you are. Sure a white rabbit was snared a Sunday last, in Grady's wood; an' Teigue seen a big white rat in the haggard yesterday."

"'Twas neither rat nor rabbit was in it. Don't ye think but I'd know a rat or a rabbit from a big white cat, with green eyes as big as halfpennies, and its back riz up like a bridge, trottin' on and across me, and ready, if I dar' stop, to rub its sides against my shins and maybe to make a jump and seize my throat, if that it's a cat at all, an' not something worse?"

As he ended his description in a low tone, looking straight at the fire my father drew his big hand across his forehead once or twice, his face being damp and shining with the moisture of fear, and he sighed, or rather groaned, heavily.

My mother had relapsed into panic, and was praying again in her fear. I, too, was terribly frightened, and on the point of crying, for I knew all about the white cat.

Clapping my father on the shoulder, by way of encouragement, my mother leaned over him, kissing him, and at last began to cry. He was wringing her hands in his, and seemed in great trouble.

"There was nothin' came into the house with me?" he asked, in a very low tone, turning to me.

"There was nothin', father," I said, "but the saddie and bridle that was in your hand."

"Nothin' white kem in at the doore wid me," he repeated.

"Nothin' at all," I answered.

"So best," said my father, and making the sign of the cross, he began mumbling to himself, and I knew he was saying his prayers.

Waiting for a while, to give him time for this exercise, my mother asked him where he first saw it.

"When I was riding up the bohereen"—the Irish term meaning a little road, such as leads up to a farmhouse—"I bethought myself that the men was on the road with the cattle, and no one to look to the horse barrin' myself, so I thought I might as well leave him in the crooked field below, an' I tuck him there, he bein' cool, and not a hair turned, for I rode him aisy all the way. It was when I turned, after lettin' him go—the saddle and bridle bein' in my hand—that I saw it, pushin' out o' the long grass at the side o' the path, an' it walked across it, in front of me, an' then back again, before me, the same way, an' sometimes at one side, an' then at the other, lookin' at me wid them shinin' eyes; and I consayted I heard it growlin' as it kep' beside me—as close as ever you see—till I kem up to the doore, here, an' knocked an' called, as ye heered me."

Now, what was it, in so simple an incident, that agitated my father, my mother, myself, and finally, every member of this rustic household, with a terrible foreboding? It was this that we, one and all, believed that my father had received, in thus encountering the white cat, a warning of his approaching death.

The omen had never failed hitherto. It did not fail now. In a week after my father took the fever that was going, and before a month he was dead.

My honest friend, Dan Donovan, paused here; I could perceive that he was praying, for his lips were busy, and I concluded that it was for the repose of that departed soul.

In a little while he resumed.

It is eighty years now since that omen first attached to my family. Eighty years? Ay, is it. Ninety is nearer the mark. And I have spoken to many old people, in those earlier times, who had a distinct recollection of everything connected with it.

It happened in this way.

My grand-uncle, Connor Donovan, had the old farm of Drumgunniol in his day. He was richer than ever my father was, or my father's father either, for he took a short lease of Balraghan, and made money out of it. But money won't soften a hard heart, and I'm afraid my grand-uncle was a cruel man—a profligate man he was, surely, and that is mostly a cruel man at heart. He drank his share, too, and cursed and swore, when he was vexed, more than was good for his soul, I'm afraid.

At that time there was a beautiful girl of the Colemans, up in the mountains, not far from Capper Cullen. I'm told that there are no Colemans there now at all, and that family has passed away. The famine years made great changes.

Ellen Coleman was her name. The Colemans were not rich. But, being such a beauty, she might have made a good match. Worse than she did for herself, poor thing, she could not.

Con Donovan—my grand-uncle, God forgive him!—sometimes in his rambles saw her at fairs or patterns, and he fell in love with her, as who might not?

He used her ill. He promised her marriage, and persuaded her to come away with him; and, after all, he broke his word. It was just the old story. He tired of her, and he wanted to push himself in the world; and he married a girl of the Collopys, that had a great fortune—twenty-four cows, seventy sheep, and a hundred and twenty goats.

He married this Mary Collopy, and grew richer than before; and Ellen Coleman died broken-hearted. But that did not trouble the strong farmer much.

He would have liked to have children, but he had none, and this was the only cross he had to bear, for everything else went much as he wished.

One night he was returning from the fair of Nenagh. A shallow stream at that time crossed the road—they have thrown a bridge over it, I am told, some time since—and its channel was often dry in summer weather. When it was so, as it passes close by the old farm-house of Drumgunniol, without a great deal of winding, it makes a sort of road, which people then used as a short cut to reach the house by. Into this dry channel, as there was plenty of light from the moon, my grand-uncle turned his horse, and when he had reached the two ash trees at the meering of the farm he turned his horse short into the river field, intending to ride through the gap at the other end, under the oak tree, and so he would have been within a few hundred yards of his door.

As he approached the "gap" he saw, or thought he saw, with a slow motion, gliding along the ground towards the same point, and now and then with a soft bound, a white object, which he described as being no bigger than his hat, but what it was he could not see, as it moved along the hedge and disappeared at the point to which he was himself tending.

When he reached the gap the horse stopped short. He urged and coaxed it in vain. He got down to lead it through, but it recoiled, snorted, and fell into a wild trembling fit. He mounted it again. But its terror continued, and it obstinately resisted his caresses and his whip. It was bright moonlight, and my grand-uncle was chafed by the horse's resistance, and, seeing nothing to account for it, and being so near home, what little patience he possessed forsook him, and, plying his whip and spur in earnest, he broke into oaths and curses.

All of a sudden the horse sprang through, and Con Donovan, as he passed under the broad branch of the oak, saw clearly a woman standing on the bank beside him, her arm extended, with the hand of which, as he flew by, she struck him a blow upon the shoulders. It threw him forward upon the neck of the horse, which, in wild terror, reached the door at a gallop, and stood there quivering and steaming all over.

Less alive than dead, my grand-uncle got in. He told his story, at least, so much as he chose. His wife did not quite know what to think. But that something very bad had happened she could not doubt. He was very faint and ill, and begged that the priest should be sent for forthwith. When they were getting him to his bed they saw distinctly the marks of five fingerprints on the flesh of his shoulder, where the spectral blow had fallen. These singular marks—which they said resembled in tint the hue of a body struck by lightning—remained imprinted on his flesh, and were buried with him.

When he had recovered sufficiently to talk with the people about him—speaking, like a man at his last hour, from a burdened heart, and troubled conscience—he repeated his story, but said he did not see, or, at all events, know, the face of the figure that stood in the gap. No one believed him. He told more about it to the priest than to others. He certainly had a secret to tell. He might as well have divulged it frankly, for the neighbors all knew well enough that it was the face of dead Ellen Coleman that he had seen.

From that moment my grand-uncle never raised his head. He was a scared, silent, broken-spirited man. It was early summer then, and at the fall of the leaf in the same year he died.

Of course there was a wake, such as beseemed a strong farmer so rich as he. For some reason the arrangements of this ceremonial were a little different from the usual routine.

The usual practice is to place the body in the great room, or kitchen, as it is called, of the house. In this particular case there was as I told you, for some reason, an unusual arrangement. The body was placed in a small room that opened upon the greater one. The door of this, during the wake, stood open. There were candles about the bed, and pipes and tobacco on the table, and stools for such guests as chose to enter, the door standing open for their reception.

The body, having been laid out, was left alone, in this smaller room, during the preparations for the wake. After nightfall one of the women, approaching the bed to get a chair which she had left near it, rushed from the room with a scream, and, having recovered her speech at the farther end of the "kitchen," and surrounded by a gaping audience, she said, at last:

"May I never sin, if his face bain't riz up again the back o' the bed, and he starin' down to the doore, wid eyes as big as pewter plates, that id be shinin' in the moon ! "

"Arra, woman! Is it cracked you are?" said one of the farm boys as they are termed, being men of any age you please.

"Ahg, Molly, don't be talkin', woman! 'Tis what ye consayted it, goin' into the dark room, out o' the light. Why didn't ye take a candle in your fingers, ye aumadhaun?" said one of her female companions.

"Candle, or no candle; I seen it," insisted Molly. "An' what's more, I could a'most tak' my oath I seen his arum, too, stretchin' out o' the bed along the flure, three times as long as it should be, to take hould o' me be the fut."

"Nansinse, ye fool, what id he want o' yer fut?" exclaimed one scornfully.

"Gi' me the candle, some o' yez—in the name o' God," said old Sal Doolan, that was straight and lean, and a woman that could pray like a priest almost.

"Give her a candle," agreed all.

But whatever they might say, there wasn't one among them that did not look pale and stern enough as they followed Mrs Doolan, who was praying as fast as her lips could patter, and leading the van with a tallow candle, held like a taper, in her fingers.

The door was half open, as the panic-stricken girl had left it; and holding the candle on high the better to examine the room, she made a step or so into it.

If my grand-uncle's hand had been stretched along the floor, in the unnatural way described, he had drawn it back again under the sheet that covered him. And tall Mrs Doolan was in no danger of tripping over his arm as she entered. But she had not gone more than a step or two with her candle aloft, when, with a drowning face, she suddenly stopped short, staring at the bed which was now fully in view.

"Lord, bless us, Mrs Doolan, ma'am, come back," said the woman next her, who had fast hold of her dress, or her "coat," as they call it, and drawing her backward with a frightened pluck, while a general recoil among her followers betokened the alarm which her hesitation had inspired.

"Whisht, will yez?" said the leader, peremptorily, "I can't hear my own ears wid the noise ye're makin', an' which iv yez let the cat here, an' whose cat is it?" she asked, peering suspiciously at a white cat that was sitting on the breast of the corpse.

"Put it away, will yez?" she resumed, with horror at the profanation. "Many a corpse as I sthretched and crossed in the bed, the likes o' that I never seen yet. The man o' the house, wid a brute baste like that mounted on him, like a phooka, Lord forgi' me for namin' the like in this room. Dhrive it away, some o' yez! out o' that, this minute, I tell ye."

Each repeated the order, but no one seemed inclined to execute it. They were crossing themselves, and whispering their conjectures and misgivings as to the nature of the beast, which was no cat of that house, nor one that they had ever seen before. On a sudden, the white cat placed itself on the pillow over the head of the body, and having from that place glared for a time at them over the features of the corpse, it crept softly along the body toward them, growling low and fiercely as it drew near.

Out of the room they bounced, in dreadful confusion, shutting the door fast after them, and not for a good while did the hardiest venture to peep in again.

The white cat was sitting in its old place, on the dead man's breast, but this time it crept quietly down the side of the bed, and disappeared under it, the sheet which was spread like a coverlet, and hung down nearly to the floor, concealed it from view.

Praying, crossing themselves, and not forgetting a sprinkling of holy water, they peeped, and finally searched, poking spades, "wattles," pitchforks and such implements under the bed. But the cat was not to be found, and they concluded that it had made its escape among their feet as they stood near the threshold. So they secured the door carefully, with hasp and padlock.

But when the door was opened next morning they found the white cat sitting, as if it had never been disturbed, upon the breast of the dead man.

Again occurred very nearly the same scene with a like result, only that some said they saw the cat afterwards lurking under a big box in a corner of the outer room, where my grand-uncle kept his leases and papers, and his prayer-book and beads.

Mrs Doolan heard it growling at her heels wherever she went; and although she could not see it, she could hear it spring on the back of her chair when she sat down, and growl in her ear, so that she would bounce up with a scream and a prayer, fancying that it was on the point of taking her by the throat.

And the priest's boy, looking round the corner, under the branches of the old orchard, saw a white cat sitting under the little window of the room where my grand-uncle was laid out and looking up at the four small panes of glass as a cat will watch a bird.

The end of it was that the cat was found on the corpse again, when the room was visited, and do what they might, whenever the body was left alone, the cat was found again in the same ill-omened contiguity with the dead man. And this continued, to the scandal and fear of the neighborhood, until the door was opened finally for the wake.

My grand-uncle being dead, and, with all due solemnities, buried, I have done with him. But not quite yet with the white cat. No banshee ever yet was more inalienably attached to a family than this apparition is to mine. But there is this difference. The banshee seems to be animated with an affectionate sympathy with the bereaved family to whom it is hereditarily attached, whereas this thing has about it a suspicion of malice. It is the messenger simply of death. And its taking the shape of a cat—the coldest, and they say, the most vindictive of brutes—is indicative of the spirit of its visit.

When my grandfather's death was near, although he seemed quite well at the time, it appeared not exactly, but very nearly in the same way in which I told you it showed itself to my father.

The day before my Uncle Teigue was killed by the bursting of his gun, it appeared to him in the evening, at twilight, by the lough, in the field where I saw the woman who walked across the water, as I told you. My uncle was washing the barrel of his gun in the lough. The grass is short there, and there is no cover near it. He did not know how it approached but the first he saw of it, the white cat was walking close round his feet, in the twilight, with an angry twist of its tail, and a green glare in its eyes, and do what he would, it continued walking round and round him, in larger or smaller circles, till he reached the orchard, and there he lost it.

My poor Aunt Peg—she married one of the O'Brians, near Oolah—came to Drumgunniol to go to the funeral of a cousin who died about a mile away. She died herself, poor woman, only a month after.

Coming from the wake, at two or three o'clock in the morning, as she got over the stile into the farm of Drumgunniol, she saw the white cat at her side, and it kept close beside her, she ready to faint all the time, till she reached the door of the house, where it made a spring up into the white-thorn tree that grows close by, and so it parted from her.

And my little brother Jim saw it also, just three weeks before he died. Every member of our family who dies, or takes his death-sickness, at Drumgunniol, is sure to see the white cat, and no one of us who sees it need hope for long life after.

The Strange Case of Dr. Jekyll and Mr. Hyde

Robert Louis Stevenson

Robert Louis Stevenson (1860-1894) was the only child of a Scottish civil engineer. Stevenson's poor health caused his formal education to be sporadic. Yet he studied law at Edinburgh University and was admitted to the Scottish bar in 1875. In 1873, he began to contribute essays to periodicals. His account of a canoe trip in France and Belgium was published as *An Inland Voyage* in 1878. In 1879, Stevenson met Fanny Van de Grift Osbourne, whom he married the next year. Stevenson lived in a series of health spas throughout Europe. During this time, he produced some of his best known work, including *The New Arabian Nights* (1882), *Treasure Island* (1883), *The Strange Case of Doctor Jekyll and Mr. Hyde* (1886), *Kidnapped* (1886), and *The Merry Men and Other Tales and Fables* (1887). In 1887, after his father's death, Stevenson moved to New York. In 1889 he decided to settle in Samoa. Stevenson became involved in the protest against the white oppression of native Samoans, which led to threats of expulsion by the English and German government. He produced several more works, both by himself and in collaboration with his stepson Lloyd Osbourne. Among these works are *The Black Arrow* (1888), *The Master of Ballantrae* (1889), *The Wrong Box* (1889), *A Footnote to History* (1892), *The Wrecker* (1892), *Catriona* (1893), and *The Ebb Tide* (1894). Stevenson was working on one final novel, *The Weir of Hermiston,* when he died of a cerebral hemorrhage in 1894; it remains unfinished.

Although written some hundred years ago, the psychological subtexts make "Dr. Jekyll and Mr. Hyde" relevant today.

Story of the Door

MR UTTERSON the lawyer was a man of a rugged countenance that was never lighted by a smile; cold, scanty and embarrassed in discourse; backward in sentiment; lean, long, dusty, dreary and yet somehow lovable. At friendly meetings, and when the wine was to his taste, something eminently human beaconed from his eye; something indeed which never found its way into his talk, but which spoke not only in these silent symbols of the after-dinner face, but more often and loudly in the acts of his life. He was austere with himself; drank gin when he was alone, to mortify a taste for vintages; and though he enjoyed the theater, had not crossed the doors of one for twenty years. But he had an approved tolerance for others; sometimes wondering, almost with envy, at the high pressure of spirits involved in their misdeeds; and in any extremity inclined to help rather than to reprove. "I incline to Cain's heresy," he used to say quaintly: "I let my brother go to the devil in his own way." In this character, it was frequently his fortune to be the last reputable acquaintance and the last good influence in the lives of downgoing men. And to such as these, so long as they came about his chambers, he never marked a shade of change in his demeanor.

No doubt the feat was easy to Mr. Utterson; for he was undemonstrative at the best, and even his friendship seemed to be founded in a similar catholicity of good-nature. It is the mark of a modest man to accept his friendly circle ready-made from the hands of opportunity; and that was the lawyer's way. His friends were those of his own blood or those whom he had known the longest; his affections, like ivy, were the growth of time, they implied no aptness in the object. Hence, no doubt, the bond that united him to Mr. Richard Enfield, his distant kinsman, the well-known man about town. It was a nut to crack for many, what these two could see in each other, or what subject they could find in common. It was reported by those who encountered them in their Sunday walks, that they said nothing, looked singularly dull, and would hail with obvious relief the appearance of a friend. For all that, the two men put the greatest store by these excursions, counted them the chief jewel of each week, and not only set aside occasions of pleasure, but even resisted the calls of business, that they might enjoy them uninterrupted.

It chanced on one of these rambles that their way led them down a by-street in a busy quarter of London. The street was small and what is called quiet, but it drove a thriving trade on the week-days. The inhabitants were all doing well, it seemed, and all emulously hoping to do better still, and laying out the surplus of their gains in coquetry; so that the shop fronts stood along that thoroughfare with an air of invitation, like rows of smiling saleswomen. Even on Sunday, when it veiled its more florid charms and lay comparatively empty of passage, the street shone out in contrast to its dingy neighborhood, like a fire in a forest; and with its freshly painted shutters, well-polished brasses, and general cleanliness and gaiety of note, instantly caught and pleased the eye of the passenger.

Two doors from one corner, on the left hand going east, the line was broken by the entry of a court; and just at that point, a certain sinister block of building thrust forward its gable on the street. It was two storys high; showed no window, nothing but a door on the lower storey and a blind forehead of discolored wall on the upper; and bore in every feature, the marks of prolonged and sordid negligence. The door, which was equipped with neither bell nor knocker, was blistered and distained. Tramps slouched into the recess and struck matches on the panels; children kept shop upon the steps; the schoolboy had tried his knife on the mouldings; and for close on a generation, no one had appeared to drive away these random visitors or to repair their ravages.

Mr. Enfield and the lawyer were on the other side of the by-street; but when they came abreast of the entry, the former lifted his cane and pointed.

"Did you ever remark that door?" he asked; and when his companion had replied in the affirmative, "It is connected in my mind," added he, "with a very odd story."

"Indeed?" said Mr. Utterson, with a slight change of voice, "and what was that?"

"Well, it was this way," returned Mr. Enfield: "I was coming home from some place at the end of the world, about three o'clock of a black winter morning, and my way lay through a part of town where there was literally nothing to be seen but lamps. Street after street, and all the folks asleep—street after street, all lighted up as if for a procession and all as empty as a church—till at last I got into that state of mind when a man listens and listens and begins to long for the sight of a policeman. All at once, I saw two figures: one a little man who was stumping along eastward at a good walk, and the other a girl of maybe eight or ten who was running as hard as she was able down a cross street. Well, sir, the two ran into one another naturally enough at the corner; and then came the horrible part of the thing; for the man trampled calmly over the child's body and left her screaming on the ground. It sounds nothing to hear, but it was hellish to see. It wasn't like a man; it was like some damned Juggernaut. I gave a view halloa, took to my heels, collared my gentleman, and brought him back to where there was already quite a group about the screaming child. He was perfectly cool and made no resistance, but gave me one look, so ugly that it brought out the sweat on me like running. The people who had turned out were the girl's own family; and pretty soon, the doctor, for whom she had been sent, put in his appearance. Well, the child was not much the worse, more frightened, according to the Sawbones; and there you might have supposed would be an end to it. But there was one curious circumstance. I had taken a loathing to my gentleman at first sight. So had the child's family, which was only natural. But the doctor's case was what struck me. He was the usual cut and dry apothecary, of no particular age and color, with a strong Edinburgh accent, and about as emotional as a bagpipe. Well, sir, he was like the rest of us; every time he looked at my prisoner, I saw that Sawbones turn sick and white with the desire to kill him. I knew what was in his mind, just as he knew what was in mine; and killing being out of the question, we did the next best. We told the man we could and would make such a scandal out of this, as should make his name stink from one end of London to the other. If he had any friends or any credit, we undertook that he should lose them. And all the time, as we were pitching it in red hot, we were keeping the women off him as best we could, for they were as wild as harpies. I never saw a circle of such hateful faces; and there was the man in the middle, with a kind of black, sneering coolness— frightened too, I could see that—but carrying it off, sir, really like Satan. 'If you choose to make capital out of this accident,' said he, 'I am naturally helpless. No gentleman but wishes to avoid a scene,' says he. 'Name your figure.' Well, we screwed him up to a hundred pounds for the child's family; he would have clearly liked to stick out; but there was something about the lot of us that meant mischief, and at last he struck. The next thing was to get the money; and where do you think he carried us but to that place with the door?—whipped out a key, went in, and presently came back with the matter of ten pounds in gold and a cheque for the balance on Coutts's, drawn payable to bearer and signed with a name that I can't mention, though it's one of the points of my story, but it was a name at least very well known and often printed. The figure was stiff; but the signature was good for more than that, if it was only genuine. I took the liberty of pointing out to my gentleman that the whole business looked apocryphal, and that a man does not, in real life, walk into a cellar door at four in the morning and come out of it with another man's cheque for close upon a hundred pounds. But he was quite easy and sneering. 'Set your mind at rest,' says he, 'I will stay with you till the banks open and cash the cheque myself.' So we all set off, the doctor, and the child's father, and our friend and myself, and passed the rest of the night in my chambers; and next day, when we had breakfasted, went in a body to the bank. I gave in the cheque myself, and said I had every reason to believe it was a forgery. Not a bit of it. The cheque was genuine."

"Tut-tut," said Mr. Utterson.

"I see you feel as I do," said Mr. Enfield. "Yes, it's a bad story. For my man was a fellow that nobody could have to do with, a really damnable man; and the person that drew the cheque is the very pink of the proprieties, celebrated too, and (what makes it worse) one of your fellows who do what they call good. Black mail, I suppose; an honest man paying through the nose for some of the capers of his youth. Black Mail House is what I call that place with the door, in consequence. Though even that, you know, is far from explaining all," he added, and with the words fell into a vein of musing.

From this he was recalled by Mr. Utterson asking rather suddenly: "And you don't know if the drawer of the cheque lives there?"

"A likely place, isn't it?" returned Mr. Enfield. "But I happen to have noticed his address; he lives in some square or other."

"And you never asked about the—place with the door?" said Mr. Utterson.

"No, sir: I had a delicacy," was the reply. "I feel very strongly about putting questions; it partakes too much of the style of the day of judgment. You start a question, and it's like starting a stone. You sit quietly on the top of a hill; and away the stone goes, starting others; and presently some bland old bird (the last you would have thought of) is knocked on the head in his own back garden and the family have to change their name. No, sir, I make it a rule of mine: the more it looks like Queer Street, the less I ask."

"A very good rule, too," said the lawyer.

"But I have studied the place for myself," continued Mr. Enfield. "It seems scarcely a house. There is no other door, and nobody goes in or out of that one but, once in a great while, the gentleman of my adventure. There are three windows looking on the court on the first floor; none below; the windows are always shut but they're clean. And then there is a chimney which is generally smoking; so somebody must live there. And yet it's not so sure; for the buildings are so packed together about that court, that it's hard to say where one ends and another begins."

The pair walked on again for a while in silence; and then "Enfield," said Mr. Utterson, "that's a good rule of yours."

"Yes, I think it is," returned Enfield.

"But for all that," continued the lawyer, "there's one point I want to ask: I want to ask the name of that man who walked over the child."

"Well," said Mr. Enfield, "I can't see what harm it would do. It was a man of the name of Hyde."

"Hm," said Mr. Utterson. "What sort of a man is he to see?"

"He is not easy to describe. There is something wrong with his appearance; something displeasing, something downright detestable. I never saw a man I so disliked, and yet I scarce know why. He must be deformed somewhere; he gives a strong feeling of deformity, although I couldn't specify the point. He's an extraordinary looking man, and yet I really can name nothing out of the way. No, sir; I can make no hand of it; I can't describe him. And it's not want of memory; for I declare I can see him this moment."

Mr. Utterson again walked some way in silence and obviously under a weight of consideration. "You are sure he used a key?" he inquired at last.

"My dear sir..." began Enfield, surprised out of himself.

"Yes, I know," said Utterson; "I know it must seem strange. The fact is, if I do not ask you the name of the other party, it is because I know it already. You see, Richard, your tale has gone home. If you have been inexact in any point, you had better correct it."

"I think you might have warned me," returned the other with a touch of sullenness. "But I have been pedantically exact, as you call it. The fellow had a key; and what's more, he has it still. I saw him use it, not a week ago."

Mr. Utterson sighed deeply but said never a word; and the young man presently resumed. "Here is another lesson to say nothing," said he. "I am ashamed of my long tongue. Let us make a bargain never to refer to this again."

"With all my heart." said the lawyer. "I shake hands on that, Richard."

Search for Mr. Hyde

That evening Mr. Utterson came home to his bachelor house in somber spirits and sat down to dinner without relish. It was his custom of a Sunday, when this meal was over, to sit close by the fire, a volume of some dry divinity on his reading desk, until the clock in the neighboring church rang out the hour of twelve, when he would go soberly and gratefully to bed. On this night, however, as soon as the cloth was taken away, he took up a candle and went into his business room. There he opened his safe, took from the most private part of it a document endorsed on the envelope as Dr. Jekyll's Will, and sat down with a clouded brow to study its contents. The will was holograph, for Mr. Utterson, though he took charge of it now that it was made, had refused to lend the least assistance in the making of it; it provided not only that, in the case of the decease of Henry Jekyll, M.D., D.C.L., L.L.D., F.R.S., etc., all his possessions were to pass into the hands of his "friend and benefactor Edward Hyde," but that in case of Dr. Jekyll's "disappearance or unexplained absence for any period exceeding three calendar months," the said Edward Hyde should step into the said Henry Jekyll's shoes without further delay and free from any burthen or obligation, beyond the payment of a few small sums to the members of the doctor's household. This document had long been the lawyer's eyesore. It offended him both as a lawyer and as a lover of the sane and customary sides of life, to whom the fanciful was the immodest. And hitherto it was his ignorance of Mr. Hyde that had swelled his indignation; now, by a sudden turn, it was his knowledge. It was already bad enough when the name was but a name of which he could learn no more. It was worse when it began to be clothed upon with detestable attributes; and out of the shifting, insubstantial mists that had so long baffled his eye, there leaped up the sudden, definite presentment of a fiend.

"I thought it was madness," he said, as he replaced the obnoxious paper in the safe, "and now I begin to fear it is disgrace."

With that he blew out his candle, put on a greatcoat, and set forth in the direction of Cavendish Square, that citadel of medicine, where his friend, the great Dr. Lanyon, had his house and received his crowding patients. "If anyone knows, it will be Lanyon," he had thought.

The solemn butler knew and welcomed him; he was subjected to no stage of delay, but ushered direct from the door to the dining-room where Dr. Lanyon sat alone over his wine. This was a hearty, healthy, dapper, red-faced gentleman, with a shock of hair prematurely white, and a boisterous and decided manner. At sight of Mr. Utterson, he sprang up from his chair and welcomed him with both hands. The geniality, as was the way of the man, was somewhat theatrical to the eye; but it reposed on genuine feeling. For these two were old friends, old mates both at school and college, both thorough respecters of themselves and of each other, and, what does not always follow, men who thoroughly enjoyed each other's company.

After a little rambling talk, the lawyer led up to the subject which so disagreeably preoccupied his mind.

"I suppose, Lanyon," said he, "you and I must be the two oldest friends that Henry Jekyll has?"

"I wish the friends were younger," chuckled Dr. Lanyon. "But I suppose we are. And what of that? I see little of him now."

"Indeed?" said Utterson. "I thought you had a bond of common interest."

"We had," was the reply. "But it is more than ten years since Henry Jekyll became too fanciful for me. He began to go wrong, wrong in mind; and though of course I continue to take an interest in him for old sake's sake, as they say, I see and I have seen devilish little of the man. Such unscientific balderdash," added the doctor, flushing suddenly purple, "would have estranged Damon and Pythias."

This little spirit of temper was somewhat of a relief to Mr. Utterson. "They have only differed on some point of science," he thought; and being a man of no scientific passions (except in the matter of conveyancing), he even added: "It is nothing worse than that!" He gave his friend a few seconds to recover his composure, and then approached the question he had come to put. "Did you ever come across a protégé of his—one Hyde?" he asked.

"Hyde?" repeated Lanyon. "No. Never heard of him. Since my time."

That was the amount of information that the lawyer carried back with him to the great, dark bed on which he tossed to and fro, until the small hours of the morning began to grow large. It was a night of little ease to his toiling mind, toiling in mere darkness and besieged by questions.

Six o'clock struck on the bells of the church that was so conveniently near to Mr. Utterson's dwelling, and still he was digging at the problem. Hitherto it had touched him on the intellectual side alone; but now his imagination also was engaged, or rather enslaved; and as he lay and tossed in the gross darkness of the night and the curtained room, Mr. Enfield's tale went by before his mind in a scroll of lighted pictures. He would be aware of the great field of lamps of a nocturnal city; then of the figure of a man walking swiftly; then of a child running from the doctor's; and then these met, and that human Juggernaut trod the child down and passed on regardless of her screams. Or else he would see a room in a rich house, where his friend lay asleep, dreaming and smiling at his dreams; and then the door of that room would be opened, the curtains of the bed plucked apart, the sleeper recalled, and lo! there would stand by his side a figure to whom power was given, and even at that dead hour, he must rise and do its bidding. The figure in these two phases haunted the lawyer all night; and if at any time he dozed over, it was but to see it glide more stealthily through sleeping houses, or move the more swiftly and still the more swiftly, even to dizziness, through wider labyrinths of lamplighted city, and at every street corner crush a child and leave her screaming. And still the figure had no face by which he might know it; even in his dreams, it had no face, or one that baffled him and melted before his eyes; and thus it was that there sprang up and grew apace in the lawyer's mind a singularly strong, almost an inordinate, curiosity to behold the features of the real Mr. Hyde. If he could but once set eyes on him, he thought the mystery would lighten and perhaps roll altogether away, as was the habit of mysterious things when well examined. He might see a reason for his friend's strange preference or bondage (call it which you please) and even for the startling clause of the will. At least it would be a face worth seeing: the face of a man who was without bowels of mercy: a face which had but to show itself to raise up, in the mind of the unimpressionable Enfield, a spirit of enduring hatred.

From that time forward, Mr. Utterson began to haunt the door in the by-street of shops. In the morning before office hours, at noon when business was plenty, and time scarce, at night under the face of the fogged city moon, by all lights and at all hours of solitude or concourse, the lawyer was to be found on his chosen post.

"If he be Mr. Hyde," he had thought, "I shall be Mr. Seek."

And at last his patience was rewarded. It was a fine dry night; frost in the air; the streets as clean as a ballroom floor; the lamps, unshaken by any wind, drawing a regular pattern of light and shadow. By ten o'clock, when the shops were closed, the by-street was very solitary and, in spite of the low growl of London from all round, very silent. Small sounds carried far; domestic sounds out of the houses were clearly audible on either side of the roadway; and the rumor of the approach of any passenger preceded him by a long time. Mr. Utterson had been some minutes at his post, when he was aware of an odd, light footstep drawing near. In the course of his nightly patrols, he had long grown accustomed to the quaint effect with which the footfalls of a single person, while he is still a great way off, suddenly spring out distinct from the vast hum and clatter of the city. Yet his attention had never before been so sharply and decisively arrested; and it was with a strong, superstitious prevision of success that he withdrew into the entry of the court.

The steps drew swiftly nearer, and swelled out suddenly louder as they turned the end of the street. The lawyer, looking forth from the entry, could soon see what manner of man he had to deal with. He was small and very plainly dressed, and the look of him, even at that distance, went somehow strongly against the watcher's inclination. But he made straight for the door, crossing the roadway to save time; and as he came, he drew a key from his pocket like one approaching home.

Mr. Utterson stepped out and touched him on the shoulder as he passed. "Mr. Hyde, I think?"

Mr. Hyde shrank back with a hissing intake of the breath. But his fear was only momentary; and though he did not look the lawyer in the face, he answered coolly enough: "That is my name. What do you want?"

"I see you are going in," returned the lawyer. "I am an old friend of Dr. Jekyll's—Mr. Utterson of Gaunt Street—you must have heard of my name; and meeting you so conveniently, I thought you might admit me."

"You will not find Dr. Jekyll; he is from home," replied Mr. Hyde, blowing in the key. And then suddenly, but still without looking up, "How did you know me?" he asked.

"On your side," said Mr. Utterson, "will you do me a favor?"

"With pleasure," replied the other. "What shall it be?"

"Will you let me see your face?" asked the lawyer.

Mr. Hyde appeared to hesitate, and then, as if upon some sudden reflection, fronted about with an air of defiance; and the pair stared at each other pretty fixedly for a few seconds. "Now I shall know you again," said Mr. Utterson. "It may be useful."

"Yes," returned Mr. Hyde, "it is as well we have met; and *à propos,* you should have my address." And he gave a number of a street in Soho.

"Good God!" thought Mr. Utterson, "can he, too, have been thinking of the will?" But he kept his feelings to himself and only grunted in acknowledgment of the address.

"And now," said the other, "how did you know me?"

"By description," was the reply.

"Whose description?"

"We have common friends," said Mr. Utterson.

"Common friends?" echoed Mr. Hyde, a little hoarsely. "Who are they?"

"Jekyll, for instance," said the lawyer.

"He never told you," cried Mr. Hyde, with a flush of anger. "I did not think you would have lied."

"Come," said Mr. Utterson, "that is not fitting language."

The other snarled aloud into a savage laugh; and the next moment, with extraordinary quickness, he had unlocked the door and disappeared into the house.

The lawyer stood awhile when Mr. Hyde had left him, the picture of disquietude. Then he began slowly to mount the street, pausing every step or two and putting his hand to his brow like a man in mental perplexity. The problem he was thus debating as he walked, was one of a class that is rarely solved. Mr. Hyde was pale and dwarfish, he gave an impression of deformity without any nameable malformation, he had a displeasing smile, he had borne himself to the lawyer with a sort of murderous mixture of timidity and boldness, and he spoke with a husky, whispering and somewhat broken voice; all these were points against him, but not all of these together could explain the hitherto unknown disgust, loathing and fear with which Mr. Utterson regarded him. "There must be something else," said the perplexed gentleman. "There *is* something more, if I could find a name for it. God bless me, the man seems hardly human! Something troglodytic, shall we say? or can it be the old story of Dr. Fell? or is it the mere radiance of a foul soul that thus transpires through, and transfigures, its clay continent? The last, I think; for, O my poor old Harry Jekyll, if ever I read Satan's signature upon a face, it is on that of your new friend."

Round the corner from the by-street, there was a square of ancient, handsome houses, now for the most part decayed from their high estate and let in flats and chambers to all sorts and conditions of men; map-engravers, architects, shady lawyers and the agents of obscure enterprises. One house, however, second from the corner, was still occupied entire; and at the door of this, which wore a great air of wealth and comfort, though it was now plunged in darkness except for the fanlight, Mr. Utterson stopped and knocked. A well-dressed, elderly servant opened the door.

"Is Dr. Jekyll at home, Poole?" asked the lawyer.

"I will see, Mr. Utterson," said Poole, admitting the visitor, as he spoke, into a large, low-roofed, comfortable hall, paved with flags, warmed (after the fashion of a country house) by a bright, open fire, and furnished with costly cabinets of oak.

"Will you wait here by the fire, sir? or shall I give you a light in the dining-room?"

"Here, thank you," said the lawyer, and he drew near and leaned on the tall fender. This hall, in which he was now left alone, was a pet fancy of his friend the doctor's; and Utterson himself was wont to speak of it as the pleasantest room in London. But tonight there was a shudder in his blood; the face of Hyde sat heavy on his memory; he felt (what was rare with him) a nausea and distaste of life; and in the gloom of his spirits, he seemed to read a menace in the flickering of the firelight on the polished cabinets and the uneasy starting of the shadow on the roof. He was ashamed of his relief, when Poole presently returned to announce that Dr. Jekyll was gone out.

"I saw Mr. Hyde go in by the old dissecting-room door, Poole," he said. "Is that right, when Dr. Jekyll is from home?"

"Quite right, Mr. Utterson, sir," replied the servant. "Mr. Hyde has a key."

"Your master seems to repose a great deal of trust in that young man, Poole," resumed the other musingly.

"Yes, sir, he do indeed," said Poole. "We have all orders to obey him."

"I do not think I ever met Mr. Hyde?" asked Utterson.

"O, dear no, sir. He never *dines* here," replied the butler. "Indeed we see very little of him on this side of the house; he mostly comes and goes by the laboratory."

"Well, good-night, Poole."

"Good-night, Mr. Utterson."

And the lawyer set out homeward with a very heavy heart. "Poor Harry Jekyll," he thought, "my mind misgives me he is in deep waters! He was wild when he was young; a long while ago to be sure; but in the law of God, there is no statute of limitations. Ay, it must be that; the ghost of some old sin, the cancer of some concealed disgrace: punishment coming, *pede claudo,* years after memory has forgotten and self-love condoned the fault." And the lawyer, scared by the thought, brooded awhile on his own past, groping in all the corners of memory, lest by chance some Jack-in-the-Box of an old iniquity should leap to light there. His past was fairly blameless; few men could read the rolls of their life with less apprehension; yet he was humbled to the dust by the many ill things he had done, and raised up again into a sober and fearful gratitude by the many he had come so near to doing, yet avoided. And then by a return on his former subject, he conceived a spark of hope. "This Master Hyde, if he were studied," thought he, "must have secrets of his own; black secrets, by the look of him; secrets compared to which poor Jekyll's worst would be like sunshine.

Things cannot continue as they are. It turns me cold to think of this creature stealing like a thief to Harry's bedside; poor Harry, what a wakening! And the danger of it; for if this Hyde suspects the existence of the will, he may grow impatient to inherit. Ay, I must put my shoulder to the wheel—if Jekyll will but let me," he added, "if Jekyll will only let me." For once more he saw before his mind's eye, as clear as transparency, the strange clauses of the will.

Dr. Jekyll Was Quite at Ease

A fortnight later, by excellent good fortune, the doctor gave one of his pleasant dinners to some five or six old cronies, all intelligent, reputable men and all judges of good wine; and Mr. Utterson so contrived that he remained behind after the others had departed. This was no new arrangement, but a thing that had befallen many scores of times. Where Utterson was liked, he was liked well. Hosts loved to detain the dry lawyer, when the light-hearted and loose-tongued had already their foot on the threshold; they liked to sit awhile in his unobtrusive company, practicing for solitude, sobering their minds in the man's rich silence after the expense and strain of gaiety. To this rule, Dr. Jekyll was no exception; and as he now sat on the opposite side of the fire—a large, well-made, smooth-faced man of fifty, with something of a slyish cast perhaps, but every mark of capacity and kindness—you could see by his looks that he cherished for Mr. Utterson a sincere and warm affection.

"I have been wanting to speak to you, Jekyll," began the latter. "You know that will of yours?"

A close observer might have gathered that the topic was distasteful; but the doctor carried it off gaily. "My poor Utterson," said he, "you are unfortunate in such a client. I never saw a man so distressed as you were by my will; unless it were that hide-bound pedant, Lanyon, at what he called my scientific heresies. O, I know he's a good fellow—you needn't frown—an excellent fellow, and I always mean to see more of him; but a hide-bound pedant for all that; an ignorant, blatant pedant. I was never more disappointed in any man than Lanyon."

"You know I never approved of it," pursued Utterson, ruthlessly disregarding the fresh topic.

"My will? Yes, certainly, I know that," said the doctor, a trifle sharply. "You have told me so."

"Well, I tell you so again," continued the lawyer. "I have been learning something of young Hyde."

The large handsome face of Dr. Jekyll grew pale to the very lips, and there came a blackness about his eyes. "I do not care to hear more," said he. "This is a matter I thought we had agreed to drop."

"What I heard was abominable," said Utterson.

"It can make no change. You do not understand my position," returned the doctor, with a certain incoherency of manner. "I am painfully situated, Utterson; my position is a very strange—a very strange one. It is one of those affairs that cannot be mended by talking."

"Jekyll," said Utterson, "you know me: I am a man to be trusted. Make a clean breast of this in confidence; and I make no doubt I can get you out of it."

"My good Utterson," said the doctor, "this is very good of you, this is downright good of you, and I cannot find words to thank you in. I believe you fully; I would trust you before any man alive, ay, before myself, if I could make the choice; but indeed it isn't what you fancy; it is not as bad as that; and just to put your good heart at rest, I will tell you one thing: the moment I choose, I can be rid of Mr. Hyde. I give you my hand upon that; and I thank you again and again; and I will just add one little word, Utterson, that I'm sure you'll take in good part: this is a private matter, and I beg of you to let it sleep."

Utterson reflected a little, looking in the fire.

"I have no doubt you are perfectly right," he said at last, getting to his feet.

"Well, but since we have touched upon this business, and for the last time I hope," continued the doctor, "there is one point I should like you to understand. I have really a very great interest in poor Hyde. I know you have seen him; he told me so; and I fear he was rude. But I do sincerely take a great, a very great interest in that young man; and if I am taken away, Utterson, I wish you to promise me that you will bear with him and get his rights for him. I think you would, if you knew all; and it would be a weight off my mind if you would promise."

"I can't pretend that I shall ever like him," said the lawyer.

"I don't ask that," pleaded Jekyll, laying his hand upon the other's arm; "I only ask for justice; I only ask you to help him for my sake, when I am no longer here."

Utterson heaved an irrepressible sigh. "Well," said he, "I promise."

The Carew Murder Case

Nearly a year later, in the month of October, 18—, London was startled by a crime of singular ferocity and rendered all the more notable by the high position of the victim. The details were few and startling. A maid servant living alone in a house not far from the river, had gone upstairs to bed about eleven. Although a fog rolled over the city in the small hours, the early part of the night was cloudless, and the lane, which the maid's window overlooked, was brilliantly lit by the full moon. It seems she was romantically given, for she sat down upon her box, which stood immediately under the window, and fell into a dream of musing. Never (she used to say, with streaming tears, when she narrated that experience), never had she felt more at peace with all men or thought more kindly of the world. And as she so sat she became aware of an aged beautiful gentleman with white hair, drawing near along the lane; and advancing to meet him, another and very small gentleman, to whom at first she paid less attention. When they had come within speech (which was just under the maid's eyes) the older man bowed and accosted the other with a very pretty manner of politeness. It did not seem as if the subject of his address were of great importance; indeed, from his pointing, it sometimes appeared as if he were only inquiring his way; but the moon shone on his face as he spoke, and the girl was pleased to watch it, it seemed to breathe such an innocent and old-world kindness of disposition, yet with something high too, as of a well-founded self-content. Presently her eye wandered to the other, and she was surprised to recognize in him a certain Mr. Hyde, who had once visited her master and for whom she had conceived a dislike. He had in his hand a heavy cane, with which he was trifling; but he answered never a word, and seemed to listen with an ill-contained impatience. And then all of a sudden he broke out in a great flame of anger, stamping with his foot, brandishing the cane, and carrying on (as the maid described it) like a madman. The old gentleman took a step back, with the air of one very much surprised and a trifle hurt; and at that Mr. Hyde broke out of all bounds and clubbed him to the earth. And next moment, with ape-like fury, he was trampling his victim under foot and hailing down a storm of blows, under which the bones were audibly shattered and the body jumped upon the roadway. At the horror of these sights and sounds, the maid fainted.

It was two o'clock when she came to herself and called for the police. The murderer was gone long ago; but there lay his victim in the middle of the lane, incredibly mangled. The stick with which the deed had been done, although it was of some rare and very tough and heavy wood, had broken in the middle under the stress of this insensate cruelty; and one splintered half had rolled in the neighboring gutter—the other, without doubt, had been carried away by the murderer. A purse and gold watch were found upon the victim: but no cards or papers, except a sealed and stamped envelope, which he had been probably carrying to the post, and which bore the name and address of Mr. Utterson.

This was brought to the lawyer the next morning, before he was out of bed; and he had no sooner seen it, and been told the circumstances, than he shot out a solemn lip. "I shall say nothing till I have seen the body," said he; "this may be very serious. Have the kindness to wait while I dress." And with the same grave countenance he hurried through his breakfast and drove to the police station, whither the body had been carried. As soon as he came into the cell, he nodded.

"Yes," said he, "I recognize him. I am sorry to say that this is Sir Danvers Carew."

"Good God, sir," exclaimed the officer, "is it possible?" And the next moment his eye lighted up with professional ambition. "This will make a deal of noise," he said. "And perhaps you can help us to the man." And he briefly narrated what the maid had seen, and showed the broken stick.

Mr. Utterson had already quailed at the name of Hyde; but when the stick was laid before him, he could doubt no longer; broken and battered as it was, he recognized it for one that he had himself presented many years before to Henry Jekyll.

"Is this Mr. Hyde a person of small stature?" he inquired.

"Particularly small and particularly wicked looking, is what the maid calls him," said the officer.

Mr. Utterson reflected; and then, raising his head, "If you will come with me in my cab," he said, "I think I can take you to his house."

It was by this time about nine in the morning, and the first fog of the season. A great chocolate colored pall lowered over heaven, but the wind was continually charging and routing these embattled vapors; so that as the cab crawled from street to street, Mr. Utterson beheld a marvelous number of degrees and hues of twilight; for here it would be dark like the back end of evening; and there would be a glow of a rich, lurid brown, like the light of some strange conflagration; and here, for a moment, the fog would be quite broken up, and a haggard shaft of daylight would glance in between the swirling wreaths. The dismal quarters of Soho seen under these changing glimpses, with its muddy ways, and slatternly passengers, and its lamps, which had never been extinguished or had been kindled afresh to combat this mournful reinvasion of darkness seemed, in the lawyer's eyes, like a district of some city in nightmare. The thoughts of his mind, besides, were of the gloomiest dye; and when he glanced at the companion of his drive, he was conscious of some touch of that terror of the law and the law's officers, which may at times assail the most honest.

As the cab drew up before the address indicated, the fog lifted a little and showed him a dingy street, a gin palace, a low French eating house, a shop for the retail of penny numbers and twopenny salads, many ragged children huddled in the doorways, and many women of many different nationalities passing out, key in hand, to have a morning glass; and the next moment the fog settled down again upon that part, as brown as umber, and cut him off from his blackguardly surroundings. This was the home of Henry Jekyll's favorite; of a man who was heir to a quarter of a million sterling.

An ivory-faced and silvery-haired old woman opened the door. She had an evil face, smoothed by hypocrisy: but her manners were excellent. Yes, she said, this was Mr. Hyde's, but he was not at home; he had been in that night very late, but he had gone away again in less than an hour; there was nothing strange in that; his habits were very irregular, and he was often absent; for instance, it was nearly two months since she had seen him till yesterday.

"Very well, then, we wish to see his rooms," said the lawyer; and when the woman began to declare it was impossible, "I had better tell you who this person is," he added. "This is Inspector Newcomen of Scotland Yard."

A flash of odious joy appeared upon the woman's face. "Ah!" said she, "he is in trouble! What has he done?"

Mr. Utterson and the inspector exchanged glances. "He don't seem a very popular character," observed the latter. "And now, my good woman, just let me and this gentleman have a look about us."

In the whole extent of the house, which but for the old woman remained otherwise empty, Mr. Hyde had only used a couple of rooms; but these were furnished with luxury and good taste. A closet was filled with wine; the plate was of silver, the napery elegant; a good picture hung upon the walls, a gift (as Utterson supposed) from Henry Jekyll, who was much of a connoisseur; and the carpets were of many plies and agreeable in color. At this moment, however, the rooms bore every mark of having been recently and hurriedly ransacked; clothes lay about the floor, with their pockets inside out; lock-fast drawers stood open; and on the hearth there lay a pile of grey ashes, as though many papers had been burned. From these embers the inspector disinterred the butt end of a green cheque book, which had resisted the action of the fire; the other half of the stick was found behind the door; and as this clinched his suspicions, the officer declared himself delighted. A visit to the bank, where several thousand pounds were found to be lying to the murderer's credit, completed his gratification.

"You may depend upon it, sir," he told Mr. Utterson: "I have him in my hand. He must have lost his head, or he never would have left the stick or, above all, burned the cheque book. Why, money's life to the man. We have nothing to do but wait for him at the bank, and get out the handbills."

The last, however, was not so easy of accomplishment; for Mr. Hyde had numbered few familiars—even the master of the servant maid had only seen him twice; his family could nowhere be traced; he had never been photographed; and the few who could describe him differed widely, as common observers will. Only on one point were they agreed; and that was the haunting sense of unexpressed deformity with which the fugitive impressed his beholders.

Incident of the Letter

It was late in the afternoon, when Mr. Utterson found his way to Dr. Jekyll's door, where he was at once admitted by Poole, and carried down by the kitchen offices and across a yard which had once been a garden, to the building which was indifferently known as the laboratory or dissecting rooms. The doctor had bought the house from the heirs of a celebrated surgeon; and his own tastes being rather chemical than anatomical, had changed the destination of the block at the bottom of the garden. It was the first time that the lawyer had been received in that part of his friend's quarters; and he eyed the dingy, windowless structure with curiosity, and gazed round with a distasteful sense of strangeness as he crossed the theater, once crowded with eager students and now lying gaunt and silent, the tables laden with chemical apparatus, the floor strewn with crates and littered with packing straw, and the light falling dimly through the foggy cupola. At the further end, a flight of stairs mounted to a door covered with red baize; and through this, Mr. Utterson was at last received into the doctor's cabinet. It was a large room fitted round with glass presses, furnished, among other things, with a cheval-glass and a business table, and looking out upon the court by three dusty windows barred with iron. The fire burned in the grate; a lamp was set lighted on the chimney shelf, for even in the houses the fog began to lie thickly; and there, close up to the warmth, sat Dr. Jekyll, looking deadly sick. He did not rise to meet his visitor, but held out a cold hand and bade him welcome in a changed voice.

"And now," said Mr. Utterson, as soon as Poole had left them, "you have heard the news?"

The doctor shuddered. "They were crying it in the square," he said. "I heard them in my dining-room."

"One word," said the lawyer. "Carew was my client, but so are you, and I want to know what I am doing. You have not been mad enough to hide this fellow?"

"Utterson, I swear to God," cried the doctor, "I swear to God I will never set eyes on him again. I bind my honor to you that I am done with him in this world. It is all at an end. And indeed he does not want my help; you do not know him as I do; he is safe, he is quite safe; mark my words, he will never more be heard of."

The lawyer listened gloomily; he did not like his friend's feverish manner. "You seem pretty sure of him," said he; "and for your sake, I hope you may be right. If it came to a trial, your name might appear."

"I am quite sure of him," replied Jekyll; "I have grounds for certainty that I cannot share with anyone. But there is one thing on which you may advise me. I have—I have received a letter; and I am at a loss whether I should show it to the police. I should like to leave it in your hands, Utterson; you would judge wisely, I am sure; I have so great a trust in you."

"You fear, I suppose, that it might lead to his detection?" asked the lawyer.

"No," said the other. "I cannot say that I care what becomes of Hyde; I am quite done with him. I was thinking of my own character, which this hateful business has rather exposed."

Utterson ruminated awhile; he was surprised at his friend's selfishness, and yet relieved by it. "Well," said he, at last, "let me see the letter."

The letter was written in an odd, upright hand and signed "Edward Hyde": and it signified, briefly enough, that the writer's benefactor, Dr. Jekyll, whom he had long so unworthily repaid for a thousand generosities, need labor under no alarm for his safety, as he had means of escape on which he placed a sure dependence. The lawyer liked this letter well enough; it put a better color on the intimacy than he had looked for; and he blamed himself for some of his past suspicions.

"Have you the envelope?" he asked.

"I burned it," replied Jekyll, "before I thought what I was about. But it bore no postmark. The note was handed in."

"Shall I keep this and sleep upon it?" asked Utterson.

"I wish you to judge for me entirely," was the reply. "I have lost confidence in myself."

"Well, I shall consider," returned the lawyer. "And now one word more: it was Hyde who dictated the terms in your will about that disappearance?"

The doctor seemed seized with a qualm of faintness; he shut his mouth tight and nodded.

"I knew it," said Utterson. "He meant to murder you. You had a fine escape."

"I have had what is far more to the purpose," returned the doctor solemnly: "I have had a lesson—O God, Utterson, what a lesson I have had!" And he covered his face for a moment with his hands.

On his way out, the lawyer stopped and had a word or two with Poole. "By the bye," said he, "there was a letter handed in to-day: what was the messenger like?" But Poole was positive nothing had come except by post; "and only circulars by that," he added.

This news sent off the visitor with his fears renewed. Plainly the letter had come by the laboratory door; possibly, indeed, it had been written in the cabinet; and if that were so, it must be differently judged, and handled with the more caution.

The newsboys, as he went, were crying themselves hoarse along the footways: "Special edition. Shocking murder of an M.P." That was the funeral oration of one friend and client; and he could not help a certain apprehension lest the good name of another should be sucked down in the eddy of the scandal. It was, at least, a ticklish decision that he had to make; and self-reliant as he was by habit, he began to cherish a longing for advice. It was not to be had directly; but perhaps, he thought, it might be fished for.

Presently after, he sat on one side of his own hearth, with Mr. Guest, his head clerk, upon the other, and midway between, at a nicely calculated distance from the fire, a bottle of a particular old wine that had long dwelt unsunned in the foundations of his house. The fog still slept on the wing above the drowned city, where the lamps glimmered like carbuncles; and through the muffle and smother of these fallen clouds, the procession of the town's life was still rolling in through the great arteries with a sound as of a mighty wind. But the room was gay with firelight. In the bottle the acids were long ago resolved; the imperial dye had softened with time, as the color grows richer in stained windows; and the glow of hot autumn afternoons on hillside vineyards, was ready to be set free and to disperse the fogs of London. Insensibly the lawyer melted. There was no man from whom he kept fewer secrets than Mr. Guest; and he was not always sure that he kept as many as he meant. Guest had often been on business to the doctor's; he knew Poole; he could scarce have failed to hear of Mr. Hyde's familiarity about the house; he might draw conclusions: was it not as well, then, that he should see a letter which put that mystery to rights? and above all since Guest, being a great student and critic of handwriting, would consider the step natural and obliging? The clerk, besides, was a man of counsel; he could scarce read so strange a document without dropping a remark; and by that remark Mr. Utterson might shape his future course.

"This is a sad business about Sir Danvers," he said.

"Yes, sir, indeed. It has elicited a great deal of public feeling," returned Guest. "The man, of course, was mad."

"I should like to hear your views on that," replied Utterson. "I have a document here in his handwriting; it is between ourselves, for I scarce know what to do about it; it is an ugly business at the best. But there it is; quite in your way: a murderer's autograph."

Guest's eyes brightened, and he sat down at once and studied it with passion. "No sir," he said: "not mad; but it is an odd hand."

"And by all accounts a very odd writer," added the lawyer.

Just then the servant entered with a note.

"Is that from Dr. Jekyll, sir?" inquired the clerk. "I thought I knew the writing. Anything private, Mr. Utterson?"

"Only an invitation to dinner. Why? Do you want to see it?"

"One moment. I thank you, sir"; and the clerk laid the two sheets of paper alongside and sedulously compared their contents. "Thank you, sir," he said at last, returning both; "it's a very interesting autograph."

There was a pause, during which Mr. Utterson struggled with himself. "Why did you compare them, Guest?" he inquired suddenly.

"Well, sir," returned the clerk, "there's a rather singular resemblance; the two hands are in many points identical: only differently sloped."

"Rather quaint," said Utterson.

"It is, as you say, rather quaint," returned Guest.

"I wouldn't speak of this note, you know," said the master.

"No, sir," said the clerk. "I understand."

But no sooner was Mr. Utterson alone that night, than he locked the note into his safe, where it reposed from that time forward. "What!" he thought. "Henry Jekyll forge for a murderer!" And his blood ran cold in his veins.

Remarkable Incident of Dr. Lanyon

Time ran on; thousands of pounds were offered in reward, for the death of Sir Danvers was resented as a public injury; but Mr. Hyde had disappeared out of the ken of the police as though he had never existed. Much of his past was unearthed, indeed, and all disreputable: tales came out of the man's cruelty, at once so callous and violent; of his vile life, of his strange associates, of the hatred that seemed to have surrounded his career; but of his present whereabouts, not a whisper. From the time he had left the house in Soho on the morning of the murder, he was simply blotted out; and gradually, as time drew on, Mr. Utterson began to recover from the hotness of his alarm, and to grow more at quiet with himself. The death of Sir Danvers was, to his way of thinking, more than paid for by the disappearance of Mr. Hyde. Now that that evil influence had been withdrawn, a new life began for Dr. Jekyll. He came out of his seclusion, renewed relations with his friends, became once more their familiar guest and entertainer; and whilst he had always been known for charities, he was now no less distinguished for religion. He was busy, he was much in the open air, he did good; his face seemed to open and brighten, as if with an inward consciousness of service; and for more than two months, the doctor was at peace.

On the 8th of January Utterson had dined at the doctor's with a small party; Lanyon had been there; and the face of the host had looked from one to the other as in the old days when the trio were inseparable friends. On the 12th, and again on the 14th, the door was shut against the lawyer. "The doctor was confined to the house," Poole said, "and saw no one." On the 15th, he tried again, and was again refused; and having now been used for the last two months to see his friend almost daily, he found this return of solitude to weigh upon his spirits. The fifth night he had in Guest to dine with him; and the sixth he betook himself to Dr. Lanyon's.

There at least he was not denied admittance; but when he came in, he was shocked at the change which had taken place in the doctor's appearance. He had his death-warrant written legibly upon his face. The rosy man had grown pale; his flesh had fallen away; he was visibly balder and older; and yet it was not so much these tokens of a swift physical decay that arrested the lawyer's notice, as a look in the eye and quality of manner that seemed to testify to some deep-seated terror of the mind. It was unlikely that the doctor should fear death; and yet that was what Utterson was tempted to suspect. "Yes," he thought; "he is a doctor, he must know his own state and that his days are counted; and the knowledge is more than he can bear." And yet when Utterson remarked on his ill-looks, it was with an air of great firmness that Lanyon declared himself a doomed man.

"I have had a shock," he said, "and I shall never recover. It is a question of weeks. Well, life has been pleasant; I liked it; yes, sir, I used to like it. I sometimes think if we knew all, we should be more glad to get away."

"Jekyll is ill, too," observed Utterson. "Have you seen him?"

But Lanyon's face changed, and he held up a trembling hand. "I wish to see or hear no more of Dr. Jekyll," he said in a loud, unsteady voice. "I am quite done with that person; and I beg that you will spare me any allusion to one whom I regard as dead."

"Tut-tut," said Mr. Utterson; and then after a considerable pause, "Can't I do anything?" he inquired. "We are three very old friends, Lanyon; we shall not live to make others."

"Nothing can be done," returned Lanyon; "ask himself."

"He will not see me," said the lawyer.

"I am not surprised at that," was the reply. "Some day, Utterson, after I am dead, you may perhaps come to learn the right and wrong of this. I cannot tell you. And in the meantime, if you can sit and talk with me of other things, for God's sake, stay and do so; but if you cannot keep clear of this accursed topic, then in God's name, go, for I cannot bear it."

As soon as he got home, Utterson sat down and wrote to Jekyll, complaining of his exclusion from the house, and asking the cause of this unhappy break with Lanyon; and the next day brought him a long answer, often very pathetically worded, and sometimes darkly mysterious in drift. The quarrel with Lanyon was incurable. "I do not blame our old friend," Jekyll wrote, "but I share his view that we must never meet. I mean from henceforth to lead a life of extreme seclusion; you must not be surprised, nor must you doubt my friendship, if my door is often shut even to you. You must suffer me to go my own dark way. I have brought on myself a punishment and a danger that I cannot name. If I am the chief of sinners, I am the chief of sufferers also. I could not think that this earth contained a place for sufferings and terrors so unmanning; and you can do but one thing, Utterson, to lighten this destiny, and that is to respect my silence." Utterson was amazed; the dark influence of Hyde had been withdrawn, the doctor had returned to his old tasks and amities; a week ago, the prospect had smiled with every promise of a cheerful and an honored age; and now in a moment, friendship, and peace of mind, and the whole tenor of his life were wrecked. So great and unprepared a change pointed to madness; but in view of Lanyon's manner and words, there must lie for it some deeper ground.

A week afterwards Dr. Lanyon took to his bed, and in something less than a fortnight he was dead. The night after the funeral, at which he had been sadly affected, Utterson locked the door of his business room, and sitting there by the light of a melancholy candle, drew out and set before him an envelope addressed by the hand and sealed with the seal of his dead friend. "PRIVATE: for the hands of G. J. Utterson ALONE, and in case of his predecease *to be destroyed unread,*" so it was emphatically superscribed; and the lawyer dreaded to behold the contents. "I have buried one friend to-day," he thought: "what if this should cost me another?" And then he condemned the fear as a disloyalty, and broke the seal. Within there was another enclosure, likewise sealed, and marked upon the cover as "not to be opened till the death or disappearance of Dr. Henry Jekyll." Utterson could not trust his eyes. Yes, it was disappearance; here again, as in the mad will which he had long ago restored to its author, here again were the idea of a disappearance and the name of Henry Jekyll bracketted. But in the will, that idea had sprung from the sinister suggestion of the man Hyde; it was set there with a purpose all too plain and horrible. Written by the hand of Lanyon, what should it mean? A great curiosity came on the trustee, to disregard the prohibition and dive at once to the bottom of these mysteries; but professional honor and faith to his dead friend were stringent obligations; and the packet slept in the inmost corner of his private safe.

It is one thing to mortify curiosity, another to conquer it; and it may be doubted if, from that day forth, Utterson desired the society of his surviving friend with the same eagerness. He thought of him kindly; but his thoughts were disquieted and fearful. He went to call indeed; but he was perhaps relieved to be denied admittance; perhaps, in his heart, he preferred to speak with Poole upon the doorstep and surrounded by the air and sounds of the open city, rather than to be admitted into that house of voluntary bondage, and to sit and speak with its inscrutable recluse. Poole had, indeed, no very pleasant news to communicate. The doctor, it appeared, now more than ever confined himself to the cabinet over the laboratory, where he would sometimes even sleep; he was out of spirits, he had grown very silent, he did not read; it seemed as if he had something on his mind. Utterson became so used to the unvarying character of these reports, that he fell off little by little in the frequency of his visits.

Incident at the Window

It chanced on Sunday, when Mr. Utterson was on his usual walk with Mr. Enfield, that their way lay once again through the by-street; and that when they came in front of the door, both stopped to gaze on it.

"Well," said Enfield, "that story's at an end at least. We shall never see more of Mr. Hyde."

"I hope not," said Utterson. "Did I ever tell you that I once saw him, and shared your feeling of repulsion?"

"It was impossible to do the one without the other," returned Enfield. "And by the way, what an ass you must have thought me, not to know that this was a back way to Dr. Jekyll's! It was partly your own fault that I found it out, even when I did."

"So you found it out, did you?" said Utterson. "But if that be so, we may step into the court and take a look at the windows. To tell you the truth, I am uneasy about poor Jekyll; and even outside, I feel as if the presence of a friend might do him good."

The court was very cool and a little damp, and full of premature twilight, although the sky, high up overhead, was still bright with sunset. The middle one of the three windows was half-way open; and sitting close beside it, taking the air with an infinite sadness of mien, like some disconsolate prisoner, Utterson saw Dr. Jekyll.

"What! Jekyll!" he cried. "I trust you are better."

"I am very low, Utterson," replied the doctor drearily, "very low. It will not last long, thank God."

"You stay too much indoors," said the lawyer. "You should be out, whipping up the circulation like Mr. Enfield and me. (This is my cousin—Mr. Enfield—Dr. Jekyll.) Come now; get your hat and take a quick turn with us."

"You are very good," sighed the other. "I should like to very much; but no, no, no, it is quite impossible; I dare not. But indeed, Utterson,

I am very glad to see you; this is really a great pleasure; I would ask you and Mr. Enfield up, but the place is really not fit."

"Why then," said the lawyer, good-naturedly, "the best thing we can do is to stay down here and speak with you from where we are."

"That is just what I was about to venture to propose," returned the doctor with a smile. But the words were hardly uttered, before the smile was struck out of his face and succeeded by an expression of such abject terror and despair, as froze the very blood of the two gentlemen below. They saw it but for a glimpse for the window was instantly thrust down; but that glimpse had been sufficient, and they turned and left the court without a word. In silence, too, they traversed the by-street; and it was not until they had come into a neighboring thoroughfare, where even upon a Sunday there were still some stirrings of life, that Mr. Utterson at last turned and looked at his companion. They were both pale; and there was an answering horror in their eyes.

"God forgive us, God forgive us," said Mr. Utterson.

But Mr. Enfield only nodded his head very seriously, and walked on once more in silence.

The Last Night

Mr. Utterson was sitting by his fireside one evening after dinner, when he was surprised to receive a visit from Poole.

"Bless me, Poole, what brings you here?" he cried; and then taking a second look at him, "What ails you?" he added; "is the doctor ill?"

"Mr. Utterson," said the man, "there is something wrong."

"Take a seat, and here is a glass of wine for you," said the lawyer. "Now, take your time, and tell me plainly what you want."

"You know the doctor's ways, sir," replied Poole, "and how he shuts himself up. Well, he's shut up again in the cabinet; and I don't like it, sir—I wish I may die if I like it. Mr. Utterson, sir, I'm afraid."

"Now, my good man," said the lawyer, "be explicit. What are you afraid of?"

"I've been afraid for about a week," returned Poole, doggedly disregarding the question, "and I can bear it no more."

The man's appearance amply bore out his words; his manner was altered for the worse; and except for the moment when he had first announced his terror, he had not once looked the lawyer in the face. Even now, he sat with the glass of wine untasted on his knee, and his eyes directed to a corner of the floor. "I can bear it no more," he repeated.

"Come," said the lawyer, "I see you have some good reason, Poole; I see there is something seriously amiss. Try to tell me what it is."

"I think there's been foul play," said Poole, hoarsely.

"Foul play!" cried the lawyer, a good deal frightened and rather inclined to be irritated in consequence. "What foul play! What does the man mean?"

"I daren't say, sir," was the answer; "but will you come along with me and see for yourself?"

Mr. Utterson's only answer was to rise and get his hat and greatcoat; but he observed with wonder the greatness of the relief that appeared upon the butler's face, and perhaps with no less, that the wine was still untasted when he set it down to follow.

It was a wild, cold, seasonable night of March, with a pale moon, lying on her back as though the wind had tilted her, and a flying wrack of the most diaphanous and lawny texture. The wind made talking difficult, and flecked the blood into the face. It seemed to have swept the streets unusually bare of passengers, besides; for Mr. Utterson thought he had never seen that part of London so deserted. He could have wished it otherwise; never in his life had he been conscious of so sharp a wish to see and touch his fellow-creatures; for struggle as he might, there was borne in upon his mind a crushing anticipation of calamity. The square, when they got there, was full of wind and dust, and the thin trees in the garden were lashing themselves along the railing. Poole, who had kept all the way a pace or two ahead, now pulled up in the middle of the pavement, and in spite of the biting weather, took off his hat and mopped his brow with a red pocket-handkerchief. But for all the hurry of his coming, these were not the dews of exertion that he wiped away, but the moisture of some strangling anguish; for his face was white and his voice, when he spoke, harsh and broken.

"Well, sir," he said, "here we are, and God grant there be nothing wrong."

"Amen, Poole," said the lawyer.

Thereupon the servant knocked in a very guarded manner; the door was opened on the chain; and a voice asked from within, "Is that you, Poole?"

"It's all right," said Poole. "Open the door."

The hall, when they entered it, was brightly lighted up; the fire was built high; and about the hearth the whole of the servants, men and women, stood huddled together like a flock of sheep. At the sight of Mr. Utterson, the housemaid broke into hysterical whimpering; and the cook, crying out "Bless God! It's Mr. Utterson," ran forward as if to take him in her arms.

"What, what? Are you all here?" said the lawyer peevishly. "Very irregular, very unseemly; your master would be far from pleased."

"They're all afraid," said Poole.

Blank silence followed, no one protesting; only the maid lifted up her voice and now wept loudly.

"Hold your tongue!" Poole said to her, with a ferocity of accent that testified to his own jangled nerves; and indeed, when the girl had so suddenly raised the note of her lamentation, they had all started and turned towards the inner door with faces of dreadful expectation. "And now," continued the butler, addressing the knife-boy, "reach me a candle, and we'll get this through hands at once." And then he begged Mr. Utterson to follow him, and led the way to the back garden.

"Now, sir," said he, "you come as gently as you can. I want you to hear, and I don't want you to be heard. And see here, sir, if by any chance he was to ask you in, don't go."

Mr. Utterson's nerves, at this unlooked-for termination, gave a jerk that nearly threw him from his balance; but he recollected his courage and followed the butler into the laboratory building and through the surgical theater, with its lumber of crates and bottles, to the foot of the stair. Here Poole motioned him to stand on one side and listen; while he himself, setting down the candle and making a great and obvious call on his resolution, mounted the steps and knocked with a somewhat uncertain hand on the red baize of the cabinet door.

"Mr. Utterson, sir, asking to see you," he called; and even as he did so, once more violently signed to the lawyer to give ear.

A voice answered from within: "Tell him I cannot see anyone," it said complainingly.

"Thank you, sir," said Poole, with a note of something like triumph in his voice; and taking up his candle, he led Mr. Utterson back across the yard and into the great kitchen, where the fire was out and the beetles were leaping on the floor.

"Sir," he said, looking Mr. Utterson in the eyes, "was that my master's voice?"

"It seems much changed," replied the lawyer, very pale, but giving look for look.

"Changed? Well, yes, I think so," said the butler. "Have I been twenty years in this man's house, to be deceived about his voice? No, sir; master's made away with; he was made away with eight days ago, when we heard him cry out upon the name of God; and *who's* in there instead of him, and *why* it stays there, is a thing that cries to Heaven, Mr. Utterson!"

"This is a very strange tale, Poole; this is rather a wild tale, my man," said Mr. Utterson, biting his finger. "Suppose it were as you suppose, supposing Dr. Jekyll to have been—well, murdered, what could induce the murderer to stay? That won't hold water; it doesn't commend itself to reason."

"Well, Mr. Utterson, you are a hard man to satisfy, but I'll do it yet," said Poole. "All this last week (you must know) him, or it, whatever it is that lives in that cabinet, has been crying night and day for some sort of medicine and cannot get it to his mind. It was sometimes his way—the master's, that is—to write his orders on a sheet of paper and throw it on the stair. We've had nothing else this week back; nothing but papers, and a closed door, and the very meals left there to be smuggled in when nobody was looking. Well, sir, every day, ay, and twice and thrice in the same day, there have been orders and complaints, and I have been sent flying to all the wholesale chemists in town. Every time I brought the stuff back, there would be another paper telling me to return it, because it was not pure, and another order to a different firm. This drug is wanted bitter bad, sir, whatever for."

"Have you any of these papers?" asked Mr. Utterson.

Poole felt in his pocket and handed out a crumpled note, which the lawyer, bending nearer to the candle, carefully examined. Its contents ran thus: "Dr. Jekyll presents his compliments to Messrs. Maw. He assures them that their last sample is impure and quite useless for his present purpose. In the year 18—, Dr. J. purchased a somewhat large quantity from Messrs. M. He now begs them to search with most sedulous care, and should any of the same quality be left, to forward it to him at once. Expense is no consideration. The importance of this to Dr. J. can hardly be exaggerated." So far the letter had run composedly enough, but here with a sudden splutter of the pen, the writer's emotions had broken loose. "For God's sake," he added, "find me some of the old."

"This is a strange note," said Mr. Utterson; and then sharply, "How do you come to have it open?"

"The man at Maw's was main angry, sir, and he threw it back to me like so much dirt," returned Poole.

"This is unquestionably the doctor's hand, do you know?" resumed the lawyer.

"I thought it looked like it," said the servant rather sulkily; and then, with another voice, "But what matters hand of write?" he said. "I've seen him!"

"Seen him?" repeated Mr. Utterson. "Well?"

"That's it!" said Poole. "It was this way. I came suddenly into the theater from the garden. It seems he had slipped out to look for this drug or whatever it is; for the cabinet door was open, and there he was at the far end of the room digging among the crates. He looked up when I came in, gave a kind of cry, and whipped upstairs into the cabinet. It was but for one minute that I saw him, but the hair stood upon my head like quills. Sir, if that was my master, why had he a mask upon his face? If it was my master, why did he cry out like a rat, and run from me? I have served him long enough. And then..." The man paused and passed his hand over his face.

"These are all very strange circumstances," said Mr. Utterson, "but I think I begin to see daylight. Your master, Poole, is plainly seized with one of those maladies that both torture and deform the sufferer; hence, for aught I know, the alteration of his voice; hence the mask and the avoidance of his friends; hence his eagerness to find this drug, by means of which the poor soul retains some hope of ultimate recovery—God grant that he be not deceived! There is my explanation; it is sad enough, Poole, ay, and appalling to consider; but it is plain and natural, hangs well together, and delivers us from all exorbitant alarms."

"Sir," said the butler, turning to a sort of mottled pallor, "that thing was not my master, and there's the truth. My master"—here he looked round him and began to whisper—"is a tall, fine build of a man, and this was more of a dwarf." Utterson attempted to protest. "O, sir," cried Poole, "do you think I do not know my master after twenty years? Do you think I do not know where his head comes to in the cabinet door, where I saw him every morning of my life? No, sir, that thing in the mask was never Dr. Jekyll—God knows what it was, but it was never Dr. Jekyll; and it is the belief of my heart that there was murder done."

"Poole," replied the lawyer, "if you say that, it will become my duty to make certain. Much as I desire to spare your master's feelings, much as I am puzzled by this note which seems to prove him to be still alive, I shall consider it my duty to break in that door."

"Ah, Mr. Utterson, that's talking!" cried the butler.

"And now comes the second question," resumed Utterson: "Who is going to do it?"

"Why, you and me, sir," was the undaunted reply.

"That's very well said," returned the lawyer; "and whatever comes of it, I shall make it my business to see you are no loser."

"There is an axe in the theater," continued Poole; "and you might take the kitchen poker for yourself."

The lawyer took that rude but weighty instrument into his hand, and balanced it. "Do you know, Poole," he said, looking up, "that you and I are about to place ourselves in a position of some peril?"

"You may say so, sir, indeed," returned the butler.

"It is well, then, that we should be frank," said the other. "We both think more than we have said; let us make a clean breast. This masked figure that you saw, did you recognize it?"

"Well, sir, it went so quick, and the creature was so doubled up, that I could hardly swear to that," was the answer. "But if you mean, was it Mr. Hyde?—why, yes, I think it was! You see, it was much of the same bigness; and it had the same quick, light way with it; and then who else could have got in by the laboratory door? You have not forgot, sir, that at the time of the murder he had still the key with him? But that's not all. I don't know, Mr. Utterson, if you ever met this Mr. Hyde?"

"Yes," said the lawyer, "I once spoke with him."

"Then you must know as well as the rest of us that there was something queer about that gentleman—something that gave a man a turn—I don't know rightly how to say it, sir, beyond this: that you felt in your marrow kind of cold and thin."

"I own I felt something of what you describe," said Mr. Utterson.

"Quite so, sir," returned Poole. "Well, when that masked thing like a monkey jumped from among the chemicals and whipped into the cabinet, it went down my spine like ice. O, I know it's not evidence, Mr. Utterson; I'm book-learned enough for that; but a man has his feelings, and I give you my bible-word it was Mr. Hyde!"

"Ay, ay," said the lawyer. "My fears incline to the same point. Evil, I fear, founded—evil was sure to come—of that connection. Ay truly, I believe you; I believe poor Harry is killed; and I believe his murderer (for what purpose, God alone can tell) is still lurking in his victim's room. Well, let our name be vengeance. Call Bradshaw."

The footman came at the summons, very white and nervous.

"Pull yourself together, Bradshaw," said the lawyer. "This suspense, I know, is telling upon all of you; but it is now our intention to make an end of it. Poole, here, and I are going to force our way into the cabinet. If all is well, my shoulders are broad enough to bear the blame. Meanwhile, lest anything should really be amiss, or any malefactor seek to escape by the back, you and the boy must go round the corner with a pair of good sticks and take your post at the laboratory door. We give you ten minutes, to get to your stations."

As Bradshaw left, the lawyer looked at his watch. "And now, Poole, let us get to ours," he said; and taking the poker under his arm, led the way into the yard. The scud had banked over the moon, and it was now quite dark. The wind, which only broke in puffs and draughts into that deep well of building, tossed the light of the candle to and fro about their steps, until they came into the shelter of the theater, where they sat down silently to wait. London hummed solemnly all around; but nearer at hand, the stillness was only broken by the sounds of a footfall moving to and fro along the cabinet floor.

"So it will walk all day, sir," whispered Poole; "ay, and the better part of the night. Only when a new sample comes from the chemist, there's a bit of a break. Ah, it's an ill conscience that's such an enemy to rest! Ah, sir, there's blood foully shed in every step of it! But hark again, a little closer—put your heart in your ears, Mr. Utterson, and tell me, is that the doctor's foot?"

The steps fell lightly and oddly, with a certain swing, for all they went so slowly; it was different indeed from the heavy creaking tread of Henry Jekyll. Utterson sighed. "Is there never anything else?" he asked.

Poole nodded. "Once," he said. "Once I heard it weeping!"

"Weeping? how that?" said the lawyer, conscious of a sudden chill of horror.

"Weeping like a woman or a lost soul," said the butler. "I came away with that upon my heart, that I could have wept too."

But now the ten minutes drew to an end. Poole disinterred the axe from under a stack of packing straw; the candle was set upon the nearest table to light them to the attack; and they drew near with bated breath to where that patient foot was still going up and down, up and down, in the quiet of the night. "Jekyll," cried Utterson, with a loud voice, "I demand to see you." He paused a moment, but there came no reply. "I give you fair warning, our suspicions are aroused, and I must and shall see you," he resumed; "if not by fair means, then by foul—if not of your consent, then by brute force!"

"Utterson," said the voice, "for God's sake, have mercy!"

"Ah, that's not Jekyll's voice—it's Hyde's!" cried Utterson. "Down with the door, Poole!"

Poole swung the axe over his shoulder; the blow shook the building, and the red baize door leaped against the lock and hinges. A dismal screech, as of mere animal terror, rang from the cabinet. Up went the axe again, and again the panels crashed and the frame bounded; four times the blow fell; but the wood was tough and the fittings were of excellent workmanship; and it was not until the fifth, that the lock burst and the wreck of the door fell inwards on the carpet.

The besiegers, appalled by their own riot and the stillness that had succeeded, stood back a little and peered in. There lay the cabinet before their eyes in the quiet lamplight, a good fire glowing and chattering on the hearth, the kettle singing its thin strain, a drawer or two open, papers neatly set forth on the business table, and nearer the fire, the things laid out for tea; the quietest room, you would have said, and, but for the glazed presses full of chemicals, the most commonplace that night in London.

Right in the midst there lay the body of a man sorely contorted and still twitching. They drew near on tiptoe, turned it on its back and beheld the face of Edward Hyde. He was dressed in clothes far too large for him, clothes of the doctor's bigness; the cords of his face still moved with a semblance of life, but life was quite gone: and by the crushed phial in the hand and the strong smell of kernels that hung upon the air, Utterson knew that he was looking on the body of a self-destroyer.

"We have come too late," he said sternly, "whether to save or punish. Hyde is gone to his account; and it only remains for us to find the body of your master."

The far greater proportion of the building was occupied by the theater, which filled almost the whole ground story and was lighted from above, and by the cabinet, which formed an upper story at one end and looked upon the court. A corridor joined the theater to the door on the by-street; and with this the cabinet communicated separately by a second flight of stairs. There were besides a few dark closets and a spacious cellar. All these they now thoroughly examined. Each closet needed but a glance, for all were empty, and all, by the dust that fell from their doors, had stood long unopened. The cellar, indeed, was filled with crazy lumber, mostly dating from the times of the surgeon who was Jekyll's predecessor; but even as they opened the door they were advertised of the uselessness of further search, by the fall of a perfect mat of cobweb which had for years sealed up the entrance. Nowhere was there any trace of Henry Jekyll, dead or alive.

Poole stamped on the flags of the corridor. "He must be buried here," he said, hearkening to the sound.

"Or he may have fled," said Utterson, and he turned to examine the door in the by-street. It was locked; and lying near by on the flags, they found the key, already stained with rust.

"This does not look like use," observed the lawyer.

"Use!" echoed Poole. "Do you not see, sir, it is broken? much as if a man had stamped on it."

"Ay," continued Utterson, "and the fractures, too, are rusty." The two men looked at each other with a scare. "This is beyond me, Poole," said the lawyer. "Let us go back to the cabinet."

They mounted the stair in silence, and still with an occasional awestruck glance at the dead body, proceeded more thoroughly to examine the contents of the cabinet. At one table, there were traces of chemical work, various measured heaps of some white salt being laid on glass saucers, as though for an experiment in which the unhappy man had been prevented.

"That is the same drug that I was always bringing him," said Poole; and even as he spoke, the kettle with a startling noise boiled over.

This brought them to the fireside, where the easychair was drawn cosily up, and the tea things stood ready to the sitter's elbow, the very sugar in the cup. There were several books on a shelf; one lay beside the tea things open, and Utterson was amazed to find it a copy of a pious work, for which Jekyll had several times expressed a great esteem, annotated, in his own hand, with startling blasphemies.

Next, in the course of their review of the chamber, the searchers came to the cheval-glass, into whose depths they looked with an involuntary horror. But it was so turned as to show them nothing but the rosy glow playing on the roof, the fire sparkling in a hundred repetitions along the glazed front of the presses, and their own pale and fearful countenances stooping to look in.

"This glass has seen some strange things, sir," whispered Poole.

"And surely none stranger than itself," echoed the lawyer in the same tones. "For what did Jekyll"—he caught himself up at the word with a start, and then conquering the weakness— "what could Jekyll want with it?" he said.

"You may say that!" said Poole.

Next they turned to the business table. On the desk, among the neat array of papers, a large envelope was uppermost, and bore, in the doctor's hand, the name of Mr. Utterson. The lawyer unsealed it, and several enclosures fell to the floor. The first was a will, drawn in the same eccentric terms as the one which he had returned six months before, to serve as a testament in case of death and as a deed of gift in case of disappearance; but in place of the name of Edward Hyde, the lawyer, with indescribable amazement, read the name of Gabriel John Utterson. He looked at Poole, and then back at the paper, and last of all at the dead malefactor stretched upon the carpet.

"My head goes round," he said. "He has been all these days in possession; he had no cause to like me; he must have raged to see himself displaced; and he has not destroyed this document."

He caught up the next paper; it was a brief note in the doctor's hand and dated at the top. "O Poole!" the lawyer cried, "he was alive and here this day. He cannot have been disposed of in so short a space; he must be still alive, he must have fled! And then, why fled? and how? and in that case, can we venture to declare this suicide? O, we must be careful. I foresee that we may yet involve your master in some dire catastrophe."

"Why don't you read it, sir?" asked Poole.

"Because I fear," replied the lawyer solemnly. "God grant I have no cause for it!" And with that he brought the paper to his eyes and read as follows:

> My Dear Utterson,—When this shall fall into your hands, I shall have disappeared, under what circumstances I have not the penetration to foresee, but my instinct and all the circumstances of my nameless situation tell me that the end is sure and must be early. Go then, and first read the narrative which Lanyon warned me he was to place in your hands; and if you care to hear more, turn to the confession of
>
> Your unworthy and unhappy friend,
>
> HENRY JEKYLL.

"There was a third enclosure?" asked Utterson.

"Here, sir," said Poole, and gave into his hands a considerable packet sealed in several places.

The lawyer put it in his pocket. "I would say nothing of this paper. If your master has fled or is dead, we may at least save his credit. It is now ten; I must go home and read these documents in quiet; but I shall be back before midnight, when we shall send for the police."

They went out, locking the door of the theater behind them; and Utterson, once more leaving the servants gathered about the fire in the hall, trudged back to his office to read the two narratives in which this mystery was now to be explained.

Dr. Lanyon's Narrative

On the ninth of January, now four days ago, I received by the evening delivery a registered envelope, addressed in the hand of my colleague and old school companion, Henry Jekyll. I was a good deal surprised by this; for we were by no means in the habit of correspondence; I had seen the man, dined with him, indeed, the night before; and I could imagine nothing in our intercourse that should justify formality of registration. The contents increased my wonder; for this is how the letter ran:

10th December, 18—

Dear Lanyon,—You are one of my oldest friends; and although we may have differed at times on scientific questions, I cannot remember, at least on my side, any break in our affection. There was never a day when, if you had said to me, "Jekyll, my life, my honor, my reason, depend upon you," I would not have sacrificed my left hand to help you. Lanyon, my life, my honor, my reason, are all at your mercy; if you fail me to-night, I am lost. You might suppose, after this preface, that I am going to ask you for something dishonorable to grant. Judge for yourself.

I want you to postpone all other engagements for to-night—ay, even if you were summoned to the bedside of an emperor; to take a cab, unless your carriage should be actually at the door; and with this letter in your hand for consultation, to drive straight to my house. Poole, my butler, has his orders; you will find him waiting your arrival with a locksmith. The door of my cabinet is then to be forced: and you are to go in alone; to open the glazed press (letter E) on the left hand, breaking the lock if it be shut; and to draw out, *with all its contents as they stand,* the fourth drawer from the top or (which is the same thing) the third from the bottom. In my extreme distress of mind, I have a morbid fear of misdirecting you; but even if I am in error, you may know the right drawer by its contents: some powders, a phial and a paper book. This drawer I beg of you to carry back with you to Cavendish Square exactly as it stands.

That is the first part of the service: now for the second. You should be back, if you set out at once on the receipt of this, long before midnight; but I will leave you that amount of margin, not only in the fear of one of those obstacles that can neither be prevented nor foreseen, but because an hour when your servants are in bed is to be preferred for what will then remain to do. At midnight, then, I have to ask you to be alone in your consulting room, to admit with your own hand into the house a man who will present himself in my name, and to place in his hands the drawer that you will have brought with you from my cabinet. Then you will have played your part and earned my gratitude completely. Five minutes afterwards, if you insist upon an explanation, you will have understood that these arrangements are of capital importance; and that by the neglect of one of them, fantastic as they must appear, you might have charged your conscience with my death or the shipwreck of my reason.

Confident as I am that you will not trifle with this appeal, my heart sinks and my hand trembles at the bare thought of such a possibility. Think of me at this hour, in a strange place, laboring under a blackness of distress that no fancy can exaggerate, and yet well aware that, if you will but punctually serve me, my troubles will roll away like a story that is told. Serve me, my dear Lanyon, and save

Your friend,

H. J.

P.S.—I had already sealed this up when a fresh terror struck upon my soul. It is possible that the post-office may fail me, and this letter not come into your hands until to-morrow morning. In that case, dear Lanyon, do my errand when it shall be most convenient for you in the course of the day; and once more expect my messenger at midnight. It may then already be too late; and if that night passes without event, you will know that you have seen the last of Henry Jekyll.

Upon the reading of this letter, I made sure my colleague was insane; but till that was proved beyond the possibility of doubt, I felt bound to do as he requested. The less I understood of this farrago, the less I was in a position to judge of its importance; and an appeal so worded could not be set aside without a grave responsibility. I rose accordingly from table, got into a hansom, and drove straight to Jekyll's house. The butler was awaiting my arrival; he had received by the same post as mine a registered letter of instruction, and had sent at once for a locksmith and a carpenter. The tradesman came while we were yet speaking; and as we moved in a body to old Dr. Denman's surgical theater, from which (as you are doubtless aware) Jekyll's private cabinet is most conveniently entered. The door was very strong, the lock excellent; the carpenter avowed he would have great trouble and have to do much damage, if force were to be used; and the locksmith was near despair. But this last was a handy fellow, and after two hours' work, the door stood open. The press marked E was unlocked; and I took out the drawer, had it filled with straw and tied in a sheet, and returned with it to Cavendish Square.

Here I proceeded to examine its contents. The powders were neatly enough made up, but not with the nicety of the dispensing chemist; so that it was plain that they were of Jekyll's private manufacture: and when I opened one of the wrappers I found what seemed to me a simple crystalline salt of a white color. The phial, to which I next turned my attention, might have been about half full of a blood-red liquor, which was highly pungent to the sense of smell and seemed to me to contain phosphorous and some volatile ether. At the other ingredients I could make no guess. The book was an ordinary version book and contained little but a series of dates. These covered a period of many years, but I observed that the entries ceased nearly a year ago and quite abruptly. Here and there a brief remark was appended to a date, usually no more than a single word: "double" occuring prehaps six times in a total of several hundred entries; and once very early in the list and followed by several marks of exclamation, "total failure!!!" All this, though, whetted my curiosity, told me little that was definite. Here were a phial of some tincture, a paper of some salt, and the record of a series of experiments that had led (like too many of Jekyll's investigations) to no end of practical usefulness. How could the presence of these articles in my house affect either the honor, or the sanity, or the life of my flighty colleague? If his messenger could go to one place, why could he not go to another? And even granting some impediment, why was this gentleman to be received by me in secret? The more I reflected the more convinced I grew that I was dealing with a case of cerebral disease; and though I dismissed my servants to bed, I loaded an old revolver, that I might be found in some posture of self-defense.

Twelve o'clock had scarce rung out over London, ere the knocker sounded very gently on the door. I went myself at the summons, and found a small man crouching against the pillars of the portico.

"Are you come from Dr. Jekyll?" I asked.

He told me "yes" by a constrained gesture; and when I had bidden him enter, he did not obey me without a searching backward glance into the darkness of the square. There was a policeman not far off, advancing with his bull's eye open; and at the sight, I thought my visitor started and made greater haste.

These particulars struck me, I confess, disagreeably; and as I followed him into the bright light of the consulting room, I kept my hand ready on my weapon. Here, at last, I had a chance of clearly seeing him. I had never set eyes on him before, so much was certain. He was small, as I have said; I was struck besides with the shocking expression of his face, with his remarkable combination of great muscular activity and great apparent debility of constitution, and—last but not least—with the odd, subjective disturbance caused by his neighborhood. This bore some resemblance to incipient rigor, and was accompanied by a marked sinking of the pulse. At the time, I set it down to some idiosyncratic, personal distaste, and merely wondered at the acuteness of the symptoms; but I have since had reason to believe the cause to lie much deeper in the nature of man, and to turn on some nobler hinge than the principle of hatred.

This person (who had thus, from the first moment of his entrance, struck in me what I can only describe as a disgustful curiosity) was dressed in a fashion that would have made an ordinary person laughable; his clothes, that is to say, although they were of rich and sober fabric, were enormously too large for him in every measurement—the trousers hanging on his legs and rolled up to keep them from the ground, the waist of the coat below his haunches, and the collar sprawling wide upon his shoulders. Strange to relate, this ludicrous accoutrement was far from moving me to laughter. Rather, as there was something abnormal and misbegotten in the very essence of the creature that now faced me—something seizing, surprising and revolting—this fresh disparity seemed but to fit in with and to reinforce it; so that to my interest in the man's nature and character, there was added a curiosity as to his origin, his life, his fortune and status in the world.

These observations, though they have taken so great a space to be set down in, were yet the work of a few seconds. My visitor was, indeed, on fire with somber excitement.

"Have you got it?" he cried. "Have you got it?" And so lively was his impatience that he even laid his hand upon my arm and sought to shake me.

I put him back, conscious at his touch of a certain icy pang along my blood. "Come, sir," said I. "You forget that I have not yet the pleasure of your acquaintance. Be seated, if you please." And I showed him an example, and sat down myself in my customary seat and with as fair an imitation of my ordinary manner to a patient, as the lateness of the hour, the nature of my preoccupations, and the horror I had of my visitor, would suffer me to muster.

"I beg your pardon, Dr. Lanyon," he replied civilly enough. "What you say is very well founded; and my impatience has shown its heels to my politeness. I come here at the instance of your colleague, Dr. Henry Jekyll, on a piece of business of some moment; and I understood..." He paused and put his hand to his throat, and I could see, in spite of his collected manner, that he was wrestling against the approaches of the hysteria—"I understood, a drawer..."

But here I took pity on my visitor's suspense, and some perhaps on my own growing curiosity.

"There it is, sir," said I, pointing to the drawer, where it lay on the floor behind a table and still covered with the sheet.

He sprang to it, and then paused, and laid his hand upon his heart: I could hear his teeth grate with the convulsive action of his jaws; and his face was so ghastly to see that I grew alarmed both for his life and reason.

"Compose yourself," said I.

He turned a dreadful smile to me, and as if with the decision of despair, plucked away the sheet. At the sight of the contents, he uttered one loud sob of such immense relief that I sat petrified. And the next moment, in a voice that was already fairly well under control, "Have you a graduated glass?" he asked.

I rose from my place with something of an effort and gave him what he asked.

He thanked me with a smiling nod, measured out a few minims of the red tincture and added one of the powders. The mixture, which was at first of a reddish hue, began, in portion as the crystals melted, to brighten in color, to effervesce audibly, and to throw off small fumes of vapor. Suddenly and at the same moment, the ebullition ceased and the compound changed to a dark purple, which faded again more slowly to a watery green. My visitor, who had watched these metamorphoses with a keen eye, smiled, set down the glass upon the table, and then turned and looked upon me with an air of scrutiny.

"And now," said he, "to settle what remains. Will you be wise? will you be guided? will you suffer me to take this glass in my hand and go forth from your house without further parley? or has the greed of curiosity too much command of you? Think before you answer, for it shall be done as you decide. As you decide, you shall be left as you were before, and neither richer nor wiser, unless the sense of service rendered to a man in mortal distress may be counted as a kind of riches of the soul. Or, if you shall so perfer to choose, a new province of knowledge and new avenues to power and fame shall be laid open to you, here, in this room, upon the instant; and your sight shall be blasted by a prodigy to stagger the unbelief of Satan."

"Sir," said I, affecting a coolness that I was far from truly possessing, "you speak enigmas, and you will perhaps not wonder that I hear you with no strong impression of belief. But I have gone too far in this way of inexplicable services to pause before I see the end."

"It is well," replied my visitor, "Lanyon, you remember your vows: what follows is under the seal of our profession. And now, you who have so long been bound to the most narrow and material views, you who have denied the virtue of transcendental medicine, you who have derided your superiors—behold!"

He put the glass to his lips and drank at one gulp. A cry followed; he reeled, staggered, clutched at the table and held on, staring with injected eyes, gasping with open mouth; and as I looked there came, I thought, a change—he seemed to swell—he face became suddenly black and the features seemed to melt and alter—and the next moment, I had sprung to my feet and leaped back against the wall, my arm raised to shield me from that prodigy, my mind submerged in terror.

"O, God!" I screamed, and "O, God!" again and again; for there before my eyes—pale and shaken, and half fainting, and groping before him with his hands, like a man restored from death—there stood Henry Jekyll!

What he had told me in the next hour, I cannot bring my mind to set on paper. I saw what I saw, I heard what I heard, and my soul sickened at it; and yet now when that sight has faded from my eyes, I ask myself if I believe it, and I cannot answer. My life is shaken to its roots; sleep has left me; the deadliest terror sits by me at all hours of the day and night; and I feel that my days are numbered, and that I must die; and yet I shall die incredulous. As for the moral turpitude that man unveiled to me, even with the tears of penitence, I cannot, even in my memory, dwell on it without a start of horror. I will say but one thing, Utterson, and that (if you can bring your mind to credit it) will be more than enough. The creature who crept into my house that night was, on Jekyll's own confession, known by the name of Hyde and hunted for in every corner of the land as the murderer of Carew.

HASTIE LANYON

Henry Jekyll's Full Statement of the Case

I was born in the year 18— to a large fortune, endowed besides with excellent parts, inclined by nature to industry, fond of the respect of the wise and good among my fellowmen, and thus, as might have been supposed, with every guarantee of an honorable and distinguished future. And indeed the worst of my faults was a certain impatient gaiety of disposition, such as has made the happiness of many, but such as I found it hard to reconcile with my imperious desire to carry my head high, and wear a more than commonly grave countenance before the public. Hence it came about that I concealed my pleasures; and that when I reached years of reflection, and began to look round me and take stock of my progress and position in the world, I stood already committed to a profound duplicity of life. Many a man would have even blazoned such irregularities as I was guilty of; but from the high views that I had set before me, I regarded and hid them with an almost morbid sense of shame. It was thus rather the exacting nature of my aspirations than any particular degradation in my faults, that made me what I was, and, with even a deeper trench than in the majority of men, severed in me those provinces of good and ill which divide and compound man's dual nature. In this case, I was driven to reflect deeply and inveterately on that hard law of life, which lies at the root of religion and is one of the most plentiful springs of distress. Though so profound a double-dealer, I was in no sense a hypocrite; both sides of me were in dead earnest; I was no more myself when I laid aside restraint and plunged in shame, than when I labored, in the eye of day, at the furtherance of knowledge or the relief of sorrow and suffering. And it chanced that the direction of my scientific studies, which led wholly towards the mystic and the transcendental, reacted and shed a strong light on this consciousness of the perennial war among my members. With every day, and from both sides of my intelligence, the moral and the intellectual, I thus drew steadily nearer to that truth, by whose partial discovery I have been doomed to such a dreadful shipwreck: that man is not truly one, but truly two. I say two, because the state of my own knowledge does not pass beyond that point. Others will follow, others will outstrip me on the same lines; and I hazard the guess that man will be ultimately known for a mere polity of multifarious, incongruous and independent denizens. I, for my part, from the nature of my life, advanced infallibly in one direction and in one direction only. It was on the moral side, and in my own person, that I learned to recognize the thorough and primitive duality of man; I saw that, of the two natures that contended in the field of my consciousness, even if I could rightly be said to be either, it was only because I was radically both; and from an early date, even before the course of my scientific discoveries had begun to suggest the most naked possibility of such a miracle, I had learned to dwell with pleasure, as a beloved daydream, on the thought of the separation of these elements. If each, I told myself, could be housed in separate identities, life would be relieved of all that was unbearable; the unjust might go his way, delivered from the aspirations and remorse of his more upright twin; and the just could walk steadfastly and securely on his upward path, doing the good things in which he found his pleasure, and no longer exposed to disgrace and penitence by the hands of this extraneous evil. It was the curse of mankind that these incongruous faggots were thus bound together—that in the agonized womb of consciousness, these polar twins should be continuously struggling. How, then, were they dissociated?

I was so far in my reflection when, as I have said, a side light began to shine upon the subject from the laboratory table. I began to perceive more deeply than it has ever yet been stated, the trembling immateriality, the mistlike transience, of this seemingly so solid body in which we walk attired. Certain agents I found to have the power to shake and pluck back that fleshly vestment, even as a wind might toss the curtains of a pavilion. For two good reasons, I will not enter deeply into this scientific branch of my confession. First, because I have been made to learn that the doom and burden of our life is bound for ever on man's shoulders, and when the attempt is made to cast it off, it but returns upon us with more unfamiliar and more awful pressure. Second, because, as my narrative will make, alas! too evident, my discoveries were incomplete. Enough, then, that I not only recognized my natural body from the mere aura and effulgence of certain of the powers that made up my spirit, but managed to compound a drug by which these powers should be dethroned from their supremacy, and a second form and countenance substituted, none the less natural to me because they were the expression, and bore the stamp of lower elements in my soul.

I hesitated long before I put this theory to the test of practice. I knew well that I risked death; for any drug that so potently controlled and shook the very fortress of identity, might, by the least scruple of an overdose or at the least inopportunity in the moment of exhibition, utterly blot out that immaterial tabernacle which I looked to it to change. But the temptation of a discovery so singular and profound at last overcame the suggestions of alarm. I had long since prepared my tincture; I purchased at once, from a firm of wholesale chemists, a large quantity of a particular salt which I knew, from my experiments, to be the last ingredient required; and late one accursed night, I compounded the elements, watched them boil and smoke together in the glass, and when the ebullition had subsided, with a strong glow of courage, drank off the potion.

The most racking pangs succeeded: a grinding in the bones, deadly nausea, and a horror of the spirit that cannot be exceeded at the hour of birth or death. Then these agonies began swiftly to subside, and I came to myself as if out of a great sickness. There was something strange in my sensations, something indescribably new and, from its very novelty, incredibly sweet. I felt younger, lighter, happier in body; within I was conscious of a heady recklessness, a current of disordered sensual images running like a millrace in my fancy, a solution of the bonds of obligation, an unknown but not an innocent freedom of the soul. I knew myself, at the first breath of this new life, to be more wicked, tenfold more wicked, sold a slave to my original evil; and the thought, in that moment, braced and delighted me like wine. I stretched out my hands, exulting in the freshness of these sensations; and in the act, I was suddenly aware that I had lost in stature.

There was no mirror, at that date, in my room; that which stands beside me as I write, was brought there later on and for the very purpose of these transformations. The night, however, was far gone into the morning—the morning, black as it was, was nearly ripe for the conception of the day—the inmates of my house were locked in the most rigorous hours of slumber; and I determined, flushed as I was with hope and triumph, to venture in my new shape as far as to my bedroom. I crossed the yard, wherein the constellations looked down upon me, I could have thought, with wonder, the first creature of that sort that their unsleeping vigilance had yet disclosed to them; I stole through the corridors, a stranger in my own house; and coming to my room, I saw for the first time the appearance of Edward Hyde.

I must here speak by theory alone, saying not that which I know, but that which I suppose to be most probable. The evil side of my nature, to which I had now transferred the stamping efficacy, was less robust and less developed than the good which I had just deposed. Again, in the course of my life, which had been, after all, nine tenths a life of effort, virtue and control, it had been much less exercised and much less exhausted. And hence, as I think, it came about that Edward Hyde was so much smaller, slighter and younger than Henry Jekyll. Even as good shone upon the countenance of the one, evil was written broadly and plainly on the face of the other. Evil besides (which I must still believe to be the lethal side of man) had left on that body an imprint of deformity and decay. And yet when I looked upon that ugly idol in the glass, I was conscious of no repugnance, rather of a leap of welcome. This, too, was myself. It seemed natural and human. In my eyes it bore a livelier image of the spirit, it seemed more express and single, than the imperfect and divided countenance I had been hitherto accustomed to call mine. And in so far I was doubtless right. I have observed that when I wore the semblance of Edward Hyde, none could come near to me at first without a visible misgiving of the flesh. This, as I take it, was because all human beings, as we meet them, are commingled out of good and evil: and Edward Hyde, alone in the ranks of mankind, was pure evil.

I lingered but a moment at the mirror: the second and conclusive experiment had yet to be attempted; it yet remained to be seen if I had lost my identity beyond redemption and must flee before daylight from a house that was no longer mine; and hurrying back to my cabinet, I once more prepared and drank the cup, once more suffered the pangs of dissolution, and came to myself once more with the character, the stature and the face of Henry Jekyll.

That night I had come to the fatal cross-roads. Had I approached my discovery in a more noble spirit, had I risked the experiment while under the empire of generous or pious aspirations, all must have been otherwise, and from these agonies of death and birth, I had come forth an angel instead of a fiend. The drug had no discriminating action; it was neither diabolical nor divine; it but shook the doors of the prison-house of my disposition; and like the captives of Philippi, that which stood within ran forth. At that time my virtue slumbered; my evil kept awake by ambition, was alert and swift to seize the occasion; and the thing that was projected was Edward Hyde. Hence, although I had now two characters as well as two appearances, one was wholly evil, and the other was still the old Henry Jekyll, that incongruous compound of whose reformation and improvement I had already learned to despair. The movement was thus wholly toward the worse.

Even at that time, I had not conquered my aversions to the dryness of a life of study. I would still be merrily disposed at times; and as my pleasures were (to say the least) undignified, and I was not only well known and highly considered, but growing towards the elderly man, this incoherency of my life was daily growing more unwelcome. It was on this side that my new power tempted me until I fell in slavery. I had but to drink the cup, to doff at once the body of the noted professor, and to assume, like a thick cloak, that of Edward Hyde. I smiled at the notion; it seemed to me at the time to be humorous; and I made my preparations with the most studious care. I took and furnished that house in Soho, to which Hyde was tracked by the police; and engaged as a housekeeper a creature whom I knew well to be silent and unscrupulous. On the other side, I announced to my servants that a Mr. Hyde (whom I described) was to have full liberty and power about my house in the square; and to parry mishaps, I even called and made myself a familiar object, in my second character. I next drew up that will to which you so much objected; so that if anything befell me in the person of Dr. Jekyll, I could enter on that of Edward Hyde without pecuniary loss. And thus fortified, as I supposed, on every side, I began to profit by the strange immunities of my position.

Men have before hired bravos to transact their crimes, while their own person and reputation sat under shelter. I was the first that ever did so for his pleasures. I was the first that could plod in the public eye with a load of genial respectability, and in a moment, like a schoolboy, strip off these lendings and spring headlong into a sea of liberty. But for me, in my impenetrable mantle, the safety was complete. Think of it—I did not even exist! Let me but escape into my laboratory door, give me but a second or two to mix and swallow the draught that I had always standing ready; and whatever he had done, Edward Hyde would pass away like the stain of breath upon a mirror; and there in his stead, quietly at home, trimming the midnight lamp in his study, a man who could afford to laugh at suspicion, would be Henry Jekyll.

The pleasures which I made haste to seek in my disguise were, as I have said, undignified; I would scarce use a harder term. But in the hands of Edward Hyde, they soon began to turn toward the monstrous. When I would come back from these excursions, I was often plunged into a kind of wonder at my vicarious depravity. This familiar that I called out of my own soul, and sent forth alone to do his good pleasure, was a being inherently malign and villainous; his every act and thought centered on self; drinking pleasure with bestial avidity from any degree of torture to another; relentless like a man of stone. Henry Jekyll stood at times aghast before the acts of Edward Hyde; but the situation was apart from ordinary laws, and insidiously relaxed the grasp of conscience. It was Hyde, after all, and Hyde alone, that was guilty. Jekyll was no worse; he woke again to his good qualities seemingly unimpaired; he would even make haste, where it was possible, to undo the evil done by Hyde. And thus his conscience slumbered.

Into the details of the infamy at which I thus connived (for even now I can scarce grant that I committed it) I have no design of entering; I mean but to point out the warnings and the successive steps with which my chastisement approached. I met with one accident which, as it brought on no consequence, I shall no more than mention. An act of cruelty to a child aroused against me the anger of a passer-by, whom I recognized the other day in the person of your kinsman; the doctor and the child's family joined him; there were moments when I feared for my life; and at last, in order to pacify their too just resentment, Edward Hyde had to bring them to the door, and pay them in a cheque drawn in the name of Henry Jekyll. But this danger was easily eliminated from the future, by opening an account at another bank in the name of Edward Hyde himself; and when, by sloping my own hand backward, I had supplied my double with a signature, I thought I sat beyond the reach of fate.

Some two months before the murder of Sir Danvers, I had been out for one of my adventures, had returned at a late hour, and woke the next day in bed with somewhat odd sensations. It was in vain I looked about me; in vain I saw the decent furniture and tall proportions of my room in the square; in vain that I recognized the pattern of the bed curtains and the design of the mahogany frame; something still kept insisting that I was not where I was, that I had not wakened where I seemed to be, but in the little room in Soho where I was accustomed to sleep in the body of Edward Hyde. I smiled to myself, and, in my psychological way, began lazily to inquire into the elements of this illusion, occasionally, even as I did so, dropping back into a comfortable morning doze. I was still so engaged when, in one of my more wakeful moments, my eyes fell upon my hand. Now the hand of Henry Jekyll (as you have often remarked) was professional in shape and size: it was large, firm, white and comely. But the hand which I now saw, clearly enough, in the yellow light of a mid-London morning, lying half shut on the bedclothes, was lean, corded, knuckly, of a dusky pallor and thickly shaded with a swart growth of hair. It was the hand of Edward Hyde.

I must have stared upon it for near half a minute, sunk as I was in the mere stupidity of wonder, before terror woke up in my breast as sudden and startling as the crash of cymbals; and bounding from my bed, I rushed to the mirror. At the sight that met my eyes, my blood was changed into something exquisitely thin and icy. Yes, I had gone to bed Henry Jekyll, I had awakened Edward Hyde. How was this to be explained? I asked myself; and then, with another bound of terror—how was it to be remedied? It was well on in the morning; the servants were up; all my drugs were in the cabinet—a long journey down two pairs of stairs, through the back passage, across the open court and through the anatomical theater, from where I was then standing horror-struck. It might indeed be possible to cover my face; but of what use was that, when I was unable to conceal the alteration in my stature? And then with an overpowering sweetness of relief, it came back upon my mind that the servants were already used to the coming and going of my second self. I had soon dressed, as well as I was able, in clothes of my own size: had soon passed through the house, where Bradshaw stared and drew back at seeing Mr. Hyde at such an hour and in such a strange array; and ten minutes later, Dr. Jekyll had returned to his own shape and was sitting down, with a darkened brow, to make a feint of breakfasting.

Small indeed was my appetite. This inexplicable incident, this reversal of my previous experience, seemed, like the Babylonian finger on the wall, to be spelling out the letters of my judgment; and I began to reflect more seriously than ever before on the issues and possibilities of my double existence. That part of me which I had the power of projecting, had lately been much exercised and nourished; it had seemed to me of late as though the body of Edward Hyde had grown in stature, as though (when I wore that form) I were conscious of a more generous tide of blood; and I began to spy a danger that, if this were much prolonged, the balance of my nature might be permanently overthrown, the power of voluntary change be forfeited, and the character of Edward Hyde become irrevocably mine. The power of the drug had not been always equally displayed. Once, very early in my career, it had totally failed me; since then I had been obliged on more than one occasion to double, and once, with infinite risk of death, to treble the amount; and these rare uncertainties had cast hitherto the sole shadow on my contentment. Now, however, and in the light of that morning's accident, I was led to remark that whereas, in the beginning, the difficulty had been to throw off the body of Jekyll, it had of late gradually but decidedly transferred itself to the other side. All things therefore seemed to point to this; that I was slowly losing hold of my original and better self, and becoming slowly incorporated with my second and worse.

Between these two, I now felt I had to choose. My two natures had memory in common, but all other faculties were most unequally shared between them. Jekyll (who was composite) now with the most sensitive apprehensions, now with a greedy gusto, projected and shared in the pleasures and adventures of Hyde; but Hyde was indifferent to Jekyll, or but remembered him as the mountain bandit remembers the cavern in which he conceals himself from pursuit. Jekyll had more than a father's interest; Hyde had more than a son's indifference. To cast in my lot with Jekyll, was to die to those appetites which I had long secretly indulged and had of late begun to pamper. To cast it in with Hyde, was to die to a thousand interests and aspirations, and to become, at a blow and forever, despised and friendless. The bargain might appear unequal; but there was still another consideration in the scales; for while Jekyll would suffer smartingly in the fires of abstinence, Hyde would be not even conscious of all that he had lost. Strange as my circumstances were, the terms of this debate are as old and commonplace as man; much the same inducements and alarms cast the die for any tempted and trembling sinner; and it fell out with me, as it falls with so vast a majority of my fellows, that I chose the better part and was found wanting in the strength to keep to it.

Yes, I preferred the elderly and discontented doctor, surrounded by friends and cherishing honest hopes; and bade a resolute farewell to the liberty, the comparative youth, the light step, leaping impulses and secret pleasures, that I had enjoyed in the disguise of Hyde. I made this choice perhaps with some unconscious reservation, for I neither gave up the house in Soho, nor destroyed the clothes of Edward Hyde, which still lay ready in my cabinet. For two months, however, I was true to my determination; for two months, I led a life of such severity as I had never before attained to, and enjoyed the compensations of an approving conscience. But time began at last to obliterate the freshness of my alarm; the praises of conscience began to grow into a thing of course; I began to be tortured with throes and longings, as of Hyde struggling after freedom; and at last, in an hour of moral weakness, I once again compounded and swallowed the transforming draught.

I do not suppose that, when a drunkard reasons with himself upon his vice, he is once out of five hundred times affected by the dangers that he runs through his brutish, physical insensibility; neither had I, long as I had considered my position, made enough allowance for the complete moral insensibility and insensate readiness to evil, which were the leading characters of Edward Hyde. Yet it was by these that I was punished. My devil had been long caged, he came out roaring. I was conscious, even when I took the draught, of a more unbridled, a more furious propensity to ill. It must have been this, I suppose, that stirred in my soul that tempest of impatience with which I listened to the civilities of my unhappy victim; I declare, at least, before God, no man morally sane could have been guilty of that crime upon so pitiful a provocation; and that I struck in no more reasonable spirit than that in which a sick child may break a plaything. But I had voluntarily stripped myself of all those balancing instincts by which even the worst of us continues to walk with some degree of steadiness among temptations; and in my case, to be tempted, however slightly, was to fall.

Instantly the spirit of hell awoke in me and raged. With a transport of glee, I mauled the unresisting body, tasting delight from every blow; and it was not till weariness had begun to succeed, that I was suddenly, in the top fit of my delirium, struck through the heart by a cold thrill of terror. A mist dispersed; I saw my life to be forfeit; and fled from the scene of these excesses, at once glorying and trembling, my lust of evil gratified and stimulated, my love of life screwed to the topmost peg. I ran to the house in Soho, and (to make assurance doubly sure) destroyed my papers; thence I set out through the lamplit streets, in the same divided ecstasy of mind, gloating on my crime, light-headedly devising others in the future, and yet still hastening and still hearkening in my wake for the steps of the avenger. Hyde had a song upon his lips as he compounded the draught, and as he drank it, pledged the dead man. The pangs of transformation had not done tearing him, before Henry Jekyll, with streaming tears of gratitude and remorse, had fallen upon his knees and lifted his clasped hands to God. The veil of self-indulgence was rent from head to foot. I saw my life as a whole: I followed it up from the days of childhood, when I had walked with my father's hand, and through the self-denying toils of my professional life, to arrive again and again, with the same sense of unreality, at the damned horrors of the evening. I could have screamed aloud; I sought with tears and prayers to smother down the crowd of hideous images and sounds with which my memory swarmed against me; and still, between the petitions, the ugly face of my iniquity stared into my soul. As the acuteness of this remorse began to die away, it was succeeded by a sense of joy. The problem of my conduct was solved. Hyde was thenceforth impossible; whether I would or not, I was now confined to the better part of my existence; and O, how I rejoiced to think of it! with what willing humility I embraced anew the restrictions of natural life! with what sincere renunciation I locked the door by which I had so often gone and come, and ground the key under my heel!

The next day, came the news that the murder had been overlooked, that the guilt of Hyde was patent to the world, and that the victim was a man high in public estimation. It was not only a crime, it had been a tragic folly. I think I was glad to know it; I think I was glad to have my better impulses thus buttressed and guarded by the terrors of the scaffold. Jekyll was now my city of refuge; let but Hyde peep out an instant, and the hands of all men would be raised to take and slay him.

I resolved in my future conduct to redeem the past; and I can say with honesty that my resolve was fruitful of some good. You know yourself how earnestly, in the last months of the last year, I labored to relieve suffering; you know that much was done for others, and that the days passed quietly, almost happily for myself. Nor can I truly say that I wearied of this beneficent and innocent life; I think instead that I daily enjoyed it more completely; but I was still cursed with my duality of purpose; and as the first edge of my penitence wore off, the lower side of me, so long indulged, so recently chained down, began to growl for license. Not that I dreamed of resuscitating Hyde; the bare idea of that would startle me to frenzy: no, it was in my own person that I was once more tempted to trifle with my conscience; and it was as an ordinary secret sinner that I at last fell before the assaults of temptation.

There comes an end to all things; the most capacious measure is filled at last; and this brief condescension to my evil finally destroyed the balance of my soul. And yet I was not alarmed; the fall seemed natural, like a return to the old days before I had made my discovery. It was a fine, clear, January day, wet under foot where the frost had melted, but cloudless overhead; and the Regent's Park was full of winter chirrupings and sweet with spring odors. I sat in the sun on a bench; the animal within me licking the chops of memory; the spiritual side a little drowsed, promising subsequent penitence, but not yet moved to begin. After all, I reflected, I was like my neighbors; and then I smiled, comparing myself with other men, comparing my active good-will with the lazy cruelty of their neglect. And at the very moment of that vainglorious thought, a qualm came over me, a horrid nausea and the most deadly shuddering. These passed away, and left me faint; and then as in turn faintness subsided, I began to be aware of a change in the temper of my thoughts, a greater boldness, a contempt of danger, a solution of the bonds of obligation. I looked down; my clothes hung formlessly on my shrunken limbs; the hand that lay on my knee was corded and hairy. I was once more Edward Hyde. A moment before I had been safe of all men's respect, wealthy, beloved—the cloth laying for me in the dining-room at home; and now I was the common quarry of mankind, hunted, houseless, a known murderer, thrall to the gallows.

My reason wavered, but it did not fail me utterly. I have more than once observed that, in my second character, my faculties seemed sharpened to a point and my spirits more tensely elastic; thus it came about that, where Jekyll perhaps might have succumbed, Hyde rose to the importance of the moment. My drugs were in one of the presses of my cabinet; how was I to reach them? That was the problem that (crushing my temples in my hands) I set myself to solve. The laboratory door I had closed. If I sought to enter by the house, my own servants would consign me to the gallows. I saw I must employ another hand, and thought of Lanyon. How was he to be reached? how persuaded? Supposing that I escaped capture in the streets, how was I to make my way into his presence? and how should I, an unknown and displeasing visitor, prevail on the famous physician to rifle the study of his colleague, Dr. Jekyll? Then I remembered that of my original character, one part remained to me: I could write my own hand; and once I had conceived that kindling spark, the way that I must follow became lighted up from end to end.

Thereupon, I arranged my clothes as best I could, and summoning a passing hansom, drove to an hotel in Portland Street, the name of which I chanced to remember. At my appearance (which was indeed comical enough, however tragic a fate these garments covered) the driver could not conceal his mirth. I gnashed my teeth upon him with a gust of devilish fury; and the smile withered from his face—happily for him—yet more happily for myself, for in another instant I had certainly dragged him from his perch. At the inn, as I entered, I looked about me with so black a countenance as made the attendants tremble; not a look did they exchange in my presence; but obsequiously took my orders, led me to a private room, and brought me wherewithal to write. Hyde in danger of his life was a creature new to me; shaken with inordinate anger, strung to the pitch of murder, lusting to inflict pain. Yet the creature was astute; mastered his fury with a great effort of the will; composed his two important letters, one to Lanyon and one to Poole; and that he might receive actual evidence of their being posted, sent them out with directions that they should be registered. Thenceforward, he sat all day over the fire in the private room, gnawing his nails; there he dined, sitting alone with his fears, the waiter visibly quailing before his eye; and thence, when the night was fully come, he set forth in the corner of a closed cab, and was driven to and fro about the streets of the city. He, I say—I cannot say, I. That child of Hell had nothing human; nothing lived in him but fear and hatred. And when at last, thinking the driver had begun to grow suspicious, he discharged the cab and ventured on foot, attired in his misfitting clothes, an object marked out for observation, into the midst of the nocturnal passengers, these two base passions raged within him like a tempest. He walked fast, hunted by his fears, chattering to himself, skulking through the less frequented thoroughfares, counting the minutes that still divided him from midnight. Once a woman spoke to him, offering, I think, a box of lights. He smote her in the face, and she fled.

When I came to myself at Lanyon's, the horror of my old friend perhaps affected me somewhat: I do not know; it was at least but a drop in the sea to the abhorrence with which I looked back upon these hours. A change had come over me. It was no longer the fear of the gallows, it was the horror of being Hyde that racked me. I received Lanyon's condemnation partly in a dream; it was partly in a dream that I came home to my own house and got into bed. I slept after the prostration of the day, with a stringent and profound slumber which not even the nightmares that wrung me could avail to break. I awoke in the morning shaken, weakened, but refreshed. I still hated and feared the thought of the brute that slept within me, and I had not of course forgotten the appalling dangers of the day before; but I was once more at home, in my own house and close to my drugs; and gratitude for my escape shone so strong in my soul that it almost rivalled the brightness of hope.

I was stepping leisurely across the court after breakfast, drinking the chill of the air with pleasure, when I was seized again with those indescribable sensations that heralded the change; and I had but the time to gain the shelter of my cabinet, before I was once again raging and freezing with the passions of Hyde. It took on this occasion a double dose to recall me to myself; and alas! six hours after, as I sat looking sadly in the fire, the pangs returned, and the drug had to be re-administered. In short, from that day forth it seemed only by a great effort as of gymnastics, and only under the immediate stimulation of the drug, that I was able to wear the countenance of Jekyll. At all hours of the day and night, I would be taken with the premonitory shudder;

above all, if I slept, or even dozed for a moment in my chair, it was always as Hyde that I awakened. Under the strain of this continually impending doom and by the sleeplessness to which I now condemned myself, ay, even beyond what I had thought possible to man, I became, in my own person, a creature eaten up and emptied by fever, languidly weak both in body and mind, and solely occupied by one thought: the horror of my other self. But when I slept, or when the virtue of the medicine wore off, I would leap almost without transition (for the pangs of transformation grew daily less marked) into the possession of a fancy brimming with images of terror, a soul boiling with causeless hatreds, and a body that seemed not strong enough to contain the raging energies of life. The powers of Hyde seemed to have grown with the sickliness of Jekyll. And certainly the hate that now divided them was equal on each side. With Jekyll, it was a thing of vital instinct. He had now seen the full deformity of that creature that shared with him some of the phenomena of consciousness, and was co-heir with him to death and beyond these links of community, which in themselves made the most poignant part of his distress, he thought of Hyde, for all his energy of life, as of something not only hellish but inorganic. This was the shocking thing; that the slime of the pit seemed to utter cries and voices; that the amorphous dust gesticulated and sinned; that what was dead, and had no shape, should usurp the offices of life. And this again, that that insurgent horror was knit to him closer than a wife, closer than an eye; lay caged in his flesh, where he heard it mutter and felt it struggle to be born; and at every hour of weakness, and in the confidence of slumber, prevailed against him, and deposed him out of life. The hatred of Hyde for Jekyll was of a different order. His terror of the gallows drove him continually to commit temporary suicide, and return to his subordinate station of a part instead of a person; but he loathed the necessity, he loathed the despondency into which Jekyll was now fallen, and he resented the dislike with which he was himself regarded. Hence the ape-like tricks that he would play me, scrawling in my own hand blasphemies on the pages of my books, burning the letters and destroying the portrait of my father; and indeed, had it not been for his fear of death, he would long ago have ruined himself in order to involve me in the ruin. But his love of life is wonderful; I go further: I, who sicken and freeze at the mere thought of him, when I recall the abjection and passion of this attachment, and when I know how he fears my power to cut him off by suicide, I find it in my heart to pity him.

It is useless, and the time awfully fails me, to prolong this description; no one has ever suffered such torments, let that suffice; and yet even to these, habit brought—no, not alleviation—but a certain callousness of soul, a certain acquiescence of despair; and my punishment might have gone on for years, but for the last calamity which has now fallen, and which has finally severed me from my own face and nature. My provision of the salt, which had never been renewed since the date of the first experiment, began to run low. I sent out for a fresh supply and mixed the draught; the ebullition followed, and the first change of color, not the second; I drank it and it was without efficiency. You will learn from Poole how I have had London ransacked; it was in vain; and I am now persuaded that my first supply was impure, and that it was that unknown impurity which lent efficacy to the draught.

About a week has passed, and I am now finishing this statement under the influence of the last of the old powders. This, then, is the last time, short of a miracle, that Henry Jekyll can think his own thoughts or see his own face (now how sadly altered) in the glass. Nor must I delay too long to bring my writing to an end; for if my narrative has hitherto escaped destruction, it has been by a combination of great prudence and great good luck. Should the throes of change take me in the act of writing it, Hyde will tear it in pieces; but if some time shall have elapsed after I have laid it by, his wonderful selfishness and circumscription to the moment will probably save it once again from the action of his ape-like spite. And indeed the doom that is closing on us both has already changed and crushed him. Half an hour from now, when I shall again and forever reindue that hated personality, I know how I shall sit shuddering and weeping in my chair, or continue, with the most strained and fearstruck ecstasy of listening, to pace up and down this room (my last earthly refuge) and give ear to every sound of menace. Will Hyde die upon the scaffold? or will he find courage to release himself at the last moment? God knows; I am careless; this is my true hour of death, and what is to follow concerns another than myself. Here then, as I lay down the pen and proceed to seal up my confession, I bring the life of that unhappy Henry Jekyll to an end.

Casting the Runes

M.R. James

Montague Rhodes James (1862-1936), the master of the English Ghost Story, was born in Kent County, England. In 1865, the family moved to Livermore, and James grew up with a great love of ancient architecture. He won a scholarship to Eton and was a model student, taking home prizes in Classics, Divinity, and French. In 1882, James entered Cambridge. Five years later, he accepted a Fellowship from King's College. In 1893, James wrote his first two horror stories, "Canon Alberic's Scrap-Book" and "Lost Hearts." James wrote his stories originally to entertain friends at parties, concentrating most of his efforts on publishing scholarly books such as *Palms of the Pharises* (1891; with H.E. Pyle) and *Ancient Libraries of Canterbury and Dover* (1903). In 1903, an English publisher asked James to compile a collection of his ghost stories with his friend James McBryde. After McBryde died before completing the book's illustrations in 1904, James released it as *Ghost Stories of Antiquity,* dedicating it to his friend. In 1908, James was named Provost of King's College, a post he held until he left the college to serve as Provost of Eton in 1918. James wrote four more collections before his death: *More Ghost Stories of Antiquity* (1911), *A Thin Ghost and Others* (1919), *A Warning to the Curious* (1925), and *The Collected Ghost Stories of M.R. James* (1931).

"Casting the Runes" displays James' understated style. This story was the basis of the classic Jacques Tourneur film *The Curse of the Demon.*

April 15th, 190-

DEAR SIR,—I am requested by the Council of the Association to return to you the draft of a paper on *The Truth of Alchemy,* which you have been good enough to offer to read at our forthcoming meeting, and to inform you that the Council do not see their way to including it in the program.

I am,
Yours faithfully,
—*Secretary.*

April 18th

DEAR SIR,—I am sorry to say that my engagements do not permit of my affording you an interview on the subject of your proposed paper. Nor do our laws allow of your discussing the matter with a Committee of our Council, as you suggest. Please allow me to assure you that the fullest consideration was given to the draft which you submitted, and that it was not declined without having been referred to the judgment of a most competent authority. No personal question (it can hardly be necessary for me to add) can have had the slightest influence on the decision of the Council.

Believe me *(ut supra).*

April 20th

The Secretary of the Association begs respectfully to inform Mr. Karswell that it is impossible for him to communicate the name of any person or persons to whom the draft of Mr. Karswell's paper may have been submitted; and further desires to intimate that he cannot undertake to reply to any further letters on this subject.

"And who *is* Mr. Karswell?" inquired the Secretary's wife. She had called at his office, and (perhaps unwarrantably) had picked up the last of these three letters, which the typist had just brought in.

"Why, my dear, just at present Mr. Karswell is a very angry man. But I don't know much about him otherwise, except that he is a person of wealth, his address is Lufford Abbey, Warwickshire, and he's an alchemist, apparently, and wants to tell us all about it; and that's about all—except that I don't want to meet him for the next week or two. Now, if you're ready to leave this place, I am."

"What have you been doing to make him angry?" asked Mrs. Secretary.

"The usual thing, my dear, the usual thing: he sent in a draft of a paper he wanted to read at the next meeting, and we referred it to Edward Dunning—almost the only man in England who knows about these things—and he said it was perfectly hopeless, so we declined it. So Karswell has been pelting me with letters ever since. The last thing he wanted was the name of the man we referred his nonsense to; you saw my answer to that. But don't you say anything about it, for goodness' sake."

"I should think not, indeed. Did I ever do such a thing? I do hope, though, he won't get to know that it was poor Mr. Dunning."

"Poor Mr. Dunning? I don't know why you call him that; he's a very happy man, is Dunning. Lots of hobbies and a comfortable home, and all his time to himself."

"I only meant I should be sorry for him if this man got hold of his name, and came and bothered him."

"Oh, ah! yes. I dare say he would be poor Mr. Dunning then."

The Secretary and his wife were lunching out, and the friends to whose house they were bound were Warwickshire people. So Mrs. Secretary had already settled it in her own mind that she would question them judiciously about Mr. Karswell. But she was saved the trouble of leading up to the subject, for the hostess said to the host, before many minutes had passed, "I saw the Abbot of Lufford this morning." The host whistled. "Did you? What in the world brings him up to town?" "Goodness knows; he was coming out of the British Museum gate as I drove past." It was not unnatural that Mrs. Secretary should inquire whether this was a real Abbot who was being spoken of. "Oh no, my dear: only a neighbor of ours in the country who bought Lufford Abbey a few years ago. His real name is Karswell." "Is he a friend of yours?" asked Mr. Secretary, with a private wink to his wife. The question let loose a torrent of declamation. There was really nothing to be said for Mr. Karswell. Nobody knew what he did with himself: his servants were a horrible set of people; he had invented a new religion for himself, and practiced no one could tell what appalling rites; he was very easily offended, and never forgave anybody: he had a dreadful face (so the lady insisted, her husband somewhat demurring); he never did a kind action, and whatever influence he did exert was mischievous. "Do the poor man justice, dear," the husband interrupted. "You forget the treat he gave the school children." "Forget it, indeed! But I'm glad you mentioned it, because it gives an idea of the man. Now, Florence, listen to this. The first winter he was at Lufford this delightful neighbor of ours wrote to the clergyman of his parish (he's not ours, but we know him very well) and offered to show the school children some magic-lantern slides. He said he had some new kinds, which he thought would interest them. Well, the clergyman was rather surprised, because Mr. Karswell had shown himself inclined to be unpleasant to the children—complaining of their trespassing, or something of the sort; but of course he accepted, and the evening was fixed, and our friend went himself to see that everything went right. He said he never had been so thankful for anything as that his own children were all prevented from being there: they were at a children's party at our house, as a matter of fact. Because this Mr. Karswell had evidently set out with the intention of frightening these poor village children out of their wits, and I do believe, if he had been allowed to go on, he would actually have done so. He began with some comparatively mild things. Red Riding Hood was one, and even then, Mr. Farrer said, the wolf was so dreadful that several of the smaller children had to be taken out: and he said Mr. Karswell began the story by producing a noise like a wolf howling in the distance, which was the most gruesome thing he had ever heard. All the slides he showed, Mr. Farrer said, were most clever; they were absolutely realistic, and where he had got them or how he worked them he could not imagine. Well, the show went on, and the stories kept on becoming a little more terrifying each time, and the children were mesmerized into complete silence. At last he produced a series which represented a little boy passing through his own park—Lufford, I mean—in the evening. Every child in the room could recognize the place from the pictures. And this poor boy was followed, and at last pursued and overtaken, and either torn in pieces or somehow made away with, by a horrible hopping creature in white, which you saw first dodging about among the trees, and gradually it appeared more and more plainly. Mr. Farrer said it gave him one of the worst nightmares he ever remembered, and what it must have meant to the children doesn't bear thinking of. Of course this was too much, and he spoke very sharply indeed to Mr. Karswell, and said it couldn't go on. All *he* said was: 'Oh, you think it's time to bring our little show to an end and send them home to their beds? *Very* well!' And then, if you please, he switched on another slide, which showed a great mass of snakes, centipedes, and disgusting creatures with wings, and somehow or other he made it seem as if they were climbing out of the picture and getting in amongst the audience; and this was accompanied by a sort of dry rustling noise which sent the children nearly mad, and of course they stampeded. A good many of them were rather hurt in getting out of the room, and I don't suppose one of them closed an eye that night. There was the most dreadful trouble in the village afterwards. Of course the mothers threw a good part of the blame on poor Mr. Farrer, and, if they could have got past the gates, I believe the fathers would have broken every window in the

Abbey. Well, now, that's Mr. Karswell: that's the Abbot of Lufford, my dear, and you can imagine how we covet *his* society."

"Yes, I think he has all the possibilities of a distinguished criminal, has Karswell," said the host. "I should be sorry for anyone who got into his bad books."

"Is he the man, or am I mixing him up with someone else?" asked the Secretary (who for some minutes had been wearing the frown of the man who is trying to recollect something). "Is he the man who brought out a *History of Witchcraft* some time back—ten years or more?"

"That's the man; do you remember the reviews of it?"

"Certainly I do; and what's equally to the point, I knew the author of the most incisive of the lot. So did you: you must remember John Harrington; he was at John's in our time."

"Oh, very well indeed, though I don't think I saw or heard anything of him between the time I went down and the day I read the account of the inquest on him."

"Inquest?" said one of the ladies. "What has happened to him?"

"Why, what happened was that he fell out of a tree and broke his neck. But the puzzle was, what could have induced him to get up there. It was a mysterious business, I must say. Here was this man—not an athletic fellow, was he? and with no eccentric twist about him that was ever noticed—walking home along a country road late in the evening—no tramps about—well known and liked in the place—and he suddenly begins to run like mad, loses his hat and stick, and finally shins up a tree—quite a difficult tree—growing in the hedgerow: a dead branch gives way, and he comes down with it and breaks his neck, and there he's found next morning with the most dreadful face of fear on him that could be imagined. It was pretty evident, of course, that he had been chased by something, and people talked of savage dogs, and beasts escaped out of menageries; but there was nothing to be made of that. That was in '89, and I believe his brother Henry (whom I remember as well at Cambridge, but *you* probably don't) has been trying to get on the track of an explanation ever since. He, of course, insists there was malice in it, but I don't know. It's difficult to see how it could have come in."

After a time the talk reverted to the *History of Witchcraft*. "Did you ever look into it?" asked the host.

"Yes, I did," said the Secretary. "I went so far as to read it."

"Was it as bad as it was made out to be?"

"Oh, in point of style and form, quite hopeless. It deserved all the pulverizing it got. But, besides that, it was an evil book. The man believed every word of what he was saying, and I'm very much mistaken if he hadn't tried the greater part of his receipts."

"Well, I only remember Harrington's review of it, and I must say if I'd been the author it would have quenched my literary ambition for good. I should never have held up my head again."

"It hasn't had that effect in the present case. But come, it's half-past three; I must be off."

On the way home the Secretary's wife said, "I do hope that horrible man won't find out that Mr. Dunning had anything to do with the rejection of his paper." "I don't think there's much chance of that," said the Secretary. "Dunning won't mention it himself, for these matters are confidential, and none of us will for the same reason. Karswell won't know his name, for Dunning hasn't published anything on the same subject yet. The only danger is that Karswell might find out, if he was to ask the British Museum people who was in the habit of consulting alchemical manuscripts: I can't very well tell them not to mention Dunning, can I? It would set them talking at once. Let's hope it won't occur to him."

However, Mr. Karswell was an astute man.

This much is in the way of prologue. On an evening rather later in the same week, Mr. Edward Dunning was returning from the British Museum, where he had been engaged in Research, to the comfortable house in a suburb where he lived alone, tended by two excellent women who had been long with him. There is nothing to be added by way of description of him to what we have heard already. Let us follow him as he takes his sober course homewards.

A train took him to within a mile or two of his house, and an electric tram a stage farther. The line ended at a point some three hundred yards from his front door. He had had enough of reading when he got into the car, and indeed the light was not such as to allow him to do more than study the advertisements on the panes of glass that faced him as he sat. As was not unnatural, the advertisements in this particular line of cars were objects of his frequent contemplation, and, with the possible exception of the brilliant and convincing dialogue between Mr. Lamplough and an eminent K.C. on the subject of Pyretic Saline, none of them afforded much scope to his imagination. I am wrong: there was one at the corner of the car farthest from him which did not seem familiar. It was in blue letters on a yellow ground, and all that he could read of it was a name—John Harrington—and something like a date. It could be of no interest to him to know more; but for all that, as the car emptied, he was just curious enough to move along the seat until he could read it well. He felt to a slight extent repaid for his trouble; the advertisement was *not* of the usual type. It ran thus: "In memory of John Harrington, F.S.A., of The Laurels, Ashbrooke. Died Sept. 18th, 1889. Three months were allowed."

The car stopped. Mr. Dunning, still contemplating the blue letters on the yellow ground, had to be stimulated to rise by a word from the conductor. "I beg your pardon," he said, "I was looking at that advertisement; it's a very odd one, isn't it?" The conductor read it slowly. "Well, my word," he said, "I never see that one before. Well, that is a cure, ain't it ? Someone bin up to their jokes 'ere, I should think." He got out a duster and applied it, not without saliva, to the pane and then to the outside. "No," he said, returning, "that ain't no transfer; seems to me as if it was reg'lar *in* the glass, what I mean in the substance, as you may say. Don't you think so, sir?" Mr. Dunning examined it and rubbed it with his glove, and agreed. "Who looks after these advertisements, and gives leave for them to be put up? I wish you would inquire. I will just take a note of the words." At this moment there came a call from the driver: "Look alive, George, time's up." "All right, all right; there's somethink else what's up at this end. You come and look at this 'ere glass." "What's gorn with the glass?" said the driver, approaching. "Well, and oo's 'Arrington? What's it all about?" "I was just asking who was responsible for putting the advertisements up in your cars, and saying it would be as well to make some inquiry about this one." "Well, sir, that's all done at the Company's orfice, that work is: it's our Mr. Timms, I believe, looks into that. When we put up to-night I'll leave word, and per'aps I'll be able to tell you to-morrer if you 'appen to be coming this way."

This was all that passed that evening. Mr. Dunning did just go to the trouble of looking up Ashbrooke, and found that it was in Warwickshire.

Next day he went to town again. The car (it was the same car) was too full in the morning to allow of his getting a word with the conductor: he could only be sure that the curious advertisement had been made away with. The close of the day brought a further element of mystery into the transaction. He had missed the tram, or else preferred walking home, but at a rather late hour, while he was at work in his study, one of the maids came to say that two men from the tramways was very anxious to speak to him. This was a reminder of the advertisement, which he had, he says, nearly forgotten. He had the men in—they were the conductor and driver of the car—and when the matter of refreshment had been attended to, asked what Mr. Timms had had to say about the advertisement. "Well, sir, that's what we took the liberty to step round about," said the conductor. "Mr. Timm's 'e give William 'ere the rough side of his tongue about that: 'cordin' to 'im there warn't no advertisement of that description sent in, nor ordered, nor paid for, nor put up, nor nothink, let alone not bein' there, and we was playing the fool takin' up his time. 'Well,' I says, 'If that's the case, all I ask of you, Mr. Timms,' I says, 'is to take and look at it for yourself,' I says. 'Of course if it ain't there,' I says, 'you may take and call me what you like.' 'Right,' he says, 'I will': and we went straight off. Now, I leave it to you, sir, if that ad., as we term 'em, with 'Arrington on it warn't as plain as ever you see anythink—blue letters on yeller glass, and as I says at the time, and you borne me out, reg'lar in the glass, because, if you remember, you recollect of me swabbing it with my duster." "To be sure I do, quite clearly—well?" "You may say well, I don't think. Mr. Timms he gets in that car with a light—no, he telled William to 'old the light outside. 'Now,' he says, 'where's your precious ad. what we've 'eard so much about?' ''Ere it is,' I says, 'Mr. Timms,' and I laid my 'and on it." The conductor paused.

"Well," said Mr. Dunning, " it was gone, I suppose. Broken?"

"Broke!—not it. There warn't, if you'll believe me, no more trace of them letters—blue letters they was—on that piece o' glass, than—well, it's no good *me* talkin'. I never see such a thing. I leave it to William here if—but there, as I says, where's the benefit in me going on about it?"

"And what did Mr. Timms say?"

"Why 'e did what I give 'im leave to—called us pretty much anything he liked, and I don't know as I blame him so much neither. But what we thought, William and me did, was as we seen you take down a bit of a note about that—well, that letterin'"

"I certainly did that, and I have it now. Did you wish me to speak to Mr. Timms myself, and show it to him? Was that what you came in about?"

"There, didn't I say as much?" said William. "Deal with a gent if you can get on the track of one, that's my word. Now perhaps, George, you'll allow as I ain't took you very far wrong to-night."

"Very well, William, very well; no need for you to go on as if you'd 'ad to frog's-march me 'ere. I come quiet, didn't I? All the same for that, we 'adn't ought to take up your time this way, sir; but if it so 'appened you could find time to step round to the Company's orfice in the morning and tell Mr. Timms what you seen for yourself, we should lay under a very 'igh obligation to you for the trouble. You see it ain't bein' called—well, one thing and another, as we mind, but if they got it into their 'ead at the orfice as we seen things as warn't there, why, one thing leads to another, and where we should be a twelvemunce 'ence—well, you can understand what I mean."

Amid further elucidations of the proposition, George, conducted by William, left the room.

The incredulity of Mr. Timms (who had a nodding acquaintance with Mr. Dunning) was greatly modified on the following day by what the latter could tell and show him; and any bad mark that might have been attached to the names of William and George was not suffered to remain on the Company's books; but explanation there was none.

Mr. Dunning's interest in the matter was kept alive by an incident of the following afternoon. He was walking from his club to the train, and he noticed some way ahead a man with a handful of leaflets such as are distributed to passers-by by agents of enterprising firms. This agent had not chosen a very crowded street for his operations: in fact, Mr. Dunning did not see him get rid of a single leaflet before he himself reached the spot. One was thrust into his hand as he passed: the hand that gave it touched his, and he experienced a sort of little shock as it did so. It seemed unnaturally rough and hot. He looked in passing at the giver, but the impression he got was so unclear that, however much he tried to reckon it up subsequently, nothing would come. He was walking quickly, and as he went on glanced at the paper. It was a blue one. The name of Harrington in large capitals caught his eye. He stopped, startled, and felt for his glasses. The next instant the leaflet was twitched out of his hand by a man who hurried past, and was irrecoverably gone. He ran back a few paces, but where was the passer-by? and where the distributor?

It was in a somewhat pensive frame of mind that Mr. Dunning passed on the following day into the Select Manuscript Room of the British Museum, and filled up tickets for Harley 3586, and some other volumes. After a few minutes they were brought to him, and he was settling the one he wanted first upon the desk, when he thought he heard his own name whispered behind him. He turned round hastily, and in doing so, brushed his little portfolio of loose papers on to the floor. He saw no one he recognized except one of the staff in charge of the room, who nodded to him, and he proceeded to pick up his papers. He thought he had them all, and was turning to begin work, when a stout gentleman at the table behind him, who was just rising to leave, and had collected his own belongings, touched him on the shoulder, saying, "May I give you this? I think it should be yours," and handed him a missing quire. "It is mine, thank you," said Mr. Dunning. In another moment the man had left the room. Upon finishing his work for the afternoon, Mr. Dunning had some conversation with the assistant in charge, and took occasion to ask who the stout gentleman was. "Oh, he's a man named Karswell," said the assistant; "he was asking me a week ago who were the great authorities on alchemy, and of course I told him you were the only one in the country. I'll see if I can't catch him: he'd like to meet you, I'm sure."

"For heaven's sake don't dream of it!" said Mr. Dunning, "I'm particularly anxious to avoid him."

"Oh! very well," said the assistant, "he doesn't come here often: I dare say you won't meet him."

More than once on the way home that day Mr. Dunning confessed to himself that he did not look forward with his usual cheerfulness to a solitary evening. It seemed to him that something ill-defined and impalpable had stepped in between him and his fellow-men—had taken him in charge, as it were. He wanted to sit close up to his neighbors in the train and in the tram, but as luck would have it both train and car were markedly empty. The conductor George was thoughtful, and appeared to be absorbed in calculations as to the number of passengers. On arriving at his house he found Dr. Watson, his medical man, on his doorstep. "I've had to upset your household arrangements, I'm sorry to say, Dunning. Both your servants *hors de combat*. In fact, I've had to send them to the Nursing Home."

"Good heavens! What's the matter?"

"It's something like ptomaine poisoning, I should think: you've not suffered yourself, I can see, or you wouldn't be walking about. I think they'll pull through all right."

"Dear, dear! Have you any idea what brought it on?"

"Well, they tell me they bought some shell-fish from a hawker at their dinner-time. It's odd. I've made inquiries, but I can't find that any hawker has been to other houses in the street. I couldn't send word to you; they won't be back for a bit yet. You come and dine with me to-night, anyhow, and we can make arrangements for going on. Eight o'clock. Don't be too anxious."

The solitary evening was thus obviated; at the expense of some distress and inconvenience, it is true. Mr. Dunning spent the time pleasantly enough with the doctor (a rather recent settler), and returned to his lonely home at about 11:30. The night he passed is not one on which he looks back with any satisfaction. He was in bed and the light was out. He was wondering if the charwoman would come early enough to get him hot water next morning, when he heard the unmistakable sound of his study door opening. No step followed it on the passage floor, but the sound must mean mischief, for he knew that he had shut the door that evening after putting his papers away in his desk. It was rather shame than courage that induced him to slip out into the passage and lean over the banister in his nightgown, listening. No light was visible; no further sound came: only a gust of warm, or even hot air played for an instant round his shins. He went back and decided to lock himself into his room. There was more unpleasantness, however. Either an economical suburban company had decided that their light would not be required in the small hours, and had stopped working, or else something was wrong with the meter; the effect was in any case that the electric light was off. The obvious course was to find a match, and also to consult his watch: he might as well know how many hours of discomfort awaited him. So he put his hand into the well-known nook under the pillow: only, it did not get so far. What he touched was, according to his account, a mouth, with teeth, and with hair about it, and, he declares, not the mouth of a human being. I do not think it is any use to guess what he said or did; but he was in a spare room with the door locked and his ear to it before he was clearly conscious again. And there he spent the rest of a most miserable night, looking every moment for some fumbling at the door: but nothing came.

The venturing back to his own room in the morning was attended with many listenings and quiverings. The door stood open, fortunately, and the blinds were up (the servants had been out of the house before the hour of drawing them down); there was, to be short, no trace of an inhabitant. The watch, too, was in its usual place; nothing was disturbed, only the wardrobe door had swung open, in accordance with its confirmed habit. A ring at the back door now announced the charwoman, who had been ordered the night before, and nerved Mr. Dunning, after letting her in, to continue his search in other parts of the house. It was equally fruitless.

The day thus begun went on dismally enough. He dared not go to the Museum: in spite of what the assistant had said, Karswell might turn up there, and Dunning felt he could not cope with a probably hostile stranger. His own house was odious; he hated sponging on the doctor. He spent some little time in a call at the Nursing Home, where he was slightly cheered by a good report of his housekeeper and maid. Towards lunch-time he betook himself to his club, again experiencing a gleam of satisfaction at seeing the Secretary of the Association. At luncheon Dunning told his friend the more material of his woes, but could not bring himself to speak of those that weighed most heavily on his spirits. "My poor dear man," said the Secretary, "what an upset! Look here: we're alone at home, absolutely. You must put up with us. Yes! no excuse: send your things in this afternoon." Dunning was unable to stand out: he was, in truth, becoming acutely anxious, as the hours went on, as to what that night might have waiting for him. He was almost happy as he hurried home to pack up.

His friends, when they had time to take stock of him, were rather shocked at his lorn appearance, and did their best to keep him up to the mark. Not altogether without success: but, when the two men were smoking alone later, Dunning became dull again. Suddenly he said, "Gayton, I believe that alchemist man knows it was I who got his paper rejected." Gayton whistled. "What makes you think that?" he said. Dunning told of his conversation with the Museum assistant, and Gayton could only agree that the guess seemed likely to be correct. "Not that I care much," Dunning went on, "only it might be a nuisance if we were to meet. He's a bad-tempered party, I imagine." Conversation dropped again; Gayton became more and more strongly impressed with the desolateness that came over Dunning's face and bearing, and finally—though with a considerable effort—he asked him point-blank whether something serious was not bothering him. Dunning gave an exclamation of relief. "I was perishing to get it off my mind," he said. "Do you know anything about a man named John Harrington?" Gayton was thoroughly startled, and at the moment could only ask why. Then the complete story of Dunning's experiences came out—what had happened in the tramcar, in his own house, and in the street, the troubling of spirit that had crept over him, and still held him; and he ended with the question he had begun with. Gayton was at a loss how to answer him. To tell the story of Harrington's end would perhaps be right; only, Dunning was in a nervous state, the story was a grim one, and he could not help asking himself whether there were not a connecting link between these two cases, in the person of Karswell. It was a difficult concession for a scientific man, but it could be eased by the phrase "hypnotic suggestion." In the end he decided that his answer to-night should be guarded; he would talk the situation over with his wife. So he said that he had known Harrington at Cambridge, and believed he had died suddenly in 1889, adding a few details about the man and his published work. He did talk over the matter with Mrs. Gayton, and, as he had anticipated, she leapt at once to the conclusion which had been hovering before him. It was she who reminded him of the surviving brother, Henry Harrington, and she also who suggested that he might be got hold of by means of their hosts of the day before. "He might be a hopeless crank," objected Gayton. "That could be ascertained from the Bennetts, who knew him," Mrs. Gayton retorted; and she undertook to see the Bennetts the very next day.

It is not necessary to tell in further detail the steps by which Henry Harrington and Dunning were brought together.

The next scene that does require to be narrated is a conversation that took place between the two. Dunning had told Harrington of the strange ways in which the dead man's name had been brought before him, and had said something, besides, of his own subsequent experiences. Then he had asked if Harrington was disposed, in return, to recall any of the circumstances connected with his brother's death. Harrington's surprise at what he heard can be imagined: but his reply was readily given.

"John," he said, "was in a very odd state, undeniably, from time to time, during some weeks before, though not immediately before, the catastrophe. There were several things; the principal notion he had was that he thought he was being followed. No doubt he was an impressionable man, but he never had had such fancies as this before. I cannot get it out of my mind that there was ill-will at work, and what you tell me about yourself reminds me very much of my brother. Can you think of any possible connecting link?"

"There is just one that has been taking shape vaguely in my mind. I've been told that your brother reviewed a book very severely not long before he died, and just lately I have happened to cross the path of the man who wrote that book in a way he would resent."

"Don't tell me the man was called Karswell."

"Why not? that is exactly his name."

Henry Harrington leaned back. "That is final to my mind. Now I must explain further. From something he said, I feel sure that my brother John was beginning to believe—very much against his will—that Karswell was at the bottom of his trouble. I want to tell you what seems to me to have a bearing on the situation. My brother was a great musician, and used to run up to concerts in town. He came back, three months before he died, from one of these, and gave me his program to look at—an analytical program: he always kept them. 'I nearly missed this one,' he said. 'I suppose I must have dropped it: anyhow, I was looking for it under my seat and in my pockets and so on, and my neighbor offered me his: said "might he give it me, he had no further use for it," and he went away just afterwards. I don't know who he was—a stout, clean-shaven man. I should have been sorry to miss it; of course I could have bought another, but this cost me nothing.' At another time he told me that he had been very uncomfortable both on the way to his hotel and during the night. I piece things together now in thinking it over. Then, not very long after, he was going over these programs, putting them in order to have them bound up, and in this particular one (which by the way I had hardly glanced at), he found quite near the beginning a strip of paper with some very odd writing on it in red and black—most carefully done—it looked to me more like Runic letters than anything else. 'Why,' he said, 'this must belong to my fat neighbor. It looks as if it might be worth returning to him; it may be a copy of something; evidently someone has taken trouble over it. How can I find his address?' We talked it over for a little and agreed that it wasn't worth advertising about, and that my brother had better look out for the man at the next concert, to which he was going very soon. The paper was lying on the book and we were both by the fire; it was a cold, windy summer evening. I suppose the door blew open, though I didn't notice it: at any rate a gust—a warm gust it was—came quite suddenly between us, took the paper and blew it straight into the fire: it was light, thin paper, and flared and went up the chimney in a single ash. 'Well,' I said, 'you can't give it back now.' He said nothing for a minute: then rather crossly, 'No, I can't; but why you should keep on saying so I don't know.' I remarked that I didn't say it more than once. 'Not more than four times, you mean,' was all he said. I remember all that very clearly, without any good reason; and now to come to the point. I don't know if you looked at that book of Karswell's which my unfortunate brother reviewed. It's not likely that you should: but I did, both before his death and after it. The first time we made game of it together. It was written in no style at all—split infinitives, and every sort of thing that makes an Oxford gorge rise. Then there was nothing that the man didn't swallow: mixing up classical myths, and stories out of the *Golden Legend* with reports of savage customs of to-day—all very proper, no doubt, if you know how to use them, but he didn't: he seemed to put the *Golden Legend* and the *Golden Bough* exactly on a par, and to believe both: a pitiable exhibition, in short. Well, after the misfortune, I looked over the book again. It was no better than before, but the impression which it left this time on my mind was different. I suspected—as I told you—that Karswell had borne ill-will to my brother, even that he was in some way responsible for what had happened; and now his book seemed to me to be a very sinister performance indeed. One chapter in particular struck me, in which he spoke of 'casting the Runes' on people, either for the purpose of gaining their affection or of getting them out of the way—perhaps more especially the latter: he spoke of all this in a way that really seemed to me to imply actual knowledge. I've not time to go into details, but the upshot is that I am pretty sure from information received that the civil man at the concert was Karswell: I suspect—I more than suspect—that the paper was of importance: and I do believe that if my brother had been able to give it back, he might have been alive now. Therefore, it occurs to me to ask you whether you have anything to put beside what I have told you."

By way of answer, Dunning had the episode in the Manuscript Room at the British Museum to relate. "Then he did actually hand you some papers; have you examined them? No? because we must, if you'll allow it, look at them at once, and very carefully."

They went to the still empty house—empty, for the two servants were not yet able to return to work. Dunning's portfolio of papers was gathering dust on the writing-table. In it were the quires of small-sized scribbling paper which he used for his transcripts: and from one of these, as he took it up, there slipped and fluttered out into the room with uncanny quickness, a strip of thin light paper. The window was open, but Harrington slammed it to, just in time to intercept the paper, which he caught. "I thought so," he said; "it might be the identical thing that was given to my brother. You'll have to look out, Dunning; this may mean something quite serious for you."

A long consultation took place. The paper was narrowly examined. As Harrington had said, the characters on it were more like Runes than anything else, but not decipherable by either man, and both hesitated to copy them, for fear, as they confessed, of perpetuating whatever evil purpose they might conceal. So it has remained impossible (if I may anticipate a little) to ascertain what was conveyed in this curious message or commission. Both Dunning and Harrington are firmly convinced that it had the effect of bringing its possessors into very undesirable company. That it must be returned to the source whence it came they were agreed, and further, that the only safe and certain way was that of personal service; and here contrivance would be necessary, for Dunning was known by sight to Karswell. He must, for one thing, alter his appearance by shaving his beard. But then might not the blow fall first? Harrington thought they could time it. He knew the date of the concert at which the "black spot" had been put on his brother: it was June 18th. The death had followed on Sept. 18th. Dunning reminded him that three months had been mentioned on the inscription on the car-window. "Perhaps," he added, with a cheerless laugh, "mine may be a bill at three months too. I believe I can fix it by my diary. Yes, April 23rd was the day at the Museum; that brings us to July 23rd. Now, you know, it becomes extremely important to me to know anything you will tell me about the progress of your brother's trouble, if it is possible for you to speak of it." "Of course. Well, the sense of being watched whenever he was alone was the most distressing thing to him. After a time I took to sleeping in his room, and he was the better for that: still, he talked a great deal in his sleep. What about? Is it wise to dwell on that, at least before things are straightened out? I think not, but I can tell you this: two things came for him by post during those weeks, both with a London postmark, and addressed in a commercial hand. One was a woodcut of Bewick's, roughly torn out of the page: one which shows a moonlit road and a man walking along it, followed by an awful demon creature. Under it were written the lines out of the 'Ancient Mariner' (which I suppose the cut illustrates) about one who, having once looked round—

walks on,
And turns no more his head,
Because he knows a frightful fiend
Doth close behind him tread.

The other was a calendar, such as tradesmen often send. My brother paid no attention to this, but I looked at it after his death, and found that everything after Sept. 18 had been torn out. You may be surprised at his having gone out alone the evening he was killed, but the fact is that during the last ten days or so of his life he had been quite free from the sense of being followed or watched."

The end of the consultation was this. Harrington, who knew a neighbor of Karswell's, thought he saw a way of keeping a watch on his movements. It would be Dunning's part to be in readiness to try to cross Karswell's path at any moment, to keep the paper safe and in a place of ready access.

They parted. The next weeks were no doubt a severe strain upon Dunning's nerves: the intangible barrier which had seemed to rise about him on the day when he received the paper, gradually developed into a brooding blackness that cut him off from the means of escape to which one might have thought he might resort. No one was at hand who was likely to suggest them to him, and he seemed robbed of all initiative. He waited with inexpressible anxiety as May, June, and early July passed on, for a mandate from Harrington. But all this time Karswell remained immovable at Lufford.

At last, in less than a week before the date he had come to look upon as the end of his earthly activities, came a telegram: "Leaves Victoria by boat train Thursday night. Do not miss. I come to you to-night. Harrington."

He arrived accordingly, and they concocted plans. The train left Victoria at nine and its last stop before Dover was Croydon West. Harrington would mark down Karswell at Victoria, and look out for Dunning at Croydon, calling to him if need were by a name agreed upon. Dunning, disguised as far as might be, was to have no label or initials on any hand luggage, and must at all costs have the paper with him.

Dunning's suspense as he waited on the Croydon platform I need not attempt to describe. His sense of danger during the last days had only been sharpened by the fact that the cloud about him had perceptibly been lighter; but relief was an ominous symptom, and, if Karswell eluded him now, hope was gone: and there were so many chances of that. The rumor of the journey might be itself a device. The twenty minutes in which he paced the platform and persecuted every porter with inquiries as to the boat train were as bitter as any he had spent.

Still, the train came, and Harrington was at the window. It was important, of course, that there should be no recognition: so Dunning got in at the farther end of the corridor carriage, and only gradually made his way to the compartment where Harrington and Karswell were. He was pleased, on the whole, to see that the train was far from full.

Karswell was on the alert, but gave no sign of recognition. Dunning took the seat not immediately facing him, and attempted, vainly at first, then with increasing command of his faculties, to reckon the possibilities of making the desired transfer. Opposite to Karswell, and next to Dunning, was a heap of Karswell's coats on the seat. It would be of no use to slip the paper into these—he would not be safe, or would not feel so, unless in some way it could be proffered by him and accepted by the other. There was a handbag, open, and with papers in it. Could he manage to conceal this (so that perhaps Karswell might leave the carriage without it), and then find and give it to him? This was the plan that suggested itself. If he could only have counselled with Harrington! but that could not be. The minutes went on. More than once Karswell rose and went out into the corridor. The second time Dunning was on the point of attempting to make the bag fall off the seat, but he caught Harrington's eye, and read in it a warning. Karswell, from the corridor, was watching: probably to see if the two men recognized each other. He returned, but was evidently restless: and, when he rose the third time, hope dawned, for something did slip off his seat and fall with hardly a sound to the floor. Karswell went out once more, and passed out of range of the corridor window. Dunning picked up what had fallen, and saw that the key was in his hands in the form of one of Cook's ticket-cases, with tickets in it. These cases have a pocket in the cover, and within very few seconds the paper of which we have heard was in the packet of this one. To make the operation more secure, Harrington stood in the doorway of the compartment and fiddled with the blind. It was done, and done at the right time, for the train was now slowing down towards Dover.

In a moment more Karswell re-entered the compartment. As he did so, Dunning, managing, he knew not how, to suppress the tremble in his voice, handed him the ticket-case, saying, "May I give you this, sir? I believe it is yours." After a brief glance at the ticket inside, Karswell uttered the hoped-for response, "Yes, it is; much obliged to you, sir," and he placed it in his breast pocket.

Even in the few moments that remained—moments of tense anxiety, for they knew not to what a premature finding of the paper might lead—both men noticed that the carriage seemed to darken about them and to grow warmer; that Karswell was fidgety and oppressed; that he drew the heap of loose coats near to him and cast it back as if it repelled him; and that he then sat upright and glanced anxiously at both. They, with sickening anxiety, busied themselves in collecting their belongings; but they both thought that Karswell was on the point of speaking when the train stopped at Dover Town. It was natural that in the short space between town and pier they should both go into the corridor.

At the pier they got out, but so empty was the train that they were forced to linger on the platform until Karswell should have passed ahead of them with his porter on the way to the boat, and only then was it safe for them to exchange a pressure of the hand and a word of concentrated congratulation. The effect upon Dunning was to make him almost faint. Harrington made him lean up against the wall, while he himself went forward a few yards within sight of the gangway to the boat, at which Karswell had now arrived. The man at the head of it examined his ticket, and, laden with coats, he passed down into the boat. Suddenly the official called after him, "You, sir, beg pardon, did the other gentleman show his ticket?" "What the devil do you mean by the other gentleman?" Karswell's snarling voice called back from the deck. The man bent over and looked at him. "The devil? Well, I don't know, I'm sure," Harrington heard him say to himself, and then aloud, "My mistake, sir; must have been your rugs! ask your pardon." And then, to a subordinate near him, "'Ad he got a dog with him, or what? Funny thing: I could 'a' swore 'e wasn't alone. Well, whatever it was, they'll 'ave to see to it aboard. She's off now. Another week and we shall be gettin' the 'oliday customers." In five minutes more there was nothing but the lessening lights of the boat, the long line of the Dover lamps, the night breeze, and the moon.

Long and long the two sat in their room at the "Lord Warden." In spite of the removal of their greatest anxiety, they were oppressed with a doubt, not of the lightest. Had they been justified in sending a man to his death, as they believed they had? Ought they not to warn him, at least? "No," said Harrington, "if he is the murderer I think him, we have done no more than is just. Still, if you think it better—but how and where can you warn him?" "He was booked to Abbeville only," said Dunning. "I saw that. If I wired to the hotels there in Joanne's Guide, 'Examine your ticket-case, Dunning,' I should feel happier. This is the 21st: he will have a day. But I am afraid he has gone into the dark." So telegrams were left at the hotel office.

It is not clear whether these reached their destination, or whether, if they did, they were understood. All that is known is that, on the afternoon of the 23rd, an English traveller, examining the front of St. Wulfram's Church at Abbeville, then under extensive repair, was struck on the head and instantly killed by a stone falling from the scaffold erected round the north-western tower, there being, as was clearly proved, no workman on the scaffold at that moment: and the traveller's papers identified him as Mr. Karswell.

Only one detail shall be added. At Karswell's sale a set of Bewick, sold with all faults, was acquired by Harrington. The page with the woodcut of the traveller and the demon was, as he had expected, mutilated. Also, after a judicious interval, Harrington repeated to Dunning something of what he had heard his brother say in his sleep: but it was not long before Dunning stopped him.

The Monkey's Paw

W.W. Jacobs

William Wymark Jacobs (1863-1943), writer of one of the most famous horror stories of all time, was born in Wapping, England. After attending several private schools, Jacobs entered civil service as a clerk in the Savings Bank Department of the British Postal Service. He began contributing stories to friend Jerome K. Jerome's *The Idler* and *To-day,* and published his first novel, *The Skipper's Wooing,* in 1897. Jacobs left the post office to become a full-time writer in 1898. In 1900, he married and settled in Epping. The Jacobs lived in Berkhamstead for a time before settling permanently in London. His notable works include *A Master of Craft* (1900), *Light Freights* (1901), *The Lady of the Barge* (1902), *Captains All* (1905), *Sailor Knots* (1909), *Night Watches* (1914), *The Castaway* (1916), and *Sea Whispers* (1926).

"The Monkey's Paw" is one of the most well-known and imitated horror stories of all time. Among the works it inspired are Stephen King's *Pet Semetary* and Bob Clark's cult film *Deathdream.*

I

WITHOUT, THE NIGHT was cold and wet, but in the small parlor of Lakesnam Villa the blinds were drawn and the fire burned brightly. Father and son were at chess, the former, who possessed ideas about the game involving radical changes, putting his king into such sharp and unnecessary perils that it even provoked comment from the white-haired old lady knitting placidly by the fire.

"Hark at the wind," said Mr. White, who, having seen a fatal mistake after it was too late, was amiably desirous of preventing his son from seeing it.

"I'm listening," said the latter, grimly surveying the board as he stretched out his hand. "Check."

"I should hardly think that he'd come tonight," said his father, with his hand poised over the board.

"Mate," replied the son.

"That's the worst of living so far out," bawled Mr. White, with sudden and unlooked-for violence; "of all the beastly, slushy, out-of-the-way places to live in, this is the worst. Pathway's a bog, and the road's a torrent. I don't know what people are thinking about. I suppose because only two houses on the road are let, they think it doesn't matter."

"Never mind, dear," said his wife soothingly; "perhaps you'll win the next one."

Mr. White looked up sharply, just in time to intercept a knowing glance between mother and son. The words died away on his lips, and he hid a guilty grin in his thin gray beard.

"There he is," said Herbert White, as the gate banged to loudly and heavy footsteps came toward the door.

The old man rose with hospitable haste, and opening the door, was heard condoling with the new arrival. The new arrival also condoled with himself, so that Mrs. White said, "Tut, tut!" and coughed gently as her husband entered the room, followed by a tall burly man, beady of eye and rubicund of visage.

"Sergeant-Major Morris," he said, introducing him.

The sergeant-major shook hands, and taking the proffered seat by the fire, watched contentedly while his host got out whisky and tumblers and stood a small copper kettle on the fire.

At the third glass his eyes got brighter, and he began to talk, the little family circle regarding with eager interest this visitor from distant parts, as he squared his broad shoulders in the chair and spoke of strange scenes and doughty deeds, of wars and plagues and strange peoples.

"Twenty-one years of it," said Mr. White, nodding at his wife and son. "When he went away he was a slip of a youth in the warehouse. Now look at him."

"He don't look to have taken much harm," said Mrs. White politely.

"I'd like to go to India myself," said the old man, "just to look round a bit, you know."

"Better where you are," said the sergeant-major, shaking his head. He put down the empty glass and, sighing softly, shook it again.

"I should like to see those old temples and fakirs and jugglers," said the old man. "What was that you started telling me the other day about a monkey's paw or something, Morris?"

"Nothing," said the soldier hastily. "Leastways, nothing worth hearing."

"Monkey's paw?" said Mrs. White curiously.

"Well, it's just a bit of what you might call magic, perhaps," said the sergeant-major off-handedly.

His three listeners leaned forward eagerly. The visitor absent-mindedly put his empty glass to his lips and then set it down again. His host filled it for him.

"To look at," said the sergeant-major, fumbling in his pocket, "it's just an ordinary little paw, dried to a mummy."

He took something out of his pocket and proffered it. Mrs. White drew back with a grimace, but her son, taking it, examined it curiously.

"And what is there special about it?" inquired Mr. White, as he took it from his son and, having examined it, placed it upon the table.

"It had a spell put on it by an old fakir," said the sergeant-major, "a very holy man. He wanted to show that fate ruled people's lives and that those who interfered with it did so to their sorrow. He put a spell on it so that three separate men could each have three wishes from it."

His manner was so impressive that his hearers were conscious that their light laughter jarred somewhat.

"Well, why don't you have three, sir?" said Herbert White cleverly.

The soldier regarded him in the way that middle age is wont to regard presumptuous youth. "I have," he said quietly, and his blotchy face whitened.

"And did you really have the three wishes granted?" asked Mrs. White.

"I did," said the sergeant-major, and his glass tapped against his strong teeth.

"And has anybody else wished?" inquired the old lady.

"The first man had his three wishes, yes," was the reply. "I don't know what the first two were, but the third was for death. That's how I got the paw."

His tones were so grave that a hush fell upon the group.

"If you've had your three wishes, it's no good to you now, then, Morris," said the old man at last. "What do you keep it for?"

The soldier shook his head. "Fancy, I suppose," he said slowly. "I did have some idea of selling it, but I don't think I will. It has caused enough mischief already. Besides, people won't buy. They think it's a fairy tale, some of them, and those who do think anything of it want to try it first and pay me afterward."

"If you could have another three wishes," said the old man, eyeing him keenly, "would you have them?"

"I don't know," said the other. "I don't know."

He took the paw, and dangling it between his front finger and thumb, suddenly threw it upon the fire. White, with a slight cry, stooped down and snatched it off.

"Better let it burn," said the soldier solemnly.

"If you don't want it, Morris," said the old man, "give it to me."

"I won't," said his friend doggedly. "I threw it on the fire. If you keep it, don't blame me for what happens. Pitch it on the fire again, like a sensible man."

The other shook his head and examined his new possession closely. "How do you do it?" he inquired.

"Hold it up in your right hand and wish aloud," said the sergeant-major, "but I warn you of the consequences."

"Sounds like the *Arabian Knights,"* said Mrs. White, as she rose and began to set the supper. "Don't you think you might wish for four pairs of hands for me?"

Her husband drew the talisman from his pocket and then all three burst into laughter as the sergeant-major, with a look of alarm on his face, caught him by the arm.

"If you must wish," he said gruffly, "wish for something sensible."

Mr. White dropped it back into his pocket, and placing chairs, motioned his friend to the table. In the business of supper the talisman was partly forgotten, and afterward the three sat listening in an enthralled fashion to a second installment of the soldier's adventures in India.

"If the tale about the monkey paw is not more truthful than those he has been telling us," said Herbert, as the door closed behind their guest, just in time for him to catch the last train, "we shan't make much out of it."

"Did you give him anything for it, father?" inquired Mrs. White, regarding her husband closely.

"A trifle," said he, coloring slightly. "He didn't want it, but I made him take it. And he pressed me again to throw it away."

"Likely," said Herbert, with pretended horror. "Why, we're going to be rich, and famous, and happy. Wish to be an emperor, father, to begin with; then you can't be henpecked."

He darted round the table, pursued by the malinged Mrs. White armed with an antimacassar.

Mr. White took the paw from his pocket and eyed it dubiously. "I don't know what to wish for, and that's a fact," he said slowly. "It seems to me I've got all I want."

"If you only cleared the house, you'd be quite happy, wouldn't you?" said Herbert, with his hand on his shoulder. "Well, wish two hundred pounds, then; that'll just do it."

His father, smiling shamefacedly at his own credulity, held up the talisman, as his son, with a solemn face somewhat marred by wink at his mother, sat down at the piano and struck a few impressive chords.

"I wish for two hundred pounds," said the old man distinctly.

A fine crash from the piano greeted the words, interrupted by a shuddering cry from the old man. His wife and son ran toward him.

"It moved," he cried with a glance of disgust at the object as it lay on the floor. "As I wished it twisted in my hands like a snake."

"Well, I don't see the money," said his son, as he picked it up and placed it on the table, "and I bet I never shall."

"It must have been your fancy, father," said his wife, regarding him anxiously.

He shook his head. "Never mind, though; there's no harm done, but it gave me a shock all the same."

They sat down by the fire again while the two men finished their pipes. Outside, the wind was higher than ever, and the old man started nervously at the sound of a door banging upstairs. A silence unusual and depressing settled upon all three, which lasted until the old couple rose to retire for the night.

"I expect you'll find the cash tied up in a big bag in the middle of your bed," said Herbert, as he bade them good night, "and something horrible squatting up on top of the wardrobe watching you as you pocket your ill-gotten gains."

II

In the brightness of the wintry sun next morning as it streamed over the breakfast table Herbert laughed at his fears. There was an air of prosaic wholesomeness about the room which it had lacked on the previous night, and the dirty, shriveled little paw was pitched on the sideboard with a carelessness which betokened no great belief in its virtues.

"I suppose all old soldiers are the same," said Mrs. White. "The idea of our listening to such nonsense! How could wishes be granted in these days? And if they could, how could two hundred pounds hurt you, father?"

"Might drop on his head from the sky," said the frivolous Herbert.

"Morris said the things happened so naturally," said his father, "that you might if you so wished attribute it to coincidence."

"Well, don't break into the money before I come back," said Herbert, as he rose from the table. "I'm afraid it'll turn you into a mean, avaricious man, and we shall have to disown you."

His mother laughed, and following him to the door, watched him down the road, and returning to the breakfast table, was very happy at the expense of her husband's credulity. All of which did not prevent her from scurrying to the door at the postman's knock, nor prevent her from referring somewhat shortly to retired sergeant-majors of bibulous habits when she found that the post brought a tailor's bill.

"Herbert will have some more of his funny remarks, I expect, when he comes home," she said, as they sat at dinner.

"I dare say," said Mr. White, pouring himself out some beer; "But for all that, the thing moved in my hand; that I'll swear to."

"You thought it did," said the old lady soothingly.

"I say it did," replied the other. "There was no thought about it; I had just—What's the matter?"

His wife made no reply. She was watching the mysterious movements of a man outside, who, peering in an undecided fashion at the house, appeared to be trying to make up his mind to enter. In mental connection with the two hundred pounds, she noticed that the stranger was well dressed and wore a silk hat of glossy newness. Three times he paused at the gate, and then walked on again. The fourth time he stood with his hand upon it, and then with sudden resolution flung it open and walked up the path. Mrs. White at the same moment placed her hands behind her, and hurriedly unfastening the strings of her apron, put that useful article of apparel beneath the cushion of her chair.

She brought the stranger, who seemed ill at ease, into the room. He gazed furtively at Mrs. White, and listened in a preoccupied fashion as the old lady apologized for the appearance of the room and her husband's coat, a garment which he usually reserved for the garden. She then waited as patiently as her sex would permit for him to broach his business, but he was at first strangely silent.

"I—was asked to call," he said at last, and stooped and picked a piece of cotton from his trousers. "I come from Maw and Meggins."

The old lady started. "Is anything the matter?" she asked breathlessly. "Has anything happened to Herbert? What is it? What is it?"

Her husband interposed. "There, there, mother," he said hastily "Sit down, and don't jump to conclusions. You've not brought bad news, I'm sure, sir," and he eyed the other wistfully.

"I'm sorry—" began the visitor.

"Is he hurt?" demanded the mother.

The visitor bowed in assent. "Badly hurt," he said quietly, "but he is not in any pain."

"Oh, thank God!" said the old woman, clasping her hands. "Thank God for that! Thank—"

She broke off suddenly as the sinister meaning of the assurance dawned upon her and she saw the awful confirmation of her fears in the other's averted face. She caught her breath, and turning to her slower-witted husband, laid her trembling old hand upon his. There was a long silence.

"He was caught in the machinery," said the visitor at length, in a low voice.

"Caught in the machinery," repeated Mr. White, in a dazed fashion, "yes."

He sat staring blankly out at the window, and taking his wife's hand between his own, pressed it as he had been wont to do in their old courting days nearly forty years before.

"He was the only one left to us," he said, turning gently to the visitor. "It is hard."

The other coughed, and rising, walked slowly to the window. "The firm wished me to convey their sincere sympathy with you in your great loss," he said, without looking round. "I beg that you will understand I am only their servant and merely obeying orders."

There was no reply; the old woman's face was white, her eyes staring, and her breath inaudible; on the husband's face was a look such as his friend the sergeant might have carried into his first action.

"I was to say that Maw and Meggins disclaim all responsibility," continued the other. "They admit no liability at all, but in consideration of your son's services they wish to present you with a certain sum as compensation."

Mr. White dropped his wife's hand, and rising to his feet, gazed with a look of horror at his visitor. His dry lips shaped the words, "How much?"

"Two hundred pounds," was the answer.

Unconscious of his wife's shriek, the old man smiled faintly, put out his hands like a sightless man, and dropped, a senseless heap, to the floor.

III

In the huge new cemetery, some two miles distant, the old people buried their dead, and came back to a house steeped in shadow and silence. It was all over so quickly that at first they could hardly realize it, and remained in a state of expectation as though of something else to happen—something else which was to lighten this load, too heavy for old hearts to bear. But the days passed, and expectation gave place to resignation—the hopeless resignation of the old, sometimes miscalled apathy. Sometimes they hardly exchanged a word, for now they had nothing to talk about, and their days were long to weariness.

It was about a week after that that the old man, waking suddenly in the night, stretched out his hand and found himself alone. The room was in darkness, and the sound of subdued weeping came from the window. He raised himself in bed and listened.

"Come back," he said tenderly. "You will be cold."

"It is colder for my son," said the old woman, and wept afresh.

The sound of her sobs died away on his ears. The bed was warm, and his eyes heavy with sleep. He dozed fitfully, and then slept until a sudden wild cry from his wife awoke him with a start.

"The monkey's paw!" she cried wildly. "The monkey's paw!"

He started up in alarm. "Where? Where is it? What's the matter ?"

She came stumbling across the room toward him. "I want it," she said quietly. "You've not destroyed it?"

"It's in the parlor, on the bracket," he replied, marveling. "Why?"

She cried and laughed together, and bending over, kissed his cheek.

"I only just thought of it," she said hysterically. "Why didn't I think of it before? Why didn't you think of it?"

"Think of what?" he questioned.

"The other two wishes," she replied rapidly. "We've only had one."

"Was not that enough?" he demanded fiercely.

"No," she cried triumphantly; "we'll have one more. Go down and get it quickly, and wish our boy alive again."

The man sat up in bed and flung the bedclothes from his quaking limbs. "Good God, you are mad!" he cried, aghast.

"Get it," she panted; "get it quickly, and wish—Oh my boy, my boy!"

Her husband struck a match and lit the candle. "Get back to bed," he said unsteadily. "You don't know what you are saying."

"We had the first wish granted," said the old woman feverishly; "why not the second?"

"A coincidence," stammered the old man.

"Go and get it and wish," cried the old woman, and dragged him toward the door.

He went down in the darkness, and felt his way to the parlor, and then to the mantelpiece. The talisman was in its place, and a horrible fear that the unspoken wish might bring his mutilated son before him ere he could escape from the room seized upon him, and he caught his breath as he found that he had lost the direction of the door. His brow cold with sweat, he felt his way round the table, and groped along the wall until he found himself in the small passage with the unwholesome thing in his hand.

Even his wife's face seemed changed as he entered the room. It was white and expectant, and to his fears seemed to have an unnatural look upon it. He was afraid of her.

"Wish!" she cried, in a strong voice.

"It is foolish and wicked," he faltered.

"Wish!" repeated his wife.

He raised his hand. "I wish my son alive again."

The talisman fell to the floor, and he regarded it shudderingly. Then he sank trembling into a chair as the old woman, with burning eyes, walked to the window and raised the blind.

He sat until he was chilled with the cold, glancing occasionally at the figure of the old woman peering through the window. The candle end, which had burnt below the rim of the china candlestick, was throwing pulsating shadows on the ceiling and walls, until, with a flicker larger than the rest, it expired. The old man, with an unspeakable sense of relief at the failure of the talisman, crept back to his bed, and a minute or two afterward the old woman came silently and apathetically beside him.

Neither spoke, but both lay silently listening to the ticking of the clock. A stair creaked, and a squeaky mouse scurried noisily through the wall. The darkness was oppressive, and after lying for some time screwing up his courage, the husband took the box of matches, and striking one, went downstairs for a candle.

At the foot of the stairs the match went out, and he paused to strike another, and at the same moment a knock, so quiet and stealthy as to be scarcely audible, sounded on the front door.

The matches fell from his hand. He stood motionless, his breath suspended until the knock was repeated. Then he turned and fled swiftly back to his room, and closed the door behind him. A third knock sounded through the house.

"What's that?" cried the old woman, starting up.

"A rat," said the old man, in shaking tones—"a rat. It passed me on the stairs."

His wife sat up in bed listening. A loud knock resounded through the house.

"It's Herbert!" she screamed. "It's Herbert!"

She ran to the door, but her husband was before her, and catching her by the arm, held her tightly.

"What are you going to do?" he whispered hoarsely.

"It's my boy; it's Herbert!" she cried, struggling mechanically. "I forgot it was two miles away. What are you holding me for? Let go. I must open the door."

"For God's sake don't let it in," cried the old man, trembling.

"You're afraid of your own son," she cried, struggling.

"Let me go. I'm coming, Herbert; I'm coming."

There was another knock, and another. The old woman with a sudden wrench broke free and ran from the room. Her husband followed to the landing, and called after her appealingly as she hurried downstairs. He heard the chain rattle back and the bottom bolt drawn slowly and stiffly from the socket. Then the old woman's voice, strained and panting.

"The bolt," she cried loudly. "Come down. I can't reach it."

But her husband was on his hands and knees groping wildly on the floor in search of the paw. If he could only find it before the thing outside got in. A perfect fusillade of knocks reverberated through the house, and he heard the scraping of a chair as his wife put it down in the passage against the door. He heard the creaking of the bolt as it came slowly back, and at the same moment, he found the monkey's paw, and frantically breathed his third and last wish.

The knocking ceased suddenly, although the echoes of it were still in the house. He heard the chair drawn back and the door opened. A cold wind rushed up the staircase, and a long loud wail of disappointment and misery from his wife gave him courage to run down to her side, and then to the gate beyond. The street lamp flickering opposite shone on a quiet and deserted road.

The Outsider

H.P. Lovecraft

Howard Phillips Lovecraft (1890-1937), the creator of the influential "Cthulhu Mythos," was born in Providence, Rhode Island. Lovecraft's father was institutionalized and died in 1898. As a child, Lovecraft read extensively. He showed an early interest in New England and Arabian history. Lovecraft left high school due to a nervous condition in 1908. He lived a life of seclusion until he began participating in amateur journalism in 1915. In 1917, Lovecraft wrote the first Cthulhu story, "Dagon," with the encouragement of W. Paul Cook. In 1924, Lovecraft moved to New York and married Sonia Green. The marriage was difficult, and the couple divorced two years later. Lovecraft moved back to Rhode Island and lived with a succession of aunts, never attaining any level of wealth. Almost all of his work appeared in *Weird Tales* magazine, and only two books—*The Shunned House* (1928) and *The Shadow Over Innsmouth* (1936)—were published during his lifetime. The first collection of his work, *The Outsider and Others,* appeared in 1939. Unpublished works like the novels *The Case of Charles Dexter Ward* and *The Dream Quest of the Unknown Kadath,* continued to be published by the pulps well into the 1940's.

Lovecraft's verbose, ornate style has served as the inspiration for many of the horror writers of today. "The Outsider" is not only Lovecraft at the top of his form, but a story that moves the reader to pity as well as fear in its portrait of the main character.

That night the Baron dreamt of many a wo;
And all his warrior-guests, with shade and form
Of witch, and demon, and large coffin-worm,
Were long be-nightmared.

—KEATS

UNHAPPY IS HE to whom the memories of childhood bring only fear and sadness. Wretched is he who looks back upon lone hours in vast and dismal chambers with brown hangings and maddening rows of antique books, or upon awed watches in twilight groves of grotesque, gigantic, and vine-encumbered trees that silently have twisted branches far aloft. Such a lot the gods gave to me—to me, the dazed, the disappointed; the barren, the broken. And yet I am strangely content and cling desperately to those sere memories, when my mind momentarily threatens to reach beyond to *the other.*

I know not where I was born, save that the castle was infinitely old and infinitely horrible, full of dark passages and having high ceilings where the eye could find only cobwebs and shadows. The stones in the crumbling corridors seemed always hideously damp, and there was an accursed smell everywhere, as of the piled-up corpses of dead generations. It was never light, so that I used sometimes to light candles and gaze steadily at them for relief, nor was there any sun outdoors, since the terrible trees grew high above the topmost accessible tower. There was one black tower which reached above the trees into the unknown outer sky, but that was partly ruined and could not be ascended save by a well-nigh impossible climb up the sheer wall, stone by stone.

I must have lived years in this place, but I cannot measure the time. Beings must have cared for my needs, yet I cannot recall any person except myself, or anything alive but the noiseless rats and bats and spiders. I think that whoever nursed me must have been shockingly aged, since my first conception of a living person was that of somebody mockingly like myself, yet distorted, shrivelled, and decaying like the castle. To me there was nothing grotesque in the bones and skeletons that strewed some of the stone crypts deep down among the foundations. I fantastically associated these things with every-day events, and thought them more natural than the colored pictures of living beings which I found in many of the mouldy books. From such books I learned all that I know. No teacher urged or guided me, and I do not recall hearing any human voice in all those years—not even my own; for although I had read of speech, I had never thought to try to speak aloud. My aspect was a matter equally unthought of, for there were no mirrors in the castle, and I merely regarded myself by instinct as akin to the youthful figures I saw drawn and painted in the books. I felt conscious of youth because I remembered so little.

Outside, across the putrid moat and under the dark mute trees, I would often lie and dream for hours about what I read in the books; and would longingly picture myself amidst gay crowds in the sunny world beyond the endless forests. Once I tried to escape from the forest, but as I went farther from the castle the shade grew denser and the air more filled with brooding fear; so that I ran frantically back lest I lose my way in a labyrinth of nighted silence.

So through endless twilights I dreamed and waited, though I knew not what I waited for. Then in the shadowy solitude my longing for light grew so frantic that I could rest no more, and I lifted entreating hands to the single black ruined tower that reached above the forest into the unknown outer sky. And at last I resolved to scale that tower, fall though I might; since it were better to glimpse the sky and perish, than to live without ever beholding day.

In the dank twilight I climbed the worn and aged stone stairs till I reached the level where they ceased, and thereafter clung perilously to small footholds leading upward. Ghastly and terrible was that dead, stairless cylinder of rock; black, ruined, and deserted, and sinister with startled bats whose wings made no noise. But more ghastly and terrible still was the slowness of my progress; for climb as I might, the darkness overhead grew no thinner, and a new chill as of haunted and venerable mould assailed me. I shivered as I wondered why I did not reach the light, and would have looked down had I dared. I fancied that night had come suddenly upon me, and vainly groped with one free hand for a window embrasure, that I might peer out and above, and try to judge the height I had attained.

All at once, after an infinity of awesome, sightless, crawling up that concave and desperate precipice, I felt my head touch a solid thing, and knew I must have gained the roof, or at least some kind of floor. In the darkness I raised my free hand and tested the barrier, finding it stone and immovable. Then came a deadly circuit of the tower, clinging to whatever holds the slimy wall could give; till finally my testing hand found the barrier yielding, and I turned upward again, pushing the slab or door with my head as I used both hands in my fearful ascent. There was no light revealed above, and as my hands went higher I knew that my climb was for the nonce ended; since the slab was the trap-door of an aperture leading to a level stone surface of greater circumference than the lower tower, no doubt the floor of some lofty and capacious observation chamber. I crawled through carefully, and tried to prevent the heavy slab from falling back into place, but failed in the latter attempt. As I lay exhausted on the stone floor I heard the eerie echoes of its fall, but hoped when necessary to pry it up again.

Believing I was now at prodigious height, far above the accursed branches of the wood, I dragged myself up from the floor and fumbled about for windows, that I might look for the first time upon the sky, and the moon and stars of which I had read. But on every hand I was disappointed; since all that I found were vast shelves of marble, bearing odious oblong boxes of disturbing size. More and more I reflected, and wondered what hoary secrets might abide in this high apartment so many aeons cut off from the castle below. Then unexpectedly my hands came upon a doorway, where hung a portal of stone, rough with strange chiselling. Trying it, I found it locked; but with a supreme burst of strength I overcame all obstacles and dragged it open inward. As I did so there came to me the purest ecstasy I have ever known; for shining tranquilly through an ornate grating of iron, and down a short stone passageway of steps that ascended from the newly found doorway, was the radiant full moon, which I had never before seen save in dreams and in vague visions I dared not call memories.

Fancying now that I had attained the very pinnacle of the castle, I commenced to rush up the few steps beyond the door; but the sudden veiling of the moon by a cloud caused me to stumble, and I felt my way more slowly in the dark. It was still very dark when I reached the grating—which I tried carefully and found unlocked, but which I did not open for fear of falling from the amazing height to which I had climbed. Then the moon came out.

Most demoniacal of all shocks is that of the abysmally unexpected and grotesquely unbelievable. Nothing I had before undergone could compare in terror with what I now saw; with the bizarre marvels that sight implied. The sight itself was as simple as it was stupefying, for it was merely this: instead of a dizzying prospect of treetops seen from a lofty eminence, there stretched around me on the level through the grating nothing less than *the solid ground,* decked and diversified by marble slabs and columns, and overshadowed by an ancient stone church, whose ruined spire gleamed spectrally in the moonlight.

Half unconscious, I opened the grating and staggered out upon the white gravel path that stretched away in two directions. My mind, stunned and chaotic as it was, still held the frantic craving for light; and not even the fantastic wonder which had happened could stay my course. I neither knew nor cared whether my experience was insanity, dreaming, or magic; but was determined to gaze on brilliance and gaiety at any cost. I knew not who I was or what I was, or what my surroundings might be; though as I continued to stumble alone I became conscious of a kind of fearsome latent memory that made my progress not wholly fortuitous. I passed under an arch out of that region of slabs and columns, and wandered through the open country; sometimes following the visible road, but sometimes leaving it curiously to tread across meadows where only occasional ruins bespoke the ancient presence of a forgotten road. Once I swam across a swift river where crumbling, mossy masonry told of a bridge long vanished.

Over two hours must have passed before I reached what seemed to be my goal, a venerable ivied castle in a thickly wooded park, maddeningly familiar, yet full of perplexing strangeness to me. I saw that the moat was filled in, and that some of the well-known towers were demolished; whilst new wings existed to confuse the beholder. But what I observed with chief interest and delight were the open windows—gorgeously ablaze with light and sending forth sound of the gayest revelry. Advancing to one of these I looked in and saw an oddly dressed company, indeed; making merry, and speaking brightly to one another. I had never, seemingly, heard human speech before and could guess only vaguely what was said. Some of the faces seemed to hold expressions that brought up incredibly remote recollections, others were utterly alien.

I now stepped through the low window into the brilliantly lighted room, stepping as I did so from my single bright moment of hope to my blackest convulsion of despair and realization. The nightmare was quick to come, for as I entered, there occurred immediately one of the most terrifying demonstrations I had ever conceived. Scarcely had I crossed the sill when there descended upon the whole company a sudden and unheralded fear of hideous intensity, distorting every face and evoking the most horrible screams from nearly every throat. Flight was universal, and in the clamor and panic several fell in a swoon and were dragged away by their madly fleeing companions. Many covered their eyes with their hands, and plunged blindly and awkwardly in their race to escape, overturning furniture and stumbling against the walls before they managed to reach one of the many doors.

The cries were shocking; and as I stood in the brilliant apartment alone and dazed, listening to their vanishing echoes, I trembled at the thought of what might be lurking near me unseen. At a casual inspection the room seemed deserted, but when I moved towards one of the alcoves I thought I detected a presence there—a hint of motion beyond the golden-arched doorway leading to another and somewhat similar room. As I approached the arch I began to perceive the presence more clearly; and then, with the first and last sound I ever uttered—a ghastly ululation that revolted me almost as poignantly as its noxious cause I beheld in full, frightful vividness the inconceivable, indescribable, and unmentionable monstrosity which had by its simple appearance changed a merry company to a herd of delirious fugitives.

I cannot even hint what it was like, for it was a compound of all that is unclean, uncanny, unwelcome, abnormal, and detestable. It was the ghoulish shade of decay, antiquity, and dissolution; the putrid, dripping eidolon of unwholesome revelation, the awful baring of that which the merciful earth should always hide. God knows it was not of this world—or no longer of this world—yet to my horror I saw in its eaten-away and bone-revealing outlines a leering, abhorrent travesty on the human shape; and in its mouldy, disintegrating apparel an unspeakable quality that chilled me even more.

I was almost paralyzed, but not too much so to make a feeble effort towards flight; a backward stumble which failed to break the spell in which the nameless, voiceless monster held me. My eyes bewitched by the glassy orbs which stared loathsomely into them, refused to close; though they were mercifully blurred, and showed the terrible object but indistinctly after the first shock. I tried to raise my hand to shut out the sight, yet so stunned were my nerves that my arm could not fully obey my will. The attempt, however, was enough to disturb my balance; so that I had to stagger forward several steps to avoid falling. As I did so I became suddenly and agonizingly aware of the *nearness* of the carrion thing, whose hideous hollow breathing I half fancied I could hear. Nearly mad, I found myself yet able to throw out a hand to ward off the foetid apparition which pressed so close; when in one cataclysmic second of cosmic nightmarishness and hellish accident *my fingers touched the rotting outstretched paw of the monster beneath the golden arch.*

I did not shriek, but all the fiendish ghouls that ride the night-wind shrieked for me as in that same second there crashed down upon my mind a single and fleeting avalanche of soul-annihilating memory. I knew in that second all that had been; I remembered beyond the frightful castle and the trees, and recognized the altered edifice in which I now stood; I recognized, most terrible of all, the unholy abomination that stood leering before me as I withdrew my sullied fingers from its own.

But in the cosmos there is balm as well as bitterness, and that balm is nepenthe. In the supreme horror of that second I forgot what had horrified me, and the burst of black memory vanished in a chaos of echoing images. In a dream I fled from that haunted and accursed pile, and ran swiftly and silently in the moonlight. When I returned to the churchyard place of marble and went down the steps I found the stone trap-door immovable; but I was not sorry, for I had hated the antique castle and the trees. Now I ride with the mocking and friendly ghouls on the night-wind, and play by day amongst the catacombs of Nephren-Ka in the sealed and unknown valley of Hadoth by the Nile. I know that light is not for me, save that of the moon over the rock tombs of Neb, nor any gaiety save the unnamed feasts of Nitokris beneath the Great Pyramid; yet in my new wildness and freedom I almost welcome the bitterness of alienage.

For although nepenthe has calmed me, I know always that I am an outsider; a stranger in this century and among those who are still men. This I have known ever since I stretched out my fingers to the abomination within that great gilded frame; stretched out my fingers and touched *a cold and unyielding surface of polished glass.*

Yours Truly, Jack the Ripper

Robert Bloch

Robert Bloch (b. 1917) was born in Chicago. A correspondent of Lovecraft's, the teenaged Bloch sold his first story, "The Horror in the Abbey," to *Weird Tales* in 1934. In 1942, he began working as a copywriter for the Gustav-Marx ad agency in Milwaukee. His first collection, *The Opener of the Way,* was published in 1945. His first novel, *The Scarf,* followed two years later. In 1953, Bloch left Gustav-Marx to become a freelance writer. In the late 1950's, he moved to Los Angeles and began writing teleplays for such shows as *Alfred Hitchcock Presents* and *Thriller.* In 1959, he was awarded the Hugo for his story "The Hellbound Train." That year he wrote his most famous novel, *Psycho.* In 1960, he wrote the first of several screenplays, *The Couch.* A later screenplay for *The Night-Walker* won the 1964 Triste Film Festival award. Throughout the 1960's, Bloch produced several novels (*The Firebug,* 1961; *The Star Stalker,* 1968), collections (*Pleasant Dreams—Nightmares,* 1960; *The Skull of the Marquis de Sade and Other Stories,* 1965; *The Living Demons,* 1967) and screenplays (*Straitjacket,* 1963; *Torture Garden,* 1968). From 1970-71, he served as President of the Mystery Writers of America. In 1977, he edited *The Best of Fredric Brown.* The following year, Bloch received the Fritz Leiber Fantasy Award. Among his later novels and collections are *American Gothic* (1974), *Cold Chills* (1977), *Out of the Mouth of Graves* (1978), *Mysteries of the Worm* (1981), *Psycho II* (1982), *Night of the Ripper* (1984), *Lori* (1989), and *The Jekyll Legacy* (1990; with Andre Norton). Bloch presently lives in California.

"Yours Truly, Jack the Ripper" possesses one of the most memorable last lines in horror literature. The twist ending is still a shock in light of the many inferior imitations written throughout the years.

1

I LOOKED at the stage Englishman. He looked at me.

"Sir Guy Hollis?" I asked.

"Indeed. Have I the pleasure of addressing John Carmody, the psychiatrist?"

I nodded. My eyes swept over the figure of my distinguished visitor. Tall, lean, sandy-haired—with the traditional tufted mustache. And the tweeds. I suspected a monocle concealed in a vest pocket, and wondered if he'd left his umbrella in the outer office.

But more than that, I wondered what the devil had impelled Sir Guy Hollis of the British Embassy to seek out a total stranger here in Chicago.

Sir Guy didn't help matters any as he sat down. He cleared his throat, glanced around nervously, tapped his pipe against the side of the desk. Then he opened his mouth.

"Mr. Carmody," he said, "have you ever heard of Jack the Ripper?"

"The murderer?" I asked.

"Exactly. The greatest monster of them all. Worse than Springheel Jack or Crippen. Jack the Ripper. Red Jack."

"I've heard of him," I said.

"Do you know his history?"

"I don't think we'll get any place swapping old wives' tales about famous crimes of history."

He took a deep breath.

"This is no old wives' tale. It's a matter of life or death."

He was so wrapped up in his obsession he even talked that way. Well—I was willing to listen. We psychiatrists get paid for listening.

"Go ahead," I told him. "Let's have the story."

Sir Guy lit a cigarette and began to talk.

"London, 1888," he began. "Late summer and early fall. That was the time. Out of nowhere came the shadowy figure of Jack the Ripper—a stalking shadow with a knife, prowling through London's East End. Haunting the squalid dives of Whitechapel, Spitalfields. Where he came from no one knew. But he brought death. Death in a knife.

"Six times that knife descended to slash the throats and bodies of London's women. Drabs and alley sluts. August 7th was the date of the first butchery. They found her body lying there with thirty-nine stab wounds. A ghastly murder. On August 31st, another victim. The press became interested. The slum inhabitants were more deeply interested still.

"Who was this unknown killer who prowled in their midst and struck at will in the deserted alleyways of night-town? And what was more important—when would he strike again?

"September 8th was the date. Scotland Yard assigned special deputies. Rumors ran rampant. The atrocious nature of the slayings was the subject for shocking speculation.

"The killer used a knife—expertly. He cut throats and removed—certain portions—of the bodies after death. He chose victims and settings with a fiendish deliberation. No one saw him or heard him. But watchmen making their gray rounds in the dawn would stumble across the hacked and horrid thing that was the Ripper's handiwork.

"Who was he? What was he? A mad surgeon? A butcher? An insane scientist? A pathological degenerate escaped from an asylum? A deranged nobleman? A member of the London police?

"Then the poem appeared in the newspapers. The anonymous poem, designed to put a stop to speculations—but which only aroused public interest to a further frenzy. A mocking little stanza:

I'm not a butcher, I'm not a Yid
Nor yet a foreign skipper,
But I'm your own true loving friend,
Yours truly—Jack the Ripper.

"And on September 30th, two more throats were slashed open. There was silence, then, in London for a time. Silence, and a nameless fear. When would Red Jack strike again? They waited through October. Every figment of fog concealed his phantom presence. Concealed it well—for nothing was learned of the Ripper's identity, or his purpose. The drabs of London shivered in the raw wind of early November. Shivered, and were thankful for the coming of each morning's sun.

"November 9th. They found her in her room. She lay there very quietly, limbs neatly arranged. And beside her, with equal neatness, were laid her breasts and heart. The Ripper had outdone himself in execution.

"Then, panic. But needless panic. For though press, police, and populace alike waited in sick dread, Jack the Ripper did not strike again.

"Months passed. A year. The immediate interest died, but not the memory. They said Jack had skipped to America. That he had committed suicide. They said—and they wrote. They've written ever since. Theories, hypotheses, arguments, treatises. But to this day no one knows who Jack the Ripper was. Or why he killed. Or why he stopped killing."

Sir Guy was silent. Obviously he expected some comment from me.

"You tell the story well," I remarked.

"I suppose you want to know why I'm interested?" he said.

"Yes. That's exactly what I'd like to know."

"Because," said Sir Guy Hollis, "I am on the trail of Jack the Ripper now. I think he's here—in Chicago!"

"Say that again."

"Jack the Ripper is alive, in Chicago, and I'm out to find him."

He wasn't smiling. It wasn't a joke.

"See here," I said. "What was the date of these murders?"

"August to November, 1888."

"1888? But if Jack the Ripper was an able-bodied man in 1888, he'd surely be dead today!"

"Perhaps. Tell me, Mr. Carmody, do you think I'm crazy?"

"Frankly—no."

"Then you might listen to the reasons I believe Jack the Ripper is alive."

"I might."

"I've studied these cases for years. Been over the actual ground. Talked to officials. Talked to friends and acquaintances of the poor drabs who were killed. Visited with men and women in the neighborhood. Collected an entire library of material touching on Jack the Ripper. Studied all the wild theories or crazy notions.

"I learned a little. Not much, but a little. I won't bore you with my conclusions. But there was another branch of inquiry that yielded more fruitful return. I have studied unsolved crimes. Murders.

"I could show you clippings from the papers of half the world's greatest cities. San Francisco. Shanghai. Calcutta. Omsk. Paris. Berlin. Pretoria. Cairo. Milan. Adelaide.

"The trail is there, the pattern. Unsolved crimes. Slashed throats of women. With the peculiar disfigurations and removals. Yes, I've followed a trail of blood. From New York westward across the continent. Then to the Pacific. From there to Africa. During the World War of 1914-18 it was Europe. After that, South America. And since 1930, the United States again. Eighty-seven such murders—and to the trained criminologist, all bear the stigma of the Ripper's handiwork.

"Recently there were the so-called Cleveland torso slayings. Remember? A shocking series. And finally, two recent deaths in Chicago. Within the past six months. One out on South Dearborn. The other somewhere up on Halsted. Same type of crime, same technique. I tell you, there are unmistakable indications in all these affairs—indications of the work of Jack the Ripper!"

"A very tight theory," I said. "I'll not question your evidence at all, or the deductions you draw. You're the criminologist, and I'll take your word for it. Just one thing remains to be explained. A minor point, perhaps, but worth mentioning."

"And what is that?" asked Sir Guy.

"Just how could a man of, let us say, eighty-five years commit these crimes? For if Jack the Ripper was around thirty in 1888 and lived, he'd be eighty-five today."

"Suppose he didn't get any older?" whispered Sir Guy.

"What's that?"

"Suppose Jack the Ripper didn't grow old? Suppose he is still a young man today?

"It's a crazy theory, I grant you," he said. "All the theories about the Ripper are crazy. The idea that he was a doctor. Or a maniac. Or a woman. The reasons advanced for such beliefs are flimsy enough. There's nothing to go by. So why should my notion be any worse?"

"Because people grow older," I reasoned with him. "Doctors, maniacs, and women alike."

"What about—sorcerers?"

"Sorcerers?"

"Necromancers. Wizards. Practicers of Black Magic?"

"What's the point?"

"I studied," said Sir Guy. "I studied everything. After a while I began to study the dates of the murders. The pattern those dates formed. The rhythm. The solar, lunar, stellar rhythm. The sidereal aspect. The astrological significance.

"Suppose Jack the Ripper didn't murder for murder's sake alone? Suppose he wanted to make—a sacrifice?"

"What kind of a sacrifice?"

Sir Guy shrugged. "It is said that if you offer blood to the dark gods they grant boons. Yes, if a blood offering is made at the proper time—when the moon and the stars are right—and with the proper ceremonies—they grant boons. Gifts of youth. Eternal youth."

"But that's nonsense!"

"No. That's—Jack the Ripper."

I stood up. "A most interesting theory," I told him. "But why do you come here and tell it to me? I'm not an authority on witchcraft. I'm not a police official or criminologist. I'm a practicing psychiatrist. What's the connection?"

Sir Guy smiled.

"You are interested, then?"

"Well, yes. There must be some point."

"There is. But I wished to be assured of your interest first. Now I can tell you my plan."

"And just what is that plan?"

Sir Guy gave me a long look.

"John Carmody," he said, "you and I are going to capture Jack the Ripper."

2

That's the way it happened. I've given the gist of that first interview in all its intricate and somewhat boring detail, because I think it's important. It helps to throw some light on Sir Guy's character and attitude. And in view of what happened after that—

But I'm coming to those matters.

Sir Guy's thought was simple. It wasn't even a thought. Just a hunch.

"You know the people here," he told me. "I've inquired. That's why I came to you as the ideal man for my purpose. You number amongst your acquaintances many writers, painters, poets. The so-called intelligentsia. The lunatic fringe from the near north side.

"For certain reasons—never mind what they are—my clues lead me to infer that Jack the Ripper is a member of that element. He chooses to pose as an eccentric. I've a feeling that with you to take me around and introduce me, I might hit upon the right person."

"It's all right with me," I said. "But just how are you going to look for him? As you say, he might be anybody, anywhere. And you have no idea what he looks like. He might be young or old. Jack the Ripper—a Jack of all trades? Rich man, poor man, beggar man, thief, doctor, lawyer—how will you know?"

"We shall see." Sir Guy sighed heavily. "But I must find him. At once."

"Why the hurry?"

Sir Guy sighed again. "Because in two days he will kill again."

"Are you sure?"

"Sure as the stars. I've plotted this chart, you see. All of the murders correspond to certain astrological rhythm patterns. If, as I suspect, he makes a blood sacrifice to renew his youth, he must murder within two days. Notice the pattern of his first crimes in London. August 7th. Then August 31st. September 8th. September 30th. November 9th. Intervals of 24 days, 9 days, 22 days—he killed two this time—and then 40 days. Of course there were crimes in between. There had to be. But they weren't discovered and pinned on him.

"At any rate, I've worked out a pattern for him, based on all my data. And I say that within the next two days he kills. So I must seek him out, somehow, before then."

"And I'm still asking you what you want me to do."

"Take me out," said Sir Guy. "Introduce me to your friends."

"But where do I begin? As far as I know, my artistic friends, despite their eccentricities, are all normal people."

"So is the Ripper. Perfectly normal. Except on certain nights." Again that faraway look in Sir Guy's eyes. "Then he becomes an ageless pathological monster, crouching to kill."

"All right," I said. "All right. I'll take you."

We made our plans. And that evening I took him over to Lester Baston's studio.

As we ascended to the penthouse roof in the elevator I took the opportunity to warn Sir Guy.

"Baston's a real oddball," I cautioned him. "So are his guests. Be prepared for anything and everything."

"I am." Sir Guy Hollis was perfectly serious. He put his hand in his trousers pocket and pulled out a gun.

"If I see him I'll be ready," Sir Guy said. He didn't smile, either.

"But you can't go running around at a party with a loaded revolver in your pocket, man!"

"Don't worry, I won't behave foolishly."

I wondered. Sir Guy Hollis was not, to my way of thinking, a rational man.

We stepped out of the elevator, went toward Baston's apartment door.

"By the way," I murmured, "just how do you wish to be introduced? Shall I tell them who you are and what you are looking for?"

"I don't care. Perhaps it would be best to be frank."

"But don't you think that the Ripper—if by some miracle he or she is present—will immediately get the wind up and take cover?"

"I think the shock of the announcement that I am hunting the Ripper would provoke some kind of betraying gesture on his part," said Sir Guy.

"It's a fine theory. But I warn you, you're going to be in for a lot of ribbing.

Sir Guy smiled.

"I'm ready," he announced. "I have a little plan of my own. Don't be shocked at anything I do."

I nodded and knocked on the door.

Baston opened it and poured out into the hall. His eyes were as red as the maraschino cherries in his Manhattan. He teetered back and forth regarding us very gravely. He squinted at my square-cut homburg hat and Sir Guy's mustache.

"Aha," he intoned. "The Walrus and the Carpenter."

I introduced Sir Guy.

"Welcome," said Baston, gesturing us inside with over-elaborate courtesy. He stumbled after us into the garish parlor.

I stared at the crowd that moved restlessly through the fog of cigarette smoke.

It was the shank of the evening for this mob. Every hand held a drink. Every face held a slightly hectic flush. Over in one corner the piano was going full blast, but the imperious strains of the *March* from *The Love for Three Oranges* couldn't drown out the profanity from the crap-game in the other corner.

Prokofieff had no chance against that, and one set of ivories rattled louder than the other.

Sir Guy got a monocle-full right away. He saw LaVerne Gonnister, the poetess, hit Hymie Kralik in the eye. He saw Hymie sit down on the floor and cry until Dick Pool accidentally stepped on his stomach as he walked through to the dining room for a drink.

He heard Nadia Vilinoff, the commercial artist, tell Johnny Odcutt that she thought his tattooing was in dreadful taste, and he saw Barclay Melton crawl under the dining room table with Johnny Odcutt's wife.

His zoological observations might have continued indefinitely if Lester Baston hadn't stepped to the center of the room and called for silence by dropping a vase on the floor.

"We have distinguished visitors in our midst," bawled Lester, waving his empty glass in our direction. "None other than the Walrus and the Carpenter. The Walrus is Sir Guy Hollis, a something-or-other from the British Embassy. The Carpenter, as you all know, is our own John Carmody, the prominent dispenser of libido liniment."

He turned and grabbed Sir Guy by the arm, dragging him to the middle of the carpet. For a moment I thought Hollis might object, but a quick wink reassured me.

"It is our custom, Sir Guy," said Baston, loudly, "to subject our new friends to a little cross-examination. Just a little formality at these very formal gatherings, you understand. Are you prepared to answer questions?"

Sir Guy nodded and grinned.

"Very well," Baston muttered. "Friends—I give you this bundle from Britain. Your witness."

Then the ribbing started. I meant to listen, but at that moment Lydia Dare saw me and dragged me off into the vestibule for one of those Darling-I-waited-for-your-call-all-day routines.

By the time I got rid of her and went back, the impromptu quiz session was in full swing. From the attitude of the crowd, I gathered that Sir Guy was doing all right for himself.

Then Baston himself interjected a question that upset the apple-cart.

"And what, may I ask, brings you to our midst tonight? What is your mission, oh Walrus?"

"I'm looking for Jack the Ripper."

Nobody laughed.

Perhaps it struck them all the way it did me. I glanced at my neighbors and began to *wonder.*

LaVerne Gonnister. Hymie Kralik. Harmless. Dick Pool. Nadia Vilinoff. Johnny Odcutt and his wife. Barclay Melton. Lydia Dare. All harmless.

But what a forced smile on Dick Pool's face! And that sly, self-conscious smirk that Barclay Melton wore!

Oh, it was absurd, I grant you. But for the first time I saw these people in a new light. I wondered about their lives—their secret lives beyond the scenes of parties.

How many of them were playing a part, concealing something?

Who here would worship Hecate and grant that horrid goddess the dark boon of blood?

Even Lester Baston might be masquerading.

The mood was upon us all, for a moment. I saw questions flicker in the circle of eyes around the room.

Sir Guy stood there, and I could swear he was fully conscious of the situation he'd created, and enjoyed it.

I wondered idly just what was *really* wrong with him. Why he had this odd fixation concerning Jack the Ripper. Maybe he was hiding secrets, too.

Baston, as usual, broke the mood.

"The Walrus isn't kidding, friends," he said. He slapped Sir Guy on the back and put his arm around him as he orated. "Our English cousin is really on the trail of the fabulous Jack the Ripper. You all remember

Jack the Ripper, I presume? Quite a cut-up in the old days, as I recall. Really had some ripping good times when he went out on a tear.

"The Walrus has some idea that the Ripper is still alive, probably prowling around Chicago with a Boy Scout knife. In fact—" Baston paused impressively and shot it out in a rasping stage whisper—"in fact, he has reason to believe that Jack the Ripper might even be right here in our midst tonight."

There was the expected reaction of giggles and grins. Baston eyed Lydia Dare reprovingly. "You girls needn't laugh," he smirked. "Jack the Ripper might be a woman, too, you know. Sort of a Jill the Ripper."

"You mean you actually suspect one of us?" shrieked LaVerne Gonnister, simpering up to Sir Guy. "But that Jack the Ripper person disappeared ages ago, didn't he? In 1888?"

"Aha!" interrupted Baston. "How do you know so much about it, young lady? Sounds suspicious! Watch her, Sir Guy—she may not be as young as she appears. These lady poets have dark pasts."

The tension was gone, the mood was shattered, and the whole thing was beginning to degenerate into a trivial party joke. The man who had played the *March* was eyeing the piano with a *scherzo* gleam in his eye that augured ill for Prokofieff. Lydia Dare was glancing at the kitchen, waiting to make a break for another drink.

Then Baston caught it.

"Guess what?" he yelled. "The Walrus has a gun."

His embracing arm had slipped and encountered the hard outline of the gun in Sir Guy's pocket. He snatched it out before Hollis had the opportunity to protest.

I stared hard at Sir Guy, wondering if this thing had carried far enough. But he flicked a wink my way and I remembered he had told me not to be alarmed.

So I waited as Baston broached a drunken inspiration.

"Let's play fair with our friend the Walrus," he cried. "He came all the way from England to our party on this mission. If none of you is willing to confess, I suggest we give him a chance to find out—the hard way."

"What's up?" asked Johnny Odcutt.

"I'll turn out the lights for one minute. Sir Guy can stand here with his gun. If anyone in this room is the Ripper he can either run for it or take the opportunity to—well, eradicate his pursuer. Fair enough?"

It was even sillier than it sounds, but it caught the popular fancy. Sir Guy's protests went unheard in the ensuing babble. And before I could stride over and put in my two cents' worth, Lester Baston had reached the light switch.

"Don't anybody move," he announced, with fake solemnity. "For one minute we will remain in darkness—perhaps at the mercy of a killer. At the end of that time, I'll turn up the lights again and look for bodies. Choose your partners, ladies and gentlemen."

The lights went out.

Somebody giggled.

I heard footsteps in the darkness. Mutterings.

A hand brushed my face.

The watch on my wrist ticked violently. But even louder, rising above it, I heard another thumping. The beating of my heart.

Absurd. Standing in the dark with a group of tipsy fools. And yet there was real terror lurking here, rustling through the velvet blackness.

Jack the Ripper prowled in darkness like this. And Jack the Ripper had a knife. Jack the Ripper had a madman's brain and a madman's purpose.

But Jack the Ripper was dead, dead and dust these many years—by every human law.

Only there are no human laws when you feel yourself in the dark, when the dark hides and protects and the outer mask slips off your face and you feel something welling up within you, a brooding shapeless purpose that is brother to the blackness.

Sir Guy Hollis shrieked.

There was a grisly thud.

Baston put the lights on.

Everybody screamed.

Sir Guy Hollis lay sprawled on the floor in the center of the room. The gun was still clutched in his hand.

I glanced at the faces, marveling at the variety of expressions human beings can assume when confronting horror.

All the faces were present in the circle. Nobody had fled. And yet Sir Guy Hollis lay there.

LaVerne Gonnister was wailing and hiding her face.

"All right."

Sir Guy rolled over and jumped to his feet. He was smiling.

"Just an experiment, eh? If Jack the Ripper *were* among those present, and thought I had been murdered, he would have betrayed himself in some way when the lights went on and he saw me lying there.

"I am convinced of your individual and collective innocence. Just a gentle spoof, my friends."

Hollis stared at the goggling Baston and the rest of them crowding in behind him.

"Shall we leave, John?" he called to me. "It's getting late, I think."

It was a pretty dull party after that.

3

I met Sir Guy the following evening as we agreed, on the corner of 29th and South Halsted.

After what had happened the night before, I was prepared for almost anything. But Sir Guy seemed matter-of-fact enough as he stood huddled against a grimy doorway and waited for me to appear.

"Boo!" I said, jumping out suddenly. He smiled. Only the betraying gesture of his left hand indicated that he'd instinctively reached for his gun when I startled him.

"All ready for our wild-goose chase?" I asked.

"Yes." He took my arm and edged me along the street slowly.

"It's foggy tonight, John," said Sir Guy Hollis. "Like London."

I nodded.

"Cold, too, for November."

I nodded again and half-shivered my agreement.

"Curious," mused Sir Guy. "London fog and November. The place and the time of the Ripper murders."

I grinned through darkness. "Let me remind you, Sir Guy, that this isn't London, but Chicago. And it isn't November, 1888. It's over fifty years later."

Sir Guy returned my grin, but without mirth. "I'm not so sure, at that," he murmured. "Look about you. Those tangled alleys and twisted streets. They're like the East End. Mitre Square. And surely they are as ancient as fifty years, at least."

"You're in the black neighborhood of South Clark Street," I said shortly. "And why you dragged me down here I still don't know."

"Just a hunch on my part, John. I want to wander around down here.

"There's the same geographical conformation in these streets as in those courts where the Ripper roamed and slew. That's where we'll find him, John. Not in the bright lights, but down here in the darkness. The darkness where he waits and crouches."

"Isn't that why you brought a gun?" I asked.

"We may need a gun," said Sir Guy, gravely. "After all, tonight is the appointed night."

I sighed. We wandered on through the foggy, deserted streets. Here and there a dim light burned above a gin-mill doorway. Otherwise, all was darkness and shadow. Deep, gaping alleyways loomed as we proceeded down a slanting side-street.

We crawled through that fog, alone and silent, like two tiny maggots floundering within a shroud.

"Can't you see there's not a soul around these streets?" I said.

"He's bound to come," said Sir Guy. "He'll be drawn here. This is what I've been looking for. A *genius loci.* An evil spot that attracts evil. Always, when he slays, it's in the slums.

"You see, that must be one of his weaknesses. He has a fascination for squalor. Besides, the women he needs for sacrifice are more easily found in the dives and stewpots of a great city."

"Well, let's go into one of the dives or stewpots," I suggested. "I'm cold. Need a drink. This damned fog gets into your bones. You Britishers can stand it, but I like warmth and dry heat."

We emerged from our side street and stood upon the threshold of an alley.

Through the white clouds of mist ahead, I discerned a dim blue light, a naked bulb dangling from a beer sign above an alley bar.

"Let's take a chance," I said. "I'm beginning to shiver."

"Lead the way," said Sir Guy. I led him down the alley passage.

We entered a dingy bar. A feeble light flickered above the counter and railing, but failed to penetrate the further gloom of the back booths.

A gigantic black lolled across the bar. He scarcely stirred as we came in, but his eyes flicked open quite suddenly and I knew he noted our presence and was judging us.

"Evening," I said.

He took his time before replying. Still sizing us up. Then, he grinned.

"Evening, gents. What's your pleasure?"

"Gin," I said. "Two gins. It's a cold night."

"That's right, gents."

He poured, I paid, and took the glasses over to one of the booths. We wasted no time in emptying them.

I went over to the bar and got the bottle. Sir Guy and I poured ourselves another drink. The big man went back into his doze, with one wary eye half-open against any sudden activity.

The clock over the bar ticked on. The wind was rising outside, tearing the shroud of fog to ragged shreds. Sir Guy and I sat in the warm booth and drank our gin.

He began to talk, and the shadows crept up about us to listen.

He rambled a great deal. He went over everything he'd said in the office when I met him, just as though I hadn't heard it before.

I listened very patiently. I poured Sir Guy another drink.

But the liquor only made him more talkative. About ritual killings and prolonging the life unnaturally—the whole fantastic tale came out again.

And of course, he maintained his unyielding conviction that the Ripper was abroad tonight.

"Very well," I said, unable to keep the impatience from my voice. "Let us say that your theory is correct—even though we must overlook every natural law and swallow a lot of superstition to give it any credence.

"But let us say, for the sake of argument, that you are right. Jack the Ripper was a man who discovered how to prolong his own life through making human sacrifices. He is in Chicago now and he is planning to kill. In other words, let us suppose that everything you claim is gospel truth. So what?"

"What do you mean?" said Sir Guy.

"If all this is true it still doesn't prove that by sitting down in a dingy gin-mill on the South Side, Jack the Ripper is going to walk in here and let you kill him, or turn him over to the police. And come to think of it, I don't even know just what you intend to *do* with him if you ever did find him."

Sir Guy gulped his gin. "I'd capture the bloody swine," he said. "Capture him and turn him over to the government, together with all the papers and documentary evidence I've collected against him over a period of many years. I've spent a fortune investigating this affair, I tell you, a fortune! His capture will mean the solution of hundreds of unsolved crimes, of that I am convinced."

In vino veritas. Or was all this babbling the result of too much gin? It didn't matter. Sir Guy Hollis had another. I sat there and wondered what to do with him. The man was rapidly working up to a climax of hysterical drunkenness.

"That's enough," I said, putting out my hand as Sir Guy reached for the half-emptied bottle again. "Let's call a cab and get out of here. It's getting late and it doesn't look as though your elusive friend is going to put in his appearance. Tomorrow, if I were you, I'd plan to turn all those papers and documents over to the F.B.I. If you're so convinced of the truth of your theory, they are competent to make a very thorough investigation, and find your man."

"No," Sir Guy was drunkenly obstinate. "No cab."

"But let's get out of here anyway," I said, glancing at my watch. "It's past midnight."

He sighed, shrugged, and rose unsteadily. As he started for the door, he tugged the gun free from his pocket.

"Here, give me that!" I whispered. "You can't walk around the street brandishing that thing."

I took the gun and slipped it inside my coat. Then I got hold of his right arm and steered him out of the door. The black man didn't look up as we departed.

We stood shivering in the alleyway. The fog had increased. I couldn't see either end of the alley from where we stood. It was cold. Damp. Dark. Fog or no fog, a little wind was whispering secrets to the shadows at our backs.

Sir Guy, despite his incapacity, still stared apprehensively at the alley, as though he expected to see a figure approaching.

"Childish foolishness," I said. "Jack the Ripper, indeed! I call this carrying a hobby too far."

"Hobby?" Through the fog I could see his distorted face. "You call this a hobby?"

"Well, what is it? Just why else are you so interested in tracking down this mythical killer?"

My arm held his. But his stare held me.

"In London," he whispered. "In 1888...one of those nameless drabs the Ripper slew...was my mother."

"What?"

"Later I was recognized by my father, and legitimatized. We swore to give our lives to find the Ripper. My father was the first to search. He died in Hollywood in 1926—on the trail of the Ripper. They said he was stabbed by an unknown assailant in a brawl. But I knew who that assailant was.

"So I've taken up his work, do you see, John? I've carried on. And I will carry on until I do find him and kill him with my own hands."

I believed him then. He wouldn't give up. He wasn't just a drunken babbler anymore. He was as fanatical, as determined, as relentless as the Ripper himself.

Tomorrow he'd be sober. He'd continue the search. Perhaps he'd turn those papers over to the F.B.I. Sooner or later, with such persistence—and with his motive—he'd be successful. I'd always known he had a motive.

"Let's go," I said, steering him down the alley.

"Wait a minute," said Sir Guy. "Give me back my gun." He lurched a little. "I'd feel better with the gun on me."

He pressed me into the dark shadows of a little recess.

I tried to shrug him off, but he was insistent.

"Let me carry the gun, now, John," he mumbled.

"All right," I said.

I reached into my coat, brought my hand out.

"But that's not a gun," he protested. "That's a knife."

"I know."

"John!" he screamed.

"Never mind the 'John,'" I whispered, raising the knife. "Just call me...Jack."

The Girl with the Hungry Eyes

Fritz Leiber

Fritz Leiber (b. 1910) was born in Chicago, the son of a Shakespearean actor. A graduate of the University of Chicago, Leiber held down jobs as a minister in New Jersey, an actor, and as an editor for Consolidated Book Publishers. In 1939, his first story, "Two Sought Adventure," appeared in *Unknown.* Leiber wrote most of his early material for *Unknown,* including his first novel, *Conjure Wife,* which was serialized in the early 1940's and was published as a hardcover in 1953. Leiber served as an inspector for Douglas aircraft from 1942-44 before becoming editor of *Science Digest.* His first collection, *Night's Black Agents,* appeared in 1947. Leiber left *Science Digest* in 1956 to pursue a career as a freelance writer. He has alternated between periods of inactivity, and extreme productivity. In 1958, the title story to his collection *The Big Time* won the Hugo. In 1959, Leiber was asked to contribute stories for a special Fritz Leiber issue of *Fantastic.* Leiber won another Hugo for his novel *The Wanderer* in 1964. In 1967, Leiber's contribution for Harlan Ellison's anthology *Dangerous Vision,* "Gonna Roll Dem Bones," won both the Nebula and the Hugo. His story "Ship of Shadows" won a Hugo in 1969, and "Ill-Met At Lankhmer" won both the Nebula and the Hugo for the following year. Among his other awards are a 1975 Gandalf Award, and a 1976 August Derleth Fantasy Award. Among his more notable works are *Green Millennium* (1953), *The Sinful Ones* (1953), *Gather, Darkness!* (1956), *A Specter is Haunting Texas* (1969), *Our Lady of Darkness* (1977) and *Ghost Light* (1983). Leiber presently resides in San Francisco.

"The Girl with the Hungry Eyes" is the best of Leiber's series of urban horror stories that also includes "Smoke Ghost" and "Gonna Roll Dem Bones." It shows Leiber's talent for fusing urban elements with an almost gothic feel.

ALL RIGHT, I'll tell you why the Girl gives me the creeps. Why I can't stand to go downtown and see the mob slavering up at her on the tower, with that pop bottle or pack of cigarettes or whatever it is beside her. Why I hate to look at magazines any more because I know she'll turn up somewhere in a brassière or a bubble bath. Why I don't like to think of millions of Americans drinking in that poisonous half-smile. It's quite a story—more story than you're expecting.

No, I haven't suddenly developed any long-haired indignation at the evils of advertising and the national glamor-girl complex. That'd be a laugh for a man in my racket, wouldn't it? Though I think you'll agree there's something a little perverted about trying to capitalize on sex that way. But it's okay with me. And I know we've had the Face and the Body and the Look and what not else, so why shouldn't someone come along who sums it all up so completely, that we have to call her the Girl and blazon her on all the billboards from Times Square to Telegraph Hill?

But the Girl isn't like any of the others. She's unnatural. She's morbid. She's unholy.

Oh, these are modern times, you say, and the sort of thing I'm hinting at went out with witchcraft. But you see I'm not altogether sure myself what I'm hinting at, beyond a certain point. There are vampires and vampires, and not all of them suck blood.

And there were the murders, if they were murders. Besides, let me ask you this. Why, when America is obsessed with the Girl, don't we find out more about her? Why doesn't she rate a *Time* cover with a droll biography inside? Why hasn't there been a feature in *Life* or the *Post?* A profile in *The New Yorker?* Why hasn't *Charm* or *Mademoiselle* done her career saga? Not ready for it? Nuts!

Why haven't the movies snapped her up? Why hasn't she been on "Information, Please"? Why don't we see her kissing candidates at political rallies? Why isn't she chosen queen of some sort of junk or other at a convention?

Why don't we read about her tastes and hobbies, her views of the Russian situation? Why haven't the columnists interviewed her in a kimono on the top floor of the tallest hotel in Manhattan and told us who her boyfriends are?

Finally—and this is the real killer—why hasn't she ever been drawn or painted?

Oh no she hasn't. If you knew anything about commercial art, you'd know that. Every blessed one of those pictures was worked up from a photograph. Expertly? Of course. They've got the top artists on it. But that's how it's done.

And now I'll tell you the why of all that. It's because from the top to the bottom of the whole world of advertising, news, and business, there isn't a solitary soul who knows where the Girl came from, where she lives, what she does, who she is, even what her name is.

You heard me. What's more, not a single solitary soul ever sees her—except one poor damned photographer, who's making more money off her than he ever hoped to in his life and who's scared and miserable as hell every minute of the day.

No, I haven't the faintest idea who he is or where he has his studio. But I know there has to be such a man and I'm morally certain he feels just like I said.

Yes, I might be able to find her, if I tried. I'm not sure though—by now she probably has other safeguards. Besides, I don't want to.

Oh, I'm off my rocker, am I? That sort of thing can't happen in the Era of the Atom? People can't keep out of sight that way, not even Garbo?

Well, I happen to know they can, because last year I was that poor damned photographer I was telling you about. Yes, last year, when the Girl made her first poisonous splash right here in this big little city of ours.

Yes, I know you weren't here last year and you don't know about it. Even the Girl had to start small. But if you hunted through the files of the local newspapers, you'd find some ads, and I might be able to locate you some of the old displays—I think Lovelybelt is still using one of them. I used to have a mountain of photos myself, until I burned them.

Yes, I made my cut off her. Nothing like what that other photographer must be making, but enough so it still bought this whiskey. She was funny about money. I'll tell you about that.

But first picture me then. I had a fourth-floor studio in that rathole the Hauser Building, not far from Ardleigh Park.

I'd been working at the Marsh-Mason studios until I'd gotten my bellyful of it and decided to start in for myself. The Hauser Building was awful—I'll never forget how the stairs creaked—but it was cheap and there was a skylight.

Business was lousy. I kept making the rounds of all the advertisers and agencies, and some of them didn't object to me too much personally, but my stuff never clicked. I was pretty near broke. I was behind on my rent. Hell, I didn't even have enough money to have a girl.

It was one of those dark gray afternoons. The building was very quiet—I'd just finished developing some pix I was doing on speculation for Lovelybelt Girdles and Budford's Pool and Playground. My model had left. A Miss Leon. She was a civics teacher at one of the high schools and modeled for me on the side, just lately on speculation, too. After one look at the prints, I decided that Miss Leon probably wasn't just what Lovelybelt was looking for—or my photography either. I was about to call it a day.

And then the street door slammed four storys down and there were steps on the stairs and she came in.

She was wearing a cheap, shiny black dress. Black pumps. No stockings. And except that she had a gray cloth coat over one of them, those skinny arms of hers were bare. Her arms are pretty skinny, you know, or can't you see things like that any more?

And then the thin neck, the slightly gaunt, almost prim face, the tumbling mass of dark hair, and looking out from under it the hungriest eyes in the world.

That's the real reason she's plastered all over the country today, you know—those eyes. Nothing vulgar, but just the same they're looking at you with a hunger that's all sex and something more than sex. That's what everybody's been looking for since the Year One—something a little more than sex.

Well, boys, there I was, alone with the Girl, in an office that was getting shadowy, in a nearly empty building. A situation that a million male Americans have undoubtedly pictured to themselves with various lush details. How was I feeling? Scared.

I know sex can be frightening. That cold heart-thumping when you're alone with a girl and feel you're going to touch her. But if it was sex this time, it was overlaid with something else.

At least I wasn't thinking about sex.

I remember that I took a backward step and that my hand jerked so that the photos I was looking at sailed to the floor.

There was the faintest dizzy feeling like something was being drawn out of me. Just a little bit.

That was all. Then she opened her mouth and everything was back to normal for a while.

"I see you're a photographer, mister," she said. "Could you use a model?"

Her voice wasn't very cultivated.

"I doubt it," I told her, picking up the pix. You see, I wasn't impressed. The commercial possibilities of her eyes hadn't registered on me yet, by a long shot. "What have you done?"

Well, she gave me a vague sort of story and I began to check her knowledge of model agencies and studios and rates and what not and pretty soon I said to her, "Look here, you never modeled for a photographer in your life. You just walked in here cold."

Well, she admitted that was more or less so.

All along through our talk I got the idea she was feeling her way, like someone in a strange place. Not that she was uncertain of herself, or of me, but just of the general situation.

"And you think anyone can model?" I asked her pityingly.

"Sure," she said.

"Look," I said, "a photographer can waste a dozen negatives trying to get one halfway human photo of an average woman. How many do you think he'd have to waste before he got a real catchy, glamorous photo of her?"

"I think I could do it," she said.

Well, I should have kicked her out right then. Maybe I admired the cool way she stuck to her dumb little guns. Maybe I was touched by her underfed look. More likely I was feeling mean on account of the way my pictures had been snubbed by everybody and I wanted to take it out on her by showing her up.

"Okay, I'm going to put you on the spot," I told her. "I'm going to try a couple of shots of you. Understand it's strictly on spec. If somebody should ever want to use a photo of you, which is about one chance in two million, I'll pay you regular rates for your time. Not otherwise."

She gave me a smile. The first. "That's swell by me," she said.

Well, I took three or four shots, close-ups of her face since I didn't fancy her cheap dress, and at least she stood up to my sarcasm. Then I remembered I still had the Lovelybelt stuff and I guess the meanness was still working in me because I handed her a girdle and told her to go behind the screen and get into it and she did, without getting flustered as I'd expected, and since we'd gone that far, I figured we might as well shoot the beach scene to round it out, and that was that.

All this time I wasn't feeling anything particular one way or the other, except every once in a while I'd get one of those faint dizzy flashes and wonder if there was something wrong with my stomach or if I could have been a bit careless with my chemicals.

Still, you know, I think the uneasiness was in me all the while.

I tossed her a card and pencil. "Write your name and address and phone," I told her and made for the darkroom.

A little later she walked out. I didn't call any good-byes. I was irked because she hadn't fussed around or seemed anxious about her poses, or even thanked me, except for that one smile.

I finished developing the negatives, made some prints, glanced at them, decided they weren't a great deal worse than Miss Leon. On an impulse I slipped them in with the pictures I was going to take on the rounds next morning.

By now I'd worked long enough, so I was a bit fagged and nervous, but I didn't dare waste enough money on liquor to help that. I wasn't very hungry. I think I went to a cheap movie.

I didn't think of the Girl at all, except maybe to wonder faintly why in my present womanless state I hadn't made a pass at her. She had seemed to belong to a—well, distinctly more approachable social strata than Miss Leon. But then, of course, there were all sorts of arguable reasons for my not doing that.

Next morning I made the rounds. My first step was Munsch's Brewery. They were looking for a "Munsch Girl." Papa Munsch had a sort of affection for me, though he razzed my photography. He had a good natural judgment about that, too. Fifty years ago he might have been one of the shoestring boys who made Hollywood.

Right now he was out in the plant, pursuing his favorite occupation. He put down the beaded schooner, smacked his lips, gabbled something technical to someone about hops, wiped his fat hands on the big apron he was wearing, and grabbed my thin stack of pictures.

He was about halfway through, making noises with his tongue and teeth, when he came to her. I kicked myself for even having stuck her in.

"That's her," he said. "The photography's not so hot, but that's the girl."

It was all decided. I wonder now why Papa Munsch sensed what the Girl had right away, while I didn't. I think it was because I saw her first in the flesh, if that's the right word.

At the time I just felt faint.

"Who is she?" he asked.

"One of my new models." I tried to make it casual.

"Bring her out tomorrow morning," he told me. "And your stuff. We'll photograph her here.

"Here, don't look so sick," he added. "Have some beer."

Well, I went away telling myself it was just a fluke, so that she'd probably blow it tomorrow with her inexperience, and so on.

Just the same, when I reverently laid my next stack of pictures on Mr. Fitch, of Lovelybelt's, rose-colored blotter, I had hers on top.

Mr. Fitch went through the motions of being an art critic. He leaned over backward, squinted his eyes, waved his long fingers, and said, "Hmm. What do you think, Miss Willow? Here, in this light, of course, the photograph doesn't show the bias cut. And perhaps we should use the Lovelybelt Imp instead of the Angel. Still, the girl.... Come over here, Binns." More finger-waving. "I want a married man's reaction."

He couldn't hide the fact that he was hooked.

Exactly the same thing happened at Budford's Pool and Playground, except that Da Costa didn't need a married man's say-so.

"Hot stuff," he said, sucking his lips. "Oh boy, you photographers!"

I hotfooted it back to the office and grabbed up the card I'd given her to put down her name and address.

It was blank.

I don't mind telling you that the next five days were about the worst I ever went through, in an ordinary way. When next morning rolled around and I still hadn't got hold of her, I had to start stalling.

"She's sick," I told Papa Munsch over the phone.

"She at a hospital?" he asked me.

"Nothing that serious," I told him.

"Get her out here then. What's a little headache?"

"Sorry, I can't."

Papa Munsch got suspicious. "You really got this girl?"

"Of course I have."

"Well, I don't know. I'd think it was some New York model, except I recognized your lousy photography."

I laughed.

"Well, look, you get her here tomorrow morning, you hear?"

"I'll try."

"Try nothing. You get her out here."

He didn't know half of what I tried. I went around to all the model and employment agencies. I did some slick detective work at the photographic and art studios. I used up some of my last dimes putting advertisements in all three papers. I looked at high school yearbooks and at employee photos in local house organs. I went to restaurants and drugstores, looking at waitresses, and to dime stores and department stores, looking at clerks. I watched the crowds coming out of movie theaters. I roamed the streets.

Evenings, I spent quite a bit of time along Pickup Row. Somehow that seemed the right place.

The fifth afternoon I knew I was licked. Papa Munsch's deadline—he'd given me several, but this was it—was due to run out at six o'clock. Mr. Fitch had already canceled.

I was at the studio window, looking out at Ardleigh Park.

She walked in.

I'd gone over this moment so often in my mind that I had no trouble putting on my act. Even the faint dizzy feeling didn't throw me off.

"Hello," I said, hardly looking at her.

"Hello," she said.

"Not discouraged yet?"

"No." It didn't sound uneasy or defiant. It was just a statement.

I snapped a look at my watch, got up and said curtly, "Look here, I'm going to give you a chance. There's a client of mine looking for a girl your general type. If you do a real good job you might break into the modeling business.

"We can see him this afternoon if we hurry," I said. I picked up my stuff. "Come on. And next time if you expect favors, don't forget to leave your phone number."

"Uh-uh," she said, not moving.

"What do you mean?" I said.

"I'm not going out to see any client of yours."

"The hell you aren't," I said. "You little nut, I'm giving you a break."

She shook her head slowly. "You're not fooling me, baby. You're not fooling me at all. They want me." And she gave me the second smile.

At the time I thought she must have seen my newspaper ad. Now I'm not so sure.

"And now I'll tell you how we're going to work," she went on. "You aren't going to have my name or address or phone number. Nobody is. And we're going to do all the pictures right here. Just you and me."

You can imagine the roar I raised at that. I was everything—angry, sarcastic, patiently explanatory, off my nut, threatening, pleading.

I would have slapped her face off, except it was photographic capital.

In the end all I could do was phone Papa Munsch and tell him her conditions. I knew I didn't have a chance, but I had to take it.

He gave me a really angry bawling out, said "no" several times and hung up.

It didn't worry her. "We'll start shooting at ten o'clock tomorrow," she said.

It was just like her, using that corny line from the movie magazines.

About midnight Papa Munsch called me up.

"I don't know what insane asylum you're renting this girl from," he said, "but I'll take her. Come around tomorrow morning and I'll try to get it through your head just how I want the pictures. And I'm glad I got you out of bed!"

After that it was a breeze. Even Mr. Fitch reconsidered and, after taking two days to tell me it was quite impossible, he accepted the conditions too.

Of course you're all under the spell of the Girl, so you can't understand how much self-sacrifice it represented on Mr. Fitch's part when he agreed to forego supervising the photography of my model in the Lovelybelt Imp or Vixen or whatever it was we finally used.

Next morning she turned up on time according to her schedule, and we went to work. I'll say one thing for her, she never got tired and she never kicked at the way I fussed over shots. I got along okay, except I still had that feeling of something being shoved away gently. Maybe you've felt it just a little, looking at her picture.

When we finished I found out there were still more rules. It was about the middle of the afternoon. I started with her to get a sandwich and coffee.

"Uh-uh," she said, "I'm going down alone. And look, baby, if you ever try to follow me, if you ever so much as stick your head out of that window when I go, you can hire yourself another model."

You can imagine how all this crazy stuff strained my temper—and my imagination. I remember opening the window after she was gone—I waited a few minutes first—and standing there getting some fresh air and trying to figure out what could be behind it, whether she was hiding from the police, or was somebody's ruined daughter, or maybe had got the idea it was smart to be temperamental, or more likely Papa Munsch was right and she was partly nuts.

But I had my pictures to finish up.

Looking back, it's amazing to think how fast her magic began to take hold of the city after that. Remembering what came after, I'm frightened of what's happening to the whole country—and maybe the world. Yesterday I read something in *Time* about the Girl's picture turning up on billboards in Egypt.

The rest of my story will help show you why I'm frightened in that big, general way. But I have a theory, too, that helps explain, though it's one of those things that's beyond that "certain point." It's about the Girl. I'll give it to you in a few words.

You know how modern advertising gets everybody's mind set in the same direction, wanting the same things, imagining the same things. And you know the psychologists aren't so skeptical of telepathy as they used to be.

Add up the two ideas. Suppose the identical desires of millions of people focussed on one telepathic person. Say a girl. Shaped her in their image.

Imagine her knowing the hiddenmost hungers of millions of men. Imagine her seeing deeper into those hungers than the people that had them, seeing the hatred and the wish for death behind the lust. Imagine her shaping herself in that complete image, keeping herself as aloof as marble. Yet imagine the hunger she might feel in answer to their hunger.

But that's getting a long way from the facts of my story. And some of those facts are darn solid. Like money. We made money.

That was the funny thing I was going to tell you. I was afraid the Girl was going to hold me up. She really had me over a barrel, you know.

But she didn't ask for anything but the regular rates. Later on I insisted on pushing more money at her, a whole lot. But she always took it with that same contemptuous look, as if she were going to toss it down the first drain when she got outside.

Maybe she did.

At any rate, I had money. For the first time in months I had money enough to get drunk, buy new clothes, take taxicabs. I could make a play for any girl I wanted to. I only had to pick.

And so of course I had to go and pick...

But first let me tell you about Papa Munsch.

Papa Munsch wasn't the first of the boys to try to meet my model but I think he was the first to really go soft on her. I could watch the change in his eyes as he looked at her pictures. They began to get sentimental, reverent. Mama Munsch had been dead for two years.

He was smart about the way he planned it. He got me to drop some information which told him when she came to work, and then one morning he came pounding up the stairs a few minutes before.

"I've got to see her, Dave," he told me.

I argued with him, I kidded him, I explained he didn't know just how serious she was about her crazy ideas. I even pointed out he was cutting both our throats. I even amazed myself by bawling him out.

He didn't take any of it in his usual way. He just kept repeating, "But, Dave, I've got to see her."

The street door slammed.

"That's her," I said. lowering my voice. "You've got to get out."

He wouldn't, so I shoved him in the darkroom, "And keep quiet," I whispered. "I'll tell her I can't work today."

I knew he'd try to look at her and probably come busting in, but there wasn't anything else I could do.

The footsteps came to the fourth floor. But she never showed at the door. I got uneasy.

"Get that bum out of there!" she yelled suddenly from beyond the door. Not very loud, but in her commonest voice.

"I'm going up to the next landing," she said. "And if that fat-bellied bum doesn't march straight down to the street, he'll never get another picture of me except spitting in his lousy beer."

Papa Munsch came out of the darkroom. He was white. He didn't look at me as he went out. He never looked at her pictures in front of me again.

That was Papa Munsch. Now it's me I'm telling about. I talked around the subject with her, I hinted, eventually I made my pass.

She lifted my hand off her as if it were a damp rag.

"No, baby," she said. "This is working time."

"But afterward..." I pressed.

"The rules still hold." And I got what I think was the fifth smile.

It's hard to believe, but she never budged an inch from that crazy line. I mustn't make a pass at her in the office, because our work was very important and she loved it and there mustn't be any distractions. And I couldn't see her anywhere else, because if I tried to, I'd never snap another picture of her—and all this with more money coming in all the time and me never so stupid as to think my photography had anything to do with it.

Of course I wouldn't have been human if I hadn't made more passes. But they always got the wet-rag treatment and there weren't any more smiles.

I changed. I went sort of crazy and light-headed—only sometimes I felt my head was going to burst. And I started to talk to her all the time. About myself.

It was like being in a constant delirium that never interfered with business. I didn't pay any attention to the dizzy feeling. It seemed natural.

I'd walk around and for a moment the reflector would look like a sheet of white-hot steel, or the shadows would seem like armies of moths, or the camera would be a big black coal car. But the next instant they'd come all right again.

I think sometimes I was scared to death of her. She'd seem the strangest, most horrible person in the world. But other times....

And I talked. It didn't matter what I was doing—lighting her, posing her, fussing with props, snapping my pictures—or where she was—on the platform, behind the screen, relaxing with a magazine—I kept up a steady gab.

I told her everything I knew about myself. I told her about my first girl. I told her about my brother Bob's bicycle. I told her about running away on a freight, and the licking Pa gave me when I came home. I told her about shipping to South America and the blue sky at night. I told her about Betty. I told her about my mother dying of cancer. I told her about being beaten up in a fight in an alley behind a bar. I told her about Mildred. I told her about the first picture I ever sold. I told her how Chicago looked from a sailboat. I told her about the longest drunk I was ever on. I told her about Marsh-Mason. I told her about Gwen. I told her about how I met Papa Munsch. I told her about hunting her. I told her about how I felt now.

She never paid the slightest attention to what I said. I couldn't even tell if she heard me.

It was when we were getting our first nibble from national advertisers that I decided to follow her when she went home.

Wait, I can place it better than that. Something you'll remember from the out-of-town papers—those maybe murders I mentioned. I think there were six.

I say "maybe" because the police could never be sure they weren't heart attacks. But there's bound to be suspicion when attacks happen to people whose hearts have been okay, and always at night when they're alone and away from home and there's a question of what they were doing.

The six deaths created one of those "mystery poisoner" scares. And afterward there was a feeling that they hadn't really stopped, but were being continued in a less suspicious way.

That's one of the things that scares me now.

But at that time my only feeling was relief that I'd decided to follow her.

I made her work until dark one afternoon. I didn't need any excuses, we were snowed under with orders. I waited until the street door slammed, then I ran down. I was wearing rubber-soled shoes. I'd slipped on a dark coat she'd never seen me in, and a dark hat.

I stood in the doorway until I spotted her. She was walking by Ardleigh Park toward the heart of town. It was one of those warm fall nights. I followed her on the other side of the street. My idea for tonight was just to find out where she lived. That would give me a hold on her.

She stopped in front of a display window of Everley's department store, standing back from the flow. She stood there looking in.

I remembered we'd done a big photograph of her for Everley's, to make a flat model for a lingerie display. That was what she was looking at.

At the time it seemed all right to me that she should adore herself, if that was what she was doing.

When people passed she'd turn away a little or drift back farther into the shadows.

Then a man came by alone. I couldn't see his face very well, but he looked middle-aged. He stopped and stood looking in the window.

She came out of the shadows and stepped up beside him.

How would you boys feel if you were looking at a poster of the Girl and suddenly she was there beside you, her arm linked with yours?

This fellow's reaction showed plain as day. A crazy dream had come to life for him.

They talked for a moment. Then he waved a taxi to the curb. They got in and drove off.

I got drunk that night. It was almost as if she'd known I was following her and had picked that way to hurt me. Maybe she had. Maybe this was the finish.

But the next morning she turned up at the usual time and I was back in the delirium, only now with some new angles added.

That night when I followed her she picked a spot under a streetlight, opposite one of the Munsch Girl billboards.

Now it frightens me to think of her lurking that way.

After about twenty minutes a convertible slowed down going past her, backed up, swung into the curb.

I was closer this time. I got a good look at the fellow's face. He was a little younger, about my age.

Next morning the same face looked up at me from the front page of the paper. The convertible had been found parked on a side street. He had been in it. As in the other maybe-murders, the cause of death was uncertain.

All kinds of thoughts were spinning in my head that day, but there were only two things I knew for sure. That I'd got the first real offer from a national advertiser, and that I was going to take the Girl's arm and walk down the stairs with her when we quit work.

She didn't seem surprised. "You know what you're doing?" she said.

"I know."

She smiled. "I was wondering when you'd get around to it."

I began to feel good. I was kissing everything good-bye, but I had my arm around hers.

It was another of those warm fall evenings. We cut across into Ardleigh Park. It was dark there, but all around the sky was a sallow pink from the advertising signs.

We walked for a long time in the park. She didn't say anything and she didn't look at me, but I could see her lips twitching and after a while her hand tightened on my arm.

We stopped. We'd been walking across the grass. She dropped down and pulled me after her. She put her hands on my shoulders. I was looking down at her face. It was the faintest sallow pink from the glow in the sky. The hungry eyes were dark smudges.

I was fumbling with her blouse. She took my hand away, not like she had in the studio. "I don't want that," she said.

First I'll tell you what I did afterward. Then I'll tell you why I did it. Then I'll tell you what she said.

What I did was run away. I don't remember all of that because I was dizzy, and the pink sky was swinging against the dark trees. But after a while I staggered into the lights of the street. The next day I closed up the studio. The telephone was ringing when I locked the door and there were unopened letters on the floor. I never saw the Girl again in the flesh, if that's the right word.

I did it because I didn't want to die. I didn't want the life drawn out of me. There are vampires and vampires, and the ones that suck blood aren't the worst. If it hadn't been for the warning of those dizzy flashes, and Papa Munsch and the face in the morning paper, I'd have gone the way the others did. But I realized what I was up against while there was still time to tear myself away. I realized that wherever she came from, whatever shaped her, she's the quintessence of the horror behind the bright billboard. She's the smile that tricks you into throwing away your money and your life. She's the eyes that lead you on and on, and then show you death. She's the creature you give everything for and never really get. She's the being that takes everything you've got and gives nothing in return. When you yearn toward her face on the billboards, remember that. She's the lure. She's the bait. She's the Girl.

And this is what she said, "I want you. I want your high spots. I want everything that's made you happy and everything that's hurt you bad. I want your first girl. I want that shiny bicycle. I want that licking. I want that pinhole camera. I want Betty's legs. I want the blue sky filled with stars. I want your mother's death. I want your blood on the cobblestones. I want Mildred's mouth. I want the first picture you sold. I want the lights of Chicago. I want the gin. I want Gwen's hands. I want your wanting me. I want your life. Feed me, baby, feed me."

The Chimney

Ramsey Campbell

Ramsey Campbell (b. 1946) was raised in Liverpool. Painfully shy and suffering from glandular obesity, Campbell took to reading. He began writing at the encouragement of his mother and English teacher. In 1962, Campbell sold his first story, "The Church in High Street," to the Arkham House anthology *Dark Mind, Dark Heart.* Arkham House founder August Derleth also published Campbell's first collection, *The Inhabitant of the Lake and Other Less Welcome Tenants,* two years later. After attending St. Edward's College, Campbell worked for the Inland Revenue from 1962-66 before joining the staff of the Liverpool Public Library. In 1971, he married Jenny Chandler. He became a full-time writer in 1973 and produced his second collection, *Demons by Daylight,* later that year. Campbell supplemented his income by doing film reviews for the BBC while working on his first novel, *The Doll That Ate Its Mother* (1976). Arkham released Campbell's third collection, *Height of the Scream,* that year. His early novels, such as *The Face That Must Die* (1979) and *To Wake the Dead* (1980), were later revised at his request—the later novel being so drastically changed that it was retitled *The Parasite* (1981). The following year Campbell's fourth collection, *Dark Companions,* was released while he worked on his most ambitious novel, *Incarnate* (1983). He also edited two anthologies in 1983, *The Gruesome Book* and *New Terrors.* Campbell's later novels include *Obsession* (1985), *The Hungry Moon* (1986), *Ancient Images* (1989), and *Midnight Sun* (1990). He has also edited *Fine Frights: Stories that Scared Me* (1988), and has published a fifth collection, *Cold Print* (1987). He lives in Merseyside with his wife and two children.

"The Chimney," winner of a World Fantasy Award, is typical of Campbell's quiet brand of horror. Its unconventional topic makes it all the more terrifying.

MAYBE MOST OF IT was only fear. But not the last thing, not that. To blame my fear for that would be worst of all.

I was twelve years old and beginning to conquer my fears. I even went upstairs to do my homework, and managed to ignore the chimney. I had to be brave, because of my parents—because of my mother.

She had always been afraid for me. The very first day I had gone to school I'd seen her watching. Her expression had reminded me of the face of a girl I'd glimpsed on television, watching men lock her husband behind bars; I was frightened all that first day. And when children had hysterics or began to bully me, or the teacher lost her temper, these things only confirmed my fears—and my mother's, when I told her what had happened each day.

Now I was at grammar school. I had been there for much of a year. I'd felt awkward in my new uniform and old shoes; the building seemed enormous, crowded with too many strange children and teachers. I'd felt I was an outsider; friendly approaches made me nervous and sullen, when people laughed and I didn't know why I was sure they were laughing at me. After a while the other boys treated me as I seemed to want to be treated: the lads from the poorer districts mocked my suburban accent, the suburban boys sneered at my old shoes.

Often I'd sat praying that the teacher wouldn't ask me a question I couldn't answer, sat paralyzed by my dread of having to stand up in the waiting watchful silence. If a teacher shouted at someone my heart jumped painfully; once I'd felt the stain of my shock creeping insidiously down my thigh. Yet I did well in the end-of-term examinations, because I was terrified of failing; for nights afterward they were another reason why I couldn't sleep.

My mother read the signs of all this on my face. More and more, once I'd told her what was wrong, I had to persuade her there was nothing worse that I'd kept back. Some mornings as I lay in bed, trying to hold back half-past seven, I'd be sick; I would grope miserably downstairs, white-faced, and my mother would keep me home. Once or twice, when my fear wasn't quite enough, I made myself sick. "Look at him. You can't expect him to go like that"—but my father would only shake his head and grunt, dismissing us both.

I knew my father found me embarrassing. This year he'd had less time for me than usual; his shop—The Anything Shop, nearby in the suburbanized village—was failing to compete with the new supermarket. But before that trouble I'd often seen him staring up at my mother and me: both of us taller than him, his eyes said, yet both scared of our own shadows. At those times I glimpsed his despair.

So my parents weren't reassuring. Yet at night I tried to stay with them as long as I could—for my worst fears were upstairs, in my room.

It was a large room, two rooms knocked into one by the previous owner. It overlooked the small back gardens. The smaller of the fireplaces had been bricked up; in winter, the larger held a fire, which my mother always feared would set fire to the room—but she let it alone, for I'd screamed when I thought she was going to take that light away: even though the firelight only added to the terrors of the room.

The shadows moved things. The mesh of the fireguard fluttered enlarged on the wall; sometimes, at the edge of sleep, it became a swaying web, and its spinner came sidling down from a corner of the ceiling. Everything was unstable; walls shifted, my clothes crawled on the back of the chair. Once, when I'd left my jacket slumped over the chair, the collar's dark upturned lack of a face began to nod forward stealthily; the holes at the ends of the sleeves worked like mouths, and I didn't dare get up to hang the jacket properly. The room grew in the dark: sounds outside, footsteps and laughter, dogs encouraging each other to bark, only emphasized the size of my trap of darkness, how distant everything else was. And there was a dimmer room, in the mirror of the wardrobe beyond the foot of the bed. There was a bed in that room, and beside it a dim nightlight in a plastic lantern. Once I'd awaked to see a face staring dimly at me from the mirror; a figure had sat up when I had, and I'd almost cried out. Often I'd stared at the dim staring face, until I'd had to hide beneath the sheets.

Of course this couldn't go on for the rest of my life. On my twelfth birthday I set about the conquest of my room.

I was happy amid my presents. I had a jigsaw, a box of colored pencils, a book of space stories. They had come from my father's shop, but they were mine now. Because I was relaxed, no doubt because she wished I could always be so, my mother said, "Would you be happier if you went to another school?"

It was Saturday; I wanted to forget Monday. Besides, I imagined all schools were as frightening. "No, I'm all right," I said.

"Are you happy at school now?" she said incredulously.

"Yes, it's all right."

"Are you sure?"

"Yes, really, it's all right. I mean, I'm happy now."

The snap of the letter slot saved me from further lying. Three birthday cards: two from neighbors who talked to me when I served them in the shop—an old lady who always carried a poodle, our next-door neighbor Dr. Flynn—and a card from my parents. I'd seen all three cards in the shop, which spoilt them somehow.

As I stood in the hall I heard my father. "You've got to control yourself," he was saying. "You only upset the child. If you didn't go on at him he wouldn't be half so bad."

It infuriated me to be called a child. "But I worry so," my mother said brokenly. "He can't look after himself."

"You don't let him try. You'll have him afraid to go up to bed next."

But I already was. Was that my mother's fault? I remembered her putting the nightlight by my bed when I was very young, checking the flex and the bulb each night—I'd taken to lying awake, dreading that one or the other would fail. Standing in the hall, I saw dimly that my mother and I encouraged each other's fears. One of us had to stop. I had to stop. Even when I was frightened, I mustn't let her see. It wouldn't be the first time I'd hidden my feelings from her. In the living room I said, "I'm going upstairs to play."

Sometimes in summer I didn't mind playing there—but this was March, and a dark day. Still, I could switch the light on. And my room contained the only table I could have to myself and my jigsaw.

I spilled the jigsaw onto the table. The chair sat with its back to the dark yawn of the fireplace; I moved it hastily to the foot of the bed, facing the door. I spread the jigsaw. There was a piece of the edge, another. By lunchtime I'd assembled the edge. "You look pleased with yourself," my father said.

I didn't notice the approach of night. I was fitting together my own blue sky, above fragmented cottages. After dinner I hurried to put in the pieces I'd placed mentally while eating. I hesitated outside my room. I should have to reach into the dark for the light switch. When I did, the wallpaper filled with bright multiplied airplanes and engines. I wished we could afford to redecorate my room, it seemed childish now.

The fireplace gaped. I retrieved the fireguard from the cupboard under the stairs, where my father had stored it now the nights were a little warmer. It covered the soot-encrusted yawn. The room felt comfortable now. I'd never seen before how much space it gave me for play.

I even felt safe in bed. I switched out the nightlight—but that was too much; I grabbed the light. I didn't mind its glow on its own, without the jagged lurid jig of the shadows. And the fireguard was comforting. It made me feel that nothing could emerge from the chimney.

On Monday I took my space stories to school. People asked to look at them; eventually they lent me books. In the following weeks some of my fears began to fade. Questions darting from desk to desk still made me uneasy, but if I had to stand up without the answer at least I knew the other boys weren't sneering at me, not all of them; I was beginning to have friends. I started to sympathize with their own ignorant silences. In the July examinations I was more relaxed, and scored more marks. I was even sorry to leave my friends for the summer; I invited some of them home.

I felt triumphant. I'd calmed my mother and my room all by myself, just by realizing what had to be done. I suppose that sense of triumph helped me. It must have given me a little strength with which to face the real terror.

It was early August, the week before our holiday. My mother was worrying over the luggage, my father was trying to calculate his accounts; they were beginning to chafe against each other. I went to my room, to stay out of their way.

I was halfway through a jigsaw, which one of my friends had swapped for mine. People sat in back gardens, letting the evening settle on them; between the houses the sky was pale yellow. I inserted pieces easily, relaxed by the nearness of our holiday. I listened to the slowing of the city, a radio fluttering along a street, something moving behind the fireguard, in the chimney.

No. It was my mother in the next room, moving luggage. It was someone dragging, dragging something, anything, outside. But I couldn't deceive my ears. In the chimney something large had moved.

It might have been a bird, stunned or dying, struggling feebly—except that a bird would have sounded wilder. It could have been a mouse, even a rat, if such things are found in chimneys. But it sounded like a large body, groping stealthily in the dark: something large that didn't want me to hear it. It sounded like the worst terror of my infancy.

I'd almost forgotten that. When I was three years old my mother had let me watch television; it was bad for my eyes, but just this once, near Christmas—I'd seen two children asleep in bed, an enormous crimson man emerging from the fireplace, creeping toward them. They weren't going to wake up! "Burglar! Burglar!" I'd screamed, beginning to cry. "No, dear, it's Father Christmas," my mother said, hastily switching off the television. "He always comes out of the chimney."

Perhaps if she'd said "down" rather than "out of"... For months after that, and in the weeks before several Christmases, I lay awake listening fearfully for movement in the chimney: I was sure a fat grinning figure would creep upon me if I slept. My mother had told me the presents that appeared at the end of my bed were left by Father Christmas, but now the mysterious visitor had a face and a huge body, squeezed into the dark chimney among the soot. When I heard the wind breathing in the chimney I had to trap my screams between my lips.

Of course at last I began to suspect there was no Father Christmas: how did he manage to steal into my father's shop for my presents? He was a childish idea, I was almost sure—but I was too embarrassed to ask my parents or my friends. But I wanted not to believe in him, that silent lurker in the chimney; and now I didn't, not really. Except that something large was moving softly behind the fireguard.

It had stopped. I stared at the wire mesh, half-expecting a fat pale face to stare out of the grate. There was nothing but the fenced dark. Cats were moaning in a garden, an ice-cream van wandered brightly. After a while I forced myself to pull the fireguard away.

I was taller than the fireplace now. But I had to stoop to peer up the dark, soot-ridged throat, and then it loomed over me, darkness full of menace, of the threat of a huge figure bursting out at me, its red mouth crammed with sparkling teeth. As I peered up, trembling a little, and tried to persuade myself that what I'd heard had flown away or scurried back into its hole, soot came trickling down from the dark—and I heard the sound of a huge body squeezed into the sooty passage, settling itself carefully, more comfortably in its burrow.

I slammed the guard into place, and fled. I had to gulp to breathe. I ran onto the landing, trying to catch my breath so as to cry for help. Downstairs my mother was nervously asking whether she should pack another of my father's shirts. "Yes, if you like," he said irritably.

No, I mustn't cry out. I'd vowed not to upset her. But how could I go back into my room? Suddenly I had a thought that seemed to help. At school we'd learned how sweeps had used to send small boys up chimneys. There had hardly been room for the boys to climb. How could a large man fit in there?

He couldn't. Gradually I managed to persuade myself. At last I opened the door of my room. The chimney was silent; there was no wind. I tried not to think that he was holding himself still, waiting to squeeze out stealthily, waiting for the dark. Later, lying in the steady glow from my plastic lantern, I tried to hold onto the silence, tried to believe there was nothing near me to shatter it. There was nothing except, eventually, sleep.

Perhaps if I'd cried out on the landing I would have been saved from my fear. But I was happy with my rationality. Only once, nearly asleep, I wished the fire were lit, because it would burn anything that might be hiding in the chimney; that had never occurred to me before. But it didn't matter, for the next day we went on holiday.

My parents liked to sleep in the sunlight, beneath newspaper masks; in the evenings they liked to stroll along the wide sandy streets. I didn't, and befriended Nigel, the son of another family who were staying in the boardinghouse. My mother encouraged the friendship: such a nice boy, two years older than me; he'd look after me. He had money, and the hope of a moustache shadowing his pimply upper lip. One evening he took me to the fairground, where we met two girls; he and the older girl went to buy ice creams while her young friend and I stared at each other timidly. I couldn't believe the young girl didn't like jigsaws. Later, while I was contradicting her, Nigel and his companion disappeared behind the Ghost Train—but Nigel reappeared almost at once, red-faced, his left cheek redder. "Where's Rose?" I asked, bewildered.

"She had to go." He seemed furious that I'd asked.

"Isn't she coming back?"

"No." He was glancing irritably about for a change of subject. "What a super bike," he said, pointing as it glided between the stalls. "Have you got a bike?"

"No," I said. "I keep asking Father Christmas, but—" I wished that hadn't got past me, for he was staring at me, winking at the young girl.

"Do you still believe in him?" he demanded scornfully.

"No, of course I don't. I was only kidding." Did he believe me? He was edging toward the young girl now, putting his arm around her; soon she excused herself, and didn't come back—I never knew her name. I was annoyed he'd made her run away. "Where did Rose go?" I said persistently.

He didn't tell me. But perhaps he resented my insistence, for as the family left the boardinghouse I heard him say loudly to his mother: "He still believes in Father Christmas." My mother heard that too, and glanced anxiously at me.

Well, I didn't. There was nobody in the chimney, waiting for me to come home. I didn't care that we were going home the next day. That night I pulled away the fireguard and saw a fat pale face hanging down into the fireplace, like an underbelly, upside-down and smiling. But I managed to wake, and eventually the sea lulled me back to sleep.

As soon as we reached home I ran upstairs. I uncovered the fireplace and stood staring, to discover what I felt. Gradually I filled with the scorn Nigel would have felt, had he known of my fear. How could I have been so childish? The chimney was only a passage for smoke, a hole into which the wind wandered sometimes. That night, exhausted by the journey home, I slept at once.

The nights darkened into October; the darkness behind the mesh grew thicker. I'd used to feel, as summer waned, that the chimney was insinuating its darkness into my room. Now the sight only reminded me I'd have a fire soon. The fire would be comforting.

It was October when my father's Christmas cards arrived, on a Saturday; I was working in the shop. It annoyed him to have to anticipate Christmas so much, to compete with the supermarket. I hardly noticed the cards: my head felt muffled, my body cold—perhaps it was the weather's sudden hint of winter.

My mother came to the shop that afternoon. I watched her pretend not to have seen the cards. When I looked away she began to pick them up timidly, as if they were unfaithful letters, glancing anxiously at me. I didn't know what was in her mind. My head was throbbing. I wasn't going home sick. I earned pocket money in the shop. Besides, I didn't want my father to think I was still weak.

Nor did I want my mother to worry. That night I lay slumped in a chair, pretending to read. Words trickled down the page; I felt like dirty clothes someone had thrown on the chair. My father was at the shop taking stock. My mother sat gazing at me. I pretended harder; the words waltzed slowly. At last she said, "Are you listening?"

I was now, though I didn't look up. "Yes," I said hoarsely, unplugging my throat with a roar.

"Do you remember when you were a baby? There was a film you saw, of Father Christmas coming out of the chimney." Her voice sounded bravely careless, falsely light, as if she were determined to make some awful revelation. I couldn't look up. "Yes," I said.

Her silence made me glance up. She looked as she had on my first day at school: full of loss, of despair. Perhaps she was realizing I had to grow up, but to my throbbing head her look suggested only terror—as if she were about to deliver me up as a sacrifice. "I couldn't tell you the truth then," she said. "You were too young."

The truth was terror; her expression promised that. "Father Christmas isn't really like that," she said.

My illness must have shown by then. She gazed at me; her lips trembled. "I can't," she said, turning her face away. "Your father must tell you."

But that left me poised on the edge of terror. I felt unnerved, rustily tense. I wanted very much to lie down. "I'm going to my room," I said. I stumbled upstairs, hardly aware of doing so. As much as anything I was fleeing her unease. The stairs swayed a little, they felt unnaturally soft underfoot. I hurried dully into my room. I slapped the light switch and missed. I was walking uncontrollably forward into blinding dark. A figure came to meet me, soft and huge in the dark of my room.

I cried out. I managed to stagger back onto the landing, grabbing the light switch as I went. The lighted room was empty. My mother came running upstairs, almost falling. "What is it, what is it?" she cried.

I mustn't say. "I'm ill. I feel sick." I did, and a minute later I was. She patted my back as I knelt by the toilet. When she'd put me to bed she made to go next door, for the doctor. "Don't leave me," I pleaded. The walls of the room swayed as if tugged by firelight, the fireplace was huge and very dark. As soon as my father opened the front door she ran downstairs, crying, "He's ill, he's ill! Go for the doctor!"

The doctor came and prescribed for my fever. My mother sat up beside me. Eventually my father came to suggest it was time she went to bed. They were going to leave me alone in my room. "Make a fire," I pleaded.

My mother touched my forehead. "But you're burning," she said.

"No, I'm cold! I want a fire! Please!" So she made one, tired as she was. I saw my father's disgust as he watched me use her worry against her to get what I wanted, his disgust with her for letting herself be used.

I didn't care. My mother's halting words had overgrown my mind.

What had she been unable to tell me? Had it to do with the sounds I'd heard in the chimney? The room lolled around me; nothing was sure. But the fire would make sure for me. Nothing in the chimney could survive it.

I made my mother stay until the fire was blazing. Suppose a huge shape burst forth from the hearth, dripping fire? When at last I let her go I lay lapped by the firelight and meshy shadows, which seemed lulling now, in my warm room.

I felt feverish, but not unpleasantly. I was content to voyage on my rocking bed; the ceiling swayed past above me. While I slept the fire went out. My fever kept me warm; I slid out of bed and, pulling away the fireguard, reached up the chimney. At the length of my arms I touched something heavy, hanging down in the dark; it yielded, then soft fat fingers groped down and closed on my wrist. My mother was holding my wrist as she washed my hands. "You mustn't get out of bed," she said when she realized I was awake.

I stared stupidly at her. "You'd got out of bed. You were sleepwalking," she explained. "You had your hands right up the chimney." I saw now that she was washing caked soot from my hands; tracks of ash led toward the bed.

It had been only a dream. One moment the fat hand had been gripping my wrist, the next it was my mother's cool slim fingers. My mother played word games and timid chess with me while I stayed in bed, that day and the next.

The third night I felt better. The fire fluttered gently; I felt comfortably warm. Tomorrow I'd get up. I should have to go back to school soon, but I didn't mind that unduly. I lay and listened to the breathing of the wind in the chimney.

When I awoke the fire had gone out. The room was full of darkness. The wind still breathed, but it seemed somehow closer. It was above me. Someone was standing over me. It couldn't be either of my parents, not in the sightless darkness.

I lay rigid. Most of all I wished that I hadn't let Nigel's imagined contempt persuade me to do without a nightlight. The breathing was slow, irregular; it sounded clogged and feeble. As I tried to inch silently toward the far side of the bed, the source of the breathing stooped toward me. I felt its breath waver on my face, and the breath sprinkled me with something like dry rain.

When I had lain paralyzed for what felt like blind hours, the breathing went away. It was in the chimney, dislodging soot; it might be the wind. But I knew it had come out to let me know that whatever the fire had done to it, it hadn't been killed. It had emerged to tell me it would come for me on Christmas Eve. I began to scream.

I wouldn't tell my mother why. She washed my face, which was freckled with soot. "You've been sleepwalking again," she tried to reassure me, but I wouldn't let her leave me until daylight. When she'd gone I saw the ashy tracks leading from the chimney to the bed.

Perhaps I had been sleepwalking and dreaming. I searched vainly for my nightlight. I would have been ashamed to ask for a new one, and that helped me to feel I could do without. At dinner I felt secure enough to say I didn't know why I had screamed.

"But you must remember. You sounded so frightened. You upset me."

My father was folding the evening paper into a thick wad the size of a pocketbook, which he could read beside his plate. "Leave the boy alone," he said. "You imagine all sorts of things when you're feverish. I did when I was his age."

It was the first time he'd admitted anything like weakness to me. If he'd managed to survive his nightmares, why should mine disturb me more? Tired out by the demands of my fever, I slept soundly that night. The chimney was silent except for the flapping of flames.

But my father didn't help me again. One November afternoon I was standing behind the counter, hoping for customers. My father pottered, grumpily fingering packets of nylons, tins of pet food, Dinky toys, baby's rattles, cards, searching for signs of theft. Suddenly he snatched a Christmas card and strode to the counter. "Sit down," he said grimly.

He was waving the card at me, like evidence. I sat down on a shelf, but then a lady came into the shop; the bell thumped. I stood up to sell her nylons. When she'd gone I gazed at my father, anxious to hear the worst. "Just sit down," he said.

He couldn't stand my being taller than he was. His size embarrassed him, but he wouldn't let me see that; he pretended I had to sit down out of respect. "Your mother says she tried to tell you about Father Christmas," he said.

She must have told him that weeks earlier. He'd put off talking to me—because we'd never been close, and now we were growing further apart. "I don't know why she couldn't tell you," he said.

But he wasn't telling me either. He was looking at me as if I were a stranger he had to chat to. I felt uneasy, unsure now that I wanted to hear what he had to say. A man was approaching the shop. I stood up, hoping he'd interrupt.

He did, and I served him. Then, to delay my father's revelation, I adjusted stacks of tins. My father stared at me in disgust. "If you don't watch out you'll be as bad as your mother."

I found the idea of being like my mother strange, indefinably disturbing. But he wouldn't let me be like him, wouldn't let me near. All right, I'd be brave, I'd listen to what he had to say. But he said, "Oh, it's not worth me trying to tell you. You'll find out."

He meant I must find out for myself that Father Christmas was a childish fantasy. He didn't mean he wanted the thing from the chimney to come for me, the disgust in his eyes didn't mean that, it didn't. He meant that I had to behave like a man.

And I could. I'd show him. The chimney was silent. I needn't worry until Christmas Eve. Nor then. There was nothing to come out.

One evening as I walked home I saw Dr. Flynn in his front room. He was standing before a mirror, gazing at his red fur-trimmed hooded suit; he stooped to pick up his beard. My mother told me that he was going to act Father Christmas at the children's hospital. She seemed on the whole glad that I'd seen. So was I: it proved the pretense was only for children.

Except that the glimpse reminded me how near Christmas was. As the nights closed on the days, and the days rushed by—the end-of-term party, the turkey, decorations in the house—I grew tense, trying to prepare myself. For what? For nothing, nothing at all. Well, I would know soon—for suddenly it was Christmas Eve.

I was busy all day. I washed up as my mother prepared Christmas dinner. I brought her ingredients, and hurried to buy some she'd used up. I stuck the day's cards to tapes above the mantelpiece. I carried home a tinsel tree which nobody had bought. But being busy only made the day move faster. Before I knew it the windows were full of night.

Christmas Eve. Well, it didn't worry me. I was too old for that sort of thing. The tinsel tree rustled when anyone passed it, light rolled in tinsel globes, streamers flinched back when doors opened. Swinging restlessly on tapes above the mantelpiece, I saw half a dozen red-cheeked, smiling bearded faces.

The night piled against the windows. I chattered to my mother about her shouting father, her elder sisters, the time her sisters had locked her in a cellar. My father grunted occasionally—even when I'd run out of subjects to discuss with my mother, and tried to talk to him about the shop. At least he hadn't noticed how late I was staying up. But he had. "It's about time everyone was in bed," he said with a kind of suppressed fury.

"Can I have some more coal?" My mother would never let me have a coal scuttle in the bedroom—she didn't want me going near the fire "To put on now," I said. Surely she must say yes. "It'll be cold in the morning," I said.

"Yes, you take some. You don't want to be cold when you're looking at what Father—at your presents."

I hurried upstairs with the scuttle. Over its clatter I heard my father say, "Are you still at that? Can't you let him grow up?"

I almost emptied the scuttle into the fire, which rose roaring and crackling. My father's voice was an angry mumble, seeping through the floor. When I carried the scuttle down my mother's eyes were red, my father looked furiously determined. I'd alwavs found their arguments frightening; I was glad to hurry to my room.

It seemed welcoming. The fire was bright within the mesh. I heard my mother come upstairs. That was comforting too: she was nearer now. I heard my father go next door—to wish the doctor Happy Christmas, I supposed. I didn't mind the reminder. There was nothing of Christmas Eve in my room, except the pillowcase on the floor at the foot of the bed. I pushed it aside with one foot, the better to ignore it.

I slid into bed. My father came upstairs; I heard further mumblings of argument through the bedroom wall. At last they stopped, and I tried to relax. I lay, glad of the silence.

A wind was rushing the house. It puffed down the chimney; smoke trickled through the fireguard. Now the wind was breathing brokenly. It was only the wind. It didn't bother me.

Perhaps I'd put too much coal on the fire. The room was hot; I was sweating. I felt almost feverish. The huge mesh flicked over the wall repeatedly, nervously, like a rapid net. Within the mirror the dimmer room danced.

Suddenly I was a little afraid. Not that something would come out of the chimney, that was stupid: afraid that my feeling of fever would make me delirious again. It seemed years since I'd been disturbed by the sight of the room in the mirror, but I was disturbed now. There was something wrong with that dim jerking room.

The wind breathed. Only the wind, I couldn't hear it changing. A fat billow of smoke squeezed through the mesh. The room seemed more oppressive now, and smelled of smoke. It didn't smell entirely like coal smoke, but I couldn't tell what else was burning. I didn't want to get up to find out.

I must lie still. Otherwise I'd be writhing about trying to clutch at sleep, as I had the second night of my fever, and sometimes in summer. I must sleep before the room grew too hot. I must keep my eyes shut. I mustn't be distracted by the faint trickling of soot, nor the panting of the wind, nor the shadows and orange light that snatched at my eyes through my eyelids.

I woke in darkness. The fire had gone out. No, it was still there when I opened my eyes: subdued orange crawled on embers, a few weak flames leaped repetitively. The room was moving more slowly now. The dim room in the mirror, the face peering out at me, jerked faintly, as if almost dead.

I couldn't look at that. I slid farther down the bed, dragging the pillow into my nest. I was too hot, but at least beneath the sheets I felt safe. I began to relax. Then I realized what I'd seen. The light had been dim, but I was almost sure the fireguard was standing away from the hearth.

I must have mistaken that, in the dim light. I wasn't feverish, I couldn't have sleepwalked again. There was no need for me to look, I was comfortable. But I was beginning to admit that I had better look when I heard the slithering in the chimney.

Something large was coming down. A fall of soot: I could hear the scattering pats of soot in the grate, thrown down by the harsh halting wind. But the wind was emerging from the fireplace, into the room. It was above me, panting through its obstructed throat.

I lay staring up at the mask of my sheets. I trembled from holding myself immobile. My held breath filled me painfully as lumps of rock. I had only to lie there until whatever was above me went away. It couldn't touch me.

The clogged breath bent nearer; I could hear its dry rattling. Then something began to fumble at the sheets over my face. It plucked feebly at them, trying to grasp them, as if it had hardly anything to grasp with. My own hands clutched at the sheets from within, but couldn't hold them down entirely. The sheets were being tugged from me, a fraction at a time. Soon I would be face to face with my visitor.

I was lying there with my eyes squeezed tight when it let go of the sheets and went away. My throbbing lungs had forced me to take shallow breaths; now I breathed silently open-mouthed, though that filled my mouth with fluff. The tolling of my ears subsided, and I realized the thing had not returned to the chimney. It was still in the room.

I couldn't hear its breathing; it couldn't be near me. Only that thought allowed me to look—that, and the desperate hope that I might escape, since it moved so slowly. I peeled the sheets down from my face slowly, stealthily, until my eyes were bare. My heartbeats shook me. In the sluggishly shifting light I saw a figure at the foot of the bed.

Its red costume was thickly furred with soot. It had its back to me, its breathing was muffled by the hood. What shocked me most was its size. It occurred to me, somewhere amid my engulfing terror, that burning shrivels things. The figure stood in the mirror as well, in the dim twitching room. A face peered out of the hood in the mirror, like a charred turnip carved with a rigid grin.

The stunted figure was still moving painfully. It edged round the foot of the bed and stooped to my pillowcase. I saw it draw the pillowcase up over itself and sink down. As it sank its hood fell back, and I saw the charred turnip roll about in the hood, as if there were almost nothing left to support it.

I should have had to pass the pillowcase to reach the door. I couldn't move. The room seemed enormous, and was growing darker; my parents were far away. At last I managed to drag the sheets over my face, and pulled the pillow, like muffs, around my ears.

I had lain sleeplessly for hours when I heard movement at the foot of the bed. The thing had got out of its sack again. It was coming toward me. It was tugging at the sheets, more strongly now. Before I could catch hold of the sheets I glimpsed a red fur-trimmed sleeve, and was screaming.

"Let go, will you," my father said irritably. "Good God, it's only me."

He was wearing Dr. Flynn's disguise, which flapped about him—the jacket, at least; his pajama cuffs peeked beneath it. I stopped screaming and began to giggle hysterically. I think he would have struck me, but my mother ran in. "It's all right. All right," she reassured me, and explained to him, "It's the shock."

He was making angrily for the door when she said, "Oh, don't go yet, Albert. Stay while he opens his presents," and, lifting the bulging pillowcase from the floor, dumped it beside me.

I couldn't push it away, I couldn't let her see my terror. I made myself pull out my presents into the daylight, books, sweets, ball-points; as I groped deeper I wondered whether the charred face would crumble when I touched it. Sweat pricked my hands; they shook with horror—they could, because my mother couldn't see them.

The pillowcase contained nothing but presents and a pinch of soot. When I was sure it was empty I slumped against the headboard, panting. "He's tired," my mother said, in defense of my ingratitude. "He was up very late last night."

Later I managed an accident, dropping the pillowcase on the fire downstairs. I managed to eat Christmas dinner, and to go to bed that night. I lay awake, even though I was sure nothing would come out of the chimney now. Later I realized why my father had come to my room in the morning dressed like that; he'd intended me to catch him, to cure me of the pretense. But it was many years before I enjoyed Christmas very much.

When I left school I went to work in libraries. Ten years later I married. My wife and I crossed town weekly to visit my parents. My mother chattered, my father was taciturn. I don't think he ever quite forgave me for laughing at him.

One winter night our telephone rang. I answered it, hoping it wasn't the police. My library was then suffering from robberies. All I wanted was to sit before the fire and imagine the glittering cold outside. But it was Dr. Flynn.

"Your parents' house is on fire," he told me. "Your father's trapped in there. Your mother needs you."

They'd had a friend to stay. My mother had lit the fire in the guest room, my old bedroom. A spark had eluded the fireguard; the carpet had caught fire. Impatient for the fire engine, my father had run back into the house to put the fire out, but had been overcome. All this I learned later. Now I drove coldly across town, toward the glow in the sky.

The glow was doused by the time I arrived. Smoke scrolled over the roof. But my mother had found a coal sack and was struggling still to run into the house, to beat out the fire; her friend and Dr. Flynn held her back. She dropped the sack and ran to me. "Oh, it's your father. It's Albert," she repeated through her weeping.

The firemen withdrew their hose. The ambulance stood winking. I saw the front door open, and a stretcher carried out. The path was wet and frosty. One stretcher-bearer slipped, and the contents of the stretcher spilled over the path.

I saw Dr. Flynn glance at my mother. Only the fear that she might turn caused him to act. He grabbed the sack and, running to the path, scooped up what lay scattered there. I saw the charred head roll on the lip of the sack before it dropped within. I had seen that already, years ago.

My mother came to live with us, but we could see she was pining; my parents must have loved each other, in their way. She died a year later. Perhaps I killed them both. I know that what emerged from the chimney was in some sense my father. But surely that was a premonition. Surely my fear could never have reached out to make him die that way.

The Dead Line

Dennis Etchison

Dennis Etchison (b. 1943) was born in Stockton, California. He won his first writing award at the age of twelve, when Etchison received $250 in an essay contest. His first published short story, "Odd Boy Out," appeared in 1961. The following year, Etchison entered California State College. He transferred to UCLA, and graduated in 1967. Etchison's literary output has been almost entirely in the short story, being published mostly in small press periodicals and anthologies. In 1980, he wrote his first novel, an adaption of the film *The Fog.* He has written three other novelizations under the pseudonym "Jack Martin" (*Halloween II,* 1981; *Halloween III: Season of the Witch,* 1982; *Videodrome,* 1983). In 1982, his first collection, *The Dark Country,* was published; its title story won both the British Fantasy Award and the World Fantasy Award. In 1983, Etchison began teaching Creative Writing at UCLA. A second collection, *Red Dreams,* appeared the following year. In 1985, he served as a staff writer of the HBO series *The Hitchhiker,* and contributed the script to its premiere episode, "Remembering Melody." While Etchison has produced one more collection (*Blood Kiss,* 1988), and has edited the acclaimed *Masters of Darkness* anthology series, he has only written one original novel, *The Dark Side* (1986). He is presently developing a television series based on his short stories entitled *The Dark Country.* Etchison presently lives with his wife in California.

Etchison's chilling talent for understatement and for making even the most innocuous object terrifying has garnered him a legion of fans. "The Dead Line" is his most famous story, a story made even more frightening by its plausibility and lack of supernatural incidents.

1

THIS MORNING I put ground glass in my wife's eyes. She didn't mind. She didn't make a sound. She never does.

I took an empty bottle from the table. I wrapped it in a towel and swung it, smashing it gently against the side of her bed. When the glass shattered it made a faint, very faint sound like wind chimes in a thick fog. No one noticed, of course, least of all Karen. Then I placed it under my shoe and stepped down hard, rocking my weight back and forth until I felt fine sand underfoot. I knelt and picked up a few sharp grains on the end of my finger, rose and dropped them onto her corneas. First one, then the other. She doesn't blink, you know. It was easy.

Then I had to leave. I saw the technicians coming. But already it was too late; the damage had been done. I don't know if they found the mess under the bed. I suppose someone will. The janitors or the orderlies, perhaps. But it won't matter to them, I'm sure.

I slipped outside the glass observation wall as the technicians descended the lines, adjusting respirators, reading printouts and making notations on their pocket recorders. I remember that I thought then of clean, college-trained farmers combing rows of crops, checking the condition of the coming harvest, turning down a cover here, patting a loose mound there, touching the beds with a horticulturist's fussiness, ready to prune wherever necessary for the demands of the marketplace. They may not have seen me at all. And what if they had? What was I but a concerned husband come to pay his respects to a loved one? I might have been lectured about the risk of bringing unwanted germs into the area, though they must know how unlikely that is with the high-intensity UV lights and sonic purifiers and other sanitary precautions. I did make a point of passing near the Children's Communicable Diseases Ward on my way there, however; one always hopes.

Then, standing alone behind the windows, isolated and empty as an expectant father waiting for his flesh and blood to be delivered at last into his own hands, I had the sudden, unshakable feeling that I was being watched.

By whom?

The technicians were still intent on their readouts.

Another visitor? It was unlikely; hardly anyone else bothers to observe. A guilty few still do stop by during the lonely hours, seeking silent expiation from a friend, relative, or lover, or merely to satisfy some morbid curiosity; the most recently acquired neomorts usually receive dutiful visitations at the beginning, but invariably the newly grieved are so overwhelmed by the impersonalness of the procedure that they soon learn to stay away to preserve their own sanity.

I kept careful track of the progress of the white coats on the other side of the windows, ready to move on at the first sign of undue concern over my wife's bed.

And it was then that I saw her face shining behind my own in the pane. She was alert and standing for the first time since the stroke, nearly eighteen months ago. I gripped the handrail until my nails were white, staring in disbelief at Karen's transparent reflection.

I turned. And shrank back against the wall. The cold sweat must have been on my face, because she reached out shakily and pressed my hand.

"Can I get you anything?"

Her hair was beautiful again, not the stringy, matted mass I had come to know. Her makeup was freshly applied, her lips dark at the edges and parted just so, opening on a warm, pink interior, her teeth no longer discolored but once more a luminous bone-white. And her eyes. They were perfect.

I lunged for her.

She sidestepped gracefully and supported my arm. I looked closely at her face as I allowed her to hold me a moment longer. There was nothing wrong with that, was there?

"Are you all right?" she said.

She was so much like Karen I had to stop the backs of my fingers from stroking the soft, wispy down at her temple, as they had done so many, many times. She had always liked that. And so, I remembered, had I; it was so long ago I had almost forgotten.

"Sorry," I managed. I adjusted my clothing, smoothing my hair down from the laminar airflow around the beds. "I'm not feeling well."

"I understand."

Did she?

"My name is Emily Richterhausen," she said.

I straightened and introduced myself. If she had seen me inside the restricted area she said nothing. But she couldn't have been here that long. I would have noticed her.

"A relative?" she asked.

"My wife."

"Has...has she been here long?"

"Yes. I'm sorry. If you'll excuse me—"

"Are you sure you're all right?" She moved in front of me. "I could get you a cup of coffee, you know, from the machines. We could both have one. Or some water."

It was obvious that she wanted to talk. She needed it. Perhaps I did too. I realized that I needed to explain myself, to pass off my presence before she could guess my plan.

"Do you come here often, Emily?" It was a foolish question. I knew I hadn't seen her before.

"It's my husband," she said.

"I see."

"Oh, he's not one of...them. Not yet. He's in Intensive Care." The lovely face began to change. "A coma. It's been weeks. They say he may regain consciousness. One of the doctors said that. How long can it go on, do you know?"

I walked with her to a bench in the waiting area.

"An accident?" I said.

"A heart attack. He was driving to work. The car crossed the divider. It was awful." She fumbled for a handkerchief. I gave her mine. "They say it was a miracle he survived at all. You should have seen the car. No, you shouldn't have. No one should have. A miracle."

"Well," I told her, trying to sound comforting, "as I understand it, there is no 'usual' in comatose cases. It can go on indefinitely, as long as brain death hasn't occurred. Until then there's always hope. I saw a news item the other day about a young man who woke up after four years. He asked if he had missed his homework assignment. You've probably heard—"

"Brain death," she repeated, mouthing the words uneasily. I saw her shudder.

"That's the latest Supreme Court ruling. Even then," I went on quickly, "there's still hope. You remember that girl in New Jersey? She's still alive. She may pull out of it at any time," I lied. "And there are others like her. A great many, in fact. Why—"

"There is hope, isn't there?"

"I'm sure of it," I said, as kindly as possible.

"But then," she said, "supposing...What is it that actually happens, afterwards? How does it work? Oh, I know about the Maintenance and Cultivation Act. The doctor explained everything at the beginning, just in case." She glanced back toward the Neomort Ward and took a deep, uncertain breath. She didn't really want to know, not now. "It looks so nice and clean, doesn't it? They can still be of great service to society. The kidneys, the eyes, even the heart. It's a wonderful thing. Isn't it?"

"It's remarkable," I agreed. "Your husband, had he signed the papers?"

"No. He kept putting it off. William never liked to dwell on such matters. He didn't believe in courting disaster. Now I only wish I had forced him to talk about it, while there was still time."

"I'm sure it won't come to that," I said immediately. I couldn't bear the sight of her crying. "You'll see. The odds are very much on your side."

We sat side by side in silence as an orderly wheeled a stainless steel cleaning cart off the elevator and headed past us to the observation area. I could not help but notice the special scent of her skin. Spring flowers. It was so unlike the hospital, the antisepticized cloud that hangs over everything until it has settled into the very pores of the skin. I studied her discreetly: the tiny, exquisite whorls of her ear, the blood pulsing rapidly and naturally beneath her healthy skin. Somewhere an electronic air ionizer was whirring, and a muffled bell began to chime in a distant hallway.

"Forgive me," she said. "I shouldn't have gone on like that. But tell me about your wife." She faced me. "Isn't it strange?" We were inches apart. "It's so reassuring to talk to someone else who understands. I don't think the doctors really know how it is for us, for those who wait."

"They can't," I said.

"I'm a good listener, really I am. William always said that."

"My—my wife signed the Universal Donor Release two years ago," I began reluctantly, "the last time she renewed her driver's license." Good until her next birthday, I thought. As simple as that. Too simple. Karen, how could you have known? How could I? I should have. I should have found out. I should have stopped your hand. "She's here now. She's been here since last year. Her electroencephalogram was certified almost immediately."

"It must be a comfort to you," she said, "to know that she didn't suffer."

"Yes."

"You know, this is the first time I've been on this particular floor. What is it they call it?" She was rattling on, perhaps to distract herself.

"The Bioemporium."

"Yes, that's it. I guess I wanted to see what it would be like, just in case. For my William." She tried bravely to smile. "Do you visit her often?"

"As often as possible."

"I'm sure that must mean a great deal."

To whom? I thought, but let it pass.

"Don't worry," I said. "Your husband will recover. He'll be fine. You'll see."

Our legs were touching. It had been so long since I had felt contact with sentient flesh. I thought of asking her for that cup of coffee now, or something more, in the cafeteria. Or a drink.

"I try to believe that," she said. "It's the only thing that keeps me going. None of this seems real, does it?"

She forced the delicate corners of her mouth up into a full smile.

"I really should be going now. I could get something for him, couldn't I? You know, in the gift shop downstairs? I'm told they have a very lovely store right here in the building. And then I'll be able to give it to him during visiting hours. When he wakes up."

"That's a good idea," I said.

She said decisively, "I don't think I'll be coming to this floor again."

"Good luck," I told her. "But first, if you'd like, Emily, I thought—"

"What was...what is your wife's name? If you don't mind my asking?"

"Karen," I said. Karen. What was I thinking? Can you forgive me? You can do that, can't you, sweetheart?

"That's such a pretty name," she said.

"Thank you."

She stood. I did not try to delay her. There are some things that must be set to rest first, before one can go on. You helped remind me of that, didn't you, Karen? I nearly forgot. But you wouldn't let me.

"I suppose we won't be running into each other again," she said. Her eyes were almost cheerful.

"No."

"Would you...could you do me one small favor?"

I looked at her.

"What do you think I should get him? He has so many nice things. But you're a man. What would you like to have, if you were in the hospital? God forbid," she added, smiling warmly.

I sat there. I couldn't speak. I should have told her the truth then. But I couldn't. It would have seemed cruel, and that is not part of my nature.

What do you get, I wondered, for a man who has nothing?

2

I awaken.

The phone is silent.

I go to the medicine cabinet, swallow another fistful of L-tryptophane tablets and settle back down restlessly, hoping for a long and mercifully dreamless nap.

Soon, all too soon and not soon enough, I fall into a deep and troubled sleep.

I awaken to find myself trapped in an airtight box.

I pound on the lid, kicking until my toes are broken and my elbows are torn and bleeding. I reach into my pocket for my lighter, an antique Zippo, thumb the flint. In the sudden flare I am able to read an engraved plate set into the satin. Twenty-five Year Guarantee, it says in fancy script. I scream. My throat tears. The lighter catches the white folds and tongues of flame lick my face, spreading rapidly down my squirming body. I inhale fire.

The lid swings open.

Two attendants in white are bending over me, squirting out the flames with a water hose. One of them chuckles.

Wonder how that happened? he says.

Spontaneous combustion? says his partner.

That would make our job a hell of a lot easier, says the other. He coils the hose and I see through burned-away eyelids that it is attached to a sink at the head of a stainless steel table. The table has grooves running along the sides and a drainage hole at one end.

I scream again, but no sound comes out.

They turn away.

I struggle up out of the coffin. There is no pain. How can that be? I claw at my clothing, baring my seared flesh.

See? I cry. I'm alive!

They do not hear.

I rip at my chest with smoldering hands, the peeled skin rolling up under my fingernails. See the blood in my veins? I shout. I'm not one of them!

Do we have to do this one over? asks the attendant. It's only a cremation. Who'll know?

I see the eviscerated remains of others glistening in the sink, in the jars and plastic bags. I grab a scalpel. I slash at my arm. I cut through the smoking cloth of my shirt, laying open fresh incisions like white lips, slicing deeper into muscle and bone.

See? Do I not bleed?

They won't listen.

I stagger from the embalming chamber, gouging my sides as I bump other caskets which topple, spilling their pale contents onto the mortuary floor.

My body is steaming as I stumble out into the cold, gray dawn.

Where can I go? What is left for me? There must be a place. There must be—

A bell chimes, and I awaken.

Frantically I locate the telephone.

A woman. Her voice is relieved but shaking as she calls my name.

"Thank God you're home," she says. "I know it's late. But I didn't know who else to call. I'm terribly sorry to bother you. Do you remember me?"

No luck this time. When? I wonder. How much longer?

"You can hear me," I say to her.

"What?" She makes an effort to mask her hysteria, but I hear her cover the mouthpiece and sob. "We must have a bad connection. I'll hang up."

"No. Please." I sit forward, rubbing invisible cobwebs from my face. "Of course I remember you. Hello, Mrs. Richterhausen." What time is it? I wonder. "I'm glad you called. How did you know the number?"

"I asked Directory Information. I couldn't forget your name. You were so kind. I have to talk to someone first, before I go back to the hospital."

It's time for her, then. She must face it now; it cannot be put off, not anymore.

"How is your husband?"

"It's my husband," she says, not listening. Her voice breaks up momentarily under electrical interference. The signal reforms, but we are still separated by a grid, as if in an electronic confessional. "At twelve-thirty tonight his, what is it, now?" She bites her lips but cannot control her voice. "His EEG. It...stopped. That's what they say. A straight line. There's nothing there. They say it's nonreversible. How can that be?" she asks desperately.

I wait.

"They want you to sign, don't they, Emily?"

"Yes." Her voice is tortured as she says, "It's a good thing, isn't it? You said so yourself, this afternoon. You know about these things. Your wife..."

"We're not talking about my wife now, are we?"

"But they say it's right. The doctor said that."

"What is, Emily?"

"The life-support," she says pathetically. "The Maintenance." She still does not know what she is saying. "My husband can be of great value to medical science. Not all the usable organs can be taken at once. They may not be matched up with recipients for some time. That's why the Maintenance is so important. It's safer, more efficient than storage. Isn't that so?"

"Don't think of it as 'life-support,' Emily. Don't fool yourself. There is no longer any life to be supported."

"But he's not dead!"

"No."

"Then his body must be kept alive..."

"Not alive, either," I say. "Your husband is now—and will continue to be—neither alive nor dead. Do you understand that?"

It is too much. She breaks down. "H-how can I decide? I can't tell them to pull the plug. How could I do that to him?"

"Isn't there a decision involved in *not* pulling the plug?"

"But it's for the good of mankind, that's what they say. For people years from now, even for people not yet born. Isn't that true? Help me," she says imploringly. "You're a good man. I need to be sure that he won't suffer. Do you think he would want it this way? It was what your wife wanted, wasn't it? At least this way you're able to visit, to go on seeing her. That's important to you, isn't it?"

"He won't feel a thing, if that's what you're asking. He doesn't now, and he never will. Not ever again."

"Then it's all right?"

I wait.

"She's at peace, isn't she, despite everything? It all seems so ghastly, somehow. I don't know what to do. Help me, please..."

"Emily," I say with great difficulty. But it must be done. "Do you understand what will happen to your husband if you authorize the Maintenance?"

She does not answer.

"Only this. Listen: this is how it begins. First he will be connected to an IBM cell separator, to keep track of leucocytes, platelets, red cells, antigens that can't be stored. He will be used around the clock to manufacture an endless red tide for transfusions—"

"But transfusions save lives!"

"Not just transfusions, Emily. His veins will be a battleground for viruses, for pneumonia, hepatitis, leukemia, live cancers. And then his body will be drained off, like a stuck pig's, and a new supply of experimental toxins pumped in, so that he can go on producing antitoxins for them. Listen to me. He will begin to decay inside, Emily. He will be riddled with disease, tumors, parasites. He will stink with fever. His heart will deform, his brain fester with tubercules, his body cavities run with infection. His hair will fall, his skin yellow, his teeth splinter and rot. In the name of science, Emily, in the name of their beloved research."

I pause.

"That is, if he's one of the lucky ones."

"But the transplants..."

"Yes, that's right! You are so right, Emily. If not the blood, then the transplants. They will take him organ by organ, cell by cell. And it will take years. As long as the machines can keep the lungs and heart moving. And finally, after they've taken his eyes, his kidneys, and the rest, it will be time for his nerve tissue, his lymph nodes, his testes. They will drill out his bone marrow, and when there is no more of that left it will be time to remove his stomach and intestines, as soon as they learn how to transplant those parts too. And they will. Believe me, they will."

"No, please..."

"And when he's been thoroughly, efficiently gutted—or when his body has eaten itself from the inside out—when there is nothing left but a respirated sac bathed from within by its own excrement, do you know what they will do then? *Do you?* Then they will begin to strip the skin from his limbs, from his skull, a few millimeters at a time, for grafting and re-grafting, until—"

"Stop!"

"Take him, Emily! Take your William out of there now, tonight, before the technicians can get their bloody hands on him! Sign nothing! Take him home. Take him away and bury him forever. Do that much for him. And for yourself. Let him rest. Give him that one last, most precious gift. Grant him his final peace. You can do that much, can't you? *Can't you?*"

From far away, across miles of the city, I hear the phone drop and then clack dully into place. But only after I have heard another sound, one that I pray I will never hear again.

Godspeed, Emily, I think, weeping. *Godspeed.*

I resume my vigil.

I try to awaken, and cannot.

3

There is a machine outside my door. It eats people, chews them up and spits out only what it can't use. It wants to get me, I know it does, but I'm not going to let it.

The call I have been waiting for will never come.

I'm sure of it now. The doctor, or his nurse or secretary or dialing machine, will never announce that they are done at last, that the procedure is no longer cost-effective, that her remains will be released for burial or cremation. Not yesterday, not today, not ever.

I have cut her arteries with stolen scalpels. I have dug with an ice pick deep into her brain, hoping to sever her motor centers. I have probed for her ganglia and nerve cords. I have pierced her eardrums. I have inserted needles, trying to puncture her heart and lungs. I have hidden caustics in the folds of her throat. I have ruined her eyes. But it's no use. It will never be enough.

They will never be done with her.

When I go to the hospital today she will not be there. She will already have been given to the interns for their spinal taps and arteriograms, for surgical practice on a cadaver that is neither alive nor dead. She will belong to the meat cutters, to the first-year med students with their dull knives and stained cross-sections...

But I know what I will do.

I will search the floors and labs and secret doors of the wing, and when I find her I will steal her silently away; I will give her safe passage. I can do that much, can't I? I will take her to a place where even they can't reach, beyond the boundaries that separate the living from the dead. I will carry her over the threshold and into that realm, wherever it may be.

And there I will stay with her, to be there with her, to take refuge with her among the dead. I will tear at my body and my corruption until we are one in soft asylum. And there I will remain, living with death for whatever may be left of eternity.

Wish me Godspeed.

Science Fiction

Critical Appreciation

What is science fiction?

I do not know; you do not know; he, she, or it does not know. But there have been a great many guesses.

A more interesting question is: Why do people go on trying to define science fiction?

People who read Westerns don't bother defining them; a Western is a Western, whether it's from Zane Grey or Walter van Tilburg Clark. A horror story is a horror story, too, whether it's from Edgar Poe or Robert Bloch. If you want to read one, you look at the covers of paperbacks or the dust jackets of hardcover books, you read some blurbs, and when you've found a book that appeals to you, you take it on home and read it—if necessary, you might even pay for it first. But readers of science fiction and fans of science fiction (and there are always a lot more readers than there are fans) do this, and then tend to do something more. They become very highly territorial.

One reason may be that reading science fiction is such an active occupation. People relax in comfy armchairs and read detective stories, or Westerns, or whatever takes their fancy; but people who read science fiction tend to sit up straight out of those armchairs and argue with it. (More, they tend to write it; I've met very, very few science fiction fans, over the years, who haven't written a few stories themselves, or a few hundred.) A science fiction story tends to be a statement about the world. That statement may be as simple as People Are No Damned Good (which seems to be the statement behind H. G. Wells' "The New Accelerator") or as complex as the tribute to heroism (and cats) that is at the root of Cordwainer Smith's "The Game of Rat and Dragon"—but it is a statement, and because it is recognized as a statement, people argue with it. From there to arguing about the definition of the form itself seems to be a very small step for mankind.

And, like many arguments, it doesn't matter two cents' worth; as Damon Knight said many years ago, "science fiction" means what we mean when we point to it, and nothing more or less. "The Veldt" may not be science fiction because its emphasis is not on the science involved in getting that very odd room to work the way it does; "The Game of Rat and Dragon" may not be science fiction because its assumptions rest firmly in mid-air; if they are both good and involving stories, who cares?

Science fiction is what we mean when we point to it; but what we mean has changed a great deal over the years. And in the beginning, of course, it wasn't science fiction at all—it was just fiction.

When Jules Verne was writing "In the Year 2889" he thought he was writing a "scientific romance," a story about science, in which the story part was sugar coating for the science part. The science part, today, may seem a little weird—no, make that a lot weird—but Verne was trying to see a thousand years ahead, and anybody trying that is going to seem pretty strange long before the date arrives; what Verne did have was faith in science, of which more later.

When H. G. Wells wrote "The New Accelerator," he didn't know he was working in a genre at all; he was just imagining a new thing and writing a story about it, and he was trying to say that maybe science didn't work; it had to be carried on by human beings, after all, and as the taxi driver says in Mary Chase's wonderful play *Harvey:* "You know what sons of bitches *they* are." Wells probably couldn't have imagined that arguments over just *what sort* of new thing had been invented would become as general as arguments over whether human beings really are that awful, but they have. (If the new thing is a machine or a scientific device of some sort, it's science fiction; if it's a new sort of troll or sprite it's fantasy, or maybe horror.) Wells, if we could ask him, might not even like that sort of argument; along with the well known cockroach Archy, he might have said that the main thing was whether the stuff was art or not.

In 1906, when a man named Frank Lillie Pollack was writing "Finis," it still wasn't science fiction. A modern commentator, Sam Moskowitz, has said of its appearance that: "Catastrophe stories were already a staple of what would later be called science fiction," but that doesn't work as an implied definition either. Some catastrophe stories are science fiction, and some (*The Towering Inferno,* for instance) just aren't. This one is, and a remarkably careful sort of job it is, too, for 1906; it reads like a very early version of, say, Larry Niven's award-winning novelette, "Inconstant Moon."

By the time Isaac Asimov was writing "Nightfall," science fiction had acquired its name (Hugo Gernsback called it "scientifiction" when he started *Amazing Stories,* the first magazine devoted to the genre, in 1926, but "scientifiction" is an odd sort of word, like "televideo"—an early name for television—and got refurbished pretty quickly), its place as a genre (because anything that has popular magazines devoted to it is a genre), a status (low—because anything that had popular magazines devoted to it was low status until televideo refurbished our caste system), and a great editor.

John W. Campbell, Jr. took over a magazine called *Astounding Stories*—he'd written some science fiction adventures for the book—and began to ask for a new sort of science fiction. The science was no longer the only point. Campbell wanted stories, and that meant getting interested in the people the science was happening to.

That was a tough proposition for a lot of earlier writers of science fiction, and many dropped out of the field altogether. Youngsters like Asimov (and Robert A. Heinlein, and Jack Williamson, and Henry Kuttner, and George O. Smith, and Judith Merril, and Katherine MacLean, and a lot more) began to fill in the vacant spaces. "Nightfall" is the product of another of Campbell's notions, as recreated by Asimov.

That notion was: If everybody agrees on something, let's find out why it *isn't* so. (Campbell called these the "Yes? Well, let's see..." stories, as in: "Everybody says this is so. Yes? Well, let's see...") The Emerson quotation that heads the story is one of those sayings people nod at and agree with without thinking very much, and after all, it's Emerson, a well-known sage; he had to be right, didn't he? "Nightfall" is Asimov saying, among other things: "Well, no."

It's also Asimov telling us (as he usually does) that human beings are only human beings, after all; we needn't hate them, or ourselves, but there's no great need to go out and hunt up pedestals to put them on, either. Wells seems to have started the argument over whether human beings are worth pedestals, hatred, or something else, in stories like "The New Accelerator" (he changed his mind later, for a lot of fine novels that aren't science fiction, and then changed it again, right on back to gloom, in *Man at the End of His Tether* near the end of his life), but it goes right on, as you'll notice.

Theodore Sturgeon was one of those new writers, too (the late 1930's—when Sturgeon and Heinlein and Asimov all began showing up in what was by then *Astounding Science-Fiction,* along with many of the others I've listed, and a lot worth looking up even if they're not on the list—was Magic Time). Sturgeon was interested in people who didn't seem to be good or bad, mostly, but individuals, of all sorts and a wonderful lot of varieties—and in writing first of all, and in science not quite so much. Even his early stories are about people, though some of them aren't much about science (and he wrote a lot of fantasy for Campbell, too, for a short lived gem of a magazine called *Unknown),* and by the time we get to "The Man Who Lost the Sea" everything but the people and the writing has almost disappeared from the surface (though there is, as there usually is in Sturgeon, a lot of hard science some way under the surface, holding things together). The focus is the quality Sturgeon saw as central to people who wanted to become the best people available: the center, as always in his work (as many critics have noticed), is love.

Then there was Ray Bradbury. I remember vividly taking a story of mine to Sam Merwin, who was then editor of both *Startling Stories* and *Thrilling Wonder Stories* (science fiction by the late 1940's was not only a genre, it was a widespread genre, with almost as many magazines specializing in it as there were magazines specializing in Westerns), and having it rejected with the comment that Sam had just bought a story on the same basic theme that seemed to work out a little better, from that new guy Bradbury. I might, he thought, be interested in seeing it when it came out.

How much better it was than mine (I was about fifteen at the time, but that's not an excuse; Bradbury was not significantly older, and in fact didn't get significantly older until about 1989, when he started using his adolescent memories as story material) I cannot tell you. "The Veldt" is from a very few years later; it's a nice frightening story, and in it the science (as is usual with Bradbury, and as was slowly becoming usual for whole swatches of science fiction writers) is either very dim or entirely non-existent.

Before Bradbury there had been Arthur C. Clarke, a hard scientist if there ever was one—but Clarke was writing a carefully poetic prose that tended to baffle hard science editors, and it took the Book-of-the-Month Club (which selected a non-fiction work of his on space travel—written and published long, long before there *was* any space travel, of course) and the work of Ray Bradbury, which got awfully popular awfully fast, to start people looking at Clarke's work long enough to see what was in it.

"The Sentinel," of course, is the famous one. There aren't many people in or around it, but Clarke's work tends to push people to one side in favor of what he sees as something bigger; and it's certainly something pretty big in this tiny story. Clarke and Stanley Kubrick used it as the foundation of *2001: A Space Odyssey.* I waited for that one for two years, because while I was busy being deathly ill one week Arthur came to visit and told me a little about the work he was doing on it; and I reacted about the way Hollywood reacted before it was released, worried that the movie audience just wouldn't get it, and would avoid it in favor of *Planet of the Apes,* which was due out in the same month.

Now, of course, we know better. We don't worry about whether people are going to get *2001: A Space Odyssey*. Instead, we worry about people just not understanding something much newer. We are almost always going to be wrong about that, but many of us positively refuse to learn better, because it is a lot of superior fun to worry about all those clods out there not getting something, and it is no fun whatever to worry over the fact that you (and I, damn it) may not be any more intelligent than all those clods.

All those clods, for instance, were every bit as fast as I was to latch on to the stories of Cordwainer Smith. Smith can make for as many arguments as Bradbury: is the stuff science fiction, and if it isn't what in God's name do we call it? I call it awfully good stuff, as hard to classify as a platypus and a great deal better-looking. "The Game of Rat and Dragon" is from a magazine called *Galaxy*, and adventure doesn't get much better than this. The last paragraph or so may get to you, too, especially if you're a cat person, as sensible people tend to be. And for Smith (as for Sturgeon, and sometimes for Bradbury), science isn't good or bad; it's something people do, and people come in all sizes.

Cordwainer Smith, of course, doesn't exist and never did; the writer was a man named Paul Eric Linebarger, a career diplomat specializing in the Far East who apparently wrote his stories because it's even more fun to do that than it is to read them. Along with Robert A. Heinlein, Larry Niven, Gordon R. Dickson, Jack Vance and some others, he invented an entire history of the future, and placed his stories in it; "The Game of Rat and Dragon" takes place fairly early in that history, maybe only five hundred years after the human race starts to recover from atomic doom.

Larry Niven's future history is, of course, quite a different one. A history of the past has to agree with other histories of the past, more or less (though if you want arguments, you can get them; try reading Northern and Southern histories of the to-do between 1861 and 1865, for which each side even has its own names); a history of the future can exist all by itself.

Science fiction is not prophecy—these stories are statements, and they are stories, but they're not whatever it is a seer comes up with when he goes into his thing and tells you you're going to meet a dark stranger—and the invention of a future history only means the invention of something that is both plausible and interesting (and if you have to drop one word, drop "plausible," of course). The particular relic of this particular empire, in Niven's story, goes back at least three million years (give or take four or five months) and involves a galaxy-wide war between two intelligent races, neither of which was human, and neither of which was an ancestor of humanity.

All this is fun, and sometimes meaningful fun; the statements involved might be important and might even call for action. But when we get to Philip K. Dick, and when we get around, at long last, to Mary Wollstonecraft Shelley, we get to a point at which the statement is beginning to do what the science was doing back when the century started: it's beginning to take over the material.

In the case of Philip K. Dick this may not matter very much, because the statements are easily as thought-provoking as the stories are. "Oh, To Be a Blobel!" is not as mind-bending as Dick's novels tend to be, and you might look up *Do Androids Dream of Electric Sheep?* which has very little to do with the movie more or less based on it, *Blade Runner* (as Dick's story, "We Can Remember It For You Wholesale," has little to do with *Total Recall,* the movie based on it), but it is sufficiently odd to give you some idea of just how strange this writer could be.

And in the case of Ms. Shelley (who would have liked that "Ms."—it's arguable that she and her equally busy mother were the nineteenth-century's most frenetic fighters for Women's Rights, and for almost anything else that occurred to them to fight about) the statement—the philosophy—no longer takes over the story; to a very large extent it *is* the story.

This is the woman who wrote *Frankenstein,* after all, and that won't mean much, in this context, unless you go out and dig up the novel (and you may not want to). The movies focused in right away on the action, hurrah!—but the action, in the novel, is not what anybody remembers. In the novel, the Monster has dialogue, all right; he has pages upon pages of philosophical speculation, covering Existence, Humanity, Moral Duty, and so on, and if I may quote a character of mine named Gerald Knave: "Usually, when people start talking about Nouns like that, I make some small excuse, on the order of: 'Pardon me, I have to go now, my hair is on fire,' and get the Hell out of earshot."

Mary Shelley was interested in an idea to the precise degree that she could see a use it could be put to. *Frankenstein* is all about, believe it or not, Things We Are Not Meant to Know, and "The Mortal Immortal" is about Things We Are Not Meant to Be. Like a very few others before the twentieth Century, Mary Shelley had begun to think that Science just might not be all that good an idea.

Immortality, says the hero of this little memoir, might not be all that good an idea either (a notion more recent science fiction writers have taken up, now and then, in extraordinary stories—see A. J. Budrys' *The End of Summer,* for instance. And just by the way, I would be happier with people who now tell me that science is not a good idea if they didn't use word processors, air mail and solid-state circuitry in telling me).

And so we arrive at "How the World Was Saved." Stanislaw Lem is also interested in ideas—but for Lem ideas are things you play with. In "How the World Was Saved" he has created all sorts of new things, making me, for one, very sad that I'll never see a worch or a gruncheon.

"How the World Was Saved" is also an example of the short-short, a form science fiction writers get a lot of fun out of. (I've had some fun with them myself.) Once in a while you don't want to do anything at all with the idea you've had; you just want to toss it out there like a bomb, for laughter, instruction, or whatever (a bomb can be very instructive, if it's figurative). What is science? What are people? What (as Lem is asking) is Existence? (He and Mary Shelley get entirely different answers.) A few science fiction short-shorts have become famous—look around out there and you'll find Arthur Clarke's "The Star," Isaac Asimov's "The Feeling of Power" and "The Last Question," my own "The Question," and lots of others, each of them just a page or two long—just the idea, no frills desired.

In general, there's a *lot* of science fiction out there on the newsstands and in the bookstores (and I haven't even mentioned the movies and the televideo, which would call for at least two more essays, and a great many more arguments). Some of it is called science fiction; some of it isn't. I have no more idea why that is than you do.

The stories in this collection are called science fiction, too. You may have some doubts about that being the right name for them and the more doubts you have, and the more you express them, the more like a science fiction fan you are likely to be. If you start writing down your own ideas, of course, there's no further room for doubt; you have become a fan, and you are just going to have to live with it.

Possibly for centuries.

—Laurence M. Janifer

The Mortal Immortal

Mary Wollstonecraft Shelley

Mary Wollstonecraft Shelley (1797-1851) was the daughter of noted feminist Mary Godwin, who died in childbirth. Mary's father, William Godwin remarried in 1801, and Shelley was constantly at odds with her stepmother. Her father sent her to Dundee in 1812, and there Shelley met her future husband, Percy Bysshe Shelley. In 1814, she travelled with the poet, his wife Harriet Westbrook, and Shelley's sister Jane to Europe. After his wife's death by drowning, the poet married Shelley in 1816. The following year, Shelley wrote her first book anonymously, *History of a Six Week Tour.* In 1818, the Shelleys, Lord Byron, and Dr. Polidori participated in a ghost story writing contest; her contribution would lead to her first novel, *Frankenstein, or the Modern Prometheus.* She moved to Italy after its publication. After her husband's death by drowning in 1822, Shelley turned to professional writing to support her son. She produced five novels (*Valperga,* 1823; *The Last Man,* 1826; *The Fortunes of Perkin Warbeck,* 1830; *Lodore,* 1835; *Falkner,* 1837), five volumes of biography for the *Cabinet Cyclopedia* (1835-38), the travel book *Rambles in Germany and Italy in 1840, 1842, and 1843* (1844), and several stories and novellas for *Keepsake* magazine. In 1839, Shelley began editing her husband's literary remains, producing two volumes: *Complete Poetical Works* (1839) and *Essays, Letters From Abroad, Translations, and Fragments* (1840).

"The Mortal Immortal" originally appeared in the *Keepsake* annual of 1834, and is an excellent exploration of the effects of immortality on a normal human being.

JULY 16, 1833—This is a memorable anniversary for me; on it I complete my three hundred and twenty-third year!

The Wandering Jew?—certainly not. More than eighteen centuries have passed over his head. In comparison with him, I am a very young Immortal.

Am I, then, immortal? This is a question which I have asked myself, by day and night, for now three hundred and three years, and yet cannot answer it. I detected a gray hair amidst my brown locks this very day—that surely signifies decay. Yet it may have remained concealed there for three hundred years—for some persons have become entirely white-headed before twenty years of age.

I will tell my story, and my reader shall judge for me. I will tell my story, and so contrive to pass some few hours of a long eternity, become so wearisome to me. For ever! Can it be? to live for ever! I have heard of enchantments, in which the victims were plunged into a deep sleep, to wake after a hundred years, as fresh as ever: I have heard of the Seven Sleepers—thus to be immortal would not be so burdensome but, oh! the weight of never-ending time—the tedious passage of the still-succeeding hours! How happy was the fabled Nourjahad!—but to my task.

All the world has heard of Cornelius Agrippa. His memory is as immortal as his arts have made me. All the world has also heard of his scholar, who, unawares, raised the foul fiend during his master's absence, and was destroyed by him. The report, true or false, of this accident was attended with many inconveniences to the renowned philosopher. All his scholars at once deserted him—his servants disappeared. He had no one near him to put coals on his ever-burning fires while he slept, or to attend to the changeful colors of his medicines while he studied. Experiment after experiment failed, because one pair of hands was insufficient to complete them: the dark spirits laughed at him for not being able to retain a single mortal in his service.

I was then very young—very poor—and very much in love. I had been for about a year the pupil of Cornelius, though I was absent when this accident took place. On my return, my friends implored me not to return to the alchemist's abode. I trembled as I listened to the dire tale they told; I required no second warning; and when Cornelius came and offered me a purse of gold if I would remain under his roof, I felt as if Satan himself tempted me. My teeth chattered—my hair stood on end:—I ran off as fast as my trembling knees would permit.

My failing steps were directed whither for two years they had every evening been attracted,—a gently bubbling spring of pure living waters, beside which lingered a dark-haired girl, whose beaming eyes were fixed on the path I was accustomed each night to tread. I cannot remember the hour when I did not love Bertha; we had been neighbors and playmates from infancy—her parents, like mine, were of humble life, yet respectable—our attachment had been a source of pleasure to them. In an evil hour a malignant fever carried off both her father and mother, and Bertha became an orphan. She would have found a home beneath my paternal roof, but unfortunately, the old lady of the near castle, rich, childless, and solitary, declared her intention to adopt her. Henceforth Bertha was clad in silk—inhabited a marble palace—and was looked on as being highly favored by fortune. But in her new situation among her new associates, Bertha remained true to the friend of her humbler days; she often visited the cottage of my father, and when forbidden to go thither, she would stray towards the neighboring wood, and meet me beside its shady fountain.

She often declared that she owed no duty to her new protectress equal in sanctity to that which bound us. Yet still I was too poor to marry, and she grew weary of being tormented on my account. She had a haughty but an impatient spirit, and grew angry at the obstacles that prevented our union. We met now after an absence, and she had been sorely beset while I was away; she complained bitterly, and almost reproached me for being poor. I replied hastily,—

"I am honest, if I am poor—were I not, I might soon become rich!"

This explanation produced a thousand questions. I feared to shock her by owning the truth, but she drew it from me: and then, casting a look of disdain on me: she said

"You pretend to love, and you fear to face the Devil for my sake!"

I protested that I had only dreaded to offend her;—while she dwelt on the magnitude of the reward that I should receive. Thus encouraged—shamed by her—led on by love and hope, laughing at my late fears, with quick steps and a light heart I returned to accept the offers of the alchemist, and was instantly installed in my office.

A year passed away. I became possessed of no insignificant sum of money. Custom had banished my fears. In spite of the most painful vigilance, I had never detected the trace of a cloven foot; nor was the studious silence of our abode ever disturbed by demoniac howls. I still continued my stolen interviews with Bertha, and hope dawned on me—hope—but not perfect joy; for Bertha fancied that love and securities were enemies, and her pleasure was to divide them in my bosom. Though true of heart, she was somewhat of a coquette in manner; and I was jealous as a Turk. She slighted me in a thousand ways, yet would never acknowledge herself to be in the wrong. She would drive me mad with anger, and then force me to beg her pardon. Sometimes she fancied that I was not sufficiently submissive, and then she had some story of a rival, favored by her protectress. She was surrounded by silk-clad youths—the rich and gay—What chance had the sad-robed scholar of Cornelius compared with these?

On one occasion the philosopher made such large demands upon my time that I was unable to meet her as I was wont. He was engaged in some mighty work and I was forced to remain, day and night, feeding his furnaces and watching his chemical preparations. Bertha waited for me in vain at the fountain. Her haughty spirit fired at this neglect; and when at last I stole out during the few short minutes allotted to me for slumber, and hoped to be consoled by her, she received me with disdain, dismissed me in scorn, and vowed that any man should possess her hand rather than he who could not be in two places at once for her sake. She would be revenged!—And truly she was. In my dingy retreat I heard that she had been hunting, attended by Albert Hoffer. Albert Hoffer was favored by her protectress, and the three passed in cavalcade before my smoky window. Methought that they mentioned my name—it was followed by a laugh of derision, as her dark eyes glanced contemptuously towards my abode.

Jealously, with all its venom and all its misery, entered my breast. Now I shed a torrent of tears, to think that I should never call her mine; and, anon, I imprecated a thousand curses on her inconstancy. Yet still I must stir the fires of the alchemist, still attend on the changes of his unintelligible medicines.

Cornelius had watched for three days and nights, nor closed his eyes. The progress of his alembics was slower than he expected: in spite of his anxiety, sleep weighed upon his eyelids. Again and again he threw off drowsiness with more than human energy; again and again it stole away his senses. He eyes his crucibles wistfully. "Not ready yet," he murmured; "will another night pass before the work is accomplished? Winzy, you are vigilant—you are faithful —you have slept, my boy—you slept last night. Look at that glass vessel. The liquid it contains is of a soft rose color: the moment it begins to change its hue, awaken me—till then I may close my eyes. First, it will turn white, and then emit golden flashes: but wait not till then; when the rose-color fades, rouse me." I scarcely heard the last words muttered as they were in sleep. Even then he did not quite yield to nature. "Winzy, my boy," he again said, "do not touch the vessel—do not put it to your lips; it's a philter—a philter to cure love; you would not cease to love your Bertha—beware to drink!"

And he slept. His venerable head sunk on his breast, and I scarce heard his regular breathing. For a few minutes I watched the vessel—the rosy hue of the liquid remained unchanged. Then my thoughts wandered—they visited the fountain, and dwelt on a thousand charming scenes never to be renewed—never! Serpents and adders were in my heart as the word "Never!" half formed itself on my lips. False girl!—false and cruel! Never more would she smile on me as that evening she smiled on Albert. Worthless, detested woman! I would not remain unrevenged—she should see Albert expire at her feet—she should die beneath my vengeance. She had smiled in disdain and triumph—she knew my wretchedness and her power. Yet what power had she?—the power of exciting my hate—my utter scorn—my—oh, all but indifference. Could I attain that—could I regard her with careless eyes, transferring my *rejected* love to one fairer and more true, that were indeed a victory!

A bright flash darted before my eyes. I had forgotten the medicine of the adept; I gazed on it with wonder: flashes of admirable beauty, more bright than those which the diamond emits when the sun's rays are on it, glanced from the surface of the liquid; an odor the most fragrant and grateful stole over my sense; the vessel seemed one globe of living radiance, lovely to the eye, and most inviting to the taste. The first thought, instinctively inspired by the grosser sense, was, I will—I must drink. I raised the vessel to my lips. "It will cure me of love—of torture!" Already I had quaffed half of the most delicious liquor ever tasted by the palate of man, when the philosopher stirred. I started—I dropped the glass—the fluid flamed and glanced along the floor, while I felt Cornelius's grip at my throat, as he shrieked aloud, "Wretch! you have destroyed the labor of my life!"

The philosopher was totally unaware that I had drunk any portion of his drug. His idea was, and I gave a tacit assent to it, that I had raised the vessel from curiosity, and that, frighted at its brightness, and the flashes of intense light it gave forth, I had let it fall. I never undeceived him. The fire of the medicine was quenched—the fragrance died away—he grew calm, as a philosopher should under the heaviest trials, and dismissed me to rest.

I will not attempt to describe the sleep of glory and bliss which bathed my soul in paradise during the remaining hours of that memorable night. Words would be faint and shallow types of my enjoyment, or of the gladness that possessed my bosom when I woke. I trod air—my thoughts were in heaven. Earth appeared heaven, and my inheritance upon it was to be one trance of delight. "This it is to be cured of love," I thought; "I will see Bertha this day, and she will find her lover cold and regardless; too happy to be disdainful, yet how utterly indifferent to her!"

The hours danced away. The philosopher secure that he had once succeeded, and believing that he might again, began to concoct the same medicine once more. He was shut up with his books and drugs, and I had a holiday. I dressed myself with care; I looked in an old but polished shield, which served me for a mirror; methought my good looks had wonderfully improved. I hurried beyond the precincts of the town, joy in my soul, the beauty of heaven and earth around me. I turned my steps toward the castle—I could look on its lofty turrets with lightness of heart, for I was cured of love. My Bertha saw me afar off, as I came up the avenue. I know not what sudden impulse animated her bosom, but at the sight she sprung with a light fawn-like bound down the marble steps, and was hastening towards me. But I had been perceived by another person. The old high-born hag, who called herself her protectress, and was her tyrant, had seen me also; she hobbled, panting, up the terrace; a page, as ugly as herself, held up her train, and fanned her as she hurried along, and stopped my fair girl with a "How, now, my bold mistress? whither so fast? Back to your cage—hawks are abroad!"

Bertha clasped her hands—her eyes were still bent on my approaching figure. I saw the contest. How I abhorred the old crone who checked the kind impulses of my Bertha's softening heart. Hitherto, respect for her rank had caused me to avoid the lady of the castle; now I disdained such trivial considerations. I was cured of love and lifted above all human fears; I hastened forwards, and soon reached the terrace. How lovely Bertha looked! her eyes flashing fire, her cheeks glowing with impatience and anger, she was a thousand times more graceful and charming than ever—I no longer loved—Oh! no, I adored—worshipped—idolized her!

She had that morning been persecuted, with more than usual vehemence, to consent to an immediate marriage with my rival. She was reproached with the encouragement that she had shown him—she was threatened with being turned out of doors with disgrace and shame. Her proud spirit rose in arms at the threat; but when she remembered the scorn that she had heaped upon me, and how, perhaps, she had thus lost one whom she now regarded as her only friend, she wept with remorse and rage. At that moment I appeared, "O, Winzy!" she exclaimed, "take me to your mothers cot; swiftly let me leave the detested luxuries and wretchedness of this noble dwelling—take me to poverty and happiness."

I clasped her in my arms with transport. The old lady was speechless with fury, and broke forth into invective only when we were far on our road to my natal cottage. My mother received the fair fugitive, escaped from a gilt cage to nature and liberty, with tenderness and joy; my father, who loved her, welcomed her heartily; it was a day of rejoicing, which did not need the addition of the celestial potion of the alchemist to steep me in delight.

Soon after this eventful day I became the husband of Bertha. I ceased to be the scholar of Cornelius, but I continued his friend. I always felt grateful to him for having, unawares, procured me that delicious draught of a divine elixir, which instead of curing me of love (sad cure! solitary and joyless remedy for evils which seem blessings to the memory), had inspired me with courage and resolution, thus winning for me an inestimable treasure in by Bertha.

I often called to mind that period of trance-like inebriation with wonder. The drink of Cornelius had not fulfilled the task for which he affirmed that it had been prepared, but its effects were more potent and blissful than words can express. They had faded by degrees, yet they lingered long—and painted life in hues of splendor. Bertha often wondered at my lightness of heart and unaccustomed gaiety; for, before, I had been rather serious, or even sad, in my disposition. She loved me the better for my cheerful temper, and our days were winged by joy.

Five years afterwards I was suddenly summoned to the bedside of the dying Cornelius. He had sent for me in haste, conjuring my instant presence. I found him stretched on his pallet, enfeebled even to death; all of life that yet remained animated his piercing eyes, and they were fixed on a glass vessel, full of a roseate liquid.

"Behold," he said, in a broken and inward voice, "the vanity of human wishes! a second time my hopes are about to be crowned, a second time they are destroyed. Look at that liquor—you remember five years ago I had prepared the same, with the same success;—then, as now, my thirsting lips expected to taste the immortal elixir—you dashed it from me! and at present it is too late."

He spoke with difficulty, and fell back on his pillow. could not help saying—

"How, revered master, can a cure for love restore you to life?"

A faint smile gleamed across his face as I listened earnestly to his scarcely intelligible answer.

"A cure for love and for all things—the Elixir of Immortality. Ah! if now I might drink, I should live for ever!"

As he spoke, a golden flash gleamed from the fluid; a well remembered fragrance stole over the air; he raised himself, all weak as he was—strength seemed miraculously to reenter his frame—he stretched forth his hand—a loud explosion startled me—a ray of fire shot up from the elixir, and the glass vessel which contained it was shivered to atoms! I turned my eyes towards the philosopher; he had fallen back—his eyes were glassy—his features rigid—he was dead!

But I lived, and was to live for ever! So said the unfortunate alchemist, and for a few days I believed his words. I remembered the glorious drunkenness that had followed my stolen draught. I reflected on the change I had felt in my frame—in my soul. The bounding elasticity of the one—the buoyant lightness of the other. I surveyed myself in a mirror, and could perceive no change in my features during the space of the five years which had elapsed. I remembered the radiant hues and grateful scent of that delicious beverage—worthy the gift it was capable of bestowing—I was, then, *Immortal*!

A few days after I laughed at my credulity. The old proverb, that "a prophet is least regarded in his own country," was true with respect to me and my defunct master. I loved him as a man—I respected him as a sage—but I derided the notion that he could command the powers of darkness, and laughed at the superstitious fears with which he was regarded by the vulgar. He was a wise philosopher, but had no acquaintance with any spirits but those clad in flesh and blood. His science was simply human; and human science, I persuaded myself, could never conquer nature's laws so far as to imprison the soul for ever within its carnal habitation. Cornelius had brewed a soul-refreshing drink—more inebriating than wine—sweeter and more fragrant than any fruit: it possessed probably strong medicinal powers, imparting gladness to the heart and vigor to the limbs; but its effects would wear out; already were they diminished in my frame. I was a lucky fellow to have quaffed health and joyous spirits, and perhaps long life, at my master's hands; but my good fortune ended there: longevity was far different from immortality.

I continued to entertain this belief for many years. Sometimes a thought stole across me—Was the alchemist indeed deceived? But my habitual credence was, that I should meet the fate of all the children of Adam at my appointed time—a little late, but still at a natural age. Yet it was certain that I retained a wonderfully youthful look. I was laughed at for my vanity in consulting the mirror so often, but I consulted it in vain—my brow was untrenched—my cheeks—my eyes—my whole person continued as untarnished as in my twentieth year.

I was troubled. I looked at the faded beauty of Bertha—I seemed more like her son. By degrees our neighbors began to make similar observations, and I found at last that I went by the name of the scholar bewitched. Bertha herself grew uneasy. She became jealous and peevish, and at length she began to question me. We had no children; we were all in all to each other; and though, as she grew older, her vivacious spirit became a little allied to ill-temper, and her beauty sadly diminished. I cherished her in my heart as the mistress I had idolized, the wife I had sought and won with such perfect love.

At last our situation became intolerable: Bertha was fifty—I twenty years of age. I had in very shame, in some measure adopted the habits of a more advanced age; I no longer mingled in the dance among the young and gay, but my heart bounded along with them while I restrained my feet; and a sorry figure I cut among the Nestors of our village. But before the time I mention things were altered—we were universally shunned; we were—at least, I was—reported to have kept up an iniquitous acquaintance with some of my former master's supposed friends. Poor Bertha was pitied, but deserted. I was regarded with horror and detestation.

What was to be done? we sat by our winter fire—poverty had made itself felt, for none would buy the produce of my farm; and often I had been forced to journey twenty miles, to some place where I was not known, to dispose of our property. It was true we had saved something for an evil day—that day was come.

We sat by our lone fireside—the old-hearted youth and his antiquated wife. Again Bertha insisted on knowing the truth; she recapitulated all she had ever heard said about me, and added her own observations. She conjured me to cast off the spell; she described how much more comely gray hairs were than my chestnut locks; she descanted on the reverence and respect due to age—how preferable to the slight regard paid to mere children: could I imagine that the despicable gifts of youth and good looks outweighed disgrace, hatred, and scorn? Nay, in the end I should be burned as a dealer in the black art, while she, to whom I had not deigned to communicate any portion of my good fortune, might be stoned as my accomplice. At length she insinuated that I must share my secret with her, and bestow on her like benefits to those I myself enjoyed, or she would denounce me—and then she burst into tears.

Thus beset, methought it was the best way to tell the truth. I revealed it as tenderly as I could, and spoke only of a *very long life,* not of immortality—which representation, indeed, coincided best with my own ideas. When I ended, I rose and said,

"And now, my Bertha, will you denounce the lover of your youth?—You will not, I know. But it is too hard, my poor wife, that you should suffer from my ill-luck and the accursed arts of Cornelius. I will leave you—you have wealth enough, and friends will return in my absence. I will go; young as I seem, and strong as I am, I can work and gain my bread among strangers, unsuspected and unknown. I loved you in youth; God is my witness that I would not desert you in age, but that your safety and happiness require it."

I took my cap and moved towards the door; in a moment Bertha's arms were round my neck and her lips were pressed to mine. "No, my husband, my Winzy," she said, "you shall not go alone—take me with you; we will remove from this place, and, as you say, among strangers we shall be unsuspected and safe. I am not so very old as quite to shame you, my Winzy; and I dare say the charm will soon wear off, and, with the blessing of God, you will become more elderly-looking, as is fitting; you shall not leave me."

I returned the good soul's embrace heartily. "I will not, my Bertha, but for your sake, I had not thought of such a thing. I will be your true, faithful husband while you are spared to me, and do my duty by you to the last."

The next day we prepared secretly for our emigration. We were obliged to make great pecuniary sacrifices—it could not be helped. We realized a sum sufficient, at least, to maintain us while Bertha lived; and without saying adieu to any one, quitted our native country to take refuge in a remote part of western France.

It was a cruel thing to transport poor Bertha from her native village, and the friends of her youth, to a new country, new language, new customs. The strange secret of my destiny rendered this removal immaterial to me; but I compassionated her deeply, and was glad to perceive that she found compensation for her misfortunes in a variety of little ridiculous circumstances. Away from all tell-tale chroniclers, she sought to decrease the apparent disparity of our ages by a thousand feminine arts—rouge, youthful dress, and assumed juvenility of manner. I could not be angry—Did not I myself wear a mask? Why quarrel with hers, because it was less successful? I grieved deeply when I remembered that this was my Bertha, whom I had loved so fondly, and won with such transport—the dark-eyed, dark-haired girl, with smiles of enchanting archness and a step like a fawn—this mincing, simpering, jealous old woman. I should have revered her gray locks and withered cheeks; but thus?—It was my work I knew; but I did not the less deplore this type of human weakness.

Her jealousy never slept. Her chief occupation was to discover that, in spite of outward appearances, I was myself growing old. I verily believed that the poor soul loved me truly in her heart, but never had woman so tormenting a mode of displaying fondness. She would discern wrinkles in my face and decrepitude in my walk, while I bounded along in youthful vigor, the youngest looking of twenty youths. I never dared address another woman: on one occasion, fancying that the belle of the village regarded me with favoring eyes, she brought me a gray wig. Her constant discourse among her acquaintances was, that though I looked so young, there was ruin at work within my frame; and she affirmed that the worst symptom about me was my apparent health. My youth was a disease, she said, and I ought at all times to prepare for a sudden and awful death, at least to awake some morning white-headed, and bowed down with all the marks of advanced years. I let her talk—I often joined in her conjectures. Her warnings chimed in with my never-ceasing speculations concerning my state, and I took an earnest, though painful, interest in listening to all that her quick wit and excited imagination could say on the subject.

Why dwell on these minute circumstances? We lived on for many long years. Bertha became bed-ridden and paralytic; I nursed her as a mother might a child. She grew peevish, and still harped upon one string—of how long I should survive her. It has ever been a source of consolation to me, that I performed my duty scrupulously towards her. She had been mine in youth, she was mine in age, and at last, when I heaped the sod over her corpse, I wept to feel that I had lost all that really bound me to humanity.

Since then how many have been my cares and woes, how few and empty my enjoyments! I pause here in my history—I will pursue it no further. A sailor without rudder or compass, tossed on a stormy sea—a traveller lost on a wide-spread heath, without land mark or stone to guide him—such have I been: more lost, more hopeless than either. A nearing ship, a gleam from some far cot, may save them; but I have no beacon except the hope of death.

Death! mysterious, ill-visaged friend of weak humanity! Why alone of all mortals have you cast me from your sheltering fold? O, for the peace of the grave! the deep silence of the iron-bound tomb! that thought would cease to work in my brain, and my heart beat no more with emotions varied only by new forms of sadness!

Am I immortal? I return to my first question. In the first place, is it not more probable that the beverage of the alchemist was fraught rather with longevity than eternal life? Such is my hope. And then be it remembered, that I only drank *half* of the potion prepared by him. Was not the whole necessary to complete the charm? To have drained half the Elixir of Immortality is but to be half immortal—my For-ever is thus truncated and null.

But again, who shall number the years of the half of eternity? I often try to imagine by what rule the infinite may be divided. Sometimes I fancy age advancing upon me. One gray hair I have found. Fool! do I lament? Yes, the fear of age and death often creeps coldly into my heart; and the more I live, the more I dread death, even while I abhor life. Such an enigma is man—born to perish—when he wars, as I do, against the established laws of his nature.

But for this anomaly of feeling surely I might die: the medicine of the alchemist would not be proof against fire—sword—and the strangling waters. I have gazed upon the blue depths of many a placid lake, and the tumultuous rushing of many a mighty river, and have said, Peace inhabits those waters; yet I have turned my steps away, to live yet another day. I have asked myself, whether suicide would be a crime in one to whom thus only the portals of the other world could be open. I have done all, except presenting myself as a soldier or duellist, an object of destruction to my—no, not my fellow-mortals, and therefore I have shrunk away. They are not my fellows. The inextinguishable power of life in my frame, and their ephemeral existence, places us wide as the poles asunder. I could not raise a hand against the meanest or the most powerful among them.

Thus I have lived on for many a year—alone and weary of myself—desirous of death, yet never dying—a mortal immortal. Neither ambition nor avarice can enter my mind, and the ardent love that gnaws at my heart, never to be returned—never to find an equal on which to expend itself—lives there only to torment me.

This very day I conceived a design by which I may end all—without self-slaughter, without making another man a Cain—an expedition, which mortal frame can never survive, even endued with the youth and strength that inhabits mine. Thus I shall put my immortality to the test, and rest forever—or return, the wonder and benefactor of the human species.

Before I go, a miserable vanity has caused me to pen these pages. I would not die, and leave no name behind. Three centuries have passed since I quaffed the fatal beverage; another year shall not elapse before, encountering gigantic dangers—warring with the powers of frost in their home—beset by famine, toil, and tempest—I yield this body, too tenacious a cage for a soul which thirsts for freedom to the destructive elements of air and water—or, if I survive, my name shall be recorded as one of the most famous among the sons of men; and, my task achieved, I shall adopt more resolute means, and, by scattering and annihilating the atoms that compose my frame set at liberty the life imprisoned within, and so cruelly prevented from soaring from this dim earth to a sphere more congenial to its unmortal essence.

In the Year 2889

Jules Verne

Jules Verne (1828-1905), the father of science fiction, was born in Nantes, France. The product of a stern household, Verne defied his family by insisting on becoming a playwright. He struggled to get his plays staged (obtaining the help of Alexandre Dumas), and served as the secretary to the Theatre Lyrique from 1853-55. In 1856, Verne married Honorine Morel and became a stockbroker. In 1863, Verne met with publisher Jules Hetzel, who hired Verne to contribute novels to his magazine *les voyages extraordinaries.* Verne's first novel, *Five Weeks in a Balloon,* appeared later that year. This was quickly followed by *Voyage to the Center of the Earth* (1864) and *From the Earth to the Moon* (1865). During the Franco-Prussian War, Verne set up a Coast Guard unit in Crotoy. He published *Twenty Thousand Leagues Under the Sea* in 1870, and *The Floating City* a year later. In 1872, Verne moved to Amiens and became a full-time writer. While he was marginally popular up to this time, the publication of *Around the World in Eighty Days* in 1873 garnered him the most fame. Verne became fanatically interested in boating, and sailed to Britain and Scandanavia in 1877, the Baltic Sea in 1880, and the Mediterranean in 1884. His book sales dropped for such titles as *The Begum's Fortune* (1878) and *The Clipper of the Clouds* (1886). In 1886, Verne's nephew Gaston tried to kill him but only succeeded in shooting him in the foot. This wound left Verne lame, and made him secretive and withdrawn. Very little is known of his later life, partially because Verne burned many of his records in 1898. His later works include *The Purchase of the North Pole* (1889), *For the Flag* (1896), *The Antartic Mystery* (1897), *The Village in the Treetops* (1901), and *Master of the World* (1904).

Although Verne's writing style may seem dated today, his talent for predicting future advances is almost legendary. "In the Year 2889" features primitive prototypes of television, cryogenics, and the telephone.

LITTLE THOUGH they seem to think of it, the people of this twenty-ninth century live continually in fairyland. Surfeited as they are with marvels, they are indifferent in presence of each new marvel. To them all seems natural. Could they but duly appreciate the refinements of civilization in our day; could they but compare the present with the past, and so better comprehend the advance we have made! How much fairer they would find our modern towns, with populations amounting sometimes to 10,000,000 souls; their streets 300 feet wide, their houses 100 feet in height; with a temperature the same in all seasons; with their lines of aerial locomotion crossing the sky in every direction! If they would but picture to themselves the state of things that once existed, when through muddy streets rumbling boxes on wheels, drawn by horses—yes, by horses!—were the only means of conveyance. Think of the railroads of the olden time, and you will be able to appreciate the pneumatic tubes through which to-day one travels at the rate of 100 miles an hour. Would not our contemporaries prize the telephone and the telephote more highly if they had not forgotten the telegraph?

Singularly enough, all these transformations rest upon principles which were perfectly familiar to our remote ancestors, but which they disregarded. Heat, for instance, is as ancient as man himself; electricity was known 3000 years ago, and steam 1100 years ago. Nay, so early as ten centuries ago it was known that the differences between the several chemical and physical forces depend on the mode of vibration of the etheric particles, which is for each specifically different. When at last the kinship of all these forces was discovered, it is simply astounding that 500 years should still have to elapse before men could analyze and describe the several modes of vibration that constitute these differences. Above all, it is singular that the mode of reproducing these forces directly from one another, and of reproducing one without the others, should have remained undiscovered till less than a hundred years ago. Nevertheless, such was the course of events, for it was not till the year 2792 that the famous Oswald Nier made this great discovery.

Truly was he a great benefactor of the human race. His admirable discovery led to many another. Hence is sprung a pleiad of inventors, its brightest star being our great Joseph Jackson. To Jackson we are indebted for those wonderful instruments—the new accumulators. Some of these absorb and condense the living force contained in the sun's rays; others, the electricity stored in our globe; others again, the energy coming from whatever source, as a waterfall, a stream, the winds, etc. He, too, it was that invented the transformer, a more wonderful contrivance still, which takes the living force from the accumulator, and, on the simple pressure of a button, gives it back to space in whatever form may be desired, whether as heat, light, electricity or mechanical force, after having first obtained from it the work required. From the day when these two instruments were contrived is to be dated the era of true progress. They have put into the hands of man a power that is almost infinite. As for their applications, they are numberless. Mitigating the rigors of winter, by giving back to the atmosphere the surplus heat stored up during the summer, they had revolutionized agriculture. By supplying motive power for aerial navigation, they have given to commerce a mighty impetus. To them we are indebted for the continuous production of electricity without batteries or dynamos, of light without combustion or incandescence and for an unfailing supply of mechanical energy for all the needs of industry.

Yes, all these wonders have been wrought by the accumulator and the transformer. And can we not to them also trace, indirectly, this latest wonder of all, the great "Earth Chronicle" building in 253rd Avenue, which was dedicated the other day? If George Washington Smith, the founder of the Manhattan "Chronicle," should come back to life today, what would he think were he to be told that this palace of marble and gold belongs to his remote descendant, Fritz Napoleon Smith, who, after thirty generations have come and gone, is owner of the same newspaper which his ancestor established!

For George Washington Smith's newspaper has lived generation after generation, now passing out of the family, anon coming back to it. When, 200 years ago, the political center of the United States was transferred from Washington to Centropolis, the newspaper followed the government and assumed the name of Earth Chronicle. Unfortunately, it was unable to maintain itself at the high level of its name. Pressed on all sides by rival journals of a more modern type, it was continually in danger of collapse. Twenty years ago its subscription list contained but a few hundred thousand names, and then Mr. Fritz Napoleon Smith bought it for a mere trifle, and originated telephonic journalism.

Every one is familiar with Fritz Napoleon Smith's system—a system made possible by the enormous development of telephony during the last hundred years. Instead of being printed, the Earth Chronicle is every morning spoken to subscribers, who, in interesting conversations with reporters, statesmen and scientists, learn the news of the day. Furthermore, each subscriber owns a phonograph, and to this instrument he leaves the task of gathering the news whenever he happens not to be in a mood to listen directly himself. As for purchasers of single copies, they can at a very trifling cost learn all that is in the paper of the day at any of the innumerable phonographs set up nearly everywhere.

Fritz Napoleon Smith's innovation galvanized the old newspaper. In the course of a few years the number of subscribers grew to be 85,000,000 and Smith's wealth went on growing, till now it reaches the almost unimaginable figure of $10,000,000,000. This lucky hit has enabled him to erect his new building, a vast edifice with four *façades,* each 3,250 feet in length, over which proudly floats the hundred-starred flag of the Union. Thanks to the same lucky hit, he is to-day king of newspaperdom; indeed, he would be king of all the Americans, too, if Americans could ever accept a king. You do not believe it? Well, then, look at the plenipotentiaries of all nations and our own ministers themselves crowding about his door, entreating his counsels, begging for his approbation, imploring the aid of his all-powerful organ. Reckon up the number of scientists and artists that he supports, of inventors that he has under his pay.

Yes, a king is he. And in truth his is a royalty full of burdens. His labors are incessant, and there is no doubt at all that in earlier times any man would have succumbed under the overpowering stress of the toil which Mr. Smith has to perform. Very fortunately for him, thanks to the progress of hygiene, which, abating all the old sources of unhealthfulness, has lifted the mean of human life from 37 up to 52 years, men have stronger constitutions now than heretofore. The discovery of nutritive air is still in the future, but in the meantime men to-day consume food that is compounded and prepared according to scientific principles, and they breathe an atmosphere freed from the microorganisms that formerly used to swarm in it; hence they live longer than their forefathers and know nothing of the innumerable diseases of olden times.

Nevertheless, and notwithstanding these considerations, Fritz Napoleon Smith's mode of life may well astonish one. His iron constitution is taxed to the utmost by the heavy strain that is put upon it. Vain the attempt to estimate the amount of labor he undergoes; an example alone can give an idea of it. Let us then go about with him for one day as he attends to his multifarious concernments. What day? That matters little; it is the same every day. Let us then take at random September 25th of this present year 2889.

This morning Mr. Fritz Napoleon Smith awoke in very bad humor. His wife having left for France eight days ago, he was feeling disconsolate. Incredible though it seems, in all the ten years since their marriage, this is the first time that Mrs. Edith Smith, the professional beauty, has been so long absent from home; two or three days usually suffice for her frequent trips to Europe. The first thing that Mr. Smith does is to connect his phonotelephote, the wires of which communicate with his Paris mansion. The telephote! Here is another of the great triumphs of science in our time. The transmission of speech is an old story; the transmission of images by means of sensitive mirrors connected by wires is a thing but of yesterday. A valuable invention indeed, and Mr. Smith this morning was not niggard of blessings for the inventor, when by its aid he was able distinctly to see his wife notwithstanding the distance that separated him from her. Mrs. Smith, weary after the ball or the visit to the theater the preceding night, is still abed, though it is near noontide at Paris. She is asleep, her head sunk in the lace-covered pillows. What? She stirs? Her lips move. She is dreaming perhaps? Yes, dreaming. She is talking, pronouncing a name—his name—Fritz! The delightful vision gave a happier turn to Mr. Smith's thoughts. And now, at the call of imperative duty, light-hearted he springs from his bed and enters his mechanical dresser.

Two minutes later the machine deposited him all dressed at the threshold of his office. The round of journalistic work was now begun. First he enters the hall of the novel-writers, a vast apartment crowned with an enormous transparent cupola. In one corner is a telephone, through which a hundred Earth Chronicle *littérateurs* in turn recount to the public in daily installments a hundred novels. Addressing one of these authors who was waiting his turn, "Capital! Capital! my dear fellow," said he, "your last story. The scene where the village maid discusses interesting philosophical problems with her lover shows your very acute power of observation. Never have the ways of country folk been better portrayed. Keep on, my dear Archibald, keep on! Since yesterday, thanks to you, there is a gain of 5000 subscribers."

"Mr. John Last," he began again, turning to a new arrival, "I am not so well pleased with your work. Your story is not a picture of life; it lacks the elements of truth. And why? Simply because you run straight on to the end; because you do not analyze. Your heroes do this thing or that from this or that motive, which you assign without ever a thought of dissecting their mental and moral natures. Our feelings, you must remember, are far more complex than all that. In real life every act is the resultant of a hundred thoughts that come and go, and these you must study, each by itself, if you would create a living character. 'But,' you will say, 'in order to note these fleeting thoughts one must know them, must be able to follow them in their capricious meanderings.' Why, any child can do that, as you know. You have simply to make use of hypnotism, electrical or human, which gives one a twofold being, setting free the witness-personality so that it may see, understand and remember the reasons which determine the personality that acts. Just study yourself as you live from day to day, my dear Last. Imitate your associate whom I was complimenting a moment ago. Let yourself be hypnotized. What's that? You have tried it already? Not sufficiently, then, not sufficiently!"

Mr. Smith continues his round and enters the reporters' hall. Here 1500 reporters, in their respective places, facing an equal number of telephones, are communicating to the subscribers the news of the world as gathered during the night. The organization of this matchless service has often been described. Besides his telephone, each reporter, as the reader is aware, has in front of him a set of commutators, which enable him to communicate with any desired telephotic line. Thus the subscribers not only hear the news but see the occurrences. When an incident is described that is already past, photographs of its main features are transmitted with the narrative. And there is no confusion withal. The reporters' items, just like the different stories and all the other component parts of the journal, are classified automatically according to an ingenious system, and reach the hearer in due succession. Furthermore, the hearers are free to listen only to what specially concerns them. They may at pleasure give attention to one editor and refuse it to another.

Mr. Smith next addresses one of the ten reporters in the astronomical department—a department still in the embryonic stage, but which will yet play an important part in journalism.

"Well, Cash, what's the news?"

"We have phototelegrams from Mercury, Venus, and Mars."

"Are those from Mars of any interest?"

"Yes, indeed. There is a revolution in the Central Empire."

"And what of Jupiter?" asked Mr. Smith.

"Nothing as yet. We cannot quite understand their signals. Perhaps ours do not reach them."

"That's bad," exclaimed Mr. Smith, as he hurried away, not in the best of humor, toward the hall of the scientific editors. With their heads bent down over their electric computers, thirty scientific men were absorbed in transcendental calculations. The coming of Mr. Smith was like the falling of a bomb among them.

"Well, gentlemen, what is this I hear? No answer from Jupiter? Is it always to be thus? Come, Cooley, you have been at work now twenty years on this problem, and yet—"

"True enough," replied the man addressed. "Our science of optics is still very defective, and though our mile-and-three-quarter telescopes—"

"Listen to that, Peer," broke in Mr. Smith, turning to a second scientist. "Optical science defective! Optical science is your specialty. But," he continued, again addressing William Cooley, "failing with Jupiter, are we getting any results from the moon?"

"The case is no better there."

"This time you do not lay the blame on the science of optics. The moon is immeasurably less distant than Mars, yet with Mars our communication is fully established. I presume you will not say that you lack telescopes?"

"Telescopes? Oh no, the trouble here is about—inhabitants!"

"That's it," added Peer.

"So, then, the moon is positively uninhabited?" asked Mr. Smith.

"At least," answered Cooley, "on the face which she presents to us. As for the opposite side, who knows?"

"Ah, the opposite side! You think, then," remarked Mr. Smith, musingly, "that if one could but—"

"Could what?"

"Why, turn the moon about-face."

"Ah, there's something in that," cried the two men at once. And indeed, so confident was their air, they seemed to have no doubt as to the possibility of success in such an undertaking.

"Meanwhile," asked Mr. Smith, after a moment's silence, "have you no news of interest to-day?"

"Indeed we have," answered Cooley. "The elements of Olympus are definitely settled. That great planet gravitates beyond Neptune at the mean distance of 11,400,799,642 miles from the sun, and to traverse its vast orbit takes 1311 years, 294 days, 12 hours, 43 minutes, 9 seconds."

"Why didn't you tell me that sooner?" cried Mr. Smith. "Now inform the reporters of this straightway. You know how eager is the curiosity of the public with regard to these astronomical questions. That news must go into to-day's issue."

Then, the two men bowing to him, Mr. Smith passed into the next hall, an enormous gallery upward of 3200 feet in length, devoted to atmospheric advertising. Every one has noticed those enormous advertisements reflected from the clouds, so large that they may be seen by the populations of whole cities or even of entire countries. This, too, is one of Mr. Fritz Napoleon Smith's ideas, and in the Earth Chronicle building a thousand projectors are constantly engaged in displaying upon the clouds these mammoth advertisements.

When Mr. Smith to-day entered the sky-advertising department, he found the operators sitting with folded arms at their motionless projectors, and inquired as to the cause of their inaction. In response, the man addressed simply pointed to the sky, which was of a pure blue. "Yes," muttered Mr. Smith, "a cloudless sky! That's too bad, but what's to be done? Shall we produce rain? That we might do, but is it of any use? What we need is clouds, not rain. Go," said he, addressing the head engineer, "go see Mr. Samuel Mark, of the meteorological division of the scientific department, and tell him for me to go to work in earnest on the question of artificial clouds. It will never do for us to be always thus at the mercy of cloudless skies!"

Mr. Smith's daily tour through the several departments of his newspaper is now finished. Next, from the advertisement hall he passes to the reception chamber, where the ambassadors accredited to the American government are awaiting him, desirous of having a word of counsel or advice from the all-powerful editor. A discussion was going on when he entered. "Your Excellency will pardon me," the French Ambassador was saying to the Russian, "but I see nothing in the map of Europe that requires change. 'The North for the Slavs?' Why, yes, of course; but the South for the Latins. Our common frontier, the Rhine, it seems to me, serves very well. Besides, my government, as you must know, will firmly oppose every movement, not only against Paris, our capital, or our two great prefectures, Rome and Madrid, but also against the kingdom of Jerusalem, the dominion of Saint Peter, of which France means to be the trusty defender."

"Well said!" exclaimed Mr. Smith. "How is it," he asked, turning to the Russian ambassador, "that you Russians are not content with your vast empire, the most extensive in the world, stretching from the banks of the Rhine to the Celestial Mountains and the Kara-Korum, whose shores are washed by the Frozen Ocean, the Atlantic, the Mediterranean and the Indian Ocean? Then, what is the use of threats? Is war possible in view of modern inventions—asphyxiating shells capable of being projected a distance of 60 miles, an electric spark of 90 miles, that can at one stroke annihilate a battalion; to say nothing of the plague, the cholera, the yellow fever, that the belligerents might spread among their antagonists mutually, and which would in a few days destroy the greatest armies?"

"True," answered the Russian, "but can we do all that we wish? As for us Russians, pressed on our eastern frontier by the Chinese, we must at any cost put forth our strength for an effort toward the west."

"Oh, is that all? In that case," said Mr. Smith, "the thing can be arranged. I will speak to the Secretary of State about it. The attention of the Chinese government shall be called to the matter. This is not the first time that the Chinese have bothered us."

"Under these conditions, of course—" And the Russian ambassador declared himself satisfied.

"Ah, Sir John, what can I do for you?" asked Mr. Smith as he turned to the representative of the people of Great Britain, who till now had remained silent.

"A great deal," was the reply. "If the Earth Chronicle would but open a campaign on our behalf—"

"And for what object?"

"Simply for the annulment of the Act of Congress annexing to the United States the British islands."

Though, by a just turn-about of things here below, Great Britain has become a colony of the United States, the English are not yet reconciled to the situation. At regular intervals they are ever addressing to the American government vain complaints.

"A campaign against the annexation that has been an accomplished fact for 150 years!" exclaimed Mr. Smith. "How can your people suppose that I would do anything so unpatriotic?"

"We at home think that your people must now be sated. The Monroe Doctrine is fully applied; the whole of America belongs to the Americans. What more do you want? Besides, we will pay for what we ask."

"Indeed!" answered Mr. Smith, without manifesting the slightest irritation. "Well, you English will ever be the same. No, no, Sir John, do not count on me for help. Give up our fairest province, Britain? Why not ask France generously to renounce possession of Africa, that magnificent colony the complete conquest of which cost her the labor of 800 years? You will be well received!"

"You decline! All is over then!" murmured the British agent sadly. "The United Kingdom falls to the share of the Americans; the Indies to that of—"

"The Russians," said Mr. Smith, completing the sentence.

"Australia—"

"Has an independent government."

"Then nothing at all remains for us!" sighed Sir John, downcast.

"Nothing?" asked Mr. Smith, laughing. "Well, now, there's Gibraltar!"

With this sally the audience ended. The clock was striking twelve, the hour of breakfast. Mr. Smith returns to his chamber. Where the bed stood in the morning a table all spread comes up through the floor. For Mr. Smith, being above all a practical man, has reduced the problem of existence to its simplest terms. For him, instead of the endless suites of apartments of the olden time, one room fitted with ingenious mechanical contrivances is enough. Here he sleeps, takes his meals, in short, lives.

He seats himself. In the mirror of the phonotelephote is seen the same chamber at Paris which appeared in it this morning. A table furnished forth is likewise in readiness here, for notwithstanding the difference of hours, Mr. Smith and his wife have arranged to take their meals simultaneously. It is delightful thus to take breakfast *tête-à-tête* with one who is 3000 miles or so away. Just now, Mrs. Smith's chamber has no occupant.

"She is late! Woman's punctuality! Progress everywhere except there!" muttered Mr. Smith as he turned the tap for the first dish. For like all wealthy folk in our day, Mr. Smith has done away with the domestic kitchen and is a subscriber to the Grand Alimentation Company, which sends through a great network of tubes to subscribers' residences all sorts of dishes, as a varied assortment is always in readiness. A subscription costs money, to be sure, but the *cuisine* is of the best, and the system has this advantage, that it does away with the pestering race of the *cordons-bleus.* Mr. Smith received and ate, all alone, the *hors-d'oeuvre, entrées, rôti,* and *legumes* that constituted the repast. He was just finishing the dessert when Mrs. Smith appeared in the mirror of the telephote.

"Why, where have you been?" asked Mr. Smith through the telephone.

"What! You are already at the dessert? Then I am late," she exclaimed, with a winsome *naïveté.* "Where have I been, you ask? Why, at my dress-maker's. The hats are just lovely this season! I suppose I forgot to note the time, and so am a little late."

"Yes, a little," growled Mr. Smith; "so little that I have already quite finished breakfast. Excuse me if I leave you now, but I must be going."

"Oh certainly, my dear; good-by till evening."

Smith stepped into his air-coach, which was in waiting for him at a window. "Where do you wish to go, sir?" inquired the coachman.

"Let me see; I have three hours," Mr. Smith mused. "Jack, take me to my accumulator works at Niagara."

For Mr. Smith has obtained a lease of the great falls of Niagara. For ages the energy developed by the falls went unutilized. Smith, applying Jackson's invention, now collects this energy, and lets or sells it. His visit to the works took more time than he had anticipated. It was four o'clock when he returned home, just in time for the daily audience which he grants to callers.

One readily understands how a man situated as Smith is must be beset with requests of all kinds. Now it is an inventor needing capital; again it is some visionary who comes to advocate a brilliant scheme which must surely yield millions of profit. A choice has to be made between these projects, rejecting the worthless, examining the questionable ones, accepting the meritorious. To this work Mr. Smith devotes every day two full hours.

The callers were fewer to-day than usual—only twelve of them. Of these, eight had only impracticable schemes to propose. In fact, one of them wanted to revive painting, an art fallen into desuetude owing to the progress made in color-photography. Another, a physician, boasted that he had discovered a cure for nasal catarrh! These impracticables were dismissed in short order. Of the four projects favorably received, the first was that of a young man whose broad forehead betokened his intellectual power.

"Sir, I am a chemist," he began, "and as such I come to you."

"Well!"

"Once the elementary bodies," said the young chemist, "were held to be sixty-two in number; a hundred years ago they were reduced to ten; now only three remain irresolvable, as you are aware."

"Yes, yes."

"Well, sir, these also I will show to be composite. In a few months, a few weeks, I shall have succeeded in solving the problem. Indeed, it may take only a few days."

"And then?"

"Then, sir, I shall simply have determined the absolute. All I want is money enough to carry my research to a successful issue."

"Very well," said Mr. Smith. "And what will be the practical outcome of your discovery?"

"The practical outcome? Why, that we shall be able to produce easily all bodies whatever—stone, wood, metal, fibers—"

"And flesh and blood?" queried Mr. Smith, interrupting him. "Do you pretend that you expect to manufacture a human being out and out?"

"Why not?"

Mr. Smith advanced $100,000 to the young chemist, and engaged his services for the Earth Chronicle laboratory.

The second of the four successful applicants, starting from experiments made so long ago as the nineteenth century and again and again repeated, had conceived the idea of removing an entire city all at once from one place to another. His special project had to do with the city of Granton, situated, as everybody knows, some fifteen miles inland. He proposes to transport the city on rails and to change it into a watering-place. The profit, of course, would be enormous. Mr. Smith, captivated by the scheme, bought a half-interest in it.

"As you are aware, sir," began applicant No. 3, "by the aid of our solar and terrestrial accumulators and transformers, we are able to make all the seasons the same. I propose to do something better still. Transform into heat a portion of the surplus energy at our disposal; send this heat to the poles; then the polar regions, relieved of their snow-caps, will become a vast territory available for man's use. What think you of the scheme?"

"Leave your plans with me, and come back in a week. I will have them examined in the meantime."

Finally, the fourth announced the early solution of a weighty scientific problem. Every one will remember the bold experiment made a hundred years ago by Dr. Nathaniel Faithburn. The doctor, being a firm believer in human hibernation—in other words, in the possibility of our suspending our vital functions and of calling them into action again after a time—resolved to subject the theory to a practical test. To this end, having first made his last will and pointed out the proper method of awakening him; having also directed that his sleep was to continue a hundred years to a day from the date of his apparent death, he unhesitatingly put the theory to the proof in his own person. Reduced to the condition of a mummy, Dr. Faithburn was coffined and laid in a tomb. Time went on. September 25th, 2889, being the day set for his resurrection, it was proposed to Mr. Smith that he should permit the second part of the experiment to be performed at his residence this evening.

"Agreed. Be here at ten o'clock," answered Mr. Smith; and with that the day's audience was closed.

Left to himself, feeling tired, he lay down on an extension chair. Then, touching a knob, he established communication with the Central Concert Hall, whence our greatest *maestros* send out to subscribers their delightful successions of accords determined by recondite algebraic formulas. Night was approaching. Entranced by the harmony, forgetful of the hour, Smith did not notice that it was growing dark. It was quite dark when he was aroused by the sound of a door opening. "Who is there?" he asked, touching a commutator.

Suddenly, in consequence of the vibrations produced, the air became luminous. "Ah! you, Doctor?"

"Yes," was the reply. "How are you?"

"I am feeling well."

"Good! Let me see your tongue. All right! Your pulse. Regular! And your appetite?"

"Only passably good."

"Yes, the stomach. There's the rub. You are over-worked. If your stomach is out of repair, it must be mended. That requires study. We must think about it."

"In the meantime," said Mr. Smith, "you will dine with me."

As in the morning, the table rose out of the floor. Again, as in the morning, the *potage, rôti, ragoûts* and *legumes* were supplied through the food-pipes. Toward the close of the meal, phonotelephotic communication was made with Paris. Smith saw his wife, seated alone at the dinner-table, looking anything but pleased at her loneliness.

"Pardon me, my dear, for having left you alone," he said through the telephone. "I was with Dr. Wilkins."

"Ah, the good doctor," remarked Mrs. Smith, her countenance lighting up.

"Yes. But, pray, when are you coming home?"

"This evening."

"Very well. Do you come by tube or by air-train?"

"Oh, by tube."

"Yes; and at what hour will you arrive?"

"About eleven, I suppose."

"Eleven by Centropolis time, you mean?"

"Yes."

"Good-by, then, for a little while," said Mr. Smith as he severed communication with Paris.

Dinner over, Dr. Wilkins wished to depart. "I shall expect you at ten," said Mr. Smith. "To-day, it seems, is the day for the return to life of the famous Dr. Faithburn. You did not think of it, I suppose. The awakening is to take place here in my house. You must come and see. I shall depend on your being here."

"I will come back," answered Dr. Wilkins.

Left alone, Mr. Smith busied himself with examining his accounts—a task of vast magnitude, having to do with transactions which involve a daily expenditure of upward of $800,000. Fortunately, indeed, the stupendous progress of mechanic art in modern times makes it comparatively easy. Thanks to the Piano Electro-Reckoner, the most complex calculations can be made in a few seconds. In two hours Mr. Smith completed his task. Just in time. Scarcely had he turned over the last page when Dr. Wilkins arrived. After him came the body of Dr. Faithburn, escorted by a numerous company of men of science. They commenced work at once. The casket being laid down in the middle of the room, the telephote was got in readiness. The outer world, already notified, was anxiously expectant, for the whole world could be eyewitnesses of the performance, a reporter meanwhile, like the chorus in the ancient drama, explaining it all *viva voce* through the telephone.

"They are opening the casket," he explained. "Now they are taking Faithburn out of it—a veritable mummy, yellow, hard and dry. Strike the body and it resounds like a block of wood. They are now applying heat; now electricity. No result. These experiments are suspended for a moment while Dr. Wilkins makes an examination of the body. Dr. Wilkins, rising, declares the man to be dead. 'Dead!' exclaims every one present. 'Yes,' answers Dr. Wilkins, 'dead!' 'And how long has he been dead?' Dr. Wilkins makes another examination. 'A hundred years,' he replies."

The case stood just as the reporter said. Faithburn was dead, quite certainly dead! "Here is a method that needs improvement," remarked Mr. Smith to Dr. Wilkins, as the scientific committee on hibernation bore the casket out. "So much for that experiment. But if poor Faithburn is dead, at least he is sleeping," he continued. "I wish I could get some sleep. I am tired out, Doctor, quite tired out! Do you not think that a bath would refresh me?"

"Certainly. But you must wrap yourself up well before you go out into the hall-way. You must not expose yourself to cold."

"Hall-way? Why, Doctor, as you well know, everything is done by machinery here. It is not for me to go to the bath; the bath will come to me. Just look!" and he pressed a button. After a few seconds a faint rumbling was heard, which grew louder and louder. Suddenly the door opened, and the tub appeared.

Such, for this year of grace 2889, is the history of one day in the life of the editor of the Earth Chronicle. And the history of that one day is the history of 365 days every year, except leap-years, and then of 366 days—for as yet no means has been found of increasing the length of the terrestrial year.

The New Accelerator

H.G. Wells

H.G. Wells (1866-1946) was born in County Kent, England. The son of a maid, Wells was nevertheless exposed to Swift, Johnson, and other writers at an early age. In 1882, Wells attended the Normal School of Science in Kensington. After leaving college in 1887, Wells taught at various schools before recurring lung hemorrhages forced him to become a correspondence tutor in 1890. In 1891, he married his cousin, Isabel. Two years later, he published two biology textbooks. In 1894, he published his first novel, *The Time Machine.* The following year he divorced Isabel to marry Amy Catherine. Wells followed *The Time Machine* with *The Island of Dr. Moreau* (1896), *The Invisible Man* (1897), *The War of the Worlds* (1898), and *The First Men in the Moon* (1901). Wells became more political in later novels such as *The Food of the Gods* (1904) and *In the Days of the Comet* (1906). In 1908, Wells helped start up *The English Review,* serializing *Tono-Bungay* in its earlier issues. His next novel, *Ann Veronica* (1909), was based on his affair with Amber Reaves. In 1914, Wells' novel *The World Set Free* predicted atomic warfare. He was appointed as the Chairman of the Policy Committee of Propaganda in Enemy Countries in 1918, but resigned shortly afterwards. Novels such as *Men Like Gods* (1923), *The Dream* (1924), and *The Shape of Things to Come* (1925) reflected Well's disillusionment with politics and humanity. In 1925, he founded the British Film Society, and wrote several film scripts, including the classic *Things to Come* (1936). Wells came out against the Catholic Church in 1930, and became increasingly misanthropic in the years preceding his death. His later novels include *Mr. Bletts on Rampole Island* (1928), *Bulpington of Blup* (1932), *Apropos of Delores* (1938), and *All Aboard for Ararat* (1940).

Like Verne, Wells had a talent for prediction. "The New Accelerator," in addition to dealing with the possible effect of metabolic change, is also infused with a light comedic humor.

CERTAINLY, IF EVER a man found a guinea when he was looking for a pin it is my good friend Professor Gibberne. I have heard before of investigators overshooting the mark, but never quite to the extent that he has done. He has really, this time at any rate, without any touch of exaggeration in the phrase, found something to revolutionize human life. And that when he was simply seeking an all-round nervous stimulant to bring languid people up to the stresses of these pushful days. I have tasted the stuff now several times, and I cannot do better than to describe the effect the thing had on me. That there are astonishing experiences in store for all in search of new sensations will become apparent enough.

Professor Gibberne, as many people know, is my neighbor in Folkestone. Unless my memory plays me a trick, his portrait at various ages has already appeared in The Strand Magazine—I think late in 1899; but I am unable to look it up because I have lent that volume to someone who has never sent it back. The reader may, perhaps, recall the high forehead and the singularly long black eyebrows that give such a Mephistophelian touch to his face. He occupies one of those pleasant detached houses in the mixed style that make the western end of the Upper Sandgate Road so interesting. His is the one with the Flemish gables and the Moorish portico, and it is in the room with the mullioned bay window that he works when he is down here, and in which of an evening we have so often smoked and talked together. He is a mighty jester, but, besides, he likes to talk to me about his work; he is one of those men who find a help and stimulus in talking, and so I have been able to follow the conception of the New Accelerator right up from a very early stage. Of course, the greater portion of his experimental work is not done in Folkestone, but in Gower Street, in the fine new laboratory next to the hospital that he has been the first to use.

As everyone knows, or at least as all intelligent people know, the special department in which Gibberne has gained so great and deserved a reputation among physiologists is the action of drugs upon the nervous system. Upon soporifics, sedatives and anesthetics he is, I am told, unequaled. He is also a chemist of considerable eminence, and I suppose in the subtle and complex jungle of riddles that centers about the ganglion cell and the axis fiber there are little cleared places of his making, glades of illumination, that, until he sees fit to publish his results, are inaccessible to every other living man. And in the last few years he has been particularly assiduous upon this question of nervous stimulants, and already, before the discovery of the New Accelerator, very successful with them. Medical science has to thank him for at least three distinct and absolutely safe invigorators of unrivaled value to practicing men. In cases of exhaustion the preparation known as

Gibberne's B Syrup has, I suppose, saved more lives already than any lifeboat round the coast.

"But none of these things begin to satisfy me yet," he told me nearly a year ago. "Either they increase the central energy without affecting the nerves or they simply increase the available energy by lowering the nervous conductivity; and all of them are unequal and local in their operation. One wakes up the heart and viscera and leaves the brain stupefied, one gets at the brain champagne fashion and does nothing good for the solar plexus, and what I want—and what, if it's an earthly possibility, I mean to have—is a stimulant that stimulates all round, that wakes you up for a time from the crown of your head to the tip of your great toe, and makes you go two—or even three to everybody else's one. Eh? That's the thing I'm after."

"It would tire a man," I said.

"Not a doubt of it. And you'd eat double or treble—and all that. But just think what the thing would mean. Imagine yourself with a little phial like this"—he held up a bottle of green glass and marked his points with it—"and in this precious phial is the power to think twice as fast, move twice as quickly, do twice as much work in a given time as you could otherwise do."

"But is such a thing possible?"

"I believe so. If it isn't, I've wasted my time for a year. These various preparations of the hypophosphites, for example, seem to show that something of the sort.... Even if it was only one and a half times as fast it would do."

"It *would* do," I said.

"If you were a statesman in a corner, for example, time rushing up against you, something urgent to be done, eh?"

"He could dose his private secretary," I said.

"And gain—double time. And think if *you,* for example, wanted to finish a book."

"Usually," I said, "I wish I'd never begun 'em."

"Or a doctor, driven to death, wants to sit down and think out a case. Or a barrister—or a man cramming for an examination."

"Worth a guinea a drop," said I, "and more—to men like that."

"And in a duel again," said Gibberne, "where it all depends on your quickness in pulling the trigger."

"Or in fencing," I echoed.

"You see," said Gibberne, "if I get it as an all-round thing it will really do you no harm at all—except perhaps to an infinitesimal degree it brings you nearer old age. You will just have lived twice to other people's once."

"I suppose," I meditated, "in a duel—it would be fair?"

"That's a question for the seconds," said Gibberne.

I harked back further. "And you really think such a thing is possible?" I said.

"As possible," said Gibberne, and glanced at something that went throbbing by the window, "as a motorbus. As a matter of fact—"

He paused and smiled at me deeply, and tapped slowly on the edge of his desk with the green phial. "I think I know the stuff....Already I've got something coming." The nervous smile upon his face betrayed the gravity of his revelation. He rarely talked of his actual experimental work unless things were very near the end. "And it may be, it may be—I shouldn't be surprised—it may even do the thing at a greater rate than twice."

"It will be rather a big thing," I hazarded.

"It will be, I think, rather a big thing."

But I don't think he quite knew what a big thing it was to be, for all that.

I remember we had several subsequent talks about the stuff. "The New Accelerator" he called it, and his tone about it grew more confident on each occasion. Sometimes he talked nervously of unexpected physiological results its use might have, and then he would get a bit unhappy; at others he was frankly mercenary, and we debated long and anxiously how the preparation might be turned to commercial account. "It's a good thing," said Gibberne, "a tremendous thing. I know I'm giving the world something, and I think it only reasonable we should expect the world to pay. The dignity of science is all very well, but I think somehow I must have the monopoly of the stuff for, say, ten years. I don't see why *all* the fun in life should go to the dealers in ham."

My own interest in the coming drug certainly did not wane in the time. I have always had a queer twist towards metaphysics in my mind. I have always been given to paradoxes about space and time, and it seemed to me that Gibberne was really preparing no less than the absolute acceleration of life. Suppose a man repeatedly dosed with such a preparation: he would live an active and record life indeed, but he would be an adult at eleven, middle-aged at twenty-five, and by thirty well on the road to senile decay. It seemed to me that so far Gibberne was only going to do for anyone who took his drug exactly what Nature has done for the Jews and Orientals, who are men in their teens and aged by fifty, and quicker in thought and act than we are all the time. The marvel of drugs has always been great to my mind; you can madden a man, calm a man, make him incredibly strong and alert or a helpless log, quicken this passion and allay that, all by means of drugs, and here was a new miracle to be added to this strange armory of phials the doctors use! But Gibberne was far too eager upon his technical points to enter very keenly into my aspect of the question.

It was the 7th or 8th of August, when he told me the distillation that would decide his failure or success for a time was going forward as we talked, and it was on the 10th that he told me the thing was done and the New Accelerator a tangible reality in the world. I met him as I was going up the Sandgate Hill towards Folkestone—I think I was going to get my hair cut; and he came hurrying down to meet me—I suppose he was coming to my house to tell me at once of his success. I remember that his eyes were unusually bright and his face flushed, and I noted even then the swift alacrity of his step.

"It's done," he cried, and gripped my hand, speaking very fast; "it's more than done. Come up to my house and see."

"Really?"

"Really!" he shouted. "Incredibly! Come up and see."

"And it does—twice!"

"It does more, much more. It scares me. Come up and see the stuff. Taste it! Try it! It's the most amazing stuff on earth." He gripped my arm and, walking at such a pace that he forced me into a trot, went shouting with me up the hill. A whole charabancful of people turned and stared at us in unison after the manner of people in charabancs. It was one of those hot, clear days that Folkestone sees so much of, every color incredibly bright and every outline hard. There was a breeze, of course, but not so much breeze as sufficed under these conditions to keep me cool and dry. I panted for mercy.

"I'm not walking fast, am I?" cried Gibberne, and slackened his pace to a quick march.

"You've been taking some of this stuff," I puffed.

"No," he said. "At the utmost a drop of water that stood in a beaker from which I had washed out the last traces of the stuff. I took some last night, you know. But that is ancient history, now."

"And it goes twice?" I said, nearing his doorway in a grateful perspiration.

"It goes a thousand times, many thousand times!" cried Gibberne, with a dramatic gesture, flinging open his Early English carved oak gate.

"Phew!" said I, and followed him to the door.

"I don't know how many times it goes," he said, with his latch-key in his hand.

"And you—"

"It throws all sorts of light on nervous physiology, it kicks the theory of vision into a perfectly new shape!...Heaven knows how many thousand times. We'll try all that after—The thing is to try the stuff now."

"Try the stuff?" I said, as we went along the passage.

"Rather," said Gibberne, turning on me in his study. "There it is in that little green phial there! Unless you happen to be afraid?"

I am a careful man by nature, and only theoretically adventurous. I was afraid. But on the other hand there is pride.

"Well," I haggled. "You say you've tried it?"

"I've tried it," he said, "and I don't look hurt by it, do I? I don't even look livery and I *feel*—"

I sat down. "Give me the potion," I said. "If the worst comes to the worst it will save having my hair cut, and that I think is one of the most hateful duties of a civilized man. How do you take the mixture?"

"With water," said Gibberne, whacking down a carafe.

He stood up in front of his desk and regarded me in his easy chair; his manner was suddenly affected by a touch of the Harley Street specialist. "It's rum stuff, you know," he said.

I made a gesture with my hand.

"I must warn you in the first place as soon as you've got it down to shut your eyes, and open them very cautiously in a minute or so's time. One still sees. The sense of vision is a question of length of vibration, and not of multitude of impacts; but there's a kind of shock to the retina, a nasty giddy confusion just at the time if the eyes are open. Keep 'em shut."

"Shut," I said. "Good!"

"And the next thing is, keep still. Don't begin to whack about. You may fetch something a nasty rap if you do. Remember you will be going several thousand times faster than you ever did before, heart, lungs, muscles, brain—everything—and you will hit hard without knowing it. You won't know it, you know. You'll feel just as you do now. Only everything in the world will seem to be going ever so many thousand times slower than it ever went before. That's what makes it so deuced queer."

"Lor'," I said. "And you mean—"

"You'll see," said he, and took up a measure. He glanced at the material on his desk. "Glasses," he said, "water. All here. Mustn't take too much for the first attempt."

The little phial glucked out its precious contents. "Don't forget what I told you," he said, turning the contents of the measure into a glass in the manner of an Italian waiter measuring whisky. "Sit with the eyes tightly shut and in absolute stillness for two minutes," he said. "Then you will hear me speak."

He added an inch or so of water to the dose in each glass.

"By the bye," he said, "don't put your glass down. Keep it in your hand and rest your hand on your knee. Yes—so. And now—"

He raised his glass.

"The New Accelerator," I said.

"The New Accelerator," he answered, and we touched glasses and drank, and instantly I closed my eyes.

You know that blank non-existence into which one drops when one has taken "gas." For an indefinite interval it was like that. Then I heard Gibberne telling me to wake up, and I stirred and opened my eyes. There he stood as he had been standing, glass still in hand. It was empty, that was all the difference.

"Well?" said I.

"Nothing out of the way?"

"Nothing. A slight feeling of exhilaration, perhaps. Nothing more."

"Sounds?"

"Things are still," I said. "By Jove! yes! They *are* still. Except the sort of faint pat, patter, like rain falling on different things. What is it?"

"Analyzed sounds," I think he said, but I am not sure. He glanced at the windows. "Have you ever seen a curtain before a window fixed in that way before?"

I followed his eyes, and there was the end of the curtain, frozen, as it were, corner high, in the act of flapping briskly in the breeze.

"No," said I, "that's odd."

"And here," he said, and opened the hand that held the glass. Naturally I winced, expecting the glass to smash. But so far from smashing it did not even seem to stir; it hung in mid-air—motionless. "Roughly speaking," said Gibberne, "an object in these latitudes falls 16 feet in the first second. This glass is falling 16 feet in a second now. Only, you see, it hasn't been falling yet for the hundredth part of a second. That gives you some idea of the pace of my Accelerator." And he waved his hand round and round, over and under the slowly sinking glass. Finally he took it by the bottom, pulled it down and placed it very carefully on the table. "Eh?" he said to me, and laughed.

"That seems all right," I said, and began very gingerly to raise myself from my chair. I felt perfectly well, very light and comfortable, and quite confident in my mind. I was going fast all over. My heart, for example, was beating a thousand times a second, but that caused me no discomfort at all. I looked out of the window. An immovable cyclist, head down and with a frozen puff of dust behind his driving-wheel, scorched to overtake a galloping charabanc that did not stir. I gaped in amazement at this incredible spectacle. "Gibberne," I cried, "how long will this confounded stuff last?"

"Heaven knows!" he answered. "Last time I took it, I went to bed and slept it off. I tell you, I was frightened. It must have lasted some minutes, I think—it seemed like hours. But after a bit it slows down rather suddenly, I believe."

I was proud to observe that I did not feel frightened—I suppose because there were two of us. "Why shouldn't we go out?" I asked.

"Why not?"

"They'll see us."

"Not they. Goodness, no! Why, we shall be going a thousand times faster than the quickest conjuring trick that was ever done. Come along! Which way shall we go? Window, or door?"

And out by the window we went.

Assuredly of all the strange experiences that I have ever had, or imagined, or read of other people having or imagining, that little raid I made with Gibberne on the Folkestone Leas, under the influence of the New Accelerator, was the strangest and maddest of all. We went out by his gate into the road, and there we made a minute examination of the statuesque passing traffic. The tops of the wheels and some of the legs of the horses of this charabanc, the end of the whiplash and the lower jaw of the conductor—who was just beginning to yawn—were perceptibly in motion, but all the rest of the lumbering conveyance seemed still. And quite noiseless except for a faint rattling that came from one man's throat! And as parts of this frozen edifice there were a driver, you know, and a conductor, and eleven people! The effect as we walked about the thing began by being madly queer and ended by being—disagreeable. There they were, people like ourselves and yet not like ourselves, frozen in careless attitudes, caught in mid-gesture. A girl and a man smiled at one another, a leering smile that threatened to last for evermore; a woman in a floppy capelline rested her arm on the rail and stared at Gibberne's house with the unwinking stare of eternity; a man stroked his moustache like a figure of wax, and another stretched a tiresome stiff hand with extended fingers towards his loosened hat. We stared at them, we laughed at them, we made faces at them, and then a sort of disgust of them came upon us, and we turned away and walked round in front of the cyclist towards the Leas.

"Goodness!" cried Gibberne, suddenly; "look there!"

He pointed, and there at the tip of his finger and sliding down the air with wings flapping slowly and at the speed of an exceptionally languid snail—was a bee.

And so we came out upon the Leas. There the thing seemed madder than ever. The band was playing in the upper stand, though all the sound it made for us was a low-pitched, wheezy rattle, a sort of prolonged last sigh that passed at times into a sound like the slow, muffled ticking of some monstrous clock. Frozen people stood erect; strange, silent, self-conscious-looking dummies hung unstably in mid-stride, promenading upon the grass. I passed close to a poodle dog suspended in the act of leaping, and watched the slow movement of his legs as he sank to earth. "Lord, look *here*!" cried Gibberne, and we halted for a moment before a magnificent person in white faint-striped flannels, white shoes, and a Panama hat, who turned back to wink at two gaily-dressed ladies he had passed. A wink, studied with such leisurely deliberation as we could afford, is an unattractive thing. It loses any quality of alert gaiety, and one remarks that the winking eye does not completely close, that under its drooping lid appears the lower edge of an eyeball and a line of white. "Heaven give me memory," said I, "and I will never wink again."

"Or smile," said Gibberne, with his eye on the lady's answering teeth.

"It's infernally hot, somehow," said I. "Let's go slower."

"Oh, come along!" said Gibberne.

We picked our way among the Bath chairs in the path. Many of the people sitting in the chairs seemed amost natural in their passive poses, but the contorted scarlet of the bandsmen was not a restful thing to see. A purple-faced gentleman was frozen in the midst of a violent struggle to refold his newspaper against the wind; there were many evidences that all these people in their sluggish way were exposed to a considerable breeze, a breeze that had no existence so far as our sensations went. We came out and walked a little way from the crowd, and turned and regarded it. To see all that multitude changed to a picture, smitten rigid, as it were, into the semblance of realistic wax, was impossibly wonderful. It was absurd, of course; but it filled me with an irrational, an exultant sense of superior advantage. Consider the wonder of it! All that I had said and thought and done since the stuff had begun to work in my veins had happened, so far as those people, so far as the world in general went, in the twinkling of an eye. "The New Accelerator—" I began, but Gibberne interrupted me.

"There's that infernal old woman!" he said.

"What old woman?"

"Lives next door to me," said Gibberne. "Has a lapdog that yaps. Gods! The temptation is strong!"

There is something very boyish and impulsive about Gibberne at times. Before I could expostulate with him he had dashed forward, snatched the unfortunate animal out of visible existence, and was running violently with it towards the cliff of the Leas. It was most extraordinary. The little brute, you know, didn't bark or wriggle or make the slightest sign of vitality. It kept quite stiffly in an attitude of somnolent repose, and Gibberne held it by the neck. It was like running about with a dog of wood. "Gibberne," I cried, "put it down!" Then I said something else. "If you run like that, Gibberne," I cried, "you'll set your clothes on fire. Your linen trousers are going brown as it is!"

He clapped his hand on his thigh and stood hesitating on the verge. "Gibberne," I cried, coming up, "put it down. This heat is too much! It's our running so! Two or three miles a second! Friction of the air!"

"What?" he said, glancing at the dog.

"Friction of the air," I shouted. "Friction of the air. Going too fast. Like meteorites and things. Too hot. And, Gibberne! Gibberne! I'm all over pricking and a sort of perspiration. You can see people stirring slightly. I believe the stuff's working off! Put that dog down."

"Eh?" he said.

"It's working off," I repeated. "We're too hot and the stuff's working off! I'm wet through."

He stared at me. Then at the band, the wheezy rattle of whose performance was certainly going faster. Then with a tremendous sweep of the arm he hurled the dog away from him and it went spinning upward, still inanimate, and hung at last over the grouped parasols of a knot of chattering people. Gibberne was gripping my elbow. "By Jove!" he cried. "I believe it is! A sort of hot pricking and—yes. That man's moving his pocket-handkerchief! Perceptibly. We must get out of this sharp."

But we could not get out of it sharply enough. Luckily, perhaps! For we might have run, and if we had run we should, I believe, have burst into flames. Almost certainly we should have burst into flames! You know we had neither of us thought of that....But before we could even begin to run the action of the drug had ceased. It was the business of a minute fraction of a second. The effect of the New Accelerator passed like the drawing of a curtain, vanished in the movement of a hand. I heard Gibberne's voice in infinite alarm. "Sit down," he said, and flop, down upon the turf at the edge of the Leas I sat—scorching as I sat. There is a patch of burnt grass there still where I sat down. The whole stagnation seemed to wake up as I did so, the disarticulated vibration of the band rushed together into a blast of music, the promenaders put their feet down and walked their ways, the papers and flags began flapping, smiles passed into words, the winker finished his wink and went on his way complacently, and all the seated people moved and spoke.

The whole world had come alive again, was going as fast as we were, or rather we were going no faster than the rest of the world. It was like slowing down as one comes into a railway station. Everything seemed to spin round for a second or two, I had the most transient feeling of nausea, and that was all. And the little dog which had seemed to hang for a moment when the force of Gibberne's arm was expended fell with a swift acceleration clean through a lady's parasol!

That was the saving of us. Unless it was for one corpulent old gentleman in a Bath chair, who certainly did start at the sight of us and afterwards regarded us at intervals with a darkly suspicious eye, and finally, I believe, said something to his nurse about us, I doubt if a solitary person remarked our sudden appearance among them. Plop! We must have appeared abruptly. We ceased to smolder almost at once, though the turf beneath me was uncomfortably hot. The attention of everyone—including even the Amusements' Association band, which on this occasion, for the only time in its history, got out of tune—was arrested by the amazing fact, and the still more amazing yapping and uproar caused by the fact, that a respectable, over-fed lapdog sleeping quietly to the east of the bandstand should suddenly fall through the parasol of a lady on the west—in a slightly singed condition due to the extreme velocity of its movements through the air. In these absurd days, too, when we are all trying to be as psychic and silly and superstitious as possible! People got up and trod on other people, chairs were overturned, the Leas policeman ran. How the matter settled itself, I do not know—we were much too anxious to disentangle ourselves from the affair and get out of range of the eye of the old gentleman in the Bath chair to make minute inquiries. As soon as we were sufficiently cool and sufficiently recovered from our giddiness and nausea and confusion of mind to do so we stood up and, skirting the crowd, directed our steps back along the road below the Metropole towards Gibberne's house. But amidst the din I heard very distinctly the gentleman who had been sitting beside the lady of the ruptured sunshade using quite unjustifiable threats and language to one of those chair-attendants who have "Inspector" written on their caps. "If you didn't throw the dog," he said, "who *did*?"

The sudden return of movement and familiar noises, and our natural anxiety about ourselves (our clothes were still dreadfully hot, and the fronts of the thighs of Gibberne's white trousers were scorched a drabbish brown), prevented the minute observations I should have liked to make on all these things. Indeed, I really made no observations of any scientific value on that return. The bee, of course, had gone. I looked for that cyclist, but he was already out of sight as we came into the Upper Sandgate Road or hidden from us by traffic; the charabanc, however, with its people now all alive and stirring, was clattering along at a spanking pace almost abreast of the nearer church.

We noted, however, that the window-sill on which we had stepped in getting out of the house was slightly singed, and that the impressions of our feet on the gravel of the path were unusually deep.

So it was I had my first experience of the New Accelerator. Practically we had been running about and saying and doing all sorts of things in the space of a second or so of time. We had lived half an hour while the band had played, perhaps, two bars. But the effect it had upon us was that the whole world had stopped for our convenient inspection. Considering all things, and particularly considering our rashness in venturing out of the house, the experience might certainly have been much more disagreeable than it was. It showed, no doubt, that Gibberne has still much to learn before his preparation is a manageable convenience, but its practicability it certainly demonstrated beyond all cavil.

Since that adventure he has been steadily bringing its use under control, and I have several times, and without the slightest bad result, taken measured doses under his direction; though I must confess I have not yet ventured abroad again while under its influence. I may mention, for example, that this story has been written at one sitting and without interruption, except for the nibbling of some chocolate, by its means. I began at 6:25, and my watch is now very nearly at the minute past the half-hour. The convenience of securing a long, uninterrupted spell of work in the midst of a day full of engagements cannot be exaggerated. Gibberne is now working at the quantitative handling of his preparation, with especial reference to its distinctive effects upon different types of constitution. He then hopes to find a Retarder with which to dilute its present rather excessive potency. The Retarder will, of course, have the reverse effect to the Accelerator; used alone it should enable the patient to spread a few seconds over many hours of ordinary time, and so to maintain an apathetic inaction, a glacierlike absence of alacrity, amidst the most animated or irritating surroundings. The two things together must necessarily work an entire revolution in civilized existence. It is the beginning of our escape from that Time Garment of which Carlyle speaks. While this Accelerator will enable us to concentrate ourselves with tremendous impact upon any moment or occasion that demands our utmost sense and vigor, the Retarder will enable us to pass in passive tranquillity through infinite hardship and tedium. Perhaps I am a little optimistic about the Retarder, which has indeed still to be discovered, but about the Accelerator there is no possible sort of doubt whatever. Its appearance upon the market in a convenient, controllable and assimilable form is a matter of the next few months. It will be obtainable of all chemists and druggists in small green bottles, at a high but, considering its extraordinary qualities, by no means excessive price. Gibberne's Nervous Accelerator it will be called, and he hopes to be able to supply it in three strengths: one in 200, one in 900 and one in 2000, distinguished by yellow, pink and white labels respectively.

No doubt its use renders a great number of very extraordinary things possible; for, of course, the most remarkable and, possibly, even criminal proceedings may be effected with impunity by thus dodging, as it were, into the interstices of time. Like all potent preparations it will be liable to abuse. We have, however, discussed this aspect of the question very thoroughly, and we have decided that this is purely a matter of medical jurisprudence and altogether outside our province. We shall manufacture and sell the Accelerator, and, as for the consequences—we shall see.

Finis

Frank Lillie Pollack

Frank Lillie Pollack is an author whose life is a virtual mystery—research into his background has not even uncovered a birth or death date. His earliest work, a short story called "The Crimson Blight," appeared in *Argosy* in 1905. In addition to "Finis," Pollack is known to have written another story ("The World Wreckers," 1908) and three books (*The Treasure Trail,* 1906; *Honey of Danger: An Adventure Story,* date unknown; *The Frozen Fortune,* 1910).

"Finis" appeared in the April 1906 issue of *Argosy.* Even to this day, it stands as one of the best "End of the World" stories ever written.

"I'M GETTING TIRED," complained Davis, lounging in the window of the Physics Building, "and sleepy. It's after eleven o'clock. This makes the fourth night I've sat up to see your new star, and it'll be the last. Why, the thing was billed to appear three weeks ago."

"Are *you* tired, Miss Wardour?" asked Eastwood, and the girl glanced up with a quick flush and a negative murmur.

Eastwood made the reflection anew that she certainly was painfully shy. She was almost as plain as she was shy, though her hair had an unusual beauty of its own, fine as silk and colored like palest flame.

Probably she had brains; Eastwood had seen her reading some extremely "deep" books, but she seemed to have no amusements, few interests. She worked daily at the Art Students' League, and boarded where he did, and he had thus come to ask her with the Davises to watch for the new star from the laboratory windows on the Heights.

"Do you really think that it's worthwhile to wait any longer, professor?" inquired Mrs. Davis, concealing a yawn.

Eastwood was somewhat annoyed by the continued failure of the star to show itself and he hated to be called "professor," being only an assistant professor of physics.

"I don't know," he answered somewhat curtly. "This is the twelfth night that I have waited for it. Of course, it would have been a mathematical miracle if astronomers should have solved such a problem exactly, though they've been figuring on it for a quarter of a century."

The new Physics Building of Columbia University was about twelve stories high. The physics laboratory occupied the ninth and tenth floors, with the astronomical rooms above it, an arrangement which would have been impossible before the invention of the oil vibration cushion, which practically isolated the instrument rooms from the earth.

Eastwood had arranged a small telescope at the window, and below them spread the illuminated map of Greater New York, sending up a faintly musical roar. All the streets were crowded, as they had been every night since the fifth of the month, when the great new star, or sun, was expected to come into view.

Some error had been made in the calculations, though, as Eastwood said, astronomers had been figuring on them for twenty-five years.

It was, in fact, nearly forty years since Professor Adolphe Bernier first announced his theory of a limited universe at the International Congress of Sciences in Paris, where it was counted as little more than a masterpiece of imagination.

Professor Bernier did not believe that the universe was infinite. Somewhere, he argued, the universe must have a center, which is the pivot for its revolution.

The moon revolves around the earth, the planetary system revolves about the sun, the solar system revolves about one of the fixed stars, and this whole system in its turn undoubtedly revolves around some more distant point. But this sort of progression must definitely stop somewhere.

Somewhere there must be a central sun, a vast incandescent body which does not move at all. And as a sun is always larger and hotter than its satellites, therefore the body at the center of the universe must be of an immensity and temperature beyond anything known or imagined.

It was objected that this hypothetical body should then be large enough to be visible from the earth, and Professor Bernier replied that some day it undoubtedly would be visible. Its light had simply not yet had time to reach the earth.

The passage of light from the nearest of the fixed stars is a matter of three years, and there must be many stars so distant that their rays have not yet reached us. The great central sun must be so inconceivably remote that perhaps hundreds, perhaps thousands of years would elapse before its light should burst upon the solar system.

All this was contemptuously classed as "newspaper science" till the extraordinary mathematical revival a little after the middle of the twentieth century afforded the means of verifying it.

Following the new theorems discovered by Professor Burnside, of Princeton, and elaborated by Dr. Taneka, of Tokyo, astronomers succeeded in calculating the arc of the sun's movements through space, and its ratio to the orbit of its satellites. With this as a basis, it was possible to follow the widening circles, the consecutive systems of the heavenly bodies and their rotations.

The theory of Professor Bernier was justified. It was demonstrated that there really was a gigantic mass of incandescent matter, which, whether the central point of the universe or not, appeared to be without motion.

The weight and distance of this new sun were approximately calculated, and, the speed of light being known, it was an easy matter to reckon when its rays would reach the earth.

It was then estimated that the approaching rays would arrive at the earth in twenty-six years, and that was twenty-six years ago. Three weeks had passed since the date when the new heavenly body was expected to become visible, and it had not yet appeared.

Popular interest had risen to a high pitch, stimulated by innumerable newspaper and magazine articles, and the streets were nightly thronged with excited crowds armed with opera-glasses and star maps, while at every corner a telescope man had planted his tripod instrument at a nickel a look.

Similar scenes were taking place in every civilized city on the globe.

It was generally supposed that the new luminary would appear in size about midway between Venus and the moon. Better informed persons expected something like the sun, and a syndicate of capitalists quietly leased large areas on the coast of Greenland in anticipation of a great rise in temperature and a northward movement in population.

Even the business situation was appreciably affected by the public uncertainty and excitement. There was a decline in stocks, and a minor religious sect boldly prophesied the end of the world.

"I've had enough of this," said Davis, looking at his watch again. "Are you ready to go, Grace? By the way, isn't it getting warmer?"

It had been a sharp February day, but the temperature was certainly rising. Water was dripping from the roofs, and from the icicles that fringed the window ledges, as if a warm wave had suddenly arrived.

"What's that light?" suddenly asked Alice Wardour, who was lingering by the open window.

"It must be moonrise," said Eastwood, though the illumination of the horizon was almost like daybreak.

Davis abandoned his intention of leaving, and they watched the east grow pale and flushed till at last a brilliant white disc heaved itself above the horizon.

It resembled the full moon, but as if trebled in luster, and the streets grew almost as light as by day.

"Good heavens, that must be the new star, after all!" said Davis in an awed voice.

"No, it's only the moon. This is the hour and minute for her rising," answered Eastwood, who had grasped the cause of the phenomenon. "But the new sun must have appeared on the other side of the earth. Its light is what makes the moon so brilliant. It will rise here just as the sun does, no telling how soon. It must be brighter than was expected—and maybe hotter," he added with a vague uneasiness.

"Isn't it getting very warm in here?" said Mrs. Davis, loosening her jacket. "Couldn't you turn off some of the steam heat?"

Eastwood turned it all off, for, in spite of the open window, the room was really growing uncomfortably close. But the warmth appeared to come from without; it was like a warm spring evening, and the icicles were breaking loose from the cornices.

For half an hour they leaned from the windows with but desultory conversation and below them the streets were black with people and whitened with upturned faces. The brilliant moon rose higher, and the mildness of the night sensibly increased.

It was after midnight when Eastwood first noticed the reddish flush tinging the clouds low in the east, and he pointed it out to his companions.

"That must be it at last," he exclaimed, with a thrill of vibrating excitement at what he was going to see, a cosmic event unprecedented in intensity.

The brightness waxed rapidly.

"By Jove, see it redden!" Davis ejaculated. "It's getting lighter than day—and hot! Whew!"

The whole eastern sky glowed with a deepening pink that extended half round the horizon. Sparrows chirped from the roofs, and it looked as if the disc of the unknown star might at any moment be expected to lift above the Atlantic, but it delayed long.

The heavens continued to burn with myriad hues, gathering at last to a fiery furnace glow on the skyline.

Mrs. Davis suddenly screamed. An American flag blowing freely from its staff on the roof of the tall building had all at once burst into flame.

Low in the east lay a long streak of intense fire which broadened as they squinted with watering eyes. It was as if the edge of the world had been beated to whiteness.

The brilliant moon faded to a feathery white film in the glare. There was a confused outcry from the observatory overhead, and a crash of something being broken, and as the strange new sunlight fell through the window the onlookers leaped back as if a blast furnace had been opened before them.

The glass cracked and fell inward. Something like the sun, but magnified fifty times in size and hotness, was rising out of the sea. An iron instrument-table by the window began to smoke with an acrid smell of varnish.

"What the devil is this, Eastwood?" shouted Davis accusingly.

From the streets rose a sudden, enormous wail of fright and pain, the outcry of a million throats at once, and the roar of a stampede followed. The pavements were choked with struggling, panic-stricken people in the fierce glare, and above the din arose the clanging rush of fire engines and trucks.

Smoke began to rise from several points below Central Park, and two or three church chimes pealed crazily.

The observers from overhead came running down the stairs with a thunderous trampling, for the elevator man had deserted his post.

"Here, we've got to get out of this," shouted Davis, seizing his wife by the arm and hustling her toward the door. "This place'll be on fire directly."

"Hold on. You can't go down into that crush on the street," Eastwood cried, trying to prevent him.

But Davis broke away and raced down the stairs, half carrying his terrified wife. Eastwood got his back against the door in time to prevent Alice from following them.

"There's nothing in this building that will burn, Miss Wardour," he said as calmly as he could. "We had better stay here for the present. It would be sure death to get involved in that stampede below. Just listen to it."

The crowds on the street seemed to sway to and fro in contending waves, and the cries, curses and screams came up in a savage chorus.

The heat was already almost blistering to the skin, though they carefully avoided the direct rays, and instruments of glass in the laboratory cracked loudly one by one.

A vast cloud of dark smoke began to rise from the harbor, where the shipping must have caught fire, and something exploded with a terrific report. A few minutes later half a dozen fires broke out in the lower part of the city, rolling up volumes of smoke that faded to a thin mist in the dazzling light.

The great new sun was now fully above the horizon, and the whole east seemed ablaze. The stampede in the streets had quieted all at once, for the survivors had taken refuge in the nearest houses, and the pavements were black with motionless forms of men and women.

"I'll do whatever you say," said Alice, who was deadly pale, but remarkably collected. Even at that moment Eastwood was struck by the splendor of her ethereally brilliant hair that burned like pale flame above her pallid face. "But we can't stay here, can we?"

"No," replied Eastwood, trying to collect his faculties in the face of this catastrophic revolution of nature. "We'd better go to the basement, I think."

In the basement were deep vaults used for the storage of delicate instruments, and these would afford shelter for a time at least. It occurred to him as he spoke that perhaps temporary safety was the best that any living thing on earth could hope for.

But he led the way down the well staircase. They had gone down six or seven flights when a gloom seemed to grow upon the air, with a welcome relief.

It seemed almost cool, and the sky had clouded heavily, with the appearance of polished and heated silver.

A deep but distant roaring arose and grew from the southeast, and they stopped on the second landing to look from the window.

A vast black mass seemed to fill the space between sea and sky, and it was sweeping toward the city, probably from the harbor, Eastwood thought, at a speed that made it visibly grow as they watched it.

"A cyclone—and a waterspout!" muttered Eastwood, appalled.

He might have foreseen it from the sudden, excessive evaporation and the heating of the air. The gigantic black pillar drove toward them swaying and reeling, and a gale came with it, and a wall of impenetrable mist behind.

As Eastwood watched its progress he saw its cloudy bulk illumined momentarily by a dozen lightning-like flashes, and a moment later, above its roar, came the tremendous detonations of heavy cannon.

The forts and the warships were firing shells to break the waterspout, but the shots seemed to produce no effect. It was the city's last and useless attempt at resistance. A moment later forts and ships alike must have been engulfed.

"Hurry! This building will collapse!" Eastwood shouted.

They rushed down another flight, and heard the crash with which the monster broke over the city. A deluge of water, like the emptying of a reservoir, thundered upon the street, and the water was steaming hot as it fell.

There was a rending crash of falling walls, and in another instant the Physics Building seemed to be twisted around by a powerful hand. The walls blew out, and the whole structure sank in a chaotic mass.

But the tough steel frame was practically unwreckable, and, in fact, the upper portion was simply bent down upon the lower stories, peeling off most of the shell of masonry and stucco.

Eastwood was stunned as he was hurled to the floor, but when he came to himself he was still upon the landing, which was tilted at an alarming angle. A tangled mass of steel rods and beams hung a yard over his head, and a huge steel girder had plunged down perpendicularly from above, smashing everything in its way.

Wreckage choked the well of the staircase, a mass of plaster, bricks and shattered furniture surrounded him, and he could look out in almost every direction through the rent iron skeleton.

A yard away Alice was sitting up, mechanically wiping the mud and water from her face, and apparently uninjured. Tepid water was puring through the interstices of the wreck in torrents, though it did not appear to be raining.

A steady, powerful gale had followed the whirlwind, and it brought a little coolness with it. Eastwood inquired perfunctorily of Alice if she were hurt, without being able to feel any degree of interest in the matter. His faculty of sympathy seemed paralyzed.

"I don't know. I thought—I thought that we were all dead!" the girl murmured in a sort of daze. "What was it? Is it all over?"

"I think it's only beginning," Eastwood answered dully.

The gale had brought up more clouds and the skies were thickly overcast, but shining white-hot. Presently the rain came down in almost scalding floods and as it fell upon the hissing streets it steamed again into the air.

In three minutes all the world was choked with hot vapors, and from the roar and splash the streets seemed to be running rivers.

The downpour seemed too violent to endure, and after an hour it did cease, while the city reeked with mist. Through the whirling fog Eastwood caught glimpses of ruined buildings, vast heaps of debris, all the wreckage of the greatest city of the twentieth century.

Then the torrents fell again, like a cataract, as if the waters of the earth were shuttlecocking between sea and heaven. With a jarring tremor of the ground a landslide went down into the Hudson.

The atmosphere was like a vapor bath, choking and sickening. The physical agony of respiration aroused Alice from a sort of stupor, and she cried out pitifully that she would die.

The strong wind drove the hot spray and steam through the shattered building till it seemed impossible that human lungs could extract life from the semi-liquid that had replaced the air, but the two lived.

After hours of this parboiling the rain slackened, and, as the clouds parted, Eastwood caught a glimpse of a familiar form halfway up the heavens. It was the sun, the old sun, looking small and watery.

But the intense heat and brightness told that the enormous body still blazed behind the clouds. The rain seemed to have ceased definitely, and the hard, shining whiteness of the sky grew rapidly hotter.

The heat of the air increased to an oven-like degree; the mists were dissipated, the clouds licked up, and the earth seemed to dry itself almost immediately. The heat from the two suns beat down simultaneously till it became a monstrous terror, unendurable.

An odor of smoke began to permeate the air; there was a dazzling shimmer over the streets, and great clouds of mist arose from the bay, but these appeared to evaporate before they could darken the sky.

The piled wreck of the building sheltered the two refugees from the direct rays of the new sun, now almost overhead, but not from the penetrating heat of the air. But the body will endure almost anything, short of tearing asunder, for a time at least; it is the finer mechanism of the nerves that suffers most.

Alice lay face down among the bricks, gasping and moaning. The blood hammered in Eastwood's brain, and the strangest mirages flickered before his eyes.

Alternately he lapsed into heavy stupors, and awoke to the agony of the day. In his lucid moments he reflected that this could not last long, and tried to remember what degree of heat would cause death.

Within an hour after the drenching rains he was feverishly thirsty, and the skin felt as if peeling from his whole body.

This fever and horror lasted until he forgot that he had ever known another state: but at last the west reddened, and the flaming sun went down. It left the familiar planet high in the heavens, and there was no darkness until the usual hour, though there was a slight lowering of the temperature.

But when night did come it brought life-giving coolness, and though the heat was still intense it seemed temperate by comparison. More than all, the kindly darkness seemed to set a limit to the cataclysmic disorders of the day.

"Ouf! This is heavenly!" said Eastwood, drawing long breaths and feeling mind and body revived in the gloom.

"It won't last long," replied Alice, and her voice sounded extraordinarily calm through the darkness. "The heat will come again when the new sun rises in a few hours."

"We might find some better place in the meanwhile—a deep cellar; or we might get into the subway," Eastwood suggested.

"It would be no use. Don't you understand? I have been thinking it all out. After this, the new sun will always shine, and we could not endure it even another day. The wave of heat is passing round the world as it revolves, and in a few hours the whole earth will be a burnt-up ball. Very likely we are the only people left alive in New York, or perhaps in America."

She seemed to have taken the intellectual initiative, and spoke with an assumption of authority that amazed him.

"But there must be others," said Eastwood, after thinking for a moment. "Other people have found sheltered places, or miners, or men underground."

"They would have been drowned by the rain. At any rate, there will be none left alive by tomorrow night.

"Think of it," she went on dreamily, "for a thousand years this wave of fire has been rushing toward us, while life has been going on so happily in the world, so unconscious that the world was doomed all the time. And now this is the end of life."

"I don't know," Eastwood said slowly. "It may be the end of human life, but there must be some forms that will survive—some micro-organisms perhaps capable of resisting high temperatures, if nothing higher. The seed of life will be left at any rate, and that is everything. Evolution will begin over again, producing new types to suit the changed conditions. I only wish I could see what creatures will be here in a few thousand years.

"But I can't realize it at all—this thing!" he cried passionately, after a pause. "Is it real? Or have we all gone mad? It seems too much like a bad dream."

The rain crashed down again as he spoke, and the earth steamed, though not with the dense reek of the day. For hours the waters roared and splashed against the earth in hot billows till the streets were foaming yellow rivers, dammed by the wreck of fallen buildings.

There was a continual rumble as earth and rock slid into the East River, and at last the Brooklyn Bridge collapsed with a thunderous crash and splash that made all Manhattan vibrate. A gigantic billow like a tidal wave swept up the river from its fall.

The downpour slackened and ceased soon after the moon began to shed an obscured but brilliant light through the clouds.

Presently the east commenced to grow luminous, and this time there could be no doubt as to what was coming.

Alice crept closer to the man as the gray light rose upon the watery air.

"Kiss me!" she whispered suddenly, throwing her arms around his neck. He could feel her trembling. "Say you love me; hold me in your arms. There is only an hour."

"Don't be afraid. Try to face it bravely," stammered Eastwood.

"I don't fear it—not death. But I have never lived. I have always been timid and wretched and afraid—afraid to speak—and I've almost wished for suffering and misery or anything rather than to be stupid and dumb and dead, the way I've always been.

"I've never dared to tell anyone what I was, what I wanted. I've been afraid all my life, but I'm not afraid now. I have never lived; I have never been happy; and now we must die together!"

It seemed to Eastwood the cry of the perishing world. He held her in his arms and kissed her wet, tremulous face that was strained to his.

The twilight was gone before they knew it. The sky was blue already, with crimson flakes mounting to the zenith, and the heat was growing once more intense.

"This is the end, Alice," said Eastwood, and his voice trembled.

She looked at him, her eyes shining with an unearthly softness and brilliancy, and turned her face to the east.

There, in crimson and orange, flamed the last dawn that human eyes would ever see.

Nightfall

Isaac Asimov

Isaac Asimov (b. 1920) was born in Petrovichi, Russia. When he was three, Asimov's family moved to New York, and his father opened a candy store. Asimov was a child prodigy, and graduated from high school when he was fifteen. In 1938, Asimov met the editor John W. Campbell, who would become Asimov's mentor, buying such early work as "Strange Playfellow (1940)," and "Nightfall (1940)." He graduated from Columbia in 1939, and obtained his Masters in 1941. Asimov received his Ph.D. in chemistry from Columbia in 1948. In 1959, his first collection, *I, Robot,* and his first novel, *Pebble in the Sky,* were released. Over the course of his career, Asimov has written over three hundred and fifty books ranging from science fiction (*Foundation,* 1951; *Foundation and Empire,* 1952; *End of Eternity,* 1955; *The Rest of the Robots,* 1964; *Nightfall and Other Stories,* 1969; *The Gods Themselves,* 1972; *The Bicentennial Man and Other Stories,* 1976; *Foundation's Edge,* 1982; *The Robots of Dawn,* 1983; *Foundation and Earth,* 1986) to mystery (*Tales of the Black Widowers,* 1974; *Casebook of the Black Widowers,* 1980) to humor (*Isacc Asimov's Treasury of Humor,* 1971; *Asimov's Sherlockian Limericks,* 1977) to science (*Realm of Algebra,* 1961; *The Genetic Code,* 1963; *Understanding Physics,* 1966; *Asimov's Guide to Science,* 1972; *A Choice of Catastrophes,* 1979). A resident of New York City, Asimov has taught at Boston University's School of Medicine since 1949.

"Nightfall" is one of the most famous science fiction stories ever written. It originally appeared in *Astounding* magazine.

"If the stars should appear one night in a thousand years, how would men believe and adore, and preserve for many generations the remembrance of the city of God?"

—Emerson

ATON 77, director of Saro University, thrust out a belligerent lower lip and glared at the young newspaperman in a hot fury.

Theremon 762 took that fury in his stride. In his earlier days, when his now widely syndicated column was only a mad idea in a cub reporter's mind, he had specialized in "impossible" interviews. It had cost him bruises, black eyes, and broken bones; but it had given him an ample supply of coolness and self-confidence.

So he lowered the outthrust hand that had been so pointedly ignored and calmly waited for the aged director to get over the worst. Astronomers were queer ducks, anyway, and if Aton's actions of the last two months meant anything, this same Aton was the queer-duckiest of the lot.

Aton 77 found his voice, and though it trembled with restrained emotion, the careful, somewhat pedantic phraseology, for which the famous astronomer was noted, did not abandon him.

"Sir," he said, "you display an infernal gall in coming to me with that impudent proposition of yours."

The husky telephotographer of the Observatory, Beenay 25, thrust a tongue's tip across dry lips and interposed nervously, "Now, sir, after all—"

The director turned to him and lifted a white eyebrow. "Do not interfere, Beenay. I will credit you with good intentions in bringing this man here; but I will tolerate no insubordination now."

Theremon decided it was time to take a part. "Director Aton, if you'll let me finish what I started saying, I think—"

"I don't believe, young man," retorted Aton, "that anything you could say now would count much as compared with your daily columns of these last two months. You have led a vast newspaper campaign against the efforts of myself and my colleagues to organize the world against the menace which it is now too late to avert. You have done your best with your highly personal attacks to make the staff of this Observatory objects of ridicule."

The director lifted a copy of the Saro City *Chronicle* from the table and shook it at Theremon furiously. "Even a person of your well-known impudence should have hesitated before coming to me with a request that he be allowed to cover today's events for his paper. Of all newsmen, you!"

Aton dashed the newspaper to the floor, strode to the window, and clasped his arms behind his back.

"You may leave," he snapped over his shoulder. He stared moodily out at the skyline where Gamma, the brightest of the planet's six suns, was setting. It had already faded and yellowed into the horizon mists, and Aton knew he would never see it again as a sane man.

He whirled. "No, wait, come here!" He gestured peremptorily. "I'll give you your story."

The newsman had made no motion to leave, and now he approached the old man slowly. Aton gestured outward. "Of the six suns, only Beta is left in the sky. Do you see it?"

The question was rather unnecessary. Beta was almost at zenith, its ruddy light flooding the landscape to an unusual orange as the brilliant rays of setting Gamma died. Beta was at aphelion. It was small; smaller than Theremon had ever seen it before, and for the moment it was undisputed ruler of Lagash's sky.

Lagash's own sun, Alpha, the one about which it revolved, was at the antipodes, as were the two distant companion pairs. The red dwarf Beta—Alpha's immediate companion—was alone, grimly alone.

Aton's upturned face flushed redly in the sunlight. "In just under four hours," he said, "civilization, as we know it, comes to an end. It will do so because, as you see, Beta is the only sun in the sky." He smiled grimly. "Print that! There'll be no one to read it."

"But if it turns out that four hours pass—and another four—and nothing happens?" asked Theremon softly.

"Don't let that worry you. Enough will happen."

"Granted! And *still*—if nothing happens?"

For a second time, Beenay 25 spoke. "Sir, I think you ought to listen to him."

Theremon said, "Put it to a vote, Director Aton."

There was a stir among the remaining five members of the Observatory staff, who till now had maintained an attitude of wary neutrality.

"That," stated Aton flatly, "is not necessary." He drew out his pocket watch. "Since your good friend, Beenay, insists so urgently, I will give you five minutes. Talk away."

"Good! Now, just what difference would it make if you allowed me to take down an eyewitness account of what's to come? If your prediction comes true, my presence won't hurt; for in that case my column would never be written. On the other hand, if nothing comes of it, you will just have to expect ridicule or worse. It would be wise to leave that ridicule to friendly hands."

Aton snorted. "Do you mean yours when you speak of friendly hands?"

"Certainly!" Theremon sat down and crossed his legs. "My columns may have been a little rough, but I gave you people the benefit of the doubt every time. After all, this is not the century to preach 'The end of the world is at hand' to Lagash. You have to understand that people don't believe the *Book of Revelations* anymore, and it annoys them to have scientists turn about-face and tell us the Cultists are right after all—"

"No such thing, young man," interrupted Aton. "While a great deal of our data has been supplied us by the Cult, our results contain none of the Cult's mysticism. Facts are facts, and the Cult's so-called mythology *has* certain facts behind it. We've exposed them and ripped away their mystery. I assure you that the Cult hates us now worse than you do."

"I don't hate you. I'm just trying to tell you that the public is in an ugly humor. They're angry."

Aton twisted his mouth in derision. "Let them be angry."

"Yes, but what about tomorrow?"

"There'll be no tomorrow!"

"But if there is. Say that there is—just to see what happens. That anger might take shape into something serious. After all, you know, business has taken a nosedive these last two months. Investors don't really believe the world is coming to an end, but just the same they're being cagy with their money until it's all over. Johnny Public doesn't believe you, either, but the new spring furniture might just as well wait a few months—just to make sure.

"You see the point. Just as soon as this is all over, the business interests will be after your hide. They'll say that if crackpots—begging your pardon—can upset the country's prosperity any time they want, simply by making some cockeyed prediction—it's up to the planet to prevent them. The sparks will fly, sir."

The director regarded the columnist sternly. "And just what were you proposing to do to help the situation?"

"Well"—Theremon grinned—"I was proposing to take charge of the publicity. I can handle things so that only the ridiculous side will show. It would be hard to stand, I admit, because I'd have to make you all out to be a bunch of gibbering idiots, but if I can get people laughing at you, they might forget to be angry. In return for that, all my publisher asks is an exclusive story."

Beenay nodded and burst out, "Sir, the rest of us think he's right. These last two months we've considered everything but the million-to-one chance that there is an error somewhere in our theory or in our calculations. We ought to take care of that, too."

There was a murmur of agreement from the men grouped about the table, and Aton's expression became that of one who found his mouth full of something bitter and couldn't get rid of it.

"You may stay if you wish, then. You will kindly refrain, however, from hampering us in our duties in any way. You will also remember that I am in charge of all activities here, and in spite of your opinions as expressed in your columns, I will expect full cooperation and full respect—"

His hands were behind his back, and his wrinkled face thrust forward determinedly as he spoke. He might have continued indefinitely but for the intrusion of a new voice.

"Hello, hello, hello!" It came in a high tenor, and the plump cheeks of the newcomer expanded in a pleased smile. "What's this morgue-like atmosphere about here? No one's losing his nerve, I hope."

Aton started in consternation and said peevishly, "Now what the devil are you doing here, Sheerin? I thought you were going to stay behind in the Hideout."

Sheerin laughed and dropped his tubby figure into a chair. "Hideout be blowed! The place bored me. I wanted to be here, where things are getting hot. Don't you suppose I have my share of curiosity? I want to see these Stars the Cultists are forever speaking about." He rubbed his hands and added in a soberer tone, "It's freezing outside. The wind's enough to hang icicles on your nose. Beta doesn't seem to give any heat at all, at the distance it is."

The white-haired director ground his teeth in sudden exasperation. "Why do you go out of your way to do crazy things, Sheerin? What kind of good are you around here?"

"What kind of good am I around there?" Sheerin spread his palms in comical resignation. "A psychologist isn't worth his salt in the Hideout. They need men of action and strong, healthy women that can breed children. Me? I'm a hundred pounds too heavy for a man of action, and I wouldn't be a success at breeding children. So why bother them with an extra mouth to feed? I feel better over here."

Theremon spoke briskly. "Just what is the Hideout, sir?"

Sheerin seemed to see the columnist for the first time. He frowned and blew his ample cheeks out. "And just who in Lagash are you, redhead?"

Aton compressed his lips and then muttered sullenly, "That's Theremon 762, the newspaper fellow. I suppose you've heard of him."

The columnist offered his hand. "And, of course, you're Sheerin 501 of Saro University. I've heard of you." Then he repeated, "What is this Hideout, sir?"

"Well," said Sheerin, "we have managed to convince a few people of the validity of our prophecy of—er—doom, to be spectacular about it, and those few have taken proper measures. They consist mainly of the immediate members of the families of the Observatory staff, certain of the faculty of Saro University, and a few outsiders. Altogether, they number about three hundred, but three quarters are women and children."

"I see! They're supposed to hide where the Darkness and the—er—Stars can't get at them, and then hold out when the rest of the world goes poof."

"If they can. It won't be easy. With all of mankind insane, with the great cities going up in flames—environment will not be conducive to survival. But they have food, water, shelter, and weapons—"

"They've got more," said Aton. "They've got all our records, except for what we will collect today. Those records will mean everything to the next cycle, and *that's* what must survive. The rest can go hang."

Theremon uttered a long, low whistle and sat brooding for several minutes. The men about the table had brought out a multi-chess board and started a six-member game. Moves were made rapidly and in silence. All eyes bent in furious concentration on the board. Theremon watched them intently and then rose and approached Aton, who sat apart in whispered conversation with Sheerin.

"Listen," he said, "let's go somewhere where we won't bother the rest of the fellows. I want to ask some questions."

The aged astronomer frowned sourly at him, but Sheerin chirped up, "Certainly. It will do me good to talk. It always does. Aton was telling me about your ideas concerning world reaction to a failure of the prediction—and I agree with you. I read your column pretty regularly, by the way, and as a general thing I like your views."

"Please, Sheerin," growled Aton.

"Eh? Oh, all right. We'll go into the next room. It has softer chairs, anyway."

There were softer chairs in the next room. There were also thick red curtains on the windows and a maroon carpet on the floor. With the bricky light of Beta pouring in, the general effect was one of dried blood.

Theremon shuddered. "Say, I'd give ten credits for a decent dose of white light for just a second. I wish Gamma or Delta were in the sky."

"What are your questions?" asked Aton. "Please remember that our time is limited. In a little over an hour and a quarter we're going upstairs, and after that there will be no time for talk."

"Well, here it is." Theremon leaned back and folded his hands on his chest. "You people seem so all-fired serious about this that I'm beginning to believe you. Would you mind explaining what it's all about?"

Aton exploded, "Do you mean to sit there and tell me that you've been bombarding us with ridicule without even finding out what we've been trying to say?"

The columnist grinned sheepishly. "It's not that bad, sir. I've got the general idea. You say there is going to be a world-wide Darkness in a few hours and that all mankind will go violently insane. What I want now is the science behind it."

"No, you don't. No, you don't," broke in Sheerin. "If you ask Aton for that—supposing him to be in the mood to answer at all—he'll trot out pages of figures and volumes of graphs. You won't make head or tail of it. Now if you were to ask me, I could give you the layman's standpoint."

"All right; I ask you."

"Then first I'd like a drink." He rubbed his hands and looked at Aton.

"Water?" grunted Aton.

"Don't be silly!"

"Don't you be silly. No alcohol today. It would be too easy to get my men drunk. I can't afford to tempt them."

The psychologist grumbled wordlessly. He turned to Theremon, impaled him with his sharp eyes, and began.

"You realize, of course, that the history of civilization on Lagash displays a cyclic character—but I mean, *cyclic*!"

"I know," replied Theremon cautiously, "that that is the current archaeological theory. Has it been accepted as a fact?"

"Just about. In this last century it's been generally agreed upon. This cyclic character is—or rather, was—one of the great mysteries. We've located series of civilizations, nine of them definitely, and indications of others as well, all of which have reached heights comparable to our own, and all of which, without exception, were destroyed by fire at the very height of their culture.

"And no one could tell why. All centers of culture were thoroughly gutted by fire, with nothing left behind to give a hint as to the cause."

Theremon was following closely. "Wasn't there a Stone Age, too?"

"Probably, but as yet practically nothing is known of it, except that men of that age were little more than rather intelligent apes. We can forget about that."

"I see. Go on!"

"There have been explanations of these recurrent catastrophes, all of a more or less fantastic nature. Some say that there are periodic rains of fire; some that Lagash passes through a sun every so often; some even wilder things. But there is one theory, quite different from all of these, that has been handed down over a period of centuries."

"I know. You mean this myth of the 'Stars' that the Cultists have in their *Book of Revelations.*"

"Exactly," rejoined Sheerin with satisfaction. "The Cultists said that every two thousand and fifty years Lagash entered a huge cave, so that all the suns disappeared, and there came *total darkness all over the world*! And then, they say, things called Stars appeared, which robbed men of their souls and left them unreasoning brutes, so that they destroyed the civilization they themselves had built up. Of course they mix all this up with a lot of religio-mystic notions, but that's the central idea."

There was a short pause in which Sheerin drew a long breath. "And now we come to the Theory of Universal Gravitation." He pronounced the phrase so that the capital letters sounded—and at that point Aton turned from the window, snorted loudly, and stalked out of the room.

The two stared after him, and Theremon said, "What's wrong?"

"Nothing in particular," replied Sheerin. "Two of the men were due several hours ago and haven't shown up yet. He's terrifically short-handed, of course, because all but the really essential men have gone to the Hideout."

"You don't think the two deserted, do you?"

"Who? Faro and Yimot? Of course not. Still, if they're not back within the hour, things would be a little sticky." He got to his feet suddenly, and his eyes twinkled. "Anyway, as long as Aton is gone—"

Tiptoeing to the nearest window, he squatted, and from the low window box beneath withdrew a bottle of red liquid that gurgled suggestively when he shook it.

"I *thought* Aton didn't know about this," he remarked as he trotted back to the table. "Here! We've only got one glass so, as the guest, you can have it. I'll keep the bottle." And he filled the tiny cup with judicious care.

Theremon rose to protest, but Sheerin eyed him sternly. "Respect your elders, young man."

The newsman seated himself with a look of anguish on his face. "Go ahead, then, you old villain."

The psychologist's Adam's apple wobbled as the bottle upended, and then, with a satisfied grunt and a smack of the lips, he began again. "But what do you know about gravitation?"

"Nothing, except that it is a very recent development, not too well established, and that the math is so hard that only twelve men in Lagash are supposed to understand it."

"*Tcha*! Nonsense! Baloney! I can give you all the essential math in a sentence. The Law of Universal Gravitation states that there exists a cohesive force among all bodies of the universe, such that the amount of this force between any two given bodies is proportional to the product of their masses divided by the square of the distance between them."

"Is that all?"

"That's enough! It took four hundred years to develop it."

"Why that long? It sounded simple enough, the way you said it."

"Because great laws are not divined by flashes of inspiration, whatever you may think. It usually takes the combined work of a world full of scientists over a period of centuries. After Genovi 41 discovered that Lagash rotated about the sun Alpha rather than vice versa—and that was four hundred years ago—astronomers have been working. The complex motions of the six suns were recorded and analyzed and unwoven. Theory after theory was advanced and checked and counterchecked and modified and abandoned and revived and converted to something else. It was a devil of a job."

Theremon nodded thoughtfully and held out his glass for more liquor. Sheerin grudgingly allowed a few ruby drops to leave the bottle.

"It was twenty years ago," he continued after remoistening his own throat, "that it was finally demonstrated that the Law of Universal Gravitation accounted exactly for the orbital motions of the six suns. It was a great triumph."

Sheerin stood up and walked to the window, still clutching his bottle. "And now we're getting to the point. In the last decade, the motions of Lagash about Alpha were computed according to Gravity and *it did not account for the orbit observed*; not even when all perturbations due to the other suns were included. Either the law was invalid, or there was another, as yet unknown, factor involved."

Theremon joined Sheerin at the window and gazed out past the wooded slopes to where the spires of Saro City gleamed bloodily on the horizon. The newsman felt the tension of uncertainty grow within him as he cast a short glance at Beta. It glowered redly at zenith, dwarfed and evil.

"Go ahead, sir," he said softly.

Sheerin replied, "Astronomers stumbled about for years, each proposed theory more untenable than the one before—until Aton had the inspiration of calling in the Cult. The head of the Cult, Sor 5, had access to certain data that simplified the problem considerably. Aton set to work on a new track.

"What if there were another nonluminous planetary body such as Lagash? If there were, you know, it would shine only by reflected light, and if it were composed of bluish rock, as Lagash itself largely is, then, in the redness of the sky, the eternal blaze of the suns would make it invisible—drown it out completely."

Theremon whistled. "What a screwy idea!"

"You think *that's* screwy? Listen to this: Suppose this body rotated about Lagash at such a distance and in such an orbit and had such a mass that its attraction would exactly account for the deviations of Lagash's orbit from theory—do you know what would happen?"

The columnist shook his head.

"Well, sometimes this body would get in the way of a sun." And Sheerin emptied what remained in the bottle at a draft.

"And it does, I suppose," said Theremon flatly.

"Yes! But only one sun lies in its plane of revolution." He jerked a thumb at the shrunken sun above. "Beta! And it has been shown that the eclipse will occur only when the arrangement of the suns is such that Beta is alone in its hemisphere and at maximum distance, at which time the moon is invariably at minimum distance. The eclipse that results, with the moon seven times the apparent diameter of Beta, covers all of Lagash and lasts well over half a day, so that no spot on the planet escapes the effects. *That eclipse comes once every two thousand and forty-nine years.*"

Theremon's face was drawn into an expressionless mask. "And that's my story?"

The psychologist nodded. "That's all of it. First the eclipse—which will start in three quarters of an hour—then univesal Darkness and, maybe, these mysterious Stars—then madness, and end of the cycle."

He brooded. "We had two months' leeway—we at the Observatory—and that wasn't enough time to persuade Lagash of the danger. Two centuries might not have been enough. But our records are at the Hideout, and today we photograph the eclipse. The next cycle will *start off* with the truth, and when the *next* eclipse comes, mankind will at last be ready for it. Come to think of it, that's part of your story too."

A thin wind ruffled the curtains at the window as Theremon opened it and leaned out. It played coldly with his hair as he stared at the crimson sunlight on his hand. Then he turned in sudden rebellion.

"What is there in Darkness to drive *me* mad?"

Sheerin smiled to himself as he spun the empty liquor bottle with abstracted motions of his hand. "Have you ever experienced Darkness, young man?"

The newsman leaned against the wall and considered. "No. Can't say I have. But I know what it is. Just—uh—" He made vague motions with his fingers and then brightened. "Just no light. Like in caves."

"Have you ever been in a cave?"

"In a *cave*! Of course not!"

"I thought not. I tried last week—just to see—but I got out in a hurry. I went in until the mouth of the cave was just visible as a blur of light, with black everywhere else. I never thought a person my weight could run that fast."

Theremon's lip curled. "Well, if it comes to that, I guess I wouldn't have run if I had been there."

The psychologist studied the young man with an annoyed frown.

"My, don't you talk big! I dare you to draw the curtain."

Theremon looked his surprise and said, "What for? If we had four or five suns out there, we might want to cut the light down a bit for comfort, but now we haven't enough light as it is."

"That's the point. Just draw the curtain; then come here and sit down."

"All right." Theremon reached for the tasseled string and jerked. The red curtain slid across the wide window, the brass rings hissing their way along the crossbar, and a dusk-red shadow clamped down on the room.

Theremon's footsteps sounded hollowly in the silence as he made his way to the table, and then they stopped halfway. "I can't see you, sir," he whispered.

"Feel your way," ordered Sheerin in a strained voice.

"But I can't see you, sir." The newsman was breathing harshly. "I can't see anything."

"What did you expect?" came the grim reply. "Come here and sit down!"

The footsteps sounded again, waveringly, approaching slowly. There was the sound of someone fumbling with a chair. Theremon's voice came thinly, "Here I am. I feel...*ulp*...all right."

"You like it, do you?"

"N—no. It's pretty awful. The walls seem to be—" He paused. "They seem to be closing in on me. I keep wanting to push them away. But I'm not going *mad*! In fact, the feeling isn't as bad as it was."

"All right. Draw the curtain back again."

There were cautious footsteps through the dark, the rustle of Theremon's body against the curtain as he felt for the tassel, and then the triumphant *ro-o-osh* of the curtain slithering back. Red light flooded the room, and with a cry of joy Theremon looked up at the sun.

Sheerin wiped the moistness off his forehead with the back of a hand and said shakily, "And that was just a dark room."

"It can be stood," said Theremon lightly.

"Yes, a dark room can. But were you at the Jonglor Centennial Exposition two years ago?"

"No, it so happens I never got around to it. Six thousand miles was just a bit too much to travel, even for the exposition."

"Well, I was there. You remember hearing about the 'Tunnel of Mystery' that broke all records in the amusement area—for the first month or so, anyway?"

"Yes. Wasn't there some fuss about it?"

"Very little. It was hushed up. You see, that Tunnel of Mystery was just a mile-long tunnel—with no lights. You got into a little open car and jolted along through Darkness for fifteen minutes. It was very popular—while it lasted."

"Popular?"

"Certainly. There's a fascination in being frightened *when it's part of a game.* A baby is born with three instinctive fears: of loud noises, of falling, and of the absence of light. That's why it's considered so funny to jump at someone and shout 'Boo!' That's why it's such fun to ride a roller coaster. And that's why that Tunnel of Mystery started cleaning up. People came out of that Darkness shaking, breathless, half dead with fear, but they kept on paying to get in."

"Wait a while, I remember now. Some people came out dead, didn't they? There were rumors of that after it shut down."

The psychologist snorted. "Bah! Two or three died. That was nothing! They paid off the families of the dead ones and argued the Jonglor City Council into forgetting it. After all, they said, if people with weak hearts want to go through the tunnel, it was at their own risk—and besides, it wouldn't happen again. So they put a doctor in the front office and had every customer go through a physical examination before getting into the car. That actually *boosted* ticket sales."

"Well, then?"

"But you see, there was something else. People sometimes came out in perfect order, except that they refused to go into buildings—any buildings; including palaces, mansions, apartment houses, tenements, cottages, huts, shacks, lean-tos, and tents."

Theremon looked shocked. "You mean they refused to come in out of the open? Where'd they sleep?"

"In the open."

"They should have *forced* them inside."

"Oh, they did, they did. Whereupon these people went into violent hysterics and did their best to bat their brains out against the nearest wall. Once you got them inside, you couldn't keep them there without a strait jacket or a heavy dose of tranquilizer.

"They must have been crazy."

"Which is exactly what they were. One person out of every ten who went into that tunnel came out that way. They called in the psychologists, and we did the only thing possible. We closed down the exhibit." He spread his hands.

"What was the matter with these people?" asked Theremon finally.

"Essentially the same thing that was the matter with you when you thought the walls of the room were crushing in on you in the dark. There is a psychological term for mankind's instinctive fear of the absence of light. We call it 'claustrophobia,' because the lack of light is always tied up with enclosed places, so that fear of one is fear of the other. You see?"

"And those people of the tunnel?"

"Those people of the tunnel consisted of those unfortunates whose mentality did not quite possess the resiliency to overcome the claustrophobia that overtook them in the Darkness. Fifteen minutes without light is a long time; you only had two or three minutes, and I believe you were fairly upset.

"The people of the tunnel had what is called a 'claustrophobic fixation.' Their latent fear of Darkness and enclosed places had crystalized and become active, and, as far as we can tell, permanent. That's what fifteen minutes in the dark will do."

There was a long silence, and Theremon's forehead wrinkled slowly into a frown. "I don't believe it's that bad."

"You mean you don't want to believe," snapped Sheerin. "You're afraid to believe. Look out the window!"

Theremon did so, and the psychologist continued without pausing. "Imagine Darkness—everywhere. No light, as far as you can see. The houses, the trees, the fields, the earth, the sky—black! And Stars thrown in, for all I know—whatever *they* are. Can you conceive it?"

"Yes, I can," declared Theremon truculently.

And Sheerin slammed his fist down upon the table in sudden passion. "You lie! You can't conceive that. Your brain wasn't built for the conception any more than it was built for the conception of infinity or of eternity. You can only talk about it. A fraction of the reality upsets you, and when the real thing comes, your brain is going to be presented with the phenomenon outside its limits of comprehension. You will go mad, completely and permanently! There is no question of it!"

He added sadly, "And another couple of millennia of painful struggle comes to nothing. Tomorrow there won't be a city standing unharmed in all Lagash."

Theremon recovered part of his mental equilibrium. "That doesn't follow. I still don't see that I can go loony just because there isn't a sun in the sky—but even if I did, and everyone else did, how does that harm the cities? Are we going to blow them down?"

But Sheerin was angry, too. "If you were in Darkness, what would you want more than anything else; what would it be that every instinct would call for? Light, damn you, *light*!"

"Well?"

"And how would you get light?"

"I don't know," said Theremon flatly.

"What's the *only* way to get light, short of a sun?"

"How should I know?"

They were standing face to face and nose to nose.

Sheerin said, "You burn something, mister. Ever see a forest fire? Ever go camping and cook a stew over a wood fire? Heat isn't the only thing burning wood gives off, you know. It gives off light, and people know that. And when it's dark they want light, and they're going to get it."

"So they burn wood?"

"So they burn whatever they can get. They've got to have light. They've got to burn something, and wood isn't handy—so they'll burn whatever is nearest. They'll have their light—and every center of habitation goes up in flames!"

Eyes held each other as though the whole matter were a personal affair of respective will powers, and then Theremon broke away wordlessly. His breathing was harsh and ragged, and he scarcely noted the sudden hubbub that came from the adjoining room behind the closed door.

Sheerin spoke, and it was with an effort that he made it sound matter-of-fact. "I think I heard Yimot's voice. He and Faro are probably back. Let's go in and see what kept them."

"Might as well!" muttered Theremon. He drew a long breath and seemed to shake himself. The tension was broken.

The room was in an uproar, with members of the staff clustering about two young men who were removing outer garments even as they parried the miscellany of questions being thrown at them.

Aton bustled through the crowd and faced the newcomers angrily. "Do you realize that it's less than half an hour before deadline? Where have you two been?"

Faro 24 seated himself and rubbed his hands. His cheeks were red with the outdoor chill. "Yimot and I have just finished carrying through a little crazy experiment of our own. We've been trying to see if we couldn't construct an arrangement by which we could simulate the appearance of Darkness and Stars so as to get an advance notion as to how it looked."

There was a confused murmur from the listeners, and a sudden look of interest entered Aton's eyes. "There wasn't anything said of this before. How did you go about it?"

"Well," said Faro, "the idea came to Yimot and myself long ago, and we've been working it out in our spare time. Yimot knew of a low one-story house down in the city with a domed roof—it had once been used as a museum, I think. Anyway, we bought it—"

"Where did you get the money?" interrupted Aton peremptorily.

"Our bank accounts," grunted Yimot 70. "It cost two thousand credits." Then, defensively, "Well, what of it? Tomorrow, two thousand credits will be two thousand pieces of paper. That's all."

"Sure," agreed Faro. "We bought the place and rigged it up with black velvet from top to bottom so as to get as perfect a Darkness as possible. Then we punched tiny holes in the ceiling and through the roof and covered them with little metal caps, all of which could be shoved aside simultaneously at the close of a switch. At least we didn't do that part ourselves; we got a carpenter and an electrician and some others—money didn't count. The point was that we could get the light to shine through those holes in the roof, so that we could get a starlike effect."

Not a breath was drawn during the pause that followed. Aton said stiffly, "You had no right to make a private—"

Faro seemed abashed. "I know, sir—but frankly, Yimot and I thought the experiment was a little dangerous. If the effect really worked, we half expected to go mad—from what Sheerin says about all this, we thought that would be rather likely. We wanted to take the risk ourselves. Of course if we found we could retain sanity, it occurred to us that we might develop immunity to the real thing, and then expose the rest of you the same way. But things didn't work out at all—"

"Why, what happened?"

It was Yimot who answered. "We shut ourselves in and allowed our eyes to get accustomed to the dark. It's an extremely creepy feeling because the total Darkness makes you feel as if the walls and ceiling are crushing in on you. But we got over that and pulled the switch. The caps fell away and the roof glittered all over with little dots of light—"

"Well?"

"Well—nothing. That was the whacky part of it. Nothing happened. It was just a roof with holes in it, and that's just what it looked like. We tried it over and over again—that's what kept us so late—but there just isn't any effect at all."

There followed a shocked silence, and all eyes turned to Sheerin, who sat motionless, mouth open.

Theremon was the first to speak. "You know what this does to this whole theory you've built up, Sheerin, don't you?" He was grinning with relief.

But Sheerin raised his hand. "Now wait a while. Just let me think this through." And then he snapped his fingers, and when he lifted his head there was neither surprise nor uncertainty in his eyes. "Of course—"

He never finished. From somewhere up above there sounded a sharp clang, and Beenay, starting to his feet, dashed up the stairs with a "What the devil!"

The rest followed after.

Things happened quickly. Once up in the dome, Beenay cast one horrified glance at the shattered photographic plates and at the man bending over them; and then hurled himself fiercely at the intruder, getting a death grip on his throat. There was a wild threshing, and as others of the staff joined in, the stranger was swallowed up and smothered under the weight of half a dozen angry men.

Aton came up last, breathing heavily. "Let him up!"

There was a reluctant unscrambling and the stranger, panting harshly, with his clothes torn and his forehead bruised, was hauled to his feet. He had a short yellow beard curled elaborately in the style affected by the Cultists.

Beenay shifted his hold to a collar grip and shook the man savagely. "All right, rat, what's the idea? These plates—"

"I wasn't after *them*," retorted the Cultist coldly. "That was an accident."

Beenay followed his glowering stare and snarled, "I see. You were after the cameras themselves. The accident with the plates was a stroke of luck for you, then. If you had touched Snapping Bertha or any of the others, you would have died by slow torture. As it is—" He drew his fist back.

Aton grabbed his sleeve. "Stop that! Let him go!"

The young technician wavered, and his arm dropped reluctantly. Aton pushed him aside and confronted the Cultist. "You're Latimer, aren't you?"

The Cultist bowed stiffly and indicated the symbol upon his hip. "I am Latimer 25, adjutant of the third class to his serenity, Sor 5."

"And"—Aton's white eyebrows lifted—"you were with his serenity when he visited me last week, weren't you?"

Latimer bowed a second time.

"Now, then, what do you want?"

"Nothing that you would give me of your own free will."

"Sor 5 sent you, I suppose—or is this your own idea?"

"I won't answer that question."

"Will there be any further visitors?"

"I won't answer that, either."

Aton glanced at his timepiece and scowled. "Now, man, what is it your master wants of me? I have fulfilled my end of the bargain."

Latimer smiled faintly, but said nothing.

"I asked him," continued Aton angrily, "for data only the Cult could supply, and it was given to me. For that, thank you. In return I promised to prove the essential truth of the creed of the Cult."

"There was no need to prove that," came the proud retort. "It stands proven by the *Book of Revelations*."

"For the handful that constitute the Cult, yes. Don't pretend to mistake my meaning. I offered to present scientific backing for your beliefs. And I did!"

The Cultist's eyes narrowed bitterly. "Yes, you did—with a fox's subtlety, for your pretended explanation backed our beliefs, and at the same time removed all necessity for them. You made of the Darkness and of the Stars a natural phenomenon and removed all its real significance. That was blasphemy."

"If so, the fault isn't mine. The facts exist. What can I do but state them?"

"Your 'facts' are a fraud and a delusion."

Aton stamped angrily. "How do you know?"

And the answer came with the certainty of absolute faith. "I know!"

The director purpled and Beenay whispered urgently. Aton waved him silent. "And what does Sor 5 want us to do? He still thinks, I suppose, that in trying to warn the world to take measures against the menace of madness, we are placing innumerable souls in jeopardy. We aren't succeeding, if that means anything to him."

"The attempt itself has done harm enough, and your vicious effort to gain information by means of your devilish instruments must be stopped. We obey the will of the Stars, and I only regret that my clumsiness prevented me from wrecking your infernal devices."

"It wouldn't have done you too much good," returned Aton. "All our data, except for the direct evidence we intend collecting right now, is already safely cached and well beyond possibility of harm." He smiled grimly. "But that does not affect your present status as an attempted burglar and criminal."

He turned to the men behind him. "Someone call the police at Saro City."

There was a cry of distaste from Sheerin. "Damn it, Aton, what's wrong with you? There's no time for that. Here"—he bustled his way forward—"let me handle this."

Aton stared down his nose at the psychologist. "This is not the time for your monkeyshines, Sheerin. Will you please let me handle this my own way? Right now you are a complete outsider here, and don't forget it."

Sheerin's mouth twisted eloquently. "Now why should we go to the impossible trouble of calling the police—with Beta's eclipse a matter of minutes from now—when this young man here is perfectly willing to pledge his word of honor to remain and cause no trouble whatsoever?"

The Cultist answered promptly, "I will do no such thing. You're free to do what you want, but it's only fair to warn you that just as soon as I get my chance I'm going to finish what I came out here to do. If it's my word of honor you're relying on, you'd better call the police."

Sheerin smiled in a friendly fashion. "You're a determined cuss, aren't you? Well, I'll explain something. Do you see that young man at the window? He's a strong, husky fellow, quite handy with his fists, and he's an outsider besides. Once the eclipse starts there will be nothing for him to do except keep an eye on you. Besides him, there will be myself—a little too stout for active fisticuffs, but still able to help."

"Well, what of it?" demanded Latimer frozenly.

"Listen and I'll tell you," was the reply. "Just as soon as the eclipse starts, we're going to take you, Theremon and I, and deposit you in a little closet with one door, to which is attached one giant lock and no windows. You will remain there for the duration."

"And afterward," breathed Latimer fiercely, "there'll be no one to let me out. I know as well as you do what the coming of the Stars means—I know it far better than you. With all your minds gone, you are not likely to free me. Suffocation or slow starvation, is it? About what I might have expected from a group of scientists. But I don't give my word. It's a matter of principle, and I won't discuss it further."

Aton seemed perturbed. His faded eyes were troubled. "Really, Sheerin, locking him—"

"Please!" Sheerin motioned him impatiently to silence. "I don't think for a moment things will go that far. Latimer has just tried a clever little bluff, but I'm not a psychologist just because I like the sound of the word." He grinned at the Cultist. "Come now, you don't really think I'm trying anything as crude as slow starvation. My dear Latimer, if I lock you in the closet, you are not going to see the Darkness, and you are not going to see the Stars. It does not take much knowledge of the fundamental creed of the Cult to realize that for you to be hidden from the Stars when they appear means the loss of your immortal soul. Now, I believe you to be an honorable man. I'll accept your word of honor to make no further effort to disrupt proceedings, if you'll offer it."

A vein throbbed in Latimer's temple, and he seemed to shrink within himself as he said thickly, "You have it!" And then he added with swift fury, "But it is my consolation that you will all be damned for your deeds of today." He turned on his heel and stalked to the high three-legged stool by the door.

Sheerin nodded to the columnist. "Take a seat next to him, Theremon—just as a formality. Hey, Theremon!"

But the newspaperman didn't move. He had gone pale to the lips. "Look at that!" The finger he pointed toward the sky shook, and his voice was dry and cracked.

There was one simultaneous gasp as every eye followed the pointing finger and, for one breathless moment, stared frozenly.

Beta was chipped on one side!

The tiny bit of encroaching blackness was perhaps the width of a fingernail, but to the staring watchers it magnified itself into the crack of doom.

Only for a moment they watched, and after that there was a shrieking confusion that was even shorter of duration and which gave way to an orderly scurry of activity—each man at his prescribed job. At the crucial moment there was no time for emotion. The men were merely scientists with work to do. Even Aton had melted away.

Sheerin said prosaically, "First contact must have been made fifteen minutes ago. A little early, but pretty good considering the uncertainties involved in the calculation." He looked about him and then tiptoed to Theremon, who still remained staring out the window, and dragged him away gently.

"Aton is furious," he whispered, "so stay away. He missed first contact on account of this fuss with Latimer, and if you get in his way he'll have you thrown out the window."

Theremon nodded shortly and sat down. Sheerin stared in surprise at him.

"The devil, man," he exclaimed, "you're shaking."

"Eh?" Theremon licked dry lips and then tried to smile. "I don't feel very well, and that's a fact."

The psychologist's eyes hardened. "You're not losing your nerve?"

"No!" cried Theremon in a flash of indignation. "Give me a chance, will you? I haven't really believed this rigmarole—not way down beneath, anyway—till just this minute. Give me a chance to get used to the idea. You've been preparing yourself for two months or more."

"You're right, at that," replied Sheerin thoughtfully. "Listen! Have you got a family—parents, wife, children?"

Theremon shook his head. "You mean the Hideout, I suppose. No, you don't have to worry about that. I have a sister, but she's two thousand miles away. I don't even know her exact address."

"Well, then, what about yourself? You've got time to get there, and they're one short anyway, since I left. After all, you're not needed here, and you'd make a darned fine addition—"

Theremon looked at the other wearily. "You think I'm scared stiff, don't you? Well, get this, mister, I'm a newspaperman and I've been assigned to cover a story. I intend covering it."

There was a faint smile on the psychologist's face. "I see. Professional honor, is that it?"

"You might call it that. But, man, I'd give my right arm for another bottle of that sockeroo juice even half the size of the one you hogged. If ever a fellow needed a drink, I do."

He broke off. Sheerin was nudging him violently. "Do you hear that? Listen!"

Theremon followed the motion of the other's chin and stared at the Cultist, who, oblivious to all about him, faced the window, a look of wild elation on his face, droning to himself the while in singsong fashion.

"What's he saying?" whispered the columnist.

"He's quoting *Book of Revelations*, fifth chapter," replied Sheerin. Then, urgently, "Keep quiet and listen, I tell you."

The Cultist's voice had risen in a sudden increase of fervor: "'And it came to pass that in those days the Sun, Beta, held lone vigil in the sky for ever longer periods as the revolutions passed; until such time as for full half a revolution, it alone, shrunken and cold, shone down upon Lagash.

"'And men did assemble in the public squares and in the highways, there to debate and to marvel at the sight, for a strange depression had seized them. Their minds were troubled and their speech confused, for the souls of men awaited the coming of the Stars.

"'And in the city of Trigon, at high noon, Vendret 2 came forth and said unto the men of Trigon, "Lo, ye sinners! Though ye scorn the ways of righteousness, yet will the time of reckoning come. Even now the Cave approaches to swallow Lagash; yea, and all it contains."

"'And even as he spoke the lip of the Cave of Darkness passed the edge of Beta so that to all Lagash it was hidden from sight. Loud were the cries of men as it vanished, and great the fear of soul that fell upon them.

"'It came to pass that the Darkness of the Cave fell upon Lagash, and there was no light on all the surface of Lagash. Men were even as blinded, nor could one man see his neighbor, though he felt his breath upon his face.

"'And in this blackness there appeared the Stars, in countless numbers, and to the strains of music of such beauty that the very leaves of the trees cried out in wonder.

"'And in that moment the souls of men departed from them, and their abandoned bodies became even as beasts; yea, even as brutes of the wild; so that through the blackened streets of the cities of Lagash they prowled with wild cries.

"'From the Stars there then reached down the Heavenly Flame, and where it touched, the cities of Lagash flamed to utter destruction, so that of man and of the works of man nought remained.

"'Even then—'"

There was a subtle change in Latimer's tone. His eyes had not shifted, but somehow he had become aware of the absorbed attention of the other two. Easily, without pausing for breath, the timbre of his voice shifted and the syllables became more liquid.

Theremon, caught by surprise, stared. The words seemed on the border of familiarity. There was an elusive shift in the accent, a tiny change in the vowel stress; nothing more—yet Latimer had become thoroughly unintelligible.

Sheerin smiled slyly. "He shifted to some old-cycle tongue, probably their traditional second cycle. That was the language in which the *Book of Revelations* was originally written, you know."

"It doesn't matter; I've heard enough." Theremon shoved his chair back and brushed his hair back with hands that no longer shook. "I feel much better now."

"You do?" Sheerin seemed mildly surprised.

"I'll say I do. I had a bad case of jitters just a while back. Listening to you and your gravitation and seeing that eclipse start almost finished me. But this"—he jerked a contemptuous thumb at the yellow-bearded Cultist—"*this* is the sort of thing my nurse used to tell me. I've been laughing at that sort of thing all my life. I'm not going to let it scare me *now*."

He drew a deep breath and said with a hectic gaiety, "But if I expect to keep on the good side of myself, I'm going to turn my chair away from the window."

Sheerin said, "Yes, but you'd better talk lower. Aton just lifted his head out of that box he's got it stuck into and gave you a look that should have killed you."

Theremon made a mouth. "I forgot about the old fellow." With elaborate care he turned the chair from the window, cast one distasteful look over his shoulder, and said, "It has occurred to me that there must be considerable immunity against this Star madness."

The psychologist did not answer immediately. Beta was past its zenith now, and the square of bloody sunlight that outlined the window upon the floor had lifted into Sheerin's lap. He stared at its dusky color thoughtfully and then bent and squinted into the sun itself.

The chip in its side had grown to a black encroachment that covered a third of Beta. He shuddered, and when he straightened once more his florid cheeks did not contain quite as much color as they had had previously.

With a smile that was almost apologetic, he reversed his chair also. "There are probably two million people in Saro City that are all trying to join the Cult at once in one gigantic revival." Then, ironically, "The Cult is in for an hour of unexampled prosperity. I trust they'll make the most of it. Now, what was it you said?"

"Just this. How did the Cultists manage to keep the *Book of Revelations* going from cycle to cycle, and how on Lagash did it get written in the first place? There must have been some sort of immunity, for if everyone had gone mad, who would be left to write the book?"

Sheerin stared at his questioner ruefully. "Well, now, young man, there isn't any eyewitness answer to that, but we've got a few damned good notions as to what happened. You see, there are three kinds of people who might remain relatively unaffected. First, the very few who don't see the Stars at all: the seriously retarded or those who drink themselves into a stupor at the beginning of the eclipse and remain so to the end. We leave them out—because they aren't really witnesses.

"Then there are children below six, to whom the world as a whole is too new and strange for them to be too frightened at Stars and Darkness. They would be just another item in an already surprising world. You see that, don't you?"

The other nodded doubtfully. "I suppose so."

"Lastly, there are those whose minds are too coarsely grained to be entirely toppled. The very insensitive would be scarcely affected—oh, such people as some of our older, work-broken peasants. Well, the children would have fugitive memories, and that, combined with the confused, incoherent babblings of the half-mad morons, formed the basis for the *Book of Revelations.*

"Naturally, the book was based, in the first place, on the testimony of those least qualified to serve as historians; that is, children and morons; and was probably edited and re-edited through the cycles."

"Do you suppose," broke in Theremon, "that they carried the book through the cycles the way we're planning on handing on the secret of gravitation?"

Sheerin shrugged. "Perhaps, but their exact method is unimportant. They do it, somehow. The point I was getting at was that the book can't help but be a mass of distortion, even if it is based on fact. For instance, do you remember the experiment with the holes in the roof that Faro and Yimot tried—the one that didn't work?"

"Yes."

"You know why it didn't w—" He stopped and rose in alarm, for Aton was approaching, his face a twisted mask of consternation.

"What's happened?"

Aton drew him aside and Sheerin could feel the fingers on his elbow twitching.

"Not so loud!" Aton's voice was low and tortured. "I've just gotten word from the Hideout on the private line."

Sheerin broke in anxiously. "They are in trouble?"

"Not *they*." Aton stressed the pronoun significantly. "They sealed themselves off just a while ago, and they're going to stay buried till day after tomorrow. They're safe. But the *city*, Sheerin—it's a shambles. You have no idea—" He was having difficulty in speaking.

"Well?" snapped Sheerin impatiently. "What of it? It will get worse. What are you shaking about?" Then, suspiciously, "How do you feel?"

Aton's eyes sparked angrily at the insinuation, and then faded to anxiety once more. "You don't understand. The Cultists are active. They're rousing the people to storm the Observatory—promising them immediate entrance into grace, promising them salvation, promising them anything. What are we to do, Sheerin?"

Sheerin's head bent, and he stared in long abstraction at his toes. He tapped his chin with one knuckle, then looked up and said crisply, "Do? What is there to do? Nothing at all. Do the men know of this?"

"No, of course not!"

"Good! Keep it that way. How long till totality?"

"Not quite an hour."

"There's nothing to do but gamble. It will take time to organize any really formidable mob, and it will take more time to get them out here. We're a good five miles from the city—"

He glared out the window, down the slopes to where the farmed patches gave way to clumps of white houses in the suburbs; down to where the metropolis itself was a blur on the horizon—a mist in the waning blaze of Beta.

He repeated without turning, "It will take time. Keep on working and pray that totality comes first."

Beta was cut in half, the line of division pushing a slight concavity into the still-bright portion of the Sun. It was like a gigantic eyelid shutting slantwise over the light of a world.

The faint clatter of the room in which he stood faded into oblivion, and he sensed only the thick silence of the fields outside. The very insects seemed frightened mute. And things were dim.

He jumped at the voice in his ear. Theremon said, "Is something wrong?"

"Eh? Er—no. Get back to the chair. We're in the way." They slipped back to their corner, but the psychologist did not speak for a time. He lifted a finger and loosened his collar. He twisted his neck back and forth but found no relief. He looked up suddenly.

"Are you having any difficulty in breathing?"

The newspaperman opened his eyes wide and drew two or three long breaths. "No. Why?"

"I looked out the window too long, I suppose. The dimness got me. Difficulty in breathing is one of the first symptoms of a claustrophobic attack."

Theremon drew another long breath. "Well, it hasn't got me yet. Say, here's another of the fellows."

Beenay had interposed his bulk between the light and the pair in the corner, and Sheerin squinted up at him anxiously. "Hello, Beenay."

The astronomer shifted his weight to the other foot and smiled feebly. "You won't mind if I sit down awhile and join in the talk? My cameras are set, and there's nothing to do till totality." He paused and eyed the Cultist, who fifteen minutes earlier had drawn a small, skin-bound book from his sleeve and had been poring intently over it ever since. "That rat hasn't been making trouble, has he?"

Sheerin shook his head. His shoulders were thrown back and he frowned his concentration as he forced himself to breathe regularly. He said, "Have you had any trouble breathing, Beenay?"

Beenay sniffed the air in his turn. "It doesn't seem stuffy to me."

"A touch of claustrophobia," explained Sheerin apologetically.

"Ohhh! It worked itself differently with me. I get the impression that my eyes are going back on me. Things seem to blur and—well, nothing is clear. And it's cold, too."

"Oh, it's cold, all right. That's no illusion." Theremon grimaced. "My toes feel as if I've been shipping them cross-country in a refrigerating car."

"What we need," put in Sheerin, "is to keep our minds busy with extraneous affairs. I was telling you a while ago, Theremon, why Faro's experiments with the holes in the roof came to nothing."

"You were just beginning," replied Theremon. He encircled a knee with both arms and nuzzled his chin against it.

"Well, as I started to say, they were misled by taking the *Book of Revelations* literally. There probably wasn't any sense in attaching any physical significance to the Stars. It might be, you know, that in the presence of total Darkness, the mind finds it absolutely necessary to create light. This illusion of light might be all the Stars there really are."

"In other words," interposed Theremon, "you mean the Stars are the results of the madness and not one of the causes. Then, what good will Beenay's photographs be?"

"To prove that it is an illusion, maybe; or to prove the opposite; for all I know. Then again—"

But Beenay had drawn his chair closer, and there was an expression of sudden enthusiasm on his face. "Say, I'm glad you two got onto this subject." His eyes narrowed and he lifted one finger. "I've been thinking about these Stars and I've got a really cute notion. Of course it's strictly ocean foam, and I'm not trying to advance it seriously, but I think it's interesting. Do you want to hear it?"

He seemed half reluctant, but Sheerin leaned back and said, "Go ahead! I'm listening."

"Well, then, supposing there were other suns in the universe." He broke off a little bashfully. "I mean suns that are so far away that they're too dim to see. It sounds as if I've been reading some of that fantastic fiction, I suppose."

"Not necessarily. Still, isn't that possibility eliminated by the fact that, according to the Law of Gravitation, they would make themselves evident by their attractive forces?"

"Not if they were far enough off," rejoined Beenay, "really far off—maybe as much as four light years, or even more. We'd never be able to detect perturbations then, because they'd be too small. Say that there were a lot of suns that far off; a dozen or two, maybe."

Theremon whistled melodiously. "What an idea for a good Sunday supplement article. Two dozen suns in a universe eight light years across. Wow! That would shrink our world into insignificance. The readers would eat it up."

"Only an idea," said Beenay with a grin, "but you see the point. During an eclipse, these dozen suns would become visible because there'd be no *real* sunlight to drown them out. Since they're so far off, they'd appear small, like so many little marbles. Of course the Cultists talk of millions of Stars, but that's probably exaggeration. There just isn't any place in the universe you could put a million suns—unless they touch one another."

Sheerin had listened with gradually increasing interest. "You've hit something there, Beenay. And exaggeration is just exactly what would happen. Our minds, as you probably know, can't grasp directly any number higher than five; above that there is only the concept of 'many.' A dozen would become a million just like that. A damn good idea!"

"And I've got another cute little notion," Beenay said. "Have you ever thought what a simple problem gravitation would be if only you had a sufficiently simple system? Supposing you had a universe in which there was a planet with only one sun. The planet would travel in a perfect ellipse and the exact nature of the gravitational force would be so evident it could be accepted as an axiom. Astronomers on such a world would start off with gravity probably before they even invented the telescope. Naked eye observation would be enough."

"But would such a system be dynamically stable?" questioned Sheerin doubtfully.

"Sure! They call it the 'one-and-one' case. It's been worked out mathematically, but it's the philosophical implications that interest me."

"It's nice to think about," admitted Sheerin, "as a pretty abstraction—like a perfect gas, or absolute zero."

"Of course," continued Beenay, "there's the catch that life would be impossible on such a planet. It wouldn't get enough heat and light, and if it rotated there would be total Darkness half of each day. You couldn't expect life—which is fundamentally dependent upon light—to develop under those conditions. Besides—"

Sheerin's chair went over backward as he sprang to his feet in a rude interruption. "Aton's brought out the lights."

Beenay said, "Huh," turned to stare, and then grinned halfway around his head in open relief.

There were half a dozen foot-long, inch-thick rods cradled in Aton's arms. He glared over them at the assembled staff members.

"Get back to work, all of you. Sheerin, come here and help me!"

Sheerin trotted to the older man's side and, one by one, in utter silence, the two adjusted the rods in makeshift metal holders suspended from the walls.

With the air of one carrying through the most sacred item of a religious ritual, Sheerin scraped a large, clumsy match into spluttering life and passed it to Aton, who carried the flame to the upper end of one of the rods.

It hesitated there awhile, playing futilely about the tip, until a sudden, crackling flare cast Aton's lined face into yellow highlights. He withdrew the match and a spontaneous cheer rattled the window.

The rod was topped by six inches of wavering flame! Methodically, the other rods were lighted, until six independent fires turned the rear of the room yellow.

The light was dim, dimmer even than the tenuous sunlight. The flames reeled crazily, giving birth to drunken, swaying shadows. The torches smoked devilishly and smelled like a bad day in the kitchen. But they emitted yellow light.

There was something about yellow light, after four hours of somber, dimming Beta. Even Latimer had lifted his eyes from his book and stared in wonder.

Sheerin warmed his hands at the nearest, regardless of the soot that gathered upon them in a fine, gray powder, and muttered ecstatically to himself. "Beautiful! Beautiful! I never realized before what a wonderful color yellow is."

But Theremon regarded the torches suspiciously. He wrinkled his nose at the rancid odor and said, "What are those things?"

"Wood," said Sheerin shortly.

"Oh, no, they're not. They aren't burning. The top inch is charred and the flame just keeps shooting up out of nothing."

"That's the beauty of it. This is a really efficient artificial-light mechanism. We made a few hundred of them, but most went to the Hideout, of course. You see"—he turned and wiped his blackened hands upon his handkerchief—"you take the pithy core of coarse water reeds, dry them thoroughly, and soak them in animal grease. Then you set fire to it and the grease burns, little by little. These torches will burn for almost half an hour without stopping. Ingenious, isn't it? It was developed by one of our own young men at Saro University."

After the momentary sensation, the dome had quieted. Latimer had carried his chair directly beneath a torch and continued reading, lips moving in the monotonous recital of invocations to the Stars. Beenay had drifted away to his cameras once more, and Theremon seized the opportunity to add to his notes on the article he was going to write for the Saro City *Chronicle* the next day—a procedure he had been following for the last two hours in a perfectly methodical, perfectly conscientious and, as he was well aware, perfectly meaningless fashion.

But, as the gleam of amusement in Sheerin's eyes indicated, careful note-taking occupied his mind with something other than the fact that the sky was gradually turning a horrible deep purple-red, as if it were one gigantic, freshly peeled beet; and so it fulfilled its purpose.

The air grew, somehow, denser. Dusk, like a palpable entity, entered the room, and the dancing circle of yellow light about the torches etched itself into ever-sharper distinction against the gathering grayness beyond. There was the odor of smoke and the presence of little chuckling sounds that the torches made as they burned; the soft pad of one of the men circling the table at which he worked, on hesitant tiptoes; the occasional indrawn breath of someone trying to retain composure in a world that was retreating into the shadow.

It was Theremon who first heard the extraneous noise. It was a vague, unorganized *impression* of sound that would have gone unnoticed but for the dead silence that prevailed within the dome.

The newsman sat upright and replaced his notebook. He held his breath and listened; then, with considerable reluctance, threaded his way between the solarscope and one of Beenay's cameras and stood before the window.

The silence ripped to fragments at his startled shout: *"Sheerin!"*

Work stopped! The psychologist was at his side in a moment. Aton joined him. Even Yimot 70, high in his little lean-back seat at the eyepiece of the gigantic solarscope, paused and looked downward.

Outside, Beta was a mere smoldering splinter, taking one last desperate look at Lagash. The eastern horizon, in the direction of the city, was lost in Darkness, and the road from Saro to the Observatory was a dull-red line bordered on both sides by wooded tracts, the trees of which had somehow lost individuality and merged into a continuous shadowy mass.

But it was the highway itself that held attention, for along it there surged another, and infinitely menacing, shadowy mass.

Aton cried in a cracked voice, "The madmen from the city! They've come!"

"How long to totality?" demanded Sheerin.

"Fifteen minutes, but...but they'll be here in five."

"Never mind, keep the men working. We'll hold them off. This place is built like a fortress. Aton, keep an eye on our young Cultist just for luck. Theremon, come with me."

Sheerin was out the door, and Theremon was at his heels. The stairs stretched below them in tight, circular sweeps about the central shaft, fading into a dank and dreary grayness.

The first momentum of their rush had carried them fifty feet down, so that the dim, flickering yellow from the open door of the dome had disappeared and both above and below the same dusky shadow crushed in upon them.

Sheerin paused, and his pudgy hand clutched at his chest. His eyes bulged and his voice was a dry cough. "I can't...breathe.... Go down...yourself. Close all doors—"

Theremon took a few downward steps, then turned. "Wait! Can you hold out a minute?" He was panting himself. The air passed in and out his lungs like so much molasses, and there was a little germ of screeching panic in his mind at the thought of making his way into the mysterious Darkness below by himself.

Theremon, after all, was afraid of the dark!

"Stay here," he said. "I'll be back in a second." He dashed upward two steps at a time, heart pounding—not altogether from the exertion—tumbled into the dome and snatched a torch from its holder. It was foul-smelling, and the smoke smarted his eyes almost blind, but he clutched that torch as if he wanted to kiss it for joy, and its flame streamed backward as he hurtled down the stairs again.

Sheerin opened his eyes and moaned as Theremon bent over him. Theremon shook him roughly. "All right, get a hold on yourself. We've got light."

He held the torch at tiptoe height and, propping the tottering psychologist by an elbow, made his way downward in the middle of the protecting circle of illumination.

The offices on the ground floor still possessed what light there was, and Theremon felt the horror about him relax.

"Here," he said brusquely, and passed the torch to Sheerin. "You can hear *them* outside."

And they could. Little scraps of hoarse, wordless shouts.

But Sheerin was right; the Observatory was built like a fortress. Erected in the last century, when the neo-Gavottian style of architecture was at its ugly height, it had been designed for stability and durability rather than for beauty.

The windows were protected by the grillwork of inch-thick iron bars sunk deep into the concrete sills. The walls were solid masonry that an earthquake couldn't have touched, and the main door was a huge oaken slab reinforced with iron. Theremon shot the bolts and they slid shut with a dull clang.

At the other end of the corridor, Sheerin cursed weakly. He pointed to the lock of the back door which had been neatly jimmied into uselessness.

"That must be how Latimer got in," he said.

"Well, don't stand there," cried Theremon impatiently. "Help drag up the furniture—and keep that torch out of my eyes. The smoke's killing me."

He slammed the heavy table up against the door as he spoke, and in two minutes had built a barricade which made up for what it lacked in beauty and symmetry by the sheer inertia of its massiveness.

Somewhere, dimly, far off, they could hear the battering of naked fists upon the door; and the screams and yells from outside had a sort of half reality.

That mob had set off from Saro City with only two things in mind: the attainment of Cultist salvation by the destruction of the Observatory, and a maddening fear that all but paralyzed them. There was no time to think of ground cars, or of weapons, or of leadership, or even of organization. They made for the Observatory on foot and assaulted it with bare hands.

And now that they were there, the last flash of Beta, the last ruby-red drop of flame, flickered feebly over a humanity that had left only stark, universal fear!

Theremon groaned, "Let's get back to the dome!"

In the dome, only Yimot, at the solarscope, had kept his place. The rest were clustered about the cameras, and Beenay was giving his instructions in a hoarse, strained voice.

"Get it straight, all of you. I'm snapping Beta just before totality and changing the plate. That will leave one of you to each camera. You all know about...about times of exposure—"

There was a breathless murmur of agreement.

Beenay passed a hand over his eyes. "Are the torches still burning? Never mind, I see them!" He was leaning hard against the back of a chair. "Now remember, don't...don't try to look for good shots. Don't waste time trying to get t-two stars at a time in the scope field. One is enough. And...and if you feel yourself going, *get away from the camera.*"

At the door, Sheerin whispered to Theremon, "Take me to Aton. I don't see him."

The newsman did not answer immediately. The vague forms of the astronomers wavered and blurred, and the torches overhead had become only yellow splotches.

"It's dark," he whimpered.

Sheerin held out his hand. "Aton." He stumbled forward. "Aton!"

Theremon stepped after and seized his arm. "Wait, I'll take you." Somehow he made his way across the room. He closed his eyes against the Darkness and his mind against the chaos within it.

No one heard them or paid attention to them. Sheerin stumbled against the wall. "Aton!"

The psychologist felt shaking hands touching him, then withdrawing, and a voice muttering, "Is that you, Sheerin?"

"Aton!" He strove to breathe normally. "Don't worry about the mob. The place will hold them off."

Latimer, the Cultist, rose to his feet, and his face twisted in desperation. His word was pledged, and to break it would mean placing his soul in mortal peril. Yet that word had been forced from him and had not been given freely. The Stars would come soon! He could not stand by and allow—And yet his word was pledged.

Beenay's face was dimly flushed as it looked upward at Beta's last ray, and Latimer, seeing him bend over his camera, made his decision. His nails cut the flesh of his palms as he tensed himself.

He staggered crazily as he started his rush. There was nothing before him but shadows; the very floor beneath his feet lacked substance. And then someone was upon him and he went down with clutching fingers at his throat.

He doubled his knee and drove it hard into his assailant. "Let me up or I'll kill you."

Theremon cried out sharply and muttered through a blinding haze of pain. "You double-crossing rat!"

The newsman seemed conscious of everything at once. He heard Beenay croak, "I've got it. At your cameras, men!" and then there was the strange awareness that the last thread of sunlight had thinned out and snapped.

Simultaneously he heard one last choking gasp from Beenay, and a queer little cry from Sheerin, a hysterical giggle that cut off in a rasp—and a sudden silence, a strange, deadly silence from outside.

And Latimer had gone limp in his loosening grasp. Theremon peered into the Cultist's eyes and saw the blankness of them, staring upward, mirroring the feeble yellow of the torches. He saw the bubble of froth upon Latimer's lips and heard the low animal whimper in Latimer's throat.

With the slow fascination of fear, he lifted himself on one arm and turned his eyes toward the blood-curdling blackness of the window.

Through it shone the Stars!

Not Earth's feeble thirty-six hundred Stars visible to the eye; Lagash was in the center of a giant cluster. Thirty thousand mighty suns shone down in a soul-searing splendor that was more frighteningly cold in its awful indifference than the bitter wind that shivered across the cold, horribly bleak world.

Theremon staggered to his feet, his throat constricting him to breathlessness, all the muscles of his body writhing in an intensity of terror and sheer fear beyond bearing. He was going mad and knew it, and somewhere deep inside a bit of sanity was screaming, struggling to fight off the hopeless flood of black terror. It was very horrible to go mad and know that you were going mad—to know that in a little minute you would be here physically and yet all the real essence would be dead and drowned in the black madness. For this was the Dark—the Dark and the Cold and the Doom. The bright walls of the universe were shattered and their awful black fragments were falling down to crush and squeeze and obliterate him.

He jostled someone crawling on hands and knees, but stumbled somehow over him. Hands groping at his tortured throat, he limped toward the flame of the torches that filled all his mad vision.

"Light!" he screamed.

Aton, somewhere, was crying, whimpering horribly like a terribly frightened child. "Stars—all the Stars—we didn't know at all. We didn't know anything. We thought six stars in a universe is something the Stars didn't notice is Darkness forever and ever and ever and the walls are breaking in and we didn't know we couldn't know and anything—"

Someone clawed at the torch, and it fell and snuffed out. In the instant, the awful splendor of the indifferent Stars leaped nearer to them.

On the horizon outside the window, in the direction of Saro City, a crimson glow began growing, strengthening in brightness, that was not the glow of a sun.

The long night had come again.

The Man Who Lost the Sea

Theodore Sturgeon

Theodore Sturgeon (1918-1985) was born Edward Hamilton Waldo. He had originally planned to attend Temple University on a gymnastic scholarship, but a severe bout of rheumatic fever forced him to retire from athletic competition. Sturgeon went to sea in 1936, and sold his first story to *McClure's* in 1937. The sale of "God in a Garden" in 1939 prompted him to take up writing full-time. During World War II, he travelled the country taking odd jobs. In 1946, John W. Campbell convinced Sturgeon to begin writing again. Two of the stories he wrote during that time, "Bianca's Hands" (1947) and "Killdozer" (1949), are considered some of his finest works. In 1950, he published his first novel, *The Dreaming Jewels.* In 1953, *More Than Human* was published; it received tremendous critical attention outside the science fiction press. During the 1950's, Sturgeon concentrated primarily on short stories, producing only one more novel, *Venus Plus X* (1960). His vampire novel, *Some of Your Blood,* was released in 1961 and became his most popular and controversial effort. Sturgeon did very little writing in the 1960's, most significantly contributing the story "If All Men Were Brothers, Would You Let One Marry Your Sister?" to Harlan Ellison's anthology *Dangerous Visions* (1967). He began writing fairly prolifically in 1970, and his story "Soft Sculpture" won both the Hugo and the Nebula. His first collection in over a decade, *Theodore Sturgeon is Alive and Well...* surfaced in 1971. Sturgeon moved to Oregon, his literary output dwindling away to almost nothing until his death.

"The Man Who Lost the Sea" was originally published in *Galaxy* magazine. Sturgeon's conversational style is sharp and effective, masterfully setting up the reader for its surprise ending.

SAY YOU'RE A KID, and one dark night you're running along the cold sand with this helicopter in your hand, saying very fast *witchy-witchy-witchy.* You pass the sick man and he wants you to shove off with that thing. Maybe he thinks you're too old to play with toys. So you squat next to him in the sand and tell him it isn't a toy, it's a model. You tell him look here, here's something most people don't know about helicopters. You take a blade of the rotor in your fingers and show him how it can move in the hub, up and down a little, back and forth a little, and twist a little, to change pitch. You start to tell him how this flexibility does away with the gyroscopic effect, but he won't listen. He doesn't want to think about flying, about helicopters, or about you, and he most especially does not want explanations about anything by anybody. Not now. Now, he wants to think about the sea. So you go away.

The sick man is buried in the cold sand with only his head and his left arm showing. He is dressed in a pressure suit and looks like a man from Mars. Built into his left sleeve is a combination time-piece and pressure gauge, the gauge with a luminous blue indicator which makes no sense, the clock hands luminous red. He can hear the pounding of surf and the soft swift pulse of his pumps. One time long ago when he was swimming he went too deep and stayed down too long and came up too fast, and when he came to it was like this: they said, "Don't move, boy. You've got the bends. Don't even *try* to move." He had tried anyway. It hurt. So now, this time, he lies in the sand without moving, without trying.

His head isn't working right. But he knows clearly that it isn't working right, which is a strange thing that happens to people in shock sometimes. Say you were that kid, you could say how it was, because once you woke up lying in the gym office in high school and asked what had happened. They explained how you tried something on the parallel bars and fell on your head. You understood exactly, though you couldn't remember falling. Then a minute later you asked again what had happened and they told you. You understood it. And a minute later...forty-one times they told you, and you understood. It was just that no matter how many times they pushed it into your head, it wouldn't stick there; but all the while you *knew* that your head would start working again in time. And in time it did.... Of course, if you were that kid, always explaining things to people and to yourself, you wouldn't want to bother the sick man with it now.

Look what you've done already, making him send you away with that angry shrug of the mind (which, with the eyes, are the only things which will move just now). The motionless effort costs him a wave of nausea. He has felt seasick before but he has never *been* seasick, and the formula for that is to keep your eyes on the horizon and stay busy. Now! Then he'd better get busy—now; for there's one place especially not to be seasick in, and that's locked up in a pressure suit. Now!

So he busies himself as best he can, with the seascape, landscape, sky. He lies on high ground, his head propped on a vertical wall of black rock. There is another such outcrop before him, whip-topped with white sand and with smooth flat sand. Beyond and down is valley, salt-flat, estuary; he cannot yet be sure. He is sure of the line of footprints, which begin behind him, pass to his left, disappear in the outcrop shadows, and reappear beyond to vanish at last into the shadows of the valley.

Stretched across the sky is old mourning-cloth, with starlight burning holes in it, and between the holes the black is absolute—wintertime, mountaintop sky-black.

(Far off on the horizon within himself, he sees the swell and crest of approaching nausea; he counters with an undertow of weakness, which meets and rounds and settles the wave before it can break. Get busier. *Now.)*

Burst in on him, then, with the X-15 model. That'll get him. Hey, how about this for a gimmick? Get too high for the thin air to give you any control, you have these little jets in the wingtips, see? and on the sides of the empennage: bank, roll, yaw, whatever, with squirts of compressed air.

But the sick man curls his sick lip: oh, git, kid, git, will you?—that has nothing to do with the sea. So you git.

Out and out the sick man forces his view, etching all he sees with a meticulous intensity, as if it might be his charge, one day, to duplicate all this. To his left is only starlit sea, windless. In front of him across the valley, rounded hills with dim white epaulettes of light. To his right, the jutting corner of the black wall against which his helmet rests. (He thinks the distant moundings of nausea becalmed, but he will not look yet.) So he scans the sky, black and bright, calling Sirius, calling Pleiades, Polaris, Ursa Minor, calling that...that...Why, it *moves.* Watch it: yes, it moves! It is a fleck of light, seeming to be wrinkled, fissured, rather like a chip of boiled cauliflower in the sky. (Of course, he knows better than to trust his own eyes just now.) But that movement...

As a child he had stood on cold sand in a frosty Cape Cod evening, watching Sputnik's steady spark rise out of the haze (madly, dawning a little north of west); and after that he had sleeplessly wound special coils for his receiver, risked his life restringing high antennas, all for the brief capture of an unreadable *tweetle-eep-tweetle* in his earphones from Vanguard, Explorer, Lunik, Discoverer, Mercury. He knew them all (well, some people collect match-covers, stamps) and he knew especially that unmistakable steady sliding in the sky.

This moving fleck was a satellite, and in a moment, motionless, uninstrumented but for his chronometer and his part-brain, he will know which one. (He is grateful beyond expression—without that sliding chip of light, there were only those footprints, those wandering footprints, to tell a man he was not alone in the world.)

Say you were a kid, eager and challengeable and more than a little bright, you might in a day or so work out a way to measure the period of a satellite with nothing but a timepiece and a brain; you might eventually see that the shadow in the rocks ahead had been there from the first only because of the light from the rising satellite. Now if you check the time exactly at the moment when the shadow on the sand is equal to the height of the outcrop, and time it again when the light is at the zenith and the shadow gone, you will multiply this number of minutes by 8—think why, now: horizon to zenith is one-fourth of the orbit, give or take a little, and halfway up the sky is half that quarter—and you will then know this satellite's period. You know all the periods—ninety minutes, two, two-and-a-half hours; with that and the appearance of this bird, you'll find out which one it is.

But if you were that kid, eager or resourceful or whatever, you wouldn't jabber about it to the sick man, for not only does he not want to be bothered with you, he's thought of all that long since and is even now watching the shadows for that triangular split second of measurement. *Now!* His eyes drop to the face of his chronometer: 0400, near as makes no never mind.

He has minutes to wait now—ten?...thirty?...twenty-three?—while this baby moon eats up its slice of shadowpie; and that's too bad, the waiting, for though the inner sea is calm there are currents below, shadows that shift and swim. Be busy. Be busy. He must not swim near that great invisible ameba, whatever happens: its first cold pseudopod is even now reaching for the vitals.

Being a knowledgeable young fellow, not quite a kid any more, wanting to help the sick man too, you want to tell him everything you know about that cold-in-the-gut, that reaching invisible surrounding implacable ameba. You know all about it—listen, you want to yell at him, don't let that touch of cold bother you. Just know what it is, that's all. Know what it is that is touching your gut. You want to tell him, listen:

Listen, this is how you met the monster and dissected it. Listen, you were skin-diving in the Grenadines, a hundred tropical shoal-water islands; you had a new blue snorkel mask, the kind with face-plate and breathing-tube all in one, and new blue flippers on your feet, and a new blue spear-gun—all this new because you'd only begun, you see; you were a beginner, aghast with pleasure at your easy intrusion into this underwater otherworld. You'd been out in a boat, you were coming back, you'd just reached the mouth of the little bay, you'd taken the notion to swim the rest of the way. You'd said as much to the boys and slipped into the warm silky water. You brought your gun.

Not far to go at all, but then beginners find wet distances deceiving. For the first five minutes or so it was only delightful, the sun hot on your back and the water so warm it seemed not to have any temperature at all and you were flying. With your face under the water, your mask was not so much attached as part of you, your wide blue flippers trod away yards, your gun rode all but weightless in your hand, the taut rubber sling making an occasional hum as your passage plucked it in the sunlit green. In your ears crooned the breathy monotone of the snorkel tube, and through the invisible disk of plate glass you saw wonders. The bay was shallow—ten, twelve feet or so—and sandy, with great growths of brain-, bone-, and fire-coral; intricate waving sea-fans, and fish—such fish! Scarlet and green and aching azure, gold and rose and slate-color studded with sparks of enamel-blue, pink and peach and silver. And that *thing* got into you, that...monster.

There were enemies in this otherworld: the sand-colored spotted sea-snake with his big ugly head and turned-down mouth, who would not retreat but lay watching the intruder pass; and the mottled moray with jaws like bolt-cutters; and somewhere around, certainly, the barracuda with his undershot face and teeth turned inward so that he must take away whatever he might strike. There were urchins—the plump white sea-egg with its thick fur of sharp quills and the black ones with the long slender spines that would break off in unwary flesh and fester there for weeks; and file-fish and stone-fish with their poisoned barbs and lethal meat; and the stingaree who could drive his spike through a leg bone. Yet these were not *monsters,* and could not matter to you, the invader churning along above them all. For you were above them in so many ways—armed, rational, comforted by the close shore (ahead the beach, the rocks on each side) and by the presence of the boat not too far behind. Yet you were...attacked.

At first it was uneasiness, not pressing, but pervasive, a contact quite as intimate as that of the sea; you were sheathed in it. And also there was the touch—the cold inward contact. Aware of it at last, you laughed: for Pete's sake, what's there to be scared of?

The monster, the ameba.

You raised your head and looked back in air. The boat had edged in to the cliff at the right; someone was giving a last poke around for lobster. You waved at the boat; it was your gun you waved, and emerging from the water it gained its latent ounces so that you sank a bit, and as if you had no snorkel on, you tipped your head back to get a breath. But tipping your head back plunged the end of the tube under water; the valve closed; you drew in a hard lungful of nothing at all. You dropped your face under; up came the tube; you got your air, and along with it a bullet of seawater which struck you somewhere inside the throat. You coughed it out and floundered, sobbing as you sucked in air, inflating your chest until it hurt, and the air you got seemed no good, no good at all, a worthless devitalized inert gas.

You clenched your teeth and headed for the beach, kicking strongly and knowing it was the right thing to do; and then below and to the right you saw a great bulk mounding up out of the sand floor of the sea. You knew it was only the reef, rocks and coral and weed, but the sight of it made you scream; you didn't care what you knew. You turned hard left to avoid it, fought by as if it would reach for you, and you couldn't get air, couldn't get air, for all the unobstructed hooting of your snorkel tube. You couldn't bear the mask, suddenly, not for another second, so you shoved it upward clear of your mouth and rolled over, floating on your back and opening your mouth to the sky and breathing with a quacking noise.

It was then and there that the monster well and truly engulfed you, mantling you round and about within itself—formless, borderless, the illimitable ameba. The beach, mere yards away, and the rocky arms of the bay, and the not-too-distant boat—these you could identify but no longer distinguish, for they were all one and the same thing...the thing called unreachable.

You fought that way for a time, on your back, dangling the gun under and behind you and straining to get enough warm sun-stained air into your chest. And in time some particles of sanity began to swirl in the roil of your mind, and to dissolve and tint it. The air pumping in and out of your square-grinned frightened mouth began to be meaningful at last, and the monster relaxed away from you.

You took stock, saw surf, beach, a leaning tree. You felt the new scend of your body as the rollers humped to become breakers. Only a dozen firm kicks brought you to where you could roll over and double up; your shin struck coral with a lovely agony and you stood in foam and waded ashore. You gained the wet sand, hard sand, and ultimately, with two more paces powered by bravado, you crossed high-water mark and lay in the dry sand, unable to move.

You lay in the sand, and before you were able to move or to think, you were able to feel a triumph—a triumph because you were alive and knew that much without thinking at all.

When you *were* able to think, your first thought was of the gun, and the first move you were able to make was to let go at last of the thing. You had nearly died because you had not let it go before; without it you would not have been burdened and you would not have panicked. You had (you began to understand) kept it because someone else would have had to retrieve it—easily enough—and you could not have stood the laughter. You had almost died because They might laugh at you.

This was the beginning of the dissection, analysis, study of the monster. It began then; it had never finished. Some of what you had learned from it was merely important; some of the rest—vital.

You had learned, for example, never to swim farther with a snorkel than you could swim back without one. You learned never to burden yourself with the unnecessary in an emergency: even a hand or a foot might be as expendable as a gun; pride was expendable, dignity was. You learned never to dive alone, even if They laugh at you, even if you have to shoot a fish yourself and say afterward "we" shot it. Most of all, you learned that fear has many fingers, and one of them—a simple one, made of too great a concentration of carbon dioxide in your blood, as from too-rapid breathing in and out of the same tube—is not really fear at all but feels like fear, and can turn into panic and kill you.

Listen, you want to say, listen, there isn't anything wrong with such an experience or with all the study it leads to, because a man who can learn enough from it could become fit enough, cautious enough, foresighted, unafraid, modest, teachable enough to be chosen, to be qualified for—

You lose the thought, or turn it away, because the sick man feels that cold touch deep inside, feels it right now, feels it beyond ignoring, above and beyond anything that you, with all your experience and certainty, could explain to him even if he would listen, which he won't. Make him, then; tell him the cold touch is some simple explainable thing like anoxia, like gladness even: some triumph that he will be able to appreciate when his head is working right again.

Triumph? Here he's alive after...whatever it is, and that doesn't seem to be triumph enough, though it was in the Grenadines, and that other time, when he got the bends, saved his own life, saved two other lives. Now, somehow, it's not the same: there seems to be a reason why just being alive afterward isn't a triumph.

Why not triumph? Because not twelve, not twenty, not even thirty minutes is it taking the satellite to complete its eighth-of-an-orbit: fifty minutes are gone, and still there's a slice of shadow yonder. It is this, *this* which is placing the cold finger upon his heart, and he doesn't know why, he doesn't know why, he *will* not know why; he is afraid he shall when his head is working again....

Oh, where's the kid? Where is any way to busy the mind, apply it to something, anything else but the watchhand which outruns the moon? Here, kid: come over here—what you got there?

If you were the kid, then you'd forgive everything and hunker down with your new model, not a toy, not a helicopter or a rocket-plane, but the big one, the one that looks like an overgrown cartridge. It's so big, even as a model, that even an angry sick man wouldn't call it a toy. A giant cartridge, but watch: the lower four-fifths is Alpha—all muscle—over a million pounds thrust. (Snap it off, throw it away.) Half the rest is Beta—all brains—it puts you on your way. (Snap it off, throw it away.) And now look at the polished fraction which is left. Touch a control somewhere and see—see? it has wings—wide triangular wings. This is Gamma, the one with wings, and on its back is a small sausage; it is a moth with a sausage on its back. The sausage (click! it comes free) is Delta. Delta is the last, the smallest: Delta is the way home.

What will they think of next? Quite a toy. Quite a toy. Beat it, kid. The satellite is almost overhead, the sliver of shadow going—going—almost gone and...gone.

Check: 0459. Fifty-nine minutes? give or take a few. Times eight...472...is, uh, 7 hours 52 minutes.

Seven hours fifty-two minutes? Why, there isn't a satellite round earth with a period like that. In all the solar system there's only...

The cold finger turns fierce, implacable.

The east is paling and the sick man turns to it, wanting the light, the sun, an end to questions whose answers couldn't be looked upon. The sea stretches endlessly out to the growing light, and endlessly, somewhere out of sight, the surf roars. The paling east bleaches the sandy hilltops and throws the line of footprints into aching relief. That would be the buddy, the sick man knows, gone for help. He cannot at the moment recall who the buddy is, but in time he will, and meanwhile the footprints make him less alone.

The sun's upper rim thrusts itself above the horizon with a flash of green, instantly gone. There is no dawn, just the green flash and then a clear white blast of unequivocal sunup. The sea could not be whiter, more still, if it were frozen and snow-blanketed. In the west, stars still blaze, and overhead the crinkled satellite is scarcely abashed by the growing light. A formless jumble in the valley below begins to resolve itself into a sort of tent-city, or installation of some kind, with tubelike and sail-like buildings. This would have meaning for the sick man if his head were working right. Soon, it would. Will. (Oh...)

The sea, out on the horizon just under the rising sun, is behaving strangely, for in that place where properly belongs a pool of unbearable brightness, there is instead a notch of brown. It is as if the white fire of the sun is drinking dry the sea—for look, look! the notch becomes a bow and the bow a crescent, racing ahead of the sunlight, white sea ahead of it and behind it a cocoa-dry stain spreading across and down toward where he watches.

Beside the finger of fear which lies on him, another finger places itself, and another, making ready for that clutch, that grip, that ultimate insane squeeze of panic. Yet beyond that again, past that squeeze when it comes, to be savored if the squeeze is only fear and not panic, lies triumph—triumph, and a glory. It is perhaps this which constitutes his whole battle: to fit himself, prepare himself to bear the utmost that fear could do, for if he can do that, there is a triumph on the other side. But...not yet. Please, not yet awhile.

Something flies (or flew, or will fly—he is a little confused on this point) toward him, from the far right where the stars still shine. It is not a bird and it is unlike any aircraft on earth, for the aerodynamics are wrong. Wings so wide and so fragile would be useless, would melt and tear away in any of earth's atmosphere but the outer fringes. He sees then (because he prefers to see it so) that it is the kid's model, or part of it, and for a toy it does very well indeed.

It is the part called Gamma, and it glides in, balancing, parallels the sand and holds away, holds away slowing, then settles, all in slow motion, throwing up graceful sheet-fountains of fine sand from its skids. And it runs along the ground for an impossible distance, letting down its weight by the ounce and stingily the ounce, until *look out* until a skid *look out* fits itself into a bridged crevasse *look out, look out!* and still moving on, it settles down to the struts. Gamma then, tired, digs her wide left wingtip carefully into the racing sand, digs it in hard; and as the wing breaks off, Gamma slews, sidles, slides slowly, pointing her other triangular tentlike wing at the sky, and broadside crushes into the rocks at the valley's end.

As she rolls smashing over, there breaks from her broad back the sausage, the little Delta, which somersaults away to break its back upon the rocks, and through the broken hull spill smashed shards of graphite from the moderator of her power-pile. *Look out! Look out!* and at the same instant from the finally checked mass of Gamma there explodes a doll, which slides and tumbles into the sand, into the rocks and smashed hot graphite from the wreck of Delta.

The sick man numbly watches this toy destroy itself: what will they think of next?—and with a gelid horror prays at the doll lying in the raging rubble of the atomic pile: *don't stay there, man—get away! get away! that's hot, you know?* But it seems like a night and a day and half another night before the doll staggers to its feet and, clumsy in its pressure-suit, runs away up the valleyside, climbs a sand-topped outcrop, slips, falls, lies under a slow cascade of cold ancient sand until, but for an arm and the helmet, it is buried.

The sun is high now, high enough to show the sea is not a sea, but brown plain with the frost burned off it, as now it burns away from the hills, diffusing in air and blurring the edges of the sun's disk, so that in a very few minutes there is no sun at all, but only a glare in the east. Then the valley below loses its shadows, and, like an arrangement in a diorama, reveals the form and nature of the wreckage below: no tent-city this, no installation, but the true real ruin of Gamma and the eviscerated hulk of Delta. (Alpha was the muscle, Beta the brain; Gamma was a bird, but Delta, Delta was the way home.)

And from it stretches the line of footprints, to and by the sick man, above to the bluff, and gone with the sandslide which had buried him there. Whose footprints?

He knows whose, whether or not he knows that he knows, or wants to or not. He knows what satellite has (give or take a bit) a period like that (want it exactly?—it's 7.66 hours). He knows what world has such a night, and such a frosty glare by day. He knows these things as he knows how spilled radioactives will pour the crash and mutter of surf into a man's earphones.

Say you were that kid: say, instead, at last, that you are the sick man, for they are the same; surely then you can understand why of all things, even while shattered, shocked, sick with radiation calculated (leaving) radiation computed (arriving) and radiation past all bearing (lying in the wreckage of Delta) you would want to think of the sea. For no farmer who fingers the soil with love and knowledge, no poet who sings of it, artist, contractor, engineer, even child bursting into tears at the inexpressible beauty of a field of daffodils—none of these is as intimate with Earth as those who live on, live with, breathe and drift in its seas. So of these things you must think; with these you must dwell until you are less sick and more ready to face the truth.

The truth, then, is that the satellite fading here is Phobos, that those footprints are your own, that there is no sea here, that you have crashed and are killed and will in a moment be dead. The cold hand ready to squeeze and still your heart is not anoxia or even fear, it is death. Now, if there is something more important than this, now is the time for it to show itself.

The sick man looks at the line of his own footprints, which testify that he is alone, and at the wreckage below, which states that there is no way back, and at the white east and the mottled west and the paling fleck-like satellite above. Surf sounds in his ears. He hears his pumps. He hears what is left of his breathing. The cold clamps down and folds him round past measuring, past all limit.

Then he speaks, cries out: then with joy he takes his triumph at the other side of death, as one takes a great fish, as one completes a skilled and mighty task, rebalances at the end of some great daring leap; and as he used to say "we shot a fish" he uses no "I":

"God," he cries, dying on Mars, "God, we made it!"

The Veldt

Ray Bradbury

Ray Bradbury (b. 1920) was born in Waukegon, Illinois. In 1934, Bradbury's family moved to Los Angeles, where he has lived ever since. In 1937, he joined the Los Angeles Science Fiction League; his first story, "Hollerbochen's Delimma," appeared in a copy of that organization's fanzine, *Imaginator!* His first professional sale, a collaboration with Henry Hasse called "Pendulum," appeared in the November, 1941 issue of *Super Science Stories.* Bradbury produced his first collection, *Dark Carnival,* in 1947. By the late 1940's, his material appeared in *American Mercury, Harper, The New Yorker,* and other mainstream magazines. In 1949, he was voted Best Science Fiction Writer by the National Fantasy Fan Federation. Bradbury's second collection, *The Martian Chronicles* (1950), was praised by mainstream critics like Christopher Isherwood. After a third collection (*The Illustrated Man,* 1951), Bradbury wrote his first novel, *Fahrenheit 451* (1953). In 1954, he wrote the screenplay to John Huston's *Moby Dick.* A year later, Bradbury published another collection, *October Country.* His first non-genre work, the novel *Dandelion Wine,* was published in 1957. *The Meadow,* Bradbury's first play, was produced in 1960. In 1962, Bradbury wrote one of his most famous works, *Something Wicked This Way Comes.* Several collections repackaged his earlier work in the 1960's (*R is for Rocket,* 1962; *The Autumn People,* 1965) while he concentrated on theater and film. In 1969, his first original collection in years, *I Sing the Body Electric,* was published. A collection of poems, *When Elephants Last in Dooryards Bloomed,* appeared in 1973. Bradbury's later works include *Long After Midnight* (1976), *The Stories of Ray Bradbury* (1980), and *The Ghosts of Forever* (1981).

"The Veldt" is the first story from *The Illustrated Man.* An early depiction of virtual reality technology, "The Veldt" is also one of the most frightneing stories ever written in any genre.

"GEORGE, I WISH you'd look at the nursery."

"What's wrong with it?"

"I don't know."

"Well, then."

"I just want you to look at it, is all, or call a psychologist in to look at it."

"What would a psychologist want with a nursery?"

"You know very well what he'd want." His wife paused in the middle of the kitchen and watched the stove busy humming to itself, making supper for four.

"It's just that the nursery is different now than it was."

"All right, let's have a look."

They walked down the hall of their soundproofed, Happylife Home, which had cost them thirty thousand dollars installed, this house which clothed and fed and rocked them to sleep and played and sang and was good to them. Their approach sensitized a switch somewhere and the nursery light flicked on when they came within ten feet of it. Similarly, behind them, in the halls, lights went on and off as they left them behind, with a soft automaticity.

"Well," said George Hadley.

They stood on the thatched floor of the nursery. It was forty feet across by forty feet long and thirty feet high; it had cost half again as much as the rest of the house. "But nothing's too good for our children," said George.

The nursery was silent. It was empty as a jungle glade at hot high noon. The walls were blank and two dimensional. Now, as George and Lydia Hadley stood in the center of the room, the walls began to purr and recede into crystalline distance, it seemed, and presently an African veldt appeared, in three dimensions, on all sides, in color, reproduced to the final pebble and bit of straw. The ceiling above them became a deep sky with a hot yellow sun.

George Hadley felt the perspiration start on his brow.

"Let's get out of this sun," he said. "This is a little too real. But I don't see anything wrong."

"Wait a moment, you'll see," said his wife.

Now the hidden odorophonics were beginning to blow a wind of odor at the two people in the middle of the baked veldtland. The hot straw smell of lion grass, the cool green smell of the hidden water hole, the great rusty smell of animals, the smell of dust like a red paprika in the hot air. And now the sounds: the thump of distant antelope feet on grassy sod, the papery rustling of vultures. A shadow passed through the sky. The shadow flickered on George Hadley's upturned, sweating face.

"Filthy creatures," he heard his wife say.

"The vultures."

"You see, there are the lions, far over, that way. Now they're on their way to the water hole. They've just been eating," said Lydia. "I don't know what."

"Some animal." George Hadley put his hand up to shield off the burning light from his squinted eyes. "A zebra or a baby giraffe, maybe."

"Are you sure?" His wife sounded peculiarly tense.

"No, it's a little late to be sure," he said, amused. "Nothing over there I can see but cleaned bone, and the vultures dropping for what's left."

"Did you hear that scream?" she asked.

"No."

"About a minute ago?"

"Sorry, no."

The lions were coming. And again George Hadley was filled with admiration for the mechanical genius who had conceived this room. A miracle of efficiency selling for an absurdly low price. Every home should have one. Oh, occasionally they frightened you with their clinical accuracy, they startled you, gave you a twinge, but most of the time what fun for everyone, not only your own son and daughter, but for yourself when you felt like a quick jaunt to a foreign land, a quick change of scenery. Well, here it was!

And here were the lions now, fifteen feet away, so real, so feverishly and startlingly real that you could feel the prickling fur on your hand, and your mouth was stuffed with the dusty upholstery smell of their heated pelts, and the yellow of them was in your eyes like the yellow of an exquisite French tapestry, the yellows of lions and summer grass, and the sound of the matted lion lungs exhaling on the silent noontide, and the smell of meat from the panting, dripping mouths.

The lions stood looking at George and Lydia Hadley with terrible green-yellow eyes.

"Watch out!" screamed Lydia.

The lions came running at them.

Lydia bolted and ran. Instinctively, George sprang after her. Outside, in the hall, with the door slammed, he was laughing and she was crying, and they both stood appalled at the other's reaction.

"George!"

"Lydia! Oh, my dear poor sweet Lydia!"

"They almost got us!"

"Walls, Lydia, remember; crystal walls, that's all they are. Oh, they look real, I must admit—Africa in your parlor—but it's all dimensional superreactionary, supersensitive color film and mental tape film behind glass screens. It's all odorophonics and sonics, Lydia. Here's my handkerchief."

"I'm afraid." She came to him and put her body against him and cried steadily. "Did you see? Did you *feel*? It's too real."

"Now, Lydia..."

"You've got to tell Wendy and Peter not to read any more on Africa."

"Of course—of course." He patted her.

"Promise?"

"Sure."

"And lock the nursery for a few days until I get my nerves settled."

"You know how difficult Peter is about that. When I punished him a month ago by locking the nursery for even a few hours—the tantrum he threw! And Wendy too. They *live* for the nursery."

"It's got to be locked, that's all there is to it."

"All right." Reluctantly he locked the huge door. "You've been working too hard. You need a rest."

"I don't know—I don't know," she said, blowing her nose, sitting down in a chair that immediately began to rock and comfort her. "Maybe I don't have enough to do. Maybe I have time to think too much. Why don't we shut the whole house off for a few days and take a vacation?"

"You mean you want to fry my eggs for me?"

"Yes." She nodded.

"And darn my socks?"

"Yes." A frantic, watery-eyed nodding.

"And sweep the house?"

"Yes, yes—oh, yes!"

"But I thought that's why we bought this house, so we wouldn't have to do anything?"

"That's just it. I feel like I don't belong here. The house is wife and mother now and nursemaid. Can I compete with an African veldt? Can I give a bath and scrub the children as efficiently or quickly as the automatic scrub bath can? I cannot. And it isn't just me. It's you. You've been awfully nervous lately."

"I suppose I have been smoking too much."

"You look as if you didn't know what to do with yourself in this house, either. You smoke a little more every morning and drink a little more every afternoon and need a little more sedative every night. You're beginning to feel unnecessary too."

"Am I?" He paused and tried to feel into himself to see what was really there.

"Oh, George!" She looked beyond him, at the nursery door. "Those lions can't get out of there, can they?"

He looked at the door and saw it tremble as if something had jumped against it from the other side.

"Of course not," he said.

At dinner they ate alone, for Wendy and Peter were at a special plastic carnival across town and had televised home to say they'd be late, to go ahead eating. So George Hadley, bemused, sat watching the dining-room table produce warm dishes of food from its mechanical interior.

"We forgot the ketchup," he said.

"Sorry," said a small voice within the table, and ketchup appeared.

As for the nursery, thought George Hadley, it won't hurt for the children to be locked out of it awhile. Too much of anything isn't good for anyone. And it was clearly indicated that the children had been spending a little too much time on Africa. That sun. He could feel it on his neck, still, like a hot paw. And the *lions.* And the smell of blood. Remarkable how the nursery caught the telepathic emanations of the children's minds and created life to fill their every desire. The children thought lions, and there were lions. The children thought zebras, and there were zebras. Sun—sun. Giraffes—giraffes. Death and death.

That *last.* He chewed tastelessly on the meat that the table had cut for him. Death thoughts. They were awfully young, Wendy and Peter, for death thoughts. Or, no, you were never too young, really. Long before you knew what death was you were wishing it on someone else. When you were two years old you were shooting people with cap pistols.

But this—the long, hot African veldt—the awful death in the jaws of a lion. And repeated again and again.

"Where are you going?"

He didn't answer Lydia. Preoccupied, he let the lights glow softly on ahead of him, extinguish behind him as he padded to the nursery door. He listened against it. Far away, a lion roared.

He unlocked the door and opened it. Just before he stepped inside, he heard a faraway scream. And then another roar from the lions, which subsided quickly.

He stepped into Africa. How many times in the last year had he opened this door and found Wonderland, Alice, the Mock Turtle, or Aladdin and his Magical Lamp, or Jack Pumpkinhead of Oz, or Dr. Doolittle, or the cow jumping over a very real-appearing moon—all the delightful contraptions of a make-believe world. How often had he seen Pegasus flying in the sky ceiling, or seen fountains of red fireworks, or heard angel voices singing. But now, this yellow hot Africa, this bake oven with murder in the heat. Perhaps Lydia was right. Perhaps they needed a little vacation from the fantasy which was growing a bit too real for ten-year-old children. It was all right to exercise one's mind with gymnastic fantasies, but when the lively child mind settled on one pattern...? It seemed that, at a distance, for the past month, he had heard lions roaring, and smelled their strong odor seeping as far away as his study door. But, being busy, he had paid it no attention.

George Hadley stood on the African grassland alone. The lions looked up from their feeding, watching him. The only flaw to the illusion was the open door through which he could see his wife, far down the dark hall, like a framed picture, eating her dinner abstractedly.

"Go away," he said to the lions.

They did not go.

He knew the principle of the room exactly. You sent out your thoughts. Whatever you thought would appear.

"Let's have Aladdin and his lamp," he snapped.

The veldtland remained; the lions remained.

"Come on, room! I demand Aladdin!" he said.

Nothing happened. The lions mumbled in their baked pelts.

"Aladdin!"

He went back to dinner. "The fool room's out of order," he said. "It won't respond."

"Or—"

"Or what?"

"Or it *can't* respond," said Lydia, "because the children have thought about Africa and lions and killing so many days that the room's in a rut."

"Could be."

"Or Peter's set it to remain that way."

"Set it?"

"He may have got into the machinery and fixed something."

"Peter doesn't know machinery."

"He's a wise one for ten. That I.Q. of his—"

"Nevertheless—"

"Hello, Mom. Hello, Dad."

The Hadleys turned. Wendy and Peter were coming in the front door, cheeks like peppermint candy, eyes like bright blue agate marbles, a smell of ozone on their jumpers from their trip in the helicopter.

"You're just in time for supper," said both parents.

"We're full of strawberry ice cream and hot dogs," said the children, holding hands. "But we'll sit and watch."

"Yes, come tell us about the nursery," said George Hadley.

The brother and sister blinked at him and then at each other. "Nursery?"

"All about Africa and everything," said the father with false joviality.

"I don't understand," said Peter.

"Your mother and I were just traveling through Africa with rod and reel; Tom Swift and his Electric Lion," said George Hadley.

"There's no Africa in the nursery," said Peter simply.

"Oh, come now, Peter. We know better."

"I don't remember any Africa," said Peter to Wendy. "Do you?"

"No."

"Run see and come tell."

She obeyed.

"Wendy, come back here!" said George Hadley, but she was gone. The house lights followed her like a flock of fireflies. Too late, he realized he had forgotten to lock the nursery door after his last inspection.

"Wendy'll look and come tell us," said Peter.

"She doesn't have to tell me. I've seen it."

"I'm sure you're mistaken, Father."

"I'm not, Peter. Come along now."

But Wendy was back. "It's not Africa," she said breathlessly.

"We'll see about this," said George Hadley, and they all walked down the hall together and opened the nursery door.

There was a green, lovely forest, a lovely river, a purple mountain, high voices singing, and Rima, lovely and mysterious, lurking in the trees with colorful flights of butterflies, like animated bouquets, lingering in her long hair. The African veldtland was gone. The lions were gone. Only Rima was here now, singing a song so beautiful that it brought tears to your eyes.

George Hadley looked in at the changed scene. "Go to bed," he said to the children.

They opened their mouths.

"You heard me," he said.

They went off to the air closet, where a wind sucked them like brown leaves up the flue to their slumber rooms.

George Hadley walked through the singing glade and picked up something that lay in the corner near where the lions had been. He walked slowly back to his wife.

"What is that?" she asked.

"An old wallet of mine," he said.

He showed it to her. The smell of hot grass was on it and the smell of a lion. There were drops of saliva on it, it had been chewed, and there were blood smears on both sides.

He closed the nursery door and locked it, tight.

In the middle of the night he was still awake and he knew his wife was awake. "Do you think Wendy changed it?" she said at last, in the dark room.

"Of course."

"Made it from a veldt into a forest and put Rima there instead of lions?"

"Yes."

"Why?"

"I don't know. But it's staying locked until I find out."

"How did your wallet get there?"

"I don't know anything," he said, "except that I'm beginning to be sorry we bought that room for the children. If children are neurotic at all, a room like that—"

"It's supposed to help them work off their neuroses in a healthful way."

"I'm starting to wonder." He stared at the ceiling.

"We've given the children everything they ever wanted. Is this our reward—secrecy, disobedience?"

"Who was it said, 'Children are carpets, they should be stepped on occasionally'? We've never lifted a hand. They're insufferable—let's admit it. They come and go when they like; they treat us as if we were offspring. They're spoiled and we're spoiled."

"They've been acting funny ever since you forbade them to take the rocket to New York a few months ago."

"They're not old enough to do that alone, I explained."

"Nevertheless, I've noticed they've been decidedly cool toward us since."

"I think I'll have David McClean come tomorrow morning to have a look at Africa."

"But it's not Africa now, it's Green Mansions country and Rima."

"I have a feeling it'll be Africa again before then."

A moment later they heard the screams.

Two screams. Two people screaming from downstairs. And then a roar of lions.

"Wendy and Peter aren't in their rooms," said his wife.

He lay in his bed with his beating heart. "No," he said. "They've broken into the nursery."

"Those screams—they sound familiar."

"Do they?"

"Yes, awfully."

And although their beds tried very hard, the two adults couldn't be rocked to sleep for another hour. A smell of cats was in the night air.

"Father?" said Peter.

"Yes."

Peter looked at his shoes. He never looked at his father any more, nor at his mother. "You aren't going to lock up the nursery for good, are you?"

"That all depends."

"On what?" snapped Peter.

"On you and your sister. If you intersperse this Africa with a little variety—oh, Sweden perhaps, or Denmark or China—"

"I thought we were free to play as we wished."

"You are, within reasonable bounds."

"What's wrong with Africa, Father?"

"Oh, so now you admit you have been conjuring up Africa, do you?"

"I wouldn't want the nursery locked up," said Peter coldly. "Ever."

"Matter of fact, we're thinking of turning the whole house off for about a month. Live sort of a carefree one-for-all existence."

"That sounds dreadful! Would I have to tie my own shoes instead of letting the shoe tier do it? And brush my own teeth and comb my hair and give myself a bath?"

"It would be fun for a change, don't you think?"

"No, it would be horrid. I didn't like it when you took out the picture painter last month."

"That's because I wanted you to learn to paint all by yourself, son."

"I don't want to do anything but look and listen and smell; what else is there to do?"

"All right, go play in Africa."

"Will you shut off the house sometime soon?"

"We're considering it."

"I don't think you'd better consider it any more, Father."

"I won't have any threats from my son!"

"Very well." And Peter strolled off to the nursery.

"Am I on time?" said David McClean.

"Breakfast?" asked George Hadley.

"Thanks, had some. What's the trouble?"

"David, you're a psychologist."

"I should hope so."

"Well, then, have a look at our nursery. You saw it a year ago when you dropped by; did you notice anything peculiar about it then?"

"Can't say I did; the usual violences, a tendency toward a slight paranoia here or there, usual in children because they feel persecuted by parents constantly, but, oh, really nothing."

They walked down the hall. "I locked the nursery up," explained the father, "and the children broke back into it during the night. I let them stay so they could form the patterns for you to see."

There was a terrible screaming from the nursery.

"There it is," said George Hadley. "See what you make of it." They walked in on the children without rapping.

The screams had faded. The lions were feeding.

"Run outside a moment, children," said George Hadley. "No, don't change the mental combination. Leave the walls as they are. Get!"

With the children gone, the two men stood studying the lions clustered at a distance, eating with great relish whatever it was they had caught.

"I wish I knew what it was," said George Hadley. "Sometimes I can almost see. Do you think if I brought high-powered binoculars here and—"

David McClean laughed dryly. "Hardly." He turned to study all four walls. "How long has this been going on?"

"A little over a month."

"It certainly doesn't feel good."

"I want facts, not feelings."

"My dear George, a psychologist never saw a fact in his life. He only hears about feelings; vague things. This doesn't feel good, I tell you. Trust my hunches and my instincts. I have a nose for something bad. This is very bad. My advice to you is to have the whole damn room torn down and your children brought to me every day during the next year for treatment."

"Is it that bad?"

"I'm afraid so. One of the original uses of these nurseries was so that we could study the patterns left on the walls by the child's mind, study at our leisure, and help the child. In this case, however, the room has become a channel toward—destructive thoughts, instead of a release away from them."

"Didn't you sense this before?"

"I sensed only that you had spoiled your children more than most. And now you're letting them down in some way. What way?"

"I wouldn't let them go to New York."

"What else?"

"I've taken a few machines from the house and threatened them, a month ago, with closing up the nursery unless they did their homework. I did close it for a few days to show I meant business."

"Ah, ha!"

"Does that mean anything?"

"Everything. Where before they had a Santa Claus now they have a Scrooge. Children prefer Santas. You've let this room and this house replace you and your wife in your children's affections. This room is their mother and father, far more important in their lives than their real parents. And now you come along and want to shut it off. No wonder there's hatred here. You can feel it coming out of the sky. Feel that sun. George, you'll have to change your life. Like too many others, you've built it around creature comforts. Why, you'd starve tomorrow if something went wrong in your kitchen. You wouldn't know how to tap an egg. Nevertheless, turn everything off. Start new. It'll take time. But we'll make good children out of bad in a year, wait and see."

"But won't the shock be too much for the children, shutting the room up abruptly, for good?"

"I don't want them going any deeper into this, that's all."

The lions were finished with their red feast.

The lions were standing on the edge of the clearing watching the two men.

"Now I'm feeling persecuted," said McClean. "Let's get out of here. I never have cared for these damned rooms. Make me nervous."

"The lions look real, don't they?" said George Hadley. "I don't suppose there's any way—"

"What?"

"—that they could become real?"

"Not that I know."

"Some flaw in the machinery, a tampering or something?"

"No."

They went to the door.

"I don't imagine the room will like being turned off," said the father.

"Nothing ever likes to die—even a room."

"I wonder if it hates me for wanting to switch it off?"

"Paranoia is thick around here today," said David McClean. "You can follow it like a spoor. Hello." He bent and picked up a bloody scarf. "This yours?"

"No." George Hadley's face was rigid. "It belongs to Lydia."

They went to the fuse box together and threw the switch that killed the nursery.

The two children were in hysterics. They screamed and pranced and threw things. They yelled and sobbed and swore and jumped at the furniture.

"You can't do that to the nursery, you can't!"

"Now, children."

The children flung themselves onto a couch, weeping.

"George," said Lydia Hadley, "turn on the nursery, just for a few moments. You can't be so abrupt."

"No."

"You can't be so cruel."

"Lydia, it's off, and it stays off. And the whole damn house dies as of here and now. The more I see of the mess we've put ourselves in, the more it sickens me. We've been contemplating our mechanical, electronic navels for too long. My God, how we need a breath of honest air!"

And he marched about the house turning off the voice clocks, the stoves, the heaters, the shoe shiners, the shoe lacers, the body scrubbers and swabbers and massagers, and every other machine he could put his hand to.

The house was full of dead bodies, it seemed. It felt like a mechanical cemetery. So silent. None of the humming hidden energy of machines waiting to function at the tap of a button.

"Don't let them do it!" wailed Peter at the ceiling, as if he was talking to the house, the nursery. "Don't let Father kill everything." He turned to his father. "Oh, I hate you!"

"Insults won't get you anywhere."

"I wish you were dead!"

"We were, for a long while. Now we're going to really start living. Instead of being handled and massaged, we're going to *live*."

Wendy was still crying and Peter joined her again. "Just a moment, just one moment, just another moment of nursery," they wailed.

"Oh, George," said the wife, "it can't hurt."

"All right—all right, if they'll only just shut up. One minute, mind you, and then off forever."

"Daddy, Daddy, Daddy!" sang the children, smiling with wet faces.

"And then we're going on a vacation. David McClean is coming back in half an hour to help us move out and get to the airport. I'm going to dress. You turn the nursery on for a minute, Lydia, just a minute, mind you."

And the three of them went babbling off while he let himself be vacuumed upstairs through the air flue and set about dressing himself. A minute later Lydia appeared.

"I'll be glad when we get away," she sighed.

"Did you leave them in the nursery?"

"I wanted to dress too. Oh, that horrid Africa. What can they see in it?"

"Well, in five minutes we'll be on our way to Iowa. Lord, how did we ever get in this house? What prompted us to buy a nightmare?"

"Pride, money, foolishness."

"I think we'd bettter get downstairs before those kids get engrossed with those damned beasts again."

Just then they heard the children calling, "Daddy, Mommy, come quick—quick!"

They went downstairs in the air flue and ran down the hall. The children were nowhere in sight. "Wendy? Peter!"

They ran into the nursery. The veldtland was empty save for the lions waiting, looking at them. "Peter, Wendy?"

The door slammed.

"Wendy, Peter!"

George Hadley and his wife whirled and ran back to the door.

"Open the door!" cried George Hadley, trying the knob.

"Why, they've locked it from the outside! Peter!" He beat at the door. "Open up!"

He heard Peter's voice outside, against the door.

"Don't let them switch off the nursery and the house," he was saying.

Mr. and Mrs. George Hadley beat at the door. "Now, don't be ridiculous, children. It's time to go. Mr. McClean'll be here in a minute and..."

And then they heard the sounds.

The lions on three sides of them, in the yellow veldt grass, padding through the dry straw, rumbling and roaring in their throats.

The lions.

Mr. Hadley looked at his wife and they turned and looked back at the beasts edging slowly forward, crouching, tails stiff.

Mr. and Mrs. Hadley screamed.

And suddenly they realized why those other screams had sounded familiar.

"Well, here I am," said David McClean in the nursery doorway. "Oh, hello." He stared at the two children seated in the center of the open glade eating a little picnic lunch. Beyond them was the water hole and the yellow veldtland; above was the hot sun. He began to perspire. "Where are your father and mother?"

The children looked up and smiled. "Oh, they'll be here directly."

"Good, we must get going." At a distance Mr. McClean saw the lions fighting and clawing and then quieting down to feed in silence under the shady trees.

He squinted at the lions with his hand up to his eyes.

Now the lions were done feeding. They moved to the water hole to drink.

A shadow flickered over Mr. McClean's hot face. Many shadows flickered. The vultures were dropping down the blazing sky.

"A cup of tea?" asked Wendy in the silence.

The Game of Rat and Dragon

Cordwainer Smith

Cordwainer Smith (1913-1966) is the pseudonym of Dr. Paul Myron Anthony Linebarger. The son of a retired judge, Linebarger grew up in China, Japan, France, and Germany. He published his first piece, a poem called "War No. 81-Q" in 1928. In 1930, Linebarger served as legal advisor to Chiang Kai-shek while attending the University of Nanking. He took his Masters from John Hopkins University in 1935, and received his doctorate a year later. Linebarger taught Asian politics at Harvard, Duke, and John Hopkins before World War II. He served as an Army intelligence officer during the war, receiving a Bronze Star. Linebarger's first published book, *Ria,* was released in 1947 under the pseudonym Felix Forrest. A spy novel published in 1949, *Atomsk,* was written under the name "Carmichael Smith." In 1950, *Fantasy Book* published his first story as Cordwainer Smith, "Scanners Live in Vain." Linebarger returned to the Army during the Korean War, writing again in 1955. His sole novel, *Nostrilia*, was finished in 1960 and was split into two parts for publication (only the first part saw publication before his death). Amongst his most famous stories are "The Burning of the Brain" (1958), "A Planet Named Shoyal" (1961), "You Will Never Be the Same" (1963), and "The Dead Lady of Clown Town" (1964). Two collections were published before his death: *Space Lords* (1965) and *The Quest of Three People* (1966). Upon his death in 1966, Linebarger was buried in Arlington with full honors.

Cordwainer Smith's handful of stories and single novel paint an intriguing tapestry of ideas and principles. "The Game of Rat and Dragon" is indicative of Smith's prose, a simple tale that is deeply imagined and entertains with its skill, elegance, and grace.

1. *The Table*

PINLIGHTING IS A hell of a way to earn a living. Underhill was furious as he closed the door behind himself. It didn't make much sense to wear a uniform and look like a soldier if people didn't appreciate what you did.

He sat down in his chair, laid his head back in the headrest, and pulled the helmet down over his forehead.

As he waited for the pin-set to warm up, he remembered the girl in the outer corridor. She had looked at it, then looked at him scornfully.

"Meow." That was all she had said. Yet it had cut him like a knife.

What did she think he was—a fool, a loafer, a uniformed nonentity? Didn't she know that for every half-hour of pinlighting, he got a minimum of two months' recuperation in the hospital?

By now the set was warm. He felt the squares of space around him, sensed himself at the middle of an immense grid, a cubic grid, full of nothing. Out in that nothingness, he could sense the hollow aching horror of space itself and could feel the terrible anxiety which his mind encountered whenever it met the faintest trace of inert dust.

As he relaxed, the comforting solidity of the Sun, the clockwork of the familiar planets and the moon rang in on him. Our own solar system was as charming and as simple as an ancient cuckoo clock filled with familiar ticking and with reassuring noises. The odd little moons of Mars swung around their planet like frantic mice, yet their regularity was itself an assurance that all was well. Far above the plane of the ecliptic, he could feel half a ton of dust more or less drifting outside the lanes of human travel.

Here there was nothing to fight, nothing to challenge the mind, to tear the living soul out of a body with its roots dripping in effluvium as tangible as blood.

Nothing ever moved in on the solar system. He could wear the pin-set forever and be nothing more than a sort of telepathic astronomer, a man who could feel the hot, warm protection of the sun throbbing and burning against his living mind.

Woodley came in.

"Same old ticking world," said Underhill. "Nothing to report. No wonder they didn't develop the pin-set until they began to planoform. Down here with the hot sun around us, it feels so good and so quiet. You can feel everything spinning and turning. It's nice and sharp and compact. It's sort of like sitting around home."

Woodley grunted. He was not much given to flights of fantasy.

Undeterred, Underhill went on, "It must have been pretty good to have been an ancient man. I wonder why they burned up their world with war. They didn't have to planoform. They didn't have to go out to earn their livings among the stars. They didn't have to dodge the rats or play the game. They couldn't have invented pinlighting because they didn't have any need of it, did they, Woodley?"

Woodley grunted, "Uh-huh." Woodley was twenty-six years old and due to retire in one more year. He already had a farm picked out. He had gotten through ten years of hard work pinlighting with the best of them. He had kept his sanity by not thinking very much about his job, meeting the strains of the task whenever he had to meet them and thinking nothing more about his duties until the next emergency arose.

Woodley never made a point of getting popular among the partners. None of the partners liked him very much. Some of them even resented him. He was suspected of thinking ugly thoughts of the partners on occasion, but since none of the partners ever thought a complaint in articulate form, the other pinlighters and the chiefs of the Instrumentality left him alone.

Underhill was still full of the wonder of their job. Happily he babbled on, "What does happen to us when we planoform? Do you think it's sort of like dying? Did you ever see anybody who had his soul pulled out?"

"Pulling souls is just a way of talking about it," said Woodley. "After all these years, nobody knows whether we have souls or not."

"But I saw one once. I saw what Dogwood looked like when he came apart. There was something funny. It looked wet and sort of sticky as if it were bleeding and it went out of him—and you know what they did to Dogwood? They took him away, up in that part of the hospital where you and I never go—way up at the top part where the others are, where the others always have to go if they are alive after the rats of the up-and-out have gotten them."

Woodley sat down and lit an ancient pipe. He was burning something called tobacco in it. It was a dirty sort of habit, but it made him look very dashing and adventurous.

"Look here, youngster. You don't have to worry about that stuff. Pinlighting is getting better all the time. The partners are getting better. I've seen them pinlight two rats forty-six million miles apart in one and a half milliseconds. As long as people had to try to work the pin-sets themselves, there was always the chance that with a minimum of four-hundred milliseconds for the human mind to set a pinlight, we wouldn't light the rats up fast enough to protect our planoforming ships. The partners have changed all that. Once they get going, they're faster than rats. And they always will be. I know it's not easy, letting a partner share your mind—"

"It's not easy for them, either," said Underhill.

"Don't worry about them. They're not human. Let them take care of themselves. I've seen more pinlighters go crazy from monkeying around with partners than I have ever seen caught by the rats. How many of them do you actually know of that got grabbed by rats?"

Underhill looked down at his fingers, which shone green and purple in the vivid light thrown by the tuned-in pin-set, and counted ships. The thumb for the *Andromeda,* lost with crew and passengers, the index finger and the middle finger for *Release Ships 43* and *56,* found with their pin-sets burned out and every man, woman, and child on board dead or insane. The ring finger, the little finger, and the thumb of the other hand were the first three battleships to be lost to the rats—lost as people realized that there was something out there *underneath space itself* which was alive, capricious, and malevolent.

Planoforming was sort of funny. It felt like—

Like nothing much.

Like the twinge of a mild electric shock.

Like the ache of a sore tooth bitten on for the first time.

Like a slightly painful flash of light against the eyes.

Yet in that time, a forty-thousand-ton ship lifting free above Earth disappeared somehow or other into two dimensions and appeared half a light-year or fifty light-years off.

At one moment, he would be sitting in the Fighting Room, the pin-set ready and the familiar solar system ticking around inside his head. For a second or a year (he could never tell how long it really was, subjectively), the funny little flash went through him and then he was loose in the up-and-out, the terrible open spaces between the stars, where the stars themselves felt like pimples on his telepathic mind and the planets were too far away to be sensed or read.

Somewhere in this outer space, a gruesome death awaited, death and horror of a kind which man had never encountered until he reached out for interstellar space itself. Apparently the light of the suns kept the Dragons away.

Dragons. That was what people called them. To ordinary people, there was nothing, nothing except the shiver of planoforming and the hammer blow of sudden death or the dark spastic note of lunacy descending into their minds.

But to the telepaths, they were dragons.

In the fraction of a second between the telepaths' awareness of a hostile something out in the black, hollow nothingness of space and the impact of a ferocious, ruinous psychic blow against all living things within the ship, the telepaths had sensed entities something like the dragons of ancient human lore, beasts more clever than beasts, demons more tangible than demons, hungry vortices of aliveness and hate compounded by unknown means out of the thin, tenuous matter between the stars.

It took a surviving ship to bring back the news—a ship in which, by sheer chance, a telepath had a lightbeam ready, turning it out at the innocent dust so that, within the panorama of his mind, the dragon dissolved into nothing at all and the other passengers, themselves non-telepathic, went about their way not realizing that their own immediate deaths had been averted.

From then on, it was easy—almost.

Planoforming ships always carried telepaths. Telepaths had their sensitiveness enlarged to an immense range by the pin-sets, which were telepathic amplifiers adapted to the mammal mind. The pin-sets in turn were electronically geared into small dirigible light bombs. Light did it.

Light broke up the dragons, allowed the ships to reform three-dimensionally, skip, skip, skip, as they moved from star to star.

The odds suddenly moved down from a hundred to one against mankind to sixty to forty in mankind's favor.

This was not enough. The telepaths were trained to become ultrasensitive, trained to become aware of the dragons in less than a millisecond.

But it was found that the dragons could move a million miles in just under two milliseconds and that this was not enough for the human mind to activate the light beams.

Attempts had been made to sheath the ships in light at all times.

This defense wore out.

As mankind learned about the dragons, so too, apparently, the dragons learned about mankind. Somehow they flattened their own bulk and came in on extremely flat trajectories very quickly.

Intense light was needed, light of sunlike intensity. This could be provided only the light bombs. Pinlighting came into existence.

Pinlighting consisted of the detonation of ultra-vivid miniature photonuclear bombs, which converted a few ounces of a magnesium isotope into pure visible radiance.

The odds kept coming down in mankind's favor, yet ships were being lost.

It became so bad that people didn't even want to find the ships because the rescuers knew what they would see. It was sad to bring back to Earth three hundred bodies ready for burial and two hundred or three hundred lunatics, damaged beyond repair, to be wakened, and fed, and cleaned, and put to sleep, wakened and fed again until their lives were ended.

Telepaths tried to reach into the minds of the psychotics who had been damaged by the dragons, but they found nothing there beyond vivid spouting columns of fiery terror bursting from the primordial id itself, the volcanic source of life.

Then came the partners.

Man and partner could do together what man could not do alone. Men had the intellect. Partners had the speed.

The partners rode their tiny craft, no larger than footballs, outside the spaceships. They planoformed with the ships. They rode beside them in their six-pound craft ready to attack.

The tiny ships of the partners were swift. Each carried a dozen pinlights, bombs no bigger than thimbles.

The pinlighters threw the partners—quite literally threw—by means of mind-to-firing relays directly at the dragons.

What seemed to be dragons to the human mind appeared in the form of gigantic rats in the minds of the partners.

Out in the pitiless nothingness of space, the partners' minds responded to an instinct as old as life. The partners attacked, striking with a speed faster than man's, going from attack to attack until the rats or themselves were destroyed. Almost all the time it was the partners who won.

With the safety of the interstellar skip, skip, skip of the ships, commerce increased immensely, the population of all the colonies went up, and the demand for trained partners increased.

Underhill and Woodley were a part of the third generation of pinlighters and yet, to them, it seemed as though their craft had endured forever.

Gearing space into minds by means of the pin-set, adding the partners to those minds, keying up the minds for the tension of a fight on which all depended—this was more than human synapses could stand for long. Underhill needed his two months' rest after half an hour of fighting. Woodley needed his retirement after ten years of service. They were young. They were good. But they had limitations.

So much depended on the choice of partners, so much on the sheer luck of who drew whom.

2. *The Shuffle*

Father Moontree and the little girl named West entered the room. They were the other two pinlighters. The human complement of the Fighting Room was now complete.

Father Moontree was a red-faced man of forty-five who had lived the peaceful life of a farmer until he reached his fortieth year. Only then, belatedly, did the authorities find he was telepathic and agree to let him late in life enter upon the career of pinlighter. He did well at it, but he was fantastically old for this kind of business.

Father Moontree looked at the glum Woodley and the musing Underhill. "How're the youngsters today? Ready for a good fight?"

"Father always wants a fight," giggled the little girl named West. She was such a little little girl. Her giggle was high and childish. She looked like the last person in the world one would expect to find in the rough, sharp dueling of pinlighting.

Underhill had been amused one time when he found one of the most sluggish of the partners coming away happy from contact with the mind of the girl named West.

Usually the partners didn't care much about the human minds with which they were paired for the journey. The partners seemed to take the attitude that human minds were complex and fouled up beyond belief, anyhow. No partner ever questioned the superiority of the human mind, though very few of the partners were much impressed by that superiority.

The partners liked people. They were willing to fight with them. They were even willing to die for them. But when a partner liked an individual the way, for example, that Captain Wow or the Lady May liked Underhill, the liking had nothing to do with intellect. It was a matter of temperament, of feel.

Underhill knew perfectly well that Captain Wow regarded his, Underhill's, brains as silly. What Captain Wow liked was Underhill's friendly emotional structure, the cheerfulness and glint of wicked amusement that shot through Underhill's unconscious thought patterns, and the gaiety with which Underhill faced danger. The words, the history books, the ideas, the science—Underhill could sense all that in his own mind, reflected back from Captain Wow's mind, as so much rubbish.

Miss West looked at Underhill. "I bet you've put stickum on the stones."

"I did not!"

Underhill felt his ears grow red with embarrassment.

During his novitiate, he had tried to cheat in the lottery because he got particularly fond of a special partner, a lovely young mother named Murr. It was so much easier to operate with Murr and she was so affectionate toward him that he forgot pinlighting was hard work and that he was not instructed to have a good time with his partner. They were both designed and prepared to go into deadly battle together.

One cheating had been enough. They had found him out and he had been laughed at for years.

Father Moontree picked up the imitation-leather cup and shook the stone dice which assigned them their partners for the trip. By senior rights he took first draw.

He grimaced. He had drawn a greedy old character, a tough old male whose mind was full of slobbering thoughts of food, veritable oceans full of half-spoiled fish. Father Moontree had once said that he burped cod liver oil for weeks after drawing that particular glutton, so strongly had the telepathic image of fish impressed itself upon his mind. Yet the glutton was a glutton for danger as well as for fish. He had killed sixty-three dragons, more than any other partner in the service, and was quite literally worth his weight in gold.

The little girl West came next. She drew Captain Wow. When she saw who it was, she smiled.

"I *like* him," she said. "He's such fun to fight with. He feels so nice and cuddly in my mind."

"Cuddly, hell," said Woodley. "I've been in his mind, too. It's the most leering mind in this ship, bar none."

"Nasty man," said the little girl. She said it declaratively, without reproach.

Underhill, looking at her, shivered.

He didn't see how she could take Captain Wow so calmly. Captain Wow's mind *did* leer. When Captain Wow got excited in the middle of a battle, confused images of dragons, deadly rats, luscious beds, the smell of fish, and the shock of space all scrambled together in his mind as he and Captain Wow, their consciousnesses linked together through the pin-set, became a fantastic composite of human being and Persian cat.

That's the trouble with working with cats, thought Underhill. It's a pity that nothing else anywhere will serve as partner. Cats were all right once you got in touch with them telepathically. They were smart enough to meet the needs of the flight, but their motives and desires were certainly different from those of humans.

They were companionable enough as long as you thought tangible images at them, but their minds just closed up and went to sleep when you recited Shakespeare or Colegrove, or if you tried to tell them what space was.

It was sort of funny realizing that the partners who were so grim and mature out here in space were the same cute little animals that people had used as pets for thousands of years back on Earth. He had embarrassed himself more than once while on the ground saluting perfectly ordinary non-telepathic cats because he had forgotten for the moment that they were not partners.

He picked up the cup and shook out his stone dice.

He was lucky—he drew the Lady May.

The Lady May was the most thoughtful partner he had ever met. In her, the finely bred pedigree mind of a Persian cat had reached one of its highest peaks of development. She was more complex than any human woman, but the complexity was all one of emotions, memory, hope, and discriminated experience—experience sorted through without benefit of words.

When he had first come into contact with her mind, he was astonished at its clarity. With her he remembered her kittenhood. He remembered every mating experience she had ever had. He saw in a half-recognizable gallery all the other pinlighters with whom she had been paired for the fight. And he saw himself radiant, cheerful, and desirable.

He even thought he caught the edge of a longing—

A very nattering and yearning thought: *What a pity he is not a cat.*

Woodley picked up the last stone. He drew what he deserved—a sullen, scarred old tomcat with none of the verve of Captain Wow. Woodley's partner was the most animal of all the cats on the ship, a low, brutish type with a dull mind. Even telepathy had not refined his character. His ears were half chewed off from the first fights in which he had engaged. He was a serviceable fighter, nothing more.

Woodley grunted.

Underhill glanced at him oddly. Didn't Woodley ever do anything but grunt?

Father Moontree looked at the other three. "You might as well get your partners now. I'll let the Go-captain know we're ready to go into the up-and-out."

3. *The Deal*

Underhill spun the combination lock on the Lady May's cage. He woke her gently and took her into his arms. She humped her back luxuriously, stretched her claws, started to purr, thought better of it, and licked him on the wrist instead. He did not have the pin-set on, so their minds were closed to each other, but in the angle of her mustache and in the movement of her ears, he caught some sense of the gratification she experienced in finding him as her partner.

He talked to her in human speech, even though speech meant nothing to a cat when the pin-set was not on.

"It's a damn shame, sending a sweet little thing like you whirling around in the coldness of nothing to hunt for rats that are bigger and deadlier than all of us put together. You didn't ask for this kind of fight, did you?"

For answer, she licked his hand, purred, tickled his cheek with her long fluffy tail, turned around and faced him, golden eyes shining.

For a moment, they stared at each other, man squatting, cat standing erect on her hind legs, front claws digging into his knee. Human eyes and cat eyes looked across an immensity which no words could meet, but which affection spanned in a single glance.

"Time to get in," he said.

She walked docilely to her spheroid carrier. She climbed in. He saw to it that her miniature pin-set rested firmly and comfortably against the base of her brain. He made sure that her claws were padded so that she could not tear herself in the excitement of battle.

Softly he said to her, "Ready?"

For answer, she preened her back as much as her harness would permit and purred softly within the confines of the frame that held her.

He slapped down the lid and watched the sealant ooze around the seam. For a few hours, she was welded into her projectile until a workman with a short cutting arc would remove her after she had done her duty.

He picked up the entire projectile and slipped it into the ejection tube. He closed the door of the tube, spun the lock, seated himself in his chair, and put his own pin-set on.

Once again he flung the switch.

He sat in a small room, *small, small, warm, warm,* the bodies of the other three people moving close around him, the tangible light in the ceiling bright and heavy against his closed eyelids.

As the pin-set warmed, the room fell away. The other people ceased to be people and became small glowing heaps of fire, embers, dark red fire, with the consciousness of life burning like old red coals in a country fireplace.

As the pin-set warmed a little more, he felt Earth just below him, felt the ship slipping away, felt the turning Moon as it swung on the far side of the world, felt the planets and the hot, clear goodness of the sun which kept the dragons so far from mankind's native ground.

Finally, he reached complete awareness.

He was telepathically alive to a range of millions of miles. He felt the dust which he had noticed earlier high above the ecliptic. With a thrill of warmth and tenderness, he felt the consciousness of the Lady May pouring over into his own. Her consciousness was as gentle and clear and yet sharp to the taste of his mind as if it were scented oil. It felt relaxing and reassuring. He could sense her welcome of him. It was scarcely a thought, just a raw emotion of greeting.

At last they were one again.

In a tiny remote corner of his mind, as tiny as the smallest toy he had ever seen in his childhood, he was still aware of the room and the ship, and of Father Moontree picking up a telephone and speaking to a Go-captain in charge of the ship.

His telepathic mind caught the idea long before his ears could frame the words. The actual sound followed the idea the way that thunder on an ocean beach follows the lightning inward from far out over the seas.

"The Fighting Room is ready. Clear to planoform, sir."

4. *The Play*

Underhill was always a little exasperated the way that Lady May experienced things before he did.

He was braced for the quick vinegar thrill of planoforming, but he caught her report of it before his own nerves could register what happened.

Earth had fallen so far away that he groped for several milliseconds before he found the Sun in the upper rear right-hand corner of his telepathic mind.

That was a good jump, he thought. *This way we'll get there in four or five skips.*

A few hundred miles outside the ship, the Lady May thought back at him, "O warm, O generous, O gigantic man! O brave, O friendly, O tender and huge partner! O wonderful with you, with you so good, good, good, warm, warm, now to fight, now to go, good with you..."

He knew that she was not thinking words, that his mind took the clear amiable babble of her cat intellect and translated it into images which his own thinking could record and understand.

Neither one of them was absorbed in the game of mutual greetings. He reached out far beyond her range of perception to see if there was anything near the ship. It was funny how it was possible to do two things at once. He could scan space with his pin-set mind and yet at the same time catch a vagrant thought of hers, a lovely, affectionate thought about a son who had had a golden face and a chest covered with soft, incredibly downy white fur.

While he was still searching, he caught the warning from her.

We jump again!

And so they had. The ship had moved to a second planoform. The stars were different. The sun was immeasurably far behind. Even the nearest stars were barely in contact. This was good dragon country, this open, nasty, hollow kind of space. He reached farther, faster, sensing and looking for danger, ready to fling the Lady May at danger wherever he found it.

Terror blazed up in his mind, so sharp, so clear, that it came through as a physical wrench.

The little girl named West had found something—something immense, long, black, sharp, greedy, horrific. She flung Captain Wow at it.

Underhill tried to keep his own mind clear. "Watch out!" he shouted telepathically at the others, trying to move the Lady May around.

At one corner of the battle, he felt the lustful rage of Captain Wow as the big Persian tomcat detonated light while he approached the streak of dust which threatened the ship and the people within.

The light scored near misses.

The dust flattened itself, changing from the shape of a sting ray into the shape of a spear.

Not three milliseconds had elapsed.

Father Moontree was talking human words and was saying in a voice that moved like cold molasses out of a heavy jar, "C-a-p-t-a-i-n." Underhill knew that the sentence was going to be "Captain, move fast!"

The battle would be fought and finished before Father Moontree got through talking.

Now, fractions of a millisecond later, the Lady May was directly in line.

Here was where the skill and speed of the partners came in. She could react faster than he. She could see the threat as an immense rat coming directly at her.

She could fire the light-bombs with a discrimination which he might miss.

He was connected with her mind, but he could not follow it.

His consciousness absorbed the tearing wound inflicted by the alien enemy. It was like no wound on Earth—raw, crazy pain which started like a burn at his navel. He began to writhe in his chair.

Actually he had not yet had time to move a muscle when the Lady May struck back at their enemy.

Five evenly spaced photonuclear bombs blazed out across a hundred-thousand miles.

The pain in his mind and body vanished.

He felt a moment of fierce, terrible, feral elation running through the mind of the Lady May as she finished her kill. It was always disappointing to the cats to find out that their enemies disappeared at the moment of destruction .

Then he felt her hurt, the pain and the fear that swept over both of them as the battle, quicker than the movement of an eyelid, had come and gone. In the same instant there came the sharp and acid twinge of planoform.

Once more the ship went skip.

He could hear Woodley thinking at him. "You don't have to bother much. This old son-of-a-gun and I will take over for a while."

Twice again the twinge, the skip.

He had no idea where he was until the lights of the Caledonia space port shone below.

With a weariness that lay almost beyond the limits of thought, he threw his mind back into rapport with the pin-set, fixing the Lady May's projectile gently and neatly in its launching tube.

She was half dead with fatigue, but he could feel the beat of her heart, could listen to her panting, and he grasped the grateful edge of a "Thanks" reaching from her mind to his.

5. *The Score*

They put him in the hospital at Caledonia.

The doctor was friendly but firm. "You actually got touched by that dragon. That's as close a shave as I've ever seen. It's all so quick that it'll be a long time before we know what happened scientifically, but I suppose you'd be ready for the insane asylum now if the contact had lasted several tenths of a millisecond longer. What kind of cat did you have out in front of you?"

Underhill felt the words coming out of him slowly. Words were such a lot of trouble compared with the speed and the joy of thinking, fast and sharp and clear, mind to mind! But words were all that could reach ordinary people like this doctor.

His mouth moved heavily as he articulated words. "Don't call our partners cats. The right thing to call them is partners. They fight for us in a team. You ought to know we call them partners, not cats. How is mine?"

"I don't know," said the doctor contritely. "We'll find out for you. Meanwhile, old man, you take it easy. There's nothing but rest that can help you. Can you make yourself sleep, or would you like us to give you some kind of sedative?"

"I can sleep," said Underhill. "I just want to know about the Lady May."

The nurse joined in. She was a little antagonistic. "Don't you want to know about the other people?"

"They're okay," said Underhill. "I knew that before I came in here."

He stretched his arms and sighed and grinned at them. He could see they were relaxing and were beginning to treat him as a person instead of a patient.

"I'm all right," he said. "Just let me know when I can go see my partner."

A new thought struck him. He looked wildly at the doctor. "They didn't send her off with the ship, did they?"

"I'll find out right away," said the doctor. He gave Underhill a reassuring squeeze of the shoulder and left the room.

The nurse took a napkin off a goblet of chilled fruit juice.

Underhill tried to smile at her. There seemed to be something wrong with the girl. He wished she would go away. First she had started to be friendly and now she was distant again. *It's a nuisance being tele-*

pathic, he thought. *You keep trying to reach even when you are not making contact.*

Suddenly she swung around on him.

"You pinlighters! You and your damn cats!"

Just as she stamped out, he burst into her mind. He saw himself a radiant hero, clad in his smooth suede uniform, the pin-set crown shining like ancient royal jewels around his head. He saw his own face, handsome and masculine, shining out of her mind. He saw himself very far away and he saw himself as she hated him.

She hated him in the secrecy of her own mind. She hated him because he was—she thought—proud and strange and rich, better and more beautiful than people like her.

He cut off the sight of her mind and, as he buried his face in the pillow, he caught an image of the Lady May.

"She *is* a cat," he thought. "That's all she is—a *cat!*"

But that was not how his mind saw her—quick beyond all dreams of speed, sharp, clever, unbelievably graceful, beautiful, wordless and undemanding.

Where would he ever find a woman who could compare with her?

Oh, To Be a Blobel!

Philip K. Dick

Philip K. Dick (1928-1982) was born in Chicago. In 1947, Dick worked at a classical radio station, and opened a record store the following year. He entered the University of California at Berkeley, but left in 1950 because of the way his pacifism conflicted with the school's ROTC requirement. He sold his first story, "Roog," to *The Magazine of Fantasy and Science Fiction* in 1952. That year, Dick gave up his store to be a freelance writer. He contributed stories to *Fantasy & Science Fiction* and *Galaxy* for three years. After his first novel, *The Solar Lottery* (1955), Dick began to concentrate his efforts on novel writing. His most famous novel, *The Man in the High Castle,* won him the Hugo award in 1962. In 1977, he was awarded the John W. Campbell award for *Flow My Tears, The Policeman Said.* Among Dick's other novels are *Eye in the Sky* (1957), *Time Out of Joint* (1959), *Dr. Futurity* (1960), *The Game Players of Titan* (1963), *The Simulcra* (1964), *The Three Stigmata of Palmer Eldritch* (1965,) *Do Androids Dream of Electric Sheep?* (1968), *Ubik* (1969), *We Can Build You* (1972), and *Through a Scanner Darkly* (1977).

Dick was one of the first of the "New Wave" science fiction writers—writers concerned more with the human than the physical sciences. "Oh, To Be a Blobel" is typical, tackling the psychological problems of warfare by positing war between two violently different species.

HE PUT A twenty-dollar platinum coin into the slot and the analyst, after a pause, lit up. Its eyes shone with sociability and it swiveled about in its chair, picked up a pen and pad of long yellow paper from its desk and said,

"Good morning, sir. You may begin."

"Hello, Dr. Jones. I guess you're not the same Dr. Jones who did the definitive biography of Freud; that was a century ago." He laughed nervously; being a rather poverty-stricken man he was not accustomed to dealing with the new fully homeostatic psychoanalysts. "Um," he said, "should I free-associate or give you background material or just what?"

Dr. Jones said, "Perhaps you could begin by telling me who you are and warum mich—why you have selected me."

"I'm George Munster of catwalk 4, building WEF-395, San Francisco condominium established 1996."

"How do you do, Mr. Munster." Dr. Jones held out its hand, and George Munster shook it. He found the hand to be of a pleasant body temperature and decidedly soft. The grip, however, was manly.

"You see," Munster said, "I'm an ex-G.I., a war veteran. That's how I got my condominium apartment at WEF-395—veterans' preference."

"Ah yes," Dr. Jones said, ticking faintly as it measured the passage of time. "The war with the Blobels."

"I fought three years in that war," Munster said, nervously smoothing his long, black, thinning hair. "I hated the Blobels and I volunteered; I was only nineteen and I had a good job—but the crusade to clear the Sol System of Blobels came first in my mind."

"Um," Dr. Jones said, ticking and nodding.

George Munster continued, "I fought well. In fact I got two decorations and a battlefield citation. Corporal. That's because I singlehandedly wiped out an observation satellite full of Blobels; we'll never know exactly how many because of course, being Blobels, they tend to fuse together and unfuse confusingly." He broke off, then, feeling emotional. Even remembering and talking about the war was too much for him...he lay back on the couch, lit a cigarette, and tried to become calm.

The Blobels had emigrated originally from another star system, probably Proxima. Several thousand years ago they had settled on Mars and on Titan, doing very well at agrarian pursuits. They were developments of the original unicellular amoeba, quite large and with a highly organized nervous system, but still amoeba, with pseudopodia, reproducing by binary fission, and in the main offensive to Terran settlers.

The war itself had broken out over ecological considerations. It had been the desire of the Foreign Aid Department of the U.N. to change the atmosphere on Mars, making it more usable for Terran settlers. This change, however, had made it unpalatable for the Blobel colonies already there; hence the squabble.

And, Munster reflected, it was not possible to change *half* the atmosphere of a planet, the Brownian movement being what it was. Within a period of ten years the altered atmosphere had diffused throughout the planet, bringing suffering—at least so they alleged—to the Blobels. In retaliation, a Blobel armada had approached Terra and had put into orbit a series of technically sophisticated satellites designed eventually to alter the atmosphere of Terra. This alteration had never come about because of course the War Offfice of the U.N. had gone into action; the satellites had been detonated by self-instructing missiles...and the war was on.

Dr. Jones said, "Are you married, Mr. Munster?"

"No sir," Munster said. "And—" He shuddered. "You'll see why when I've finished telling you. See, doctor—" He stubbed out his cigarette. "I'll be frank. I was a Terran spy. That was my task; they gave the job to me because of my bravery in the field...I didn't ask for it."

"I see," Dr. Jones said.

"Do you?" Munster's voice broke. "Do you know what was necessary in those days in order to make a Terran into a successful spy among the Blobels?"

Nodding, Dr. Jones said, "Yes, Mr. Munster. You had to relinquish your human form and assume the repellent form of a Blobel."

Munster said nothing; he clenched and unclenched his fist, bitterly. Across from him Dr. Jones ticked.

That evening, back in his small apartment at WEF-395, Munster opened a fifth of Teacher's scotch and sat by himself sipping from a cup, lacking even the energy to get a glass down from the cupboard over the sink.

What had he gotten out of the session with Dr. Jones today? Nothing, as nearly as he could tell. And it had eaten deep into his meager financial resources...meager because—

Because for almost twelve hours out of the day he reverted, despite all the efforts of himself and the Veterans' Hospitalization Agency of the U.N., to his old wartime Blobel shape. To a formless unicellular-like blob, right in the middle of his own apartment at WEF-395.

His financial resources consisted of a small pension from the War Office; finding a job was impossible, because as soon as he was hired the strain caused him to revert there on the spot, in plain sight of his new employer and fellow workers.

It did not assist in forming successful work-relationships.

Sure enough, now, at eight in the evening, he felt himself once more beginning to revert; it was an old and familiar experience to him, and he loathed it. Hurriedly, he sipped the last of the cup of scotch, put the cup down on a table...and felt himself slide together into a homogenous puddle.

The telephone rang.

"I can't answer," he called to it. The phone's relay picked up his anguished message and conveyed it to the calling party. Now Munster had become a single transparent gelatinous mass in the middle of the rug; he undulated toward the phone—it was still ringing, despite his statement to it, and he felt furious resentment; didn't he have enough troubles already, without having to deal with a ringing phone?

Reaching it, he extended a pseudopodium and snatched the receiver from the hook. With great effort he formed his plastic substance into the semblance of a vocal apparatus, resonating dully. "I'm busy," he resonated in a low booming fashion into the mouthpiece of the phone. "Call later." *Call,* he thought as he hung up, *tomorrow morning. When I've been able to regain my human form.*

The apartment was quiet, now.

Sighing, Munster flowed back across the carpet, to the window, where he rose into a high pillar in order to see the view beyond; there was a light-sensitive spot on his outer surface, and although he did not possess a true lens he was able to appreciate—nostalgically—the sight of San Francisco Bay, the Golden Gate Bridge, the playground for small children which was Alcatraz Island.

Dammit, he thought bitterly. *I can't marry; I can't live a genuine human existence, reverting this way to the form the War Office bigshots forced me into back in the wartimes....*

He had not known then, when he accepted the mission, that it would leave this permanent effect. They had assured him it was "only temporary, for the duration," or some such glib phrase. *Duration my ass,* Munster thought with furious, impotent resentment. *It's been* eleven years *now.*

The psychological problems created for him, the pressure on his psyche, were immense. Hence his visit to Dr. Jones.

Once more the phone rang.

"Okay," Munster said aloud, and flowed laboriously back across the room to it. "You want to talk to me?" he said as he came closer and closer; the trip, for someone in Blobel form, was a long one. "I'll talk to you. You can even turn on the vidscreen and *look* at me." At the phone he snapped the switch which would permit visual communication as well as auditory. "Have a good look," he said, and displayed his amorphous form before the scanning tube of the video.

Dr. Jones's voice came: "I'm sorry to bother you at your home, Mr. Munster, especially when you're in this, um, awkward condition..." The homeostatic analyst paused. "But I've been devoting time to problem solving vis-à-vis your condition. I may have at least a partial solution."

"What?" Munster said, taken by surprise. "You mean to imply that medical science can now—"

"No, no," Dr. Jones said hurriedly. "The physical aspects lie out of my domain; you must keep that in mind, Munster. When you consulted me about your problems it was the psychological adjustment that—"

"I'll come right down to your office and talk to you," Munster said. And then he realized that he could not; in his Blobel form it would take him days to undulate all the way across town to Dr. Jones's office. "Jones," he said desperately, "you see the problems I face. I'm stuck here in this apartment every night beginning about eight o'clock and lasting through until almost seven in the morning...I can't even visit you and consult you and get help—"

"Be quiet, Mr. Munster," Dr. Jones interrupted. "I'm trying to tell you something. *You're not the only one in this condition.* Did you know that?"

Heavily, Munster said, "Sure. In all, eighty-three Terrans were made over into Blobels at one time or another during the war. Of the eighty-three"—he knew the facts by heart—"sixty-one survived and now there's an organization called Veterans of Unnatural Wars of which fifty are members. I'm a member. We meet twice a month, revert in unison..." He started to hang up the phone. So this was what he had gotten for his money, this stale news. "Good-bye, doctor," he murmured.

Dr. Jones whirred in agitation. "Mr. Munster, I don't mean other Terrans. I've researched this in your behalf, and I discover that according to captured records at the Library of Congress fifteen *Blobels* were formed into pseudo-Terrans to act as spies for *their* side. Do you understand?"

After a moment Munster said, "Not exactly."

"You have a mental block against being helped," Dr. Jones said. "But here's what I want, Munster; you be at my office at eleven in the morning tomorrow. We'll take up the solution to your problem then. Goodnight."

Wearily, Munster said, "When I'm in my Blobel form my wits aren't too keen, doctor. You'll have to forgive me." He hung up, still puzzled. So there were fifteen Blobels walking around on Titan this moment, doomed to occupy human forms—so what? How did that help him?

Maybe he would find out at eleven tomorrow.

When he strode into Dr. Jones's waiting room he saw, seated in a deep chair in a corner by a lamp, reading a copy of *Fortune,* an exceedingly attractive young woman.

Automatically, Munster found a place to sit from which he could eye her. Stylish dyed-white hair braided down the back of her neck...he took in the sight with delight, pretending to read his own copy of *Fortune.* Slender legs, small and delicate elbows. And her sharp, clearly-featured face. The intelligent eyes, the thin, tapered nostrils—a truly lovely girl, he thought. He drank in the sight of her...until all at once she raised her head and stared coolly back at him.

"Dull, having to wait," Munster mumbled.

The girl said, "Do you come to Dr. Jones often?"

"No," he admitted. "This is just the second time."

"I've never been here before," the girl said. "I was going to another electronic fully homeostatic psychoanalyst in Los Angeles and then late yesterday Dr. Bing, my analyst, called me and told me to fly up here and see Dr. Jones this morning. Is this one good?"

"Um," Munster said. "I guess so." *We'll see,* he thought. *That's precisely what we don't know, at this point.*

The inner office door opened and there stood Dr. Jones. "Miss Arrasmith," it said, nodding to the girl. "Mr. Munster." It nodded to George. "Won't you both come in?"

Rising to her feet, Miss Arrasmith said, "Who pays the twenty dollars then?"

But the analyst had become silent; it had turned off.

"I'll pay," Miss Arrasmith said, reaching into her purse.

"No, no," Munster said. "Let me." He got out a twenty-dollar piece and dropped it into the analyst's slot.

At once, Dr. Jones said, "You're a gentleman, Mr. Munster." Smiling it ushered the two of them into its office. "Be seated, please, Miss Arrasmith, without preamble please allow me to explain your—condition to Mr. Munster." To Munster it said, "Miss Arrasmith is a Blobel."

Munster could only stare at the girl.

"Obviously," Dr. Jones continued, "presently in human form. This, for her, is the state of involuntary reversion. During the war she operated behind Terran lines, acting for the Blobel War League. She was captured and held, but then the war ended and she was neither tried nor sentenced."

"They released me," Miss Arrasmith said in a low, carefully controlled voice. "Still in human form. I stayed here out of shame. I just couldn't go back to Titan and—" Her voice wavered.

"There is great shame attached to this condition," Dr. Jones said, "for any high-caste Blobel."

Nodding, Miss Arrasmith sat clutching a tiny Irish linen handkerchief and trying to look poised. "Correct, doctor. I did visit Titan to discuss my condition with medical authorities there. After expensive and prolonged therapy with me they were able to induce a return to my natural form for a period of"—she hesitated—"about one-fourth of the time. But the other three-fourths...I am as you perceive me now." She ducked her head and touched the handkerchief to her right eye.

"Jeez," Munster protested, "you're lucky; a human form is infinitely superior to a Blobel form—I ought to know. As a Blobel you have to creep along...you're like a big jellyfish, no skeleton to keep you erect. And binary fission—it's lousy, I say really lousy, compared to the Terran form of—you know. Reproduction." He colored.

Dr. Jones ticked and stated, "For a period of about six hours your human forms overlap. And then for about one hour your Blobel forms overlap. So all in all, the two of you possess seven hours out of twenty-four in which you both possess identical forms. In my opinion"—it toyed with its pen and paper—"seven hours is not too bad. If you follow my meaning."

After a moment Miss Arrasmith said, "But Mr. Munster and I are natural enemies."

"That was years ago," Munster said.

"Correct," Dr. Jones agreed. "True, Miss Arrasmith is basically a Blobel and you, Munster, are a Terran, but—" It gestured. "Both of you are outcasts in either civilization; both of you are stateless and hence gradually suffering a loss of ego-identity. I predict for both of you a gradual deterioration ending finally in severe mental illness. Unless you two can develop a rapprochement." The analyst was silent then.

Miss Arrasmith said softly, "I think we're very lucky, Mr. Munster. As Dr. Jones said, we do overlap for seven hours a day...we can enjoy that time together, no longer in wretched isolation." She smiled up hopefully at him, rearranging her coat. Certainly, she had a nice figure; the somewhat low-cut dress gave an ideal clue to that.

Studying her, Munster pondered.

"Give him time," Dr. Jones told Miss Arrasmith. "My analysis of him is that he will see this correctly and do the right thing."

Still rearranging her coat and dabbing at her large, dark eyes, Miss Arrasmith waited.

The phone in Dr. Jones's office rang, a number of years later. He answered it in his customary way. "Please, sir or madam, deposit twenty dollars if you wish to speak to me."

A tough male voice on the other end of the line said, "Listen, this is the U.N. Legal Office and we don't deposit twenty dollars to talk to anybody. So trip that mechanism inside you, Jones."

"Yes sir," Dr Jones said, and with his right hand tripped the lever behind his ear that caused him to come on free.

"Back in 2037," the U.N. legal expert said, "did you advise a couple to marry? A George Munster and a Vivian Arrasmith, now Mrs. Munster?"

"Why yes," Dr. Jones said, after consulting his built-in memory banks.

"Had you investigated the legal ramifications of their issue?"

"Um well," Dr. Jones said, "that's not my worry."

"You can be arraigned for advising any action contrary to U.N. law."

"There's no law prohibiting a Blobel and a Terran from marrying."

The U.N. legal expert said, "All right, doctor, I'll settle for a look at their case histories."

"Absolutely not," Dr. Jones said. "That would be a breach of ethics."

"We'll get a writ and sequester them, then."

"Go ahead." Dr. Jones reached behind his ear to shut himself off.

"Wait. It may interest you to know that the Munsters now have four children. And, following the Mendelian Law, the offspring comprise a strict one, two, one ratio. One Blobel girl, one hybrid boy, one hybrid girl, one Terran girl. The legal problem arises in that the Blobel Supreme Council claims the pure-blooded Blobel girl as a citizen of Titan and also suggests that one of the two hybrids be donated to the council's jurisdiction." The U.N. legal expert explained, "You see, the Munsters' marriage is breaking up; they're getting divorced and it's sticky finding which laws obtain regarding them and their issue."

"Yes," Dr. Jones admitted, "I would think so. What has caused their marriage to break up?"

"I don't know and don't care. Possibly the fact that both adults and two of the four children rotate daily between being Blobels and Terrans; maybe the strain got to be too much. If you want to give them psychological advice, consult them. Good-bye." The U.N. legal expert rang off.

Did I make a mistake, advising them to marry? Dr. Jones asked itself. *I wonder if I shouldn't look them up; I owe at least that to them.*

Opening the Los Angeles phonebook, it began thumbing through the M's.

These had been six difficult years for the Munsters.

First, George had moved from San Francisco to Los Angeles; he and Vivian had set up their household in a condominium apartment with three instead of two rooms. Vivian, being in Terran form three-fourths of the time, had been able to obtain a job; right out in public she gave jet flight information at the Fifth Los Angeles Airport. George, however—

His pension comprised an amount only one-fourth that of his wife's salary and he felt it keenly. To augment it, he had searched for a way of earning money at home. Finally in a magazine he had found this valuable ad:

> MAKE SWIFT PROFITS IN YOUR OWN CONDO! RAISE GIANT BULL-FROGS FROM JUPITER, CAPABLE OF EIGHTY-FOOT LEAPS. CAN BE USED IN FROG RACING (WHERE LEGAL) AND

So in 2038 he had bought his first pair of frogs imported from Jupiter and had begun raising them for swift profits, right in his own condominium apartment building, in a corner of the basement that Leopold the partially homeostatic janitor let him use gratis.

But in the relatively feeble Terran gravity the frogs were capable of enormous leaps, and the basement proved too small for them; they ricocheted from wall to wall like green Ping-Pong balls and soon died. Obviously it took more than a portion of the basement at QEK-604 Apartments to house a crop of the damned things, George realized.

And then, too, their first child had been born. It had turned out to be pure-blooded Blobel for twenty-four hours a day it consisted of a gelatinous mass and George found himself waiting in vain for it to switch over to a human form, even for a moment.

He faced Vivian defiantly in this matter, during a period when both of them were in human form.

"How can I consider it my child?" he asked her. "It's—an alien life-form to me." He was discouraged and even horrified. "Dr. Jones should have foreseen this; maybe it's *your* child—it looks just like you."

Tears filled Vivian's eyes. "You mean that insultingly."

"Damn right I do. We fought you creatures—we used to consider you no better than Portuguese stingrays." Gloomily, he put on his coat. "I'm going down to Veterans of Unnatural Wars Headquarters," he informed his wife, "and have a beer with the boys." Shortly, he was on his way to join with his old wartime buddies, glad to get out of the apartment house.

V.U.W. Headquarters was a decrepit cement building in downtown Los Angeles left over from the twentieth century and sadly in need of paint. The V.U.W. had little funds because most of its members were, like George Munster, living on U.N. pensions. However, there was a pool table and an old 3-D television set and a few dozen tapes of popular music and also a chess set. George generally drank his beer and played chess with his fellow members, either in human form or in Blobel form; this was one place in which both were accepted.

This particular evening he sat with Pete Ruggles, a fellow veteran who also had married a Blobel female reverting, as Vivian did, to human form.

"Pete, I can't go on. I've got a gelatinous blob for a child. My whole life I've wanted a kid, and now what have I got? Something that looks like it washed up on the beach."

Sipping his beer—he too was in human form at the moment— Pete answered, "Criminy, George, I admit it's a mess. But you must have known what you were getting into when you married her. And my God, according to Mendel's Law, the next kid—"

"I mean," George broke in, "I don't respect my own wife; that's the basis of it. I think of her as a *thing.* And myself, too. We're both things." He drank down his beer in one gulp.

Pete said meditatively, "But from the Blobel standpoint—"

"Listen, whose side are you on?" George demanded.

"Don't yell at me," Pete said, "or I'll deck you."

A moment later they were swinging wildly at each other. Fortunately Pete reverted to Blobel form in the nick of time; no harm was done. Now George sat alone, in human shape, while Pete oozed off somewhere else, probably to join a group of the boys who had also assumed Blobel form.

Maybe we can found a new society somewhere on a remote moon, George said to himself moodily. *Neither Terran nor Blobel.*

I've got to go back to Vivian, George resolved. *What else is there for me? I'm lucky to find her; I'd be nothing but a war veteran guzzling beer here at V.U.W. Headquarters every damn day and night, with no future, no hope, no real life...*

He had a new money-making scheme going, now. It was a home mail-order business; he had placed an ad in the *Saturday Evening Post* for MAGIC LODESTONES REPUTED TO BRING YOU LUCK. FROM ANOTHER STAR SYSTEM ENTIRELY! The stones had come from Proxima and were obtainable on Titan; it was Vivian who had made the commercial contact for him with her people. But so far, few people had sent in the dollar-fifty.

I'm a failure, George said to himself.

Fortunately the next child, born in the winter of 2039, showed itself to be a hybrid; it took human form fifty percent of the time, and so at last George had a child who was—occasionally, anyhow—a member of his own species.

He was still in the process of celebrating the birth of Maurice when a delegation of their neighbors at QEK-604 Apartments came and rapped on their door.

"We've got a petition here," the chairman of the delegation said, shuffling his feet in embarrassment, "asking that you and Mrs. Munster leave QEK-604."

"But why?" George asked, bewildered. "You haven't objected to us up until now."

"The reason is that now you've got a hybrid youngster who will want to play with ours, and we feel it's unhealthy for our kids to—"

George slammed the door in their faces.

But still, he felt the pressure, the hostility from the people on all sides of them. *And to think,* he thought bitterly, *that I fought in the war to save these people. It sure wasn't worth it.*

An hour later he was down at V.U.W. Headquarters once more, drinking beer and talking with his buddy Sherman Downs, also married to a Blobel.

"Sherman, it's no good. We're not wanted; we've got to emigrate. Maybe we'll try it on Titan, in Viv's world."

"Chrissakes," Sherman protested, "I hate to see you fold up, George. Isn't your electromagnetic reducing belt beginning to sell, finally? "

For the last few months, George had been making and selling a complex electronic reducing gadget which Vivian had helped him design; it was based in principle on a Blobel device popular on Titan but unknown on Terra. And this had gone over well; George had more orders than he could fill. But—

"I had a terrible experience, Sherm," George confided. "I was in a drugstore the other day, and they gave me a big order for my reducing belt, and I got so excited—" He broke off. "You can guess what happened. I reverted. Right in plain sight of a hundred customers. And when the buyer saw that he canceled the order for the belts. It was what we all fear...you should have seen how their attitude toward me changed."

Sherm said, "Hire someone to do your selling for you. A full-blooded Terran."

Thickly, George said "*I'm* a full-blooded Terran, and don't you forget it. Ever."

"I just mean—"

"I know what you meant," George said. And took a swing at Sherman. Fortunately he missed and in the excitement both of them reverted to Blobel form. They oozed angrily into each other for a time, but at last fellow veterans managed to separate them.

"I'm as much a Terran as anyone," George thought-radiated in the Blobel manner to Sherman. "And I'll flatten anyone who says otherwise."

In Blobel form he was unable to get home; he had to phone Vivian to come and get him. It was humiliating.

Suicide, he decided. *That's the answer.*

How best to do it? In Blobel form he was unable to feel pain; best to do it then. Several substances would dissolve him...he could for instance drop himself into a heavily-chlorinated swimming pool, such as QEK-604 maintained in its recreation room.

Vivian, in human form, found him as he reposed hesitantly at the edge of the swimming pool, late one night.

"George, I beg you—go back to Dr. Jones."

"Naw," he boomed dully, forming a quasi-vocal apparatus with a portion of his body. "It's no use, Viv. I don't *want* to go on." Even the belts; they had been Viv's idea, rather than his. He was second even there...behind her, falling constantly further behind each passing day.

Viv said, "You have so much to offer the children."

That was true. "Maybe I'll drop over to the U.N. War Office," he decided. "Talk to them, see if there's anything new that medical science has come up with that might stabilize me."

"But if you stabilize as a Terran," Vivian said, "what would become of me?"

"We'd have *eighteen entire* hours together a day. All the hours you take human form!"

"But you wouldn't want to stay married to me. Because, George, then you could meet a Terran woman."

It wasn't fair to her, he realized. So he abandoned the idea.

In the spring of 2041 their third child was born, also a girl, and like Maurice a hybrid. It was Blobel at night and Terran by day.

Meanwhile, George found a solution to some of his problems.

He got himself a mistress.

At the Hotel Elysium, a run-down wooden building in the heart of Los Angeles, he and Nina arranged to meet one another.

"Nina," George said, sipping Teacher's scotch and seated beside her on the shabby sofa which the hotel provided, "you've made my life worth living again." He fooled with the buttons on her blouse.

"I respect you," Nina Glaubman said, assisting him with the buttons, "In spite of the fact—well, you are a former enemy of our people."

"God," George protested, "we must not think about the old days—we have to close our minds to our pasts." *Nothing but our future,* he thought.

His reducing-belt enterprise had developed so well that now he employed fifteen full-time Terran employees and owned a small, modern factory on the outskirts of San Fernando. If U.N. taxes had been reasonable he would by now be a wealthy man...brooding on that, George wondered what the tax rate was in Blobel-run lands, on Io, for instance. Maybe he ought to look into it.

One night at V.U.W. Headquarters he discussed the subject with Reinholt, Nina's husband, who of course was ignorant of the modus vivendi between George and Nina.

"Reinholt," George said with difficulty, as he drank his beer, "I've got big plans. This cradle-to-grave socialism the U.N. operates...it's not for me. It's cramping me. The Munster Magic Magnetic Belt is"—he gestured—"more than Terran civilization can support. You get me?"

Coldly, Reinholt said, "But George, you are a Terran; if you emigrate to Blobel-run territory with your factory you'll be betraying your—"

"Listen," George told him, "I've got one authentic Blobel child, two half-Blobel children, and a fourth on the way. I've got strong *emotional* ties with those people out there on Titan and Io."

"You're a traitor," Reinholt said, and punched him in the mouth. "And not only that," he continued, punching George in the stomach, "you're running around with my wife. I'm going to kill you."

To escape, George reverted to Blobel form; Reinholt's blows passed harmlessly deep into his moist, jellylike substance. Reinholt then reverted too, and flowed into him murderously, trying to consume and absorb George's nucleus.

Fortunately fellow veterans pried their two bodies apart before any permanent harm was done.

Later that night, still trembling, George sat with Vivian in the living room of their eight-room suite at the great new condominium apartment building ZGF-900. It had been a close call, and now of course Reinholt would tell Viv; it was only a question of time. The marriage, as far as George could see, was over. This perhaps was their last moment together.

"Viv," he said urgently, "you have to believe me; I love you. You and the children—plus the belt business, naturally—are my complete life." A desperate idea came to him. "Let's emigrate now, tonight. Pack up the kids and go to Titan, right this minute."

"I can't go," Vivian said. "I know how my people would treat me, and treat you and the children, too. George, you go. Move the factory to Io. I'll stay here." Tears filled her dark eyes.

"Hell," George said, "what kind of life is that? With you on Terra and me on Io—that's no marriage. And who'll get the kids?" Probably Viv would get them...but his firm employed top legal talent—perhaps he could use it to solve his domestic problems.

The next morning Vivian found out about Nina. And hired an attorney of her own.

"Listen," George said, on the phone talking to his top legal talent, Henry Ramarau. "Get me custody of the fourth child; it'll be a Terran. And we'll compromise on the two hybrids; I'll take Maurice and she can have Kathy. And naturally she gets that blob, that first so-called child. As far as I'm concerned it's hers anyhow." He slammed the receiver down and then turned to the board of directors of his company. "Now where were we?" he demanded. "In our analysis of Io tax laws."

During the next weeks the idea of a move to Io appeared more and more feasible from a profit and loss standpoint.

"Go ahead and buy land on Io," George instructed his business agent in the field, Tom Hendricks. "And get it cheap; we want to start right." To his secretary Miss Nolan he said, "Now keep everyone out of my office until further notice. I feel an attack coming on. From anxiety over this major move off Terra to Io." He added, "And personal worries."

"Yes, Mr. Munster," Miss Nolan said, ushering Tom Hendricks out of George's private office. "No one will disturb you." She could be counted on to keep everyone out while George reverted to his wartime Blobel shape, as he often did, these days; the pressure on him was immense.

When, later in the day, he resumed human form, George learned from Miss Nolan that a Dr. Jones had called.

"I'll be damned," George said, thinking back to six years ago. "I thought it'd be in the junk pile by now." To Miss Nolan he said, "Call Dr. Jones, notify me when you have it; I'll take a minute off to talk to it." It was like old times, back in San Francisco.

Shortly, Miss Nolan had Dr. Jones on the line.

"Doctor," George said, leaning back in his chair and swiveling from side to side and poking at an orchid on his desk. "Good to hear from you."

The voice of the homeostatic analyst came in his ear, "Mr. Munster, I note that you now have a secretary."

"Yes," George said, "I'm a tycoon. I'm in the reducing-belt game; it's somewhat like the flea-collar that cats wear. Well, what can I do for you?"

"I understand you have four children now—"

"Actually three, plus a fourth on the way. Listen, that fourth, doctor, is vital to me; according to Mendel's Law it's a full-blooded Terran and by God I'm doing everything in my power to get custody of it." He added, "Vivian—you remember her—is now back on Titan. Among her own people, where she belongs. And I'm putting some of the finest doctors I can get on my payroll to stabilize me; I'm tired of this constant reverting, night and day; I've got too much to do for such nonsense."

Dr. Jones said, "From your tone I can see you're an important, busy man, Mr. Munster. You've certainly risen in the world, since I saw you last."

"Get to the point, doctor," George said impatiently. "Why'd you call?"

"I, um, thought perhaps I could bring you and Vivian together again."

"Bah," George said contemptuously. "That woman? Never. Listen, doctor, I have to ring off; we're in the process of finalizing on some basic business strategy, here at Munster, Incorporated."

"Mr. Munster," Dr. Jones asked, "is there another woman?"

"There's another Blobel," George said, "if that's what you mean." And he hung up the phone. *Two Blobels are better than none,* he said to himself. *And now back to business...* He pressed a button on his desk and at once Miss Nolan put her head into the office. "Miss Nolan," George said, "get me Hank Ramarau; I want to find out—"

"Mr. Ramarau is waiting on the other line," Miss Nolan said. "He says it's urgent."

Switching to the other line, George said, "Hi, Hank. What's up?"

"I've just discovered," his top legal advisor said, "that to operate your factory on Io you must be a citizen of Titan."

"We ought to be able to fix that up," George said.

"But to be a citizen of Titan—" Ramarau hesitated. "I'll break it to you as easy as I can, George. You have to be a Blobel."

"Dammit, I am a Blobel," George said. "At least part of the time. Won't that do?"

"No," Ramarau said, "I checked into that, knowing of your affliction, and it's got to be one hundred percent of the time. Night *and* day."

"Hmmm," George said. "That is bad. But we'll overcome it, somehow. Listen, Hank, I've got an appointment with Eddy Fullbright, my medical coordinator; I'll talk to you after, okay?" He rang off and then sat scowling and rubbing his jaw. *Well,* he decided, *if it has to be it has to be. Facts are facts, and we can't let them stand in our way.*

Picking up the phone he dialed his doctor, Eddy Fullbright.

The twenty-dollar platinum coin rolled down the chute and tripped the circuit. Dr. Jones came on, glanced up, and saw a stunning, sharp-breasted young woman whom it recognized—by means of a quick scan of its memory banks—as Mrs. George Munster, the former Vivian Arrasmith.

"Good day, Vivian," Dr. Jones said cordially. "But I understood you were on Titan." It rose to its feet, offering her a chair.

Dabbing at her large, dark eyes, Vivian sniffled, "Doctor, everything is collapsing around me. My husband is having an affair with another woman...all I know is that her name is Nina and all the boys down at V.U.W. Headquarters are talking about it. Presumably she's a Terran. We're both filing for divorce. And we're having a dreadful legal battle over the children." She arranged her coat modestly. "I'm expecting. Our fourth."

"This I know," Dr. Jones said. "A full-blooded Terran this time, if Mendel's Law holds...although it only applied to litters."

Mrs. Munster said miserably, "I've been on Titan talking to legal and medical experts, gynecologists, and especially marital guidance counselors; I've had all sorts of advice during the past month. Now I'm back on Terra but I can't find George—he's *gone.*"

"I wish I could help you, Vivian," Dr. Jones said. "I talked to your husband briefly, the other day, but he spoke only in generalities...evidently he's such a big tycoon now that it's hard to approach him."

"And to think," Vivian sniffled, "the he achieved it all because of an idea I gave him. A Blobel idea."

"The ironies of fate," Dr. Jones said. "Now, if you want to keep your husband, Vivian—"

"I'm determined to keep him, Dr. Jones. Frankly, I've undergone therapy on Titan, the latest and most expensive...it's because I love George so much, even more than I love my own people or my planet."

"Eh?" Dr. Jones said.

"Through the most modern developments in medical science in the Sol System," Vivian said, "I've been stabilized, Dr. Jones. Now I am in human form twenty-four hours a day instead of eighteen. I've renounced my natural form in order to keep my marriage with George."

"The supreme sacrifice," Dr. Jones said, touched.

"Now, if I can only *find* him, doctor—"

At the ground-breaking ceremonies on Io, George Munster flowed gradually to the shovel, extended a pseudopodium, seized the shovel, and with it managed to dig a symbolic amount of soil. "This is a great day," he boomed hollowly, by means of the semblance of a vocal apparatus into which he had fashioned the slimy, plastic substance which made up his unicellular body.

"Right, George," Hank Ramarau agreed, standing nearby with the legal documents.

The Ionan official, like George a great transparent blob, oozed across to Ramarau, took the documents, and boomed, "These will be transmitted to my government. I'm sure they're in order, Mr. Ramarau."

"I guarantee you," Ramarau said to the official, "Mr. Munster does not revert to human form at any time; he's made use of some of the most advanced techniques in medical science to achieve this stability at the unicellular phase of his former rotation. Munster would never cheat."

"This historic moment," the great blob that was George Munster thought-radiated to the throng of local Blobels attending the ceremonies, "means a higher standard of living for Ionans who will be employed; it will bring prosperity to this area, plus a proud sense of national achievement in the manufacture of what we recognize to be a native invention, the Munster Magic Magnetic Belt."

The throng of Blobels thought-radiated cheers.

"This is a proud day in my life," George Munster informed them, and began to ooze by degrees back to his car, where his chauffeur waited to drive him to his permanent hotel room at Io City.

Someday he would own the hotel. He was putting the profits from his business in local real estate; it was the patriotic—and the profitable—thing to do, other Ionans, other Blobels, had told him.

"I'm finally a successful man," George Munster thought-radiated to all close enough to pick up his emanations.

Amid frenzied cheers he oozed up the ramp and into his Titan-made car.

The Sentinel

Arthur C. Clarke

Arthur C. Clarke (b. 1917) was born in Minehead, England. As a child, Clarke became very interested in astronomy. In high school, Clarke began contributing science fiction to *Huish Magazine.* He joined the Royal Air Force in 1941, and was the Technical Officer for the first ground controlled approach radar system. In 1945, Clarke published a paper that proposed stationary orbiting communication satellites. He attended King's College from 1946-48, and graduated with a B.A. in physics and mathematics. In 1949, Clarke became assistant editor of *Physics Abstracts.* His first book, *Interplanetary Flight,* was released in 1950, and was quickly followed by *Exploration of Space* a year later. In 1951, he published his first fictional book, *Prelude to Space.* This was followed by *The Sands of Mars* (1952) and *Childhood's End* (1954). In 1954, Clarke moved to Sri Lanka to engage in oceanography and undersea exploration. His short story "The Star" won the Hugo in 1956. In 1967, Clarke was approached by filmmaker Stanley Kubrick about writing a script based on his story "The Sentinel." The film that resulted, *2001: A Space Odyssey,* won him a second Hugo for best screenplay. In 1972, "Meeting With Medusa" won Clarke a Nebula award. He has also won Nebulas for his novels *Rondezvous With Rama* (1973) and *Fountains of Paradise* (1979). Among Clarke's other works are *Expedition to Earth* (1953), *Earthlight* (1955), *Tales from the White Hart* (1957), *Tales of Ten Worlds* (1963), *The Nine Billion Names of God* (1967), *Imperial Earth* (1976), *The View From Serendip* (1977), and *2010: Odyssey Two* (1982). Clarke presently lives in Sri Lanka.

"The Sentinel" is demonstrative of Clarke's eye for detail and ability to create a sense of awe in the reader.

THE NEXT TIME you see the full moon high in the south, look carefully at its right-hand edge and let your eye travel upward along the curve of the disk. Round about two o'clock you will notice a small, dark oval: anyone with normal eyesight can find it quite easily. It is the great walled plain, one of the finest on the Moon, known as the Mare Crisium—the Sea of Crises. Three hundred miles in diameter, and almost completely surrounded by a ring of magnificent mountains, it had never been explored until we entered it in the late summer of 1996.

Our expedition was a large one. We had two heavy freighters which had flown our supplies and equipment from the main lunar base in the Mare Serenitatis, five hundred miles away. There were also three small rockets which were intended for short-range transport over regions which our surface vehicles couldn't cross. Luckily, most of the Mare Crisium is very flat. There are none of the great crevasses so common and so dangerous elsewhere, and very few craters or mountains of any size. As far as we could tell, our powerful caterpillar tractors would have no difficulty in taking us wherever we wished to go.

I was geologist—or selenologist, if you want to be pedantic—in charge of the group exploring the southern region of the Mare. We had crossed a hundred miles of it in a week, skirting the foothills of the mountains along the shore of what was once the ancient sea, some thousand million years before. When life was beginning on Earth, it was already dying here. The waters were retreating down the flanks of those stupendous cliffs, retreating into the empty heart of the Moon. Over the land which we were crossing, the tideless ocean had once been half a mile deep, and now the only trace of moisture was the hoarfrost one could sometimes find in caves which the searing sunlight never penetrated.

We had begun our journey early in the slow lunar dawn, and still had almost a week of Earth-time before nightfall. Half a dozen times a day we would leave our vehicle and go outside in the space-suits to hunt for interesting minerals, or to place markers for the guidance of future travelers. It was an uneventful routine. There is nothing hazardous or even particularly exciting about lunar exploration. We could live comfortably for a month in our pressurized tractors, and if we ran into trouble we could always radio for help and sit tight until one of the spaceships came to our rescue.

I said just now that there was nothing exciting about lunar exploration, but of course that isn't true. One could never grow tired of those incredible mountains, so much more rugged than the gentle hills of Earth. We never knew, as we rounded the capes and promontories of that vanished sea, what new splendors would be revealed to us. The whole southern curve of the Mare Crisium is a vast delta where a score of rivers once found their way into the ocean, fed perhaps by the torrential rains that must have lashed the mountains in the brief volcanic age when the Moon was young. Each of these ancient valleys was an invitation, challenging us to climb into the unknown uplands beyond. But we had a hundred miles still to cover, and could only look longingly at the heights which others must scale.

We kept Earth-time aboard the tractor, and precisely at 22.00 hours the final radio message would be sent out to Base and we would close down for the day. Outside, the rocks would still be burning beneath the almost vertical sun, but to us it was night until we awoke again eight hours later. Then one of us would prepare breakfast, there would be a great buzzing of electric razors, and someone would switch on the short-wave radio from Earth. Indeed, when the smell of frying sausages began to fill the cabin, it was sometimes hard to believe that we were not back on our own world—everything was so normal and homely, apart from the feeling of decreased weight and the unnatural slowness with which objects fell.

It was my turn to prepare breakfast in the corner of the main cabin that served as a galley. I can remember that moment quite vividly after all these years, for the radio had just played one of my favorite melodies, the old Welsh air, "David of the White Rock." Our driver was already outside in his space-suit, inspecting our caterpillar treads. My assistant, Louis Garnett, was up forward in the control position, making some belated entries in yesterday's log.

As I stood by the frying pan waiting, like any terrestrial housewife, for the sausages to brown, I let my gaze wander idly over the mountain walls which covered the whole of the southern horizon, marching out of sight to east and west below the curve of the Moon. They seemed only a mile or two from the tractor, but I knew that the nearest was twenty miles away. On the Moon, of course, there is no loss of detail with distance—none of that almost imperceptible haziness which softens and sometimes transfigures all far-off things on Earth.

Those mountains were ten thousand feet high, and they climbed steeply out of the plain as if ages ago some subterranean eruption had smashed them skyward through the molten crust. The base of even the nearest was hidden from sight by the steeply curving surface of the plain, for the Moon is a very little world, and from where I was standing the horizon was only two miles away.

I lifted my eyes toward the peaks which no man had ever climbed, the peaks which, before the coming of terrestrial life, had watched the retreating oceans sink sullenly into their graves, taking with them the hope and the morning promise of a world. The sunlight was beating against those ramparts with a glare that hurt the eyes, yet only a little way above them the stars were shining steadily in a sky blacker than a winter midnight on Earth.

I was turning away when my eye caught a metallic glitter high on the ridge of a great promontory thrusting out into the sea thirty miles to the west. It was a dimensionless point of light, as if a star had been clawed from the sky by one of those cruel peaks, and I imagined that some smooth rock surface was catching the sunlight and heliographing it straight into my eyes. Such things were not uncommon. When the Moon is in her second quarter, observers on Earth can sometimes see the great ranges in the Oceanus Procellarum burning with a blue-white iridescence as the sunlight flashes from their slopes and leaps again from world to world. But I was curious to know what kind of rock could be shining so brightly up there, and I climbed into the observation turret and swung our four-inch telescope round to the west.

I could see just enough to tantalize me. Clear and sharp in the field of vision, the mountain peaks seemed only half a mile away, but whatever was catching the sunlight was still too small to be resolved. Yet it seemed to have an elusive symmetry, and the summit upon which it rested was curiously flat. I stared for a long time at that glittering enigma, straining my eyes into space, until presently a smell of burning from the galley told me that our breakfast sausages had made their quarter-million-mile journey in vain.

All that morning we argued our way across the Mare Crisium while the western mountains reared higher in the sky. Even when we were out prospecting in the space-suits, the discussion would continue over the radio. It was absolutely certain, my companions argued, that there had never been any form of intelligent life on the Moon. The only living things that had ever existed there were a few primitive plants and their slightly less degenerate ancestors. I knew that as well as anyone, but there are times when a scientist must not be afraid to make a fool of himself.

"Listen," I said at last, "I'm going up there, if only for my own peace of mind. That mountain's less than twelve thousand feet high—that's only two thousand under Earth gravity—and I can make the trip in twenty hours at the outside. I've always wanted to go up into those hills, anyway, and this gives me an excellent excuse."

"If you don't break your neck," said Garnett, "you'll be the laughing-stock of the expedition when we get back to Base. That mountain will probably be called Wilson's Folly from now on."

"I won't break my neck," I said firmly. "Who was the first man to climb Pico and Helicon?"

"But weren't you rather younger in those days?" asked Louis gently.

"That," I said with great dignity, "is as good a reason as any for going."

We went to bed early that night, after driving the tractor to within half a mile of the promontory. Garnett was coming with me in the morning; he was a good climber, and had often been with me on such exploits before. Our driver was only too glad to be left in charge of the machine.

At first sight, those cliffs seemed completely unscaleable, but to anyone with a good head for heights, climbing is easy on a world where all weights are only a sixth of their normal value. The real danger in lunar mountaineering lies in overconfidence; a six-hundred-foot drop on the Moon can kill you just as thoroughly as a hundred-foot fall on Earth.

We made our first halt on a wide ledge about four thousand feet above the plain. Climbing had not been very difficult, but my limbs were stiff with the unaccustomed effort, and I was glad of the rest. We could still see the tractor as a tiny metal insect far down at the foot of the cliff, and we reported our progress to the driver before starting on the next ascent.

Inside our suits it was comfortably cool, for the refrigeration units were fighting the fierce sun and carrying away the body heat of our exertions. We seldom spoke to each other, except to pass climbing instructions and to discuss our best plan of ascent. I do not know what Garnett was thinking, probably that this was the craziest goose-chase he had ever embarked upon. I more than half agreed with him, but the joy of climbing, the knowledge that no man had ever gone this way before and the exhilaration of the steadily widening landscape gave me all the reward I needed.

I don't think I was particularly excited when I saw in front of us the wall of rock I had first inspected through the telescope from thirty miles away. It would level off about fifty feet above our heads, and there on the plateau would be the thing that had lured me over these barren wastes. It was, almost certainly, nothing more than a boulder splintered ages ago by a falling meteor, and with its cleavage planes still fresh and bright in this incorruptible, unchanging silence.

There were no hand-holds on the rock face, and we had to use a grapnel. My tired arms seemed to gain new strength as I swung the three-pronged metal anchor round my head and sent it sailing up toward the stars. The first time it broke loose and came falling slowly back when we pulled the rope. On the third attempt, the prongs gripped firmly and our combined weights could not shift it.

Garnett looked at me anxiously. I could tell that he wanted to go first, but I smiled back at him through the glass of my helmet and shook my head. Slowly, taking my time, I began the final ascent.

Even with my space-suit, I weighed only forty pounds here, so I pulled myself up hand over hand without bothering to use my feet. At the rim I paused and waved to my companion, then I scrambled over the edge and stood upright, staring ahead of me.

You must understand that until this very moment I had been almost completely convinced that there could be nothing strange or unusual for me to find here. Almost, but not quite; it was that haunting doubt that had driven me forward. Well, it was a doubt no longer, but the haunting had scarcely begun.

I was standing on a plateau perhaps a hundred feet across. It had once been smooth—too smooth to be natural—but falling meteors had pitted and scored its surface through immeasurable eons. It had been leveled to support a glittering, roughly pyramidal structure, twice as high as a man, that was set in the rock like a gigantic, many-faceted jewel.

Probably no emotion at all filled my mind in those first few seconds. Then I felt a great lifting of my heart, and a strange, inexpressible joy. For I loved the Moon, and now I knew that the creeping moss of Aristarchus and Eratosthenes was not the only life she had brought forth in her youth. The old, discredited dream of the first explorers was true. There had, after all, been a lunar civilization—and I was the first to find it. That I had come perhaps a hundred million years too late did not distress me; it was enough to have come at all.

My mind was beginning to function normally, to analyze and to ask questions. Was this a building, a shrine—or something for which my language had no name? If a building, then why was it erected in so uniquely inaccessible a spot? I wondered if it might be a temple, and I could picture the adepts of some strange priesthood calling on their gods to preserve them as the life of the Moon ebbed with the dying oceans, and calling on their gods in vain.

I took a dozen steps forward to examine the thing more closely, but some sense of caution kept me from going too near. I knew a little of archaeology, and tried to guess the cultural level of the civilization that must have smoothed this mountain and raised the glittering mirror surfaces that still dazzled my eyes.

The Egyptians could have done it, I thought, if their workmen had possessed whatever strange materials these far more ancient architects had used. Because of the thing's smallness, it did not occur to me that

I might be looking at the handiwork of a race more advanced than my own. The idea that the Moon had possessed intelligence at all was still almost too tremendous to grasp, and my pride would not let me take the final, humiliating plunge.

And then I noticed something that set the scalp crawling at the back of my neck—something so trivial and so innocent that many would never have noticed it at all. I have said that the plateau was scarred by meteors; it was also coated inches-deep with the cosmic dust that is always filtering down upon the surface of any world where there are no winds to disturb it. Yet the dust and the meteor scratches ended quite abruptly in a wide circle enclosing the little pyramid, as though an invisible wall was protecting it from the ravages of time and the slow but ceaseless bombardment from space.

There was someone shouting in my earphones, and I realized that Garnett had been calling me for some time. I walked unsteadily to the edge of the cliff and signaled him to join me, not trusting myself to speak. Then I went back toward that circle in the dust. I picked up a fragment of splintered rock and tossed it gently toward the shining enigma. If the pebble had vanished at that invisible barrier I should not have been surprised, but it seemed to hit a smooth, hemispherical surface and slide gently to the ground.

I knew then that I was looking at nothing that could be matched in the antiquity of my own race. This was not a building, but a machine, protecting itself with forces that had challenged Eternity. Those forces, whatever they might be, were still operating, and perhaps I had already come too close. I thought of all the radiations man had trapped and tamed in the past century. For all I knew, I might be as irrevocably doomed as if I had stepped into the deadly, silent aura of an unshielded atomic pile.

I remember turning then toward Garnett, who had joined me and was now standing motionless at my side. He seemed quite oblivious to me, so I did not disturb him but walked to the edge of the cliff in an effort to marshal my thoughts. There below me lay the Mare Crisium—Sea of Crises, indeed—strange and weird to most men, but reassuringly familiar to me. I lifted my eyes toward the crescent Earth, lying in her cradle of stars, and I wondered what her clouds had covered when these unknown builders had finished their work. Was it the steaming jungle of the Carboniferous, the bleak shoreline over which the first amphibians must crawl to conquer the land—or, earlier still, the long loneliness before the coming of life?

Do not ask me why I did not guess the truth sooner— the truth that seems so obvious now. In the first excitement of my discovery, I had assumed without question that this crystalline apparition had been built by some race belonging to the Moon's remote past, but suddenly, and with overwhelming force, the belief came to me that it was as alien to the Moon as I myself.

In twenty years we had found no trace of life but a few degenerate plants. No lunar civilization, whatever its doom, could have left but a single token of its existence.

I looked at the shining pyramid again, and the more remote it seemed from anything that had to do with the Moon. And suddenly I felt myself shaking with a foolish, hysterical laughter, brought on by excitement and overexertion: for I had imagined that the little pyramid was speaking to me and was saying: "Sorry, I'm a stranger here myself."

It had taken us twenty years to crack that invisible shield and to reach the machine inside those crystal walls. What we could not understand, we broke at last with the savage might of atomic power and now I have seen the fragments of the lovely, glittering thing I found up there on the mountain.

They are meaningless. The mechanisms—if indeed they are mechanisms—of the pyramid belong to a technology that lies far beyond our horizon, perhaps to the technology of para-physical forces.

The mystery haunts us all the more now that the other planets have been reached and we know that only Earth has ever been the home of intelligent life in our Universe. Nor could any lost civilization of our own world have built that machine, for the thickness of the meteoric dust on the plateau has enabled us to measure its age. It was set there upon its mountain before life had emerged from the seas of Earth.

When our world was half its present age, *something* from the stars swept through the Solar System, left this token of its passage, and went again upon its way. Until we destroyed it, that machine was still fulfilling the purpose of its builders; and as to that purpose, here is my guess.

Nearly a hundred thousand million stars are turning in the circle of the Milky Way, and long ago other races on the worlds of other suns must have scaled and passed the heights that we have reached. Think of such civilizations, far back in time against the fading afterglow of Creation, masters of a universe so young that life as yet had come only to a handful of worlds. Theirs would have been a loneliness we cannot imagine, the loneliness of gods looking out across infinity and finding none to share their thoughts.

They must have searched the star clusters as we have searched the planets. Everywhere there would be worlds, but they would be empty or peopled with crawling, mindless things. Such was our own Earth, the smoke of the great volcanoes still staining the skies, when that first ship of the peoples of the dawn came sliding in from the abyss beyond Pluto. It passed the frozen outer worlds, knowing that life could play no part in their destinies. It came to rest among the inner planets, warming themselves around the fire of the Sun and waiting for their stories to begin.

Those wanderers must have looked on Earth, circling safely in the narrow zone between fire and ice, and must have guessed that it was the favorite of the Sun's children. Here, in the distant future, would be intelligence; but there were countless stars before them still, and they might never come this way again.

So they left a sentinel, one of millions they have scattered throughout the Universe, watching over all worlds with the promise of life. It was a beacon that down the ages has been patiently signaling the fact that no one had discovered it.

Perhaps you understand now why that crystal pyramid was set upon the Moon instead of on the Earth. Its builders were not concerned with races still struggling up from savagery. They would be interested in our civilization only if we proved our fitness to survive—by crossing space and so escaping from the Earth, our cradle. That is the challenge that all intelligent races must meet, sooner or later. It is a double challenge, for it depends in turn upon the conquest of atomic energy and the last choice between life and death.

Once we had passed that crisis, it was only a matter of time before we found the pyramid and forced it open. Now its signals have ceased, and those whose duty it is will be turning their minds upon Earth. Perhaps they wish to help our infant civilization. But they must be very, very old, and the old are often insanely jealous of the young.

I can never look now at the Milky Way without wondering from which of those banked clouds of stars the emissaries are coming. If you will pardon so commonplace a simile, we have set off the fire-alarm and have nothing to do but to wait.

I do not think we will have to wait for long.

A Relic of Empire

Larry Niven

Larry Niven (b. 1938) was born in Los Angeles. A graduate of Washburn University, Niven did a year of graduate work at UCLA before pursuing a career as a science fiction writer. Niven lived off a family trust fund until the publication of his first book, *World of Ptavvs* (1966). His short story "Neutron Star" won a Hugo Award in 1967. *A Gift From Earth* was released the following year. In 1969, Niven married Marilyn Joyce Wisowaty. In 1970, Niven wrote the first book in his most famous series, *Ringworld.* His story "Inconstant Moon" won him his second Hugo in 1971. That year, he produced *The Flying Sorcerers* with David Gerrold. In 1973 he wrote *Protector,* and he collaborated with Jerry Pournelle on *The Mote in God's Eye* in 1974. Niven's partnership with Pournelle proved particularly fruitful, and they wrote two other novels during the 1970's, *Inferno* (1976) and *Lucifer's Hammer* (1977). His later works include *The Long ARM of Gil Hamilton* (1976), *A World Out of Time* (1976), *Convergent Series* (1979), *The Ringworld Engineers* (1979), *The Patchwork Girl* (1980), *Dream Park* (1982; in collaboration with Steven Barnes), *Limits* (1985), *The Barsoom Project* (1989), and *N-Space* (1990). He presently lives in California.

"A Relic of Empire" is a pivotal story in Niven's Known Space series. The series as a whole has been hailed by critics as one of the best future histories in the annals of science fiction.

WHEN THE SHIP arrived, Dr. Richard Schultz-Mann was out among the plants, flying over and around them on a lift belt. He hovered over one inspecting with proprietary interest an anomalous patch in its yellow foliage. This one would soon be ripe.

The nature-lover was a breadstick of a man, very tall and very thin, with an aristocratic head sporting a close-cropped growth of coppery hair and an asymmetric beard. A white streak ran above his right ear and there was a patch of white on each side of the chin, one coinciding with the waxed spike. As his head moved in the double sunlight, the patches changed color instantly.

He took a tissue sample frorn the grayish patch, stored it, and started to move on....

The ship came down like a daylight meteor, streaking blue-white across the vague red glare of Big Mira. It slowed and circled high overhead, weaving drunkenly across the sky, then settled toward the plain near Mann's *Explorer.* Mann watched it land, then gave up his bumblebee activities and went to welcome the newcomers. He was amazed at the coincidence. As far as he knew, his had been the first ship ever to land here. The company would be good...but what could anyone possibly want here?

Little Mira set while he was skimming back. A flash of white at the far edge of the sea, and the tiny blue-white dwarf was gone. The shadows changed abruptly, turning the world red. Mann took off his pink-tinged goggles. Big Mira was still high, sixty degrees above the horizon and two hours from second sunset.

The newcomer was huge, a thick blunt-nosed cylinder twenty times the size of the *Explorer.* It looked old: not damaged, not even weathered, but indefinably old. Its nose was still closed tight, the living bubble retracted, if indeed it had a living bubble. Nothing moved nearby. They must be waiting for his welcome before they debarked.

Mann dropped toward the newcomer.

The stunner took him a few hundred feet up. Without pain and without sound, suddenly all Mann's muscles turned to loose jelly. Fully conscious and completely helpless, he continued to dive toward the ground.

Three figures swarmed up at him from the newcomer's oversized air lock. They caught him before he hit. Tossing humorous remarks at each other in a language Mann did not know, they towed him down to the plain.

The man behind the desk wore a captain's hat and a cheerful smile. "Our supply of Verinol is limited," he said in the trade language. "If I have to use it, I will, but I'd rather save it. You may have heard that it has unpleasant side effects."

"I understand perfectly," said Mann. "You'll use it the moment you think you've caught me in a lie." Since he had not yet been injected with the stuff, he decided it was a bluff. The man had no Verinol, if indeed there was such an animal as Verinol.

But he was still in a bad hole. The ancient, renovated ship held more than a dozen men, whereas Mann seriously doubted if he could have stood up. The sonic had not entirely worn off.

His captor nodded approvingly. He was huge and square, almost a cartoon of a heavy-planet man, with muscularity as smooth and solid as an elephant's. A Jinxian, for anyone's money. His size made the tiny shipboard office seem little more than a coffin. Among the crew his captain's hat would not be needed to enforce orders. He looked like he could kick holes in hullmetal, or teach tact to an armed Kzin.

"You're quick," he said. "That's good. I'll be asking questions about you and about this planet. You'll give truthful, complete answers. If some of my questions get too personal, say so; but remember, I'll use the Verinol if I'm not satisfied. How old are you?"

"One hundred and fifty-four."

"You look much older."

"I was off boosterspice for a couple of decades."

"Tough luck. Planet of origin?"

"Wunderland."

"Thought so, with that stick-figure build. Name?"

"Doctor Richard Harvey Schultz-Mann."

"Rich Mann, hah? Are you?"

Trust a Jinxian to spot a pun. "No. After I make my reputation, I'll write a book on the Slaver Empire. Then I'll be rich."

"If you say so. Married?"

"Several times. Not at the moment."

"Rich Mann, I can't give you my real name, but you can call me Captain Kidd. What kind of beard is that?"

"You've never seen an asymmetric beard?"

"No, thank the Mist Demons. It looks like you've shaved off all your hair below the part, and everything on your face left of what looks like a one-tuft goatee. Is that the way it's supposed to go?"

"Exactly so."

"You did it on purpose then."

"Don't mock me, Captain Kidd."

"Point taken. Are they popular on Wunderland?"

Dr. Mann unconsciously sat a little straighter. "Only among those willing to take the time and trouble to keep it neat." He twisted the single waxed spike of beard at the right of his chin with unconscious complacence. This was the only straight hair on his face—the rest of the beard being close-cropped and curly—and it sprouted from one of the white patches. Mann was proud of his beard.

"Hardly seems worth it," said the Jinxian. "I assume it's to show you're one of the leisure classes. What are you doing on Mira Ceti-T?"

"I'm investigating one aspect of the Slaver Empire."

"You're a geologist, then?"

"No, a xenobiologist."

"I don't understand."

"What do you know about the Slavers?"

"A little. They used to live all through this part of the galaxy. One day the slave races decided they'd had enough, and there was a war. When it was over, everyone was dead."

"You know quite a bit. Well, Captain, a billion and a half years is a long time. The Slavers left only two kinds of evidence of their existence. There are the stasis boxes and their contents, mostly weaponry, but records have been found too. And there are the plants and animals developed for the Slavers' convenience by their tnuctip slaves, who were biological engineers."

"I know about those. We have bandersnatchi on Jinx, on both sides of the ocean."

"The bandersnatchi food animals are a special case. They can't mutate; their chromosomes are as thick as your finger, too large to be influenced by radiation. All other relics of tnuctipun engineering have mutated almost beyond recognition. Almost. For the past twelve years I've been searching out and identifying the surviving species."

"It doesn't sound like a fun way to spend a life, Rich Mann. Are there Slaver animals on this planet?"

"Not animals, but plants. Have you been outside yet?"

"Not yet."

"Then come out. I'll show you."

The ship was very large. It did not seem to be furnished with a living bubble, hence the entire lifesystem must be enclosed within the metal walls. Mann walked ahead of the Jinxian down a long unpainted corridor to the airlock, waited inside while the pressure dropped slightly, then rode the escalator to the ground. He would not try to escape yet, though the sonic had worn off. The Jinxian was affable but alert, he carried a flashlight-laser dangling from his belt, his men were all around them, and Mann's lift belt had been removed. Richard Mann was not quixotic.

It was a red, red world. They stood on a dusty plain sparsely scattered with strange yellow-headed bushes. A breeze blew things like tumbleweeds across the plain, things which on second glance were the dried heads of former bushes. No other life-forms were visible. Big Mira sat on the horizon, a vague, fiery semicircular cloud, just dim enough to look at without squinting. Outlined in sharp black silhouette against the red giant's bloody disk were three slender, improbably tall spires, unnaturally straight and regular, each with a vivid patch of yellow vegetation surrounding its base. Members of the Jinxian's crew ran, walked, or floated outside, some playing an improvised variant of baseball, others at work, still others merely enjoying themselves. None were Jinxian, and none had Mann's light-planet build. Mann noticed that a few were using the thin wire blades of variable-knives to cut down some of the straight bushes.

"Those," he said.

"The bushes?"

"Yes. They used to be tnuctip stage trees. We don't know what they looked like originally, but the old records say the Slavers stopped using them some decades before the rebellion. May I ask what those men are doing in my ship?"

Expanded from its clamshell nose, the *Explorer's* living bubble was bigger than the *Explorer.* Held taut by air pressure, isolated from the surrounding environment, proof against any atmospheric chemistry found in nature, the clear fabric hemisphere was a standard feature of all camper-model spacecraft. Mann could see biped shadows moving purposefully about inside and going between the clamshell doors into the ship proper.

"They're not stealing anything, Rich Mann. I sent them in to remove a few components from the drives and the comm systems."

"One hopes they won't damage what they remove."

"They won't. They have their orders."

"I assume you don't want me to call someone," said Mann. He noticed that the men were preparing a bonfire, using stage bushes. The bushes were like miniature trees, four to six feet tall, slender and straight, and the brilliant yellow foliage at the top was flattened like the head of a dandelion. From the low, rounded eastern mountains to the western sea, the red land was sprinkled with the yellow dots of their heads. Men were cutting off the heads and roots, then dragging the logs away to pile them in conical formation over a stack of death-dry tumbleweed heads.

"We don't want you to call the Wunderland police, who happen to be somewhere out there looking for us."

"I hate to pry—"

"No, no, you're entitled to your curiosity. We're pirates."

"Surely you jest. Captain Kidd, if you've figured out a way to make piracy pay off, you must be bright enough to make ten times the money on the stock market."

"Why?"

By the tone of his voice, by his gleeful smile, the Jinxian was baiting him. Fine; it would keep his mind off stage trees. Mann said, "Because you can't *catch* a ship in hyperspace. The only way you can match courses with a ship is to wait until it's in an inhabited system. Then the police come calling."

"I know an inhabited system where there aren't any police."

"The hell you do."

They had walked more or less aimlessly to the *Explorer's* airlock. Now the Jinxian turned and gazed out over the red plain, toward the dwindling crescent of Big Mira, which now looked like a bad forest fire. "I'm curious about those spires."

"Fine, keep your little secret. I've wondered about them myself, but I haven't had a chance to look at them yet."

"I'd think they'd interest you. They look definitely artificial to me."

"But they're a billion years too young to be Slaver artifacts."

"Rich Mann, are those bushes the only life on this planet?"

"I haven't seen anything else," Mann lied.

"Then it couldn't have been a native race that put those spires up. I never heard of a space-traveling race that builds such big things for mere monuments."

"Neither did I. Shall we look at them tomorrow?"

"Yes." Captain Kidd stepped into the *Explorer's* airlock, wrapped a vast hand gently around Mann's thin wrist and pulled his captive in beside him. The airlock cycled and Mann followed the Jinxian into the living bubble with an impression that the Jinxian did not quite trust him.

Fine.

It was dark inside the bubble. Mann hesitated before turning on the light. Outside he could see the last red sliver of Big Mira shrinking with visible haste. He saw more. A man was kneeling before the conical bonfire, and a flickering light was growing in the dried bush-head kindling.

Mann turned on the lights, obliterating the outside view. "Go on about piracy," he said.

"Oh, yes." The Jinxian dropped into a chair, frowning. "Piracy was only the end product. It started a year ago, when I found the puppeteer system."

"The—"

"Yes. The puppeteers' home system."

Richard Mann's ears went straight up. He was from Wunderland, remember?

Puppeteers are highly intelligent, herbivorous, and very old as a species. Their corner on interstellar business is as old as the human Bronze Age. And they are cowards.

A courageous puppeteer is not regarded as insane only by other puppeteers. It *is* insane, and usually shows disastrous secondary symptoms: depression, homicidal tendencies, and the like. These poor, warped minds are easy to spot. No sane puppeteer will cross a vehicular roadway or travel in any but the safest available fashion or resist a thief, even an unarmed thief. No sane puppeteer will leave his home system, wherever that may be, without his painless method of suicide, nor will it walk an alien world without guards—nonpuppeteer guards.

The location of the puppeteer system is one of the puppeteer's most closely guarded secrets. Another is the painless suicide gimmick. It may be a mere trick of preconditioning. Whatever it is, it works. Puppeteers cannot be tortured into revealing anything about their home world, though they hate pain. It must be a world with reasonably earthlike atmosphere and temperature, but beyond that nothing is known...or was known.

Suddenly Mann wished that they hadn't lit the bonfire so soon. He didn't know how long it would burn before the logs caught, and he wanted to hear more about this.

"I found it just a year ago," the Jinxian repeated. "It's best I don't tell you what I was doing up to then. The less you know about who I am, the better. But when I'd got safely out of the system, I came straight home. I wanted time to think."

"And you picked piracy? Why not blackmail?"

"I thought of that—"

"I should hope so! Can you imagine what the puppeteers would pay to keep that secret?"

"Yes. That's what stopped me. Rich Mann, how much would you have asked for in one lump sum?"

"A round billion stars and immunity from prosecution."

"Okay. Now look at it from the puppeteer point of view. That billion wouldn't buy them complete safety, because you might still talk. But if they spent a tenth of that on detectives, weapons, hit men, et cetera they could shut your mouth for keeps and also find and hit anyone you might have talked to. I couldn't figure any way to make myself safe and still collect, not with that much potential power against me.

"So I thought of piracy.

"Eight of us had gone in, but I was the only one who'd guessed just what we'd stumbled into. I let the others in on it. Some had friends they could trust, and that raised our number to fourteen. We bought a ship, a very old one, and renovated it. She's an old slowboat's ground-to-orbit auxiliary fitted out with a new hyperdrive; maybe you noticed?"

"No. I saw how old she was."

"We figured even if the puppeteers recognized her, they'd never trace her. We took her back to the puppeteer system and waited."

A flickering light glimmered outside the bubble wall. Any second now the logs would catch...Mann tried to relax.

"Pretty soon a ship came in. We waited till it was too deep in the system's gravity well to jump back into hyperspace. Then we matched courses. Naturally they surrendered right away. We went in in suits so they couldn't describe us even if they could tell humans apart. Would you believe they had six hundred million stars in currency?"

"That's pretty good pay. What went wrong?"

"My idiot crew wouldn't leave. We'd figured most of the ships coming into the puppeteer system would be carrying money. They're misers, you know. Part of being a coward is wanting security. And they do most of their mining and manufacturing on other worlds, where they can get labor. So we waited for two more ships, because we had room for lots more money. The puppeteers wouldn't dare attack us inside their own system." Captain Kidd made a sound of disgust. "I can't really blame the men. In a sense they were right. One ship with a fusion drive can do a hell of a lot of damage just by hovering over a city. So we stayed.

"Meanwhile the puppeteers registered a formal complaint with Earth.

"Earth hates people who foul up interstellar trade. We'd offered physical harm to a puppeteer. A thing like that could cause a stock-market crash. So Earth offered the services of every police force in human space. Hardly seems fair, does it?"

"They ganged up on you. But they still couldn't come after you, could they? The puppeteers would have to tell the police how to find their system. They'd hardly do that; not when some human descendant might attack them a thousand years from now."

The Jinxian dialed himself a frozen daiquiri. "They had to wait till we left. I still don't know how they tracked us. Maybe they've got something that can track a gravity warp moving faster than light. I wouldn't put it past them to build it just for us. Anyway, when we angled toward Jinx, we heard them telling the police of We Made It just where we were."

"Ouch."

"We headed for the nearest double star. Not my idea; Hermie Preston's. He thought we could hide in the dust clouds in the trojan points. Whatever the puppeteers were using probably couldn't find us in normal space." Two thirsty gulps had finished his daiquiri. He crumpled the cup, watch it evaporate, dialed another. "The nearest double star was Mira Cet. We hardly expected to find a planet in the trailing trojan point, but as long as it was there, we decided to use it."

"And here you are."

"Yeah."

"You'll be better off when you've found a way to hide that ship."

"We had to find out about you first, Rich Mann. Tomorrow we'll sink the *Puppet Master* in the ocean. Already we've shut off the fusion drive. The lifters work by battery, and the cops can't detect that."

"Fine. Now for the billion-dollar—"

"No, no, Rich Mann. I will not tell you where to find the puppeteer planet. Give up the whole idea. Shall we join the campfire group?"

Mann came joltingly alert. *How* had the stage trees lasted this long? Thinking fast, he said, "Is your autokitchen as good as mine?"

"Probably not. Why?"

"Let me treat your group to dinner, Captain Kidd."

Captain Kidd shook his head, smiling. "No offense, Rich Mann, but I can't read your kitchen controls, and there's no point in tempting you. You might rashly put someth—"

WHAM!

The living bubble bulged inward, snapped back. Captain Kidd swore and ran for the airlock. Mann stayed seated, motionless, hoping against hope that the Jinxian had forgotten him.

WHAM! WHAM! Flares of light from the region of the campfire. Captain Kidd frantically punched the cycle button, and the opaque inner door closed on him. Mann came to his feet, running.

WHAM! The concussion hurt his ears and set the bubble rippling. Burning logs must be flying in all directions. The airlock recycled, empty. No telling where the Jinxian was; the outer door was opaque too. Well, that worked both ways.

WHAM!

Mann searched through the airlock locker, pushing sections of spacesuit aside to find the lift belt. It wasn't there. He'd been wearing it; they'd taken it off him after they shot him down.

He moaned: a tormented, uncouth sound to come from a cultured Wunderlander He *had* to have a lift belt.

WHAMWHAMWHAM. Someone was screaming far away.

Mann snatched up the suit's chest-and-shoulder section and locked it around him. It was rigid vacuum armor, with a lift motor built into the back. He took an extra moment to screw down the helmet, then hit the cycle button.

No use searching for weapons. They'd have taken even a variable-knife.

The Jinxian could be just outside waiting. He might have realized the truth by now.

The door opened.... Captain Kidd was easy to find, a running misshapen shadow and a frantic booming voice. "Flatten out, you yeastheads! It's an attack!" He hadn't guessed. But he must know that the We Made It police would use stunners.

Mann twisted his lift control to full power.

The surge of pressure took him under the armpits. Two standard gees sent blood rushing to his feet, pushed him upward with four times Wunderland's gravity. A last stage log exploded under him, rocked him back and forth, and then all was dark and quiet.

He adjusted the attitude setting to slant him almost straight forward. The dark ground sped beneath him. He moved northeast. Nobody was following him—yet.

Captain Kidd's men would have been killed, hurt, or at least stunned when the campfire exploded in their faces. He'd expected Captain Kidd to chase him, but the Jinxian couldn't have caught him. Lift motors are all alike, and Mann wasn't as heavy as the Jinxian.

He flew northeast, flying very low, knowing that the only landmarks big enough to smash him were the spires to the west. When he could no longer see the ships' lights, he turned south, still very low. Still nobody followed him. He was glad he'd taken the helmet; it protected his eyes from the wind.

In the blue dawn he came awake. The sky was darker than navy blue, and the light around him was dim, like blue moonlight. Little Mira was a hurtingly bright pinpoint between two mountain peaks, bright enough to sear holes in a man's retinae. Mann unscrewed his helmet, adjusted the pink goggles over his eyes. Now it was even darker.

He poked his nose above the yellow moss. The plain and sky were empty of men. The pirates must be out looking for him, but, they hadn't gotten here yet. So far so good.

Far out across the plain there was fire. A stage tree rose rapidly into the black sky, minus its roots and flowers, the wooden flanges at its base holding it in precarious aerodynamic stability. A white rope of smoke followed it up. When the smoke cut off, the tree became invisible...until, much higher, there was a puff of white cloud like a flak burst. Now the seeds would be spreading across the sky.

Richard Mann smiled. Wonderful, how the stage trees had adapted to the loss of their masters. The Slavers had raised them on wide plantations, using the solid-fuel rocket cores inside the living bark to lift their ships from places where a fusion drive would have done damage. But the trees used the rockets for reproduction, to scatter their seeds farther than any plant before them.

Ah, well...Richard Mann snuggled deeper into the yellow woolly stuff around him and began to consider his next move. He was a hero now in the eyes of humanity-at-large. He had badly damaged the pirate crew. When the police landed, he could count on a reward from the puppeteers. Should he settle for that or go on to bigger stakes?

The *Puppet Master's* cargo was bigger stakes, certainly. But even if he could take it, which seemed unlikely, how could he fit it into his ship? How escape the police of We Made It?

No. Mann had another stake in mind, one just as valuable and infinitely easier to hide.

What Captain Kidd apparently hadn't realized was that blackmail is not immoral to a puppeteer. There are well-established rules of conduct that make blackmail perfectly safe both for blackmailer and victim. Two are that the blackmailer must submit to having certain portions of his memory erased, and must turn over all evidence against the victim. Mann was prepared to do this if he could force Captain Kidd to tell him where to find the puppeteer system.

But how?

Well, he knew one thing the Jinxian didn't....

Little Mira rose fast, arc blue, a hole into hell. Mann remained where he was, an insignificant mote in the yellow vegetation below one of the spires Captain Kidd had remarked on last night. The spire was a good half mile high. An artifact that size would seem impossibly huge to any but an Earthman. The way it loomed over him made Mann uncomfortable. In shape it was a slender cone with a base three hundred feet across. The surface near the base was gray and smooth to touch, like polished granite.

The yellow vegetation was a thick, rolling carpet. It spread out around the spire in an uneven circle half a mile in diameter and dozens of feet deep. It rose about the base in a thick turtleneck collar. Close up, the stuff wasn't even discrete plants. It looked like a cross between moss and wool, dyed flagrant yellow.

It made a good hiding place. Not perfect, of course; a heat sensor would pick him out in a flash. He hadn't thought of that last night, and now it worried him. Should he get out, try to reach the sea?

The ship would certainly carry a heat sensor, but not a portable one. A portable heat sensor would be a weapon, a nighttime gunsight, and weapons of war had been illegal for some time in human space.

But the *Puppet Master* could have stopped elsewhere to get such implements. Kzinti, for example.

Nonsense. Why would Captain Kidd have needed portable weapons with night gunsights? He certainly hadn't expected puppeteers to fight hand-to-hand! The stunners were mercy weapons; even a pirate would not dare kill a puppeteer, and Captain Kidd was no ordinary pirate.

All right. Radar? He need only burrow into the moss/wool. Sight search? Same answer. Radio? Mental note: Do not transmit anything.

Mental note? There was a dictaphone in his helmet. He used it after pulling the helmet out of the moss/wool around him.

Flying figures. Mann watched them for a long moment, trying to spot the Jinxian. There were only four, and he wasn't among them. The four were flying northwest of him, moving south. Mann ducked into the moss.

"Hello, Rich Mann."

The voice was low, contorted with fury. Mann felt the shock race through him, contracting every muscle with the fear of death. It came from behind him!

From his helmet.

"Hello, Rich Mann. Guess where I am?"

He couldn't turn it off. Spacesuit helmet radios weren't built to be turned off: a standard safety factor. If one were fool enough to ignore safety, one could insert an "off" switch; but Mann had never felt the need.

"I'm in your ship, using your ship-to-suit radio circuit. That was a good trick you played last night. I didn't even know what a stage tree was till I looked it up in your library."

He'd just have to endure it. A pity he couldn't answer back.

"You killed four of my men and put five more in the autodoc tanks. Why'd you do it, Rich Mann? You must have known we weren't going to kill you. Why should we? There's no blood on *our* hands."

You lie, Mann thought at the radio. *People die in a market crash. And the ones who live are the ones who suffer. Do you know what it's like to be suddenly poor and not know how to live poor?*

"I'll assume you want something, Rich Mann. All right. What? The money in my hold? That's ridiculous. You'd never get in. You want to turn us in for a reward? Fat chance. You've got no weapons. If we find you now, we'll kill you."

The four searchers passed far to the west, their headlamps spreading yellow light across the blue dusk. They were no danger to him now. A pity they and their fellows should have been involved in what amounted to a vendetta.

"The puppeteer planet, of course. The modern El Dorado. But you don't know where it is, do you? I wonder if I ought to give you a hint. Of course you'd never know whether I was telling the truth...."

Did the Jinxian know how to live poor? Mann shuddered. The old memories came back only rarely; but when they came, they hurt.

You have to learn not to buy luxuries before you've bought necessities. You can starve learning which is which. Necessities are food and a place to sleep, shoes and pants. Luxuries are tobacco, restaurants, fine shirts, throwing away a ruined meal while you're learning to cook, quitting a job you don't like. A union is a necessity. Boosterspice is a luxury.

The Jinxian wouldn't know about that. He'd had the money to buy his own ship.

"Ask me politely, Rich Mann. Would you like to know where I found the puppeteer system?"

Mann had leased the *Explorer* on a college grant. It had been the latest step in a long climb upward. Before that...

He was half his lifetime old when the crash came. Until then boosterspice had kept him as young as the ageless idle ones who were his friends and relatives. Overnight he was one of the hungry. A number of his partners in disaster had ridden their lift belts straight up into eternity; Richard Schultz-Mann had sold his for his final dose of boosterspice. Before he could afford boosterspice again, there were wrinkles in his forehead, the texture of his skin had changed, his sex urge had decreased, strange white patches had appeared in his hair, there were twinges in his back. He still got them.

Yet always he had maintained his beard. With the white spike and the white streak it looked better than ever. After the boosterspice restored color to his hair, he dyed the patches back in again.

"Answer me, Rich Mann!"

Go ride a bandersnatch.

It was a draw. Captain Kidd couldn't entice him into answering, and Mann would never know the pirate's secret. If Kidd dropped his ship in the sea, Mann could show it to the police. At least that would be something.

Luckily Kidd couldn't move the *Explorer*. Otherwise he could take both ships half around the planet, leaving Mann stranded.

The four pirates were far to the south. Captain Kidd had apparently given up on the radio. There were water and food syrup in his helmet; Mann would not starve.

Where in blazes were the police? On the other side of the planet?

Stalemate.

Big Mira came as a timorous peeping Tom, poking its rim over the mountains like red smoke. The land brightened, taking on tinges of lavender against long, long navy blue shadows. The shadows shortened and became vague.

The morality of his position was beginning to bother Dr. Richard Mann.

In attacking the pirates, he had done his duty as a citizen. The pirates had sullied humanity's hard-won reputation for honesty. Mann had struck back.

But his motive? Fear had been two parts of that motive. First, the fear that Captain Kidd might decide to shut his mouth. Second, the fear of being poor.

That fear had been with him for some time.

Write a book and make a fortune! It looked good on paper. The thirty-light-year sphere of human space contained nearly fifty billion readers. Persuade one percent of them to shell out half a star each for a disposable tape, and your four-percent royalties became twenty million stars. But most books nowadays were flops. You had to scream very loud nowadays to get the attention of even ten billion readers. Others were trying to drown you out.

Before Captain Kidd, that had been Richard Schultz-Mann's sole hope of success.

He'd behaved within the law. Captain Kidd couldn't make that claim; but Captain Kidd hadn't killed anybody.

Mann sighed. He'd had no choice. His major motive was honor, and that motive still held.

He moved restlessly in his nest of damp moss/wool. The day was heating up, and his suit's temperature control would not work with half a suit.

What was that?

It was the *Puppet Master,* moving effortlessly toward him on its lifters. The Jinxian must have decided to get it under water before the human law arrived.

...Or had he?

Mann adjusted his lift motor until he was just short of weightless, then moved cautiously around the spire. He saw the four pirates moving to intersect the *Puppet Master.* They'd see him if he left the spire. But if he stayed, those infrared detectors...

He'd have to chance it.

The suit's padded shoulders gouged his armpits as he streaked toward the second spire. He stopped in midair over the moss and dropped, burrowed in it. The pirates didn't swerve.

Now he'd see.

The ship slowed to a stop over the spire he'd just left.

"Can you hear me, Rich Mann?"

Mann nodded gloomily to himself. Definitely, that was it.

"I should have tried this before. Since you're nowhere in sight, you've either left the vicinity altogether or you're hiding in the thick bushes around those towers."

Should he try to keep dodging from spire to spire? Or could he outfly them?

At least one was bound to be faster. The armor increased his weight.

"I hope you took the opportunity to examine this tower. It's fascinating. Very smooth, stony surface, except at the top. A perfect cone, also except at the top. You listening? The tip of this thing swells from an eight-foot neck into an egg-shaped knob fifteen feet across. The knob isn't polished as smooth as the rest of it. Vaguely reminiscent of an asparagus spear, wouldn't you say?"

Richard Schultz-Mann cocked his head, tasting an idea.

He unscrewed his helmet, ripped out and pocketed the radio. In frantic haste he began ripping out double handfuls of the yellow moss/wool, stuffed them into a wad in the helmet, and turned his lighter on it. At first the vegetation merely smoldered, while Mann muttered through clenched teeth. Then it caught with a weak blue smokeless flame. Mann placed his helmet in a mossy nest, setting it so it would not tip over and spill its burning contents.

"I'd have said a phallic symbol, myself. What do you think, Rich Mann? If these are phallic symbols, they're pretty well distorted. Humanoid but not human, you might say."

The pirates had joined their ship. They hovered around its floating silver bulk, ready to drop on him when the *Puppet Master's* infrared detectors found him.

Mann streaked away to the west on full acceleration, staying as low as he dared. The spire would shield him for a minute or so, and then...

"This vegetation isn't stage trees, Rich Mann. It looks like some sort of grass from here. Must need something in the rock they made these erections out of. Mph. No hot spots. You're not down there after all. Well, we try the next one."

Behind him, in the moments when he dared look back, Mann saw the *Puppet Master* move to cover the second spire, the one he'd left a moment ago, the one with a gray streak in the moss at its base. Four humanoid dots clustered loosely above the ship.

"Peekaboo," came the Jinxian's voice. "And good-bye, killer."

The *Puppet Master's* fusion drive went on. Fusion flame lashed out in a blue-white spear, played down the side of the pillar and into the moss/wool below. Mann faced forward and concentrated on flying. He felt neither elation nor pity, but only disgust. The Jinxian was a fool after all. He'd seen no life on Mira Ceti-T but for the stage trees. He had Mann's word that there was none. Couldn't he reach the obvious conclusion? Perhaps the moss/wool had fooled him. It certainly did look like yellow moss, clustering around the spires as if it needed some chemical element in the stone.

A glance back told him that the pirate ship was still spraying white flame over the spire and the foliage below. He'd have been a cinder by now. The Jinxian must want him extremely dead. Well—

The spire went all at once. It sat on the lavender plain in a hemisphere of multicolored fire, engulfing the other spires and the Jinxian ship; and then it began to expand and rise. Mann adjusted his attitude to vertical to get away from the ground. A moment later the shock wave slammed into him and blew him tumbling over the desert.

Two white ropes of smoke rose straight up through the dimming explosion cloud. The other spires were taking off while still green! Fire must have reached the foliage at their bases.

Mann watched them go with his head thrown back and his body curiously loose in the vacuum armor. His expression was strangely contented. At these times he could forget himself and his ambitions in the contemplation of immortality.

Two knots formed simultaneously in the rising smoke trails. Second stage on. They rose very fast now.

"Rich Mann."

Mann flicked his transmitter on. "You'd live through anything."

"Not Me. I can't feel anything below my shoulders. Listen, Rich Mann, I'll trade secrets with you. What happened?"

"The big towers are stage trees."

"Uh?" Half question, half an expression of agony.

"A stage tree has two life cycles. One is the bush, the other is the big multistage form." Mann talked fast, fearful of losing his audience. "The forms alternate. A stage tree seed lands on a planet and grows into a bush. Later there are lots of bushes. When a seed hits a particularly fertile spot, it grows into a multistage form. You still there?"

"Yuh."

"In the big form the living part is the tap root and the photosynthetic organs around the base. That way the rocket section doesn't have to carry so much weight. It grows straight up out of the living part, but it's as dead as the center of an oak except for the seed at the top. When it's ripe, the rocket takes off. Usually it'll reach terminal velocity for the system it's in. Kidd, I can't see your ship; I'll have to wait till the smoke—"

"Just keep talking."

"I'd like to help."

"Too late. Keep talking."

"I've tracked the stage trees across twenty light-years of space. God knows where they started. They're all through the systems around here. The seed pods spend hundreds of thousands of years in space; and when they enter a system, they explode. If there's a habitable world, one seed is bound to hit it. If there isn't, there's lots more pods where that one came from. It's immortality, Captain Kidd. This one plant has traveled farther than mankind, and it's much older. A billion and a—"

"Mann."

"Yah."

"Twenty-three point six, seventy point one, six point nil. I don't know its name on the star charts. Shall I repeat that?"

Mann forgot the stage trees. "Better repeat it."

"Twenty-three point six, seventy point one, six point nothing. Hunt in that area till you find it. It's a red giant, undersized. Planet is small, dense, no moon."

"Got it."

"You're stupid if you use it. You'll have the same luck I did. That's why I told you."

"I'll use blackmail."

"They'll kill you. Otherwise I wouldn't have said. Why'd you kill me, Rich Mann?"

"I didn't like your remarks about my beard. Never insult a Wunderlander's asymmetric beard, Captain Kidd."

"I won't do it again."

"I'd like to help." Mann peered into the billowing smoke. Now it was a black pillar tinged at the edges by the twin sunlight. "Still can't see your ship."

"You will in a moment."

The pirate moaned...and Mann saw the ship. He managed to turn his head in time to save his eyes.

How the World Was Saved

Stanislaw Lem

Stanislaw Lem (b. 1921) was born in Lvov, Poland. Lem studied medicine, but his education was interrupted by the German occupation of Poland. In 1946, he finally received his M.D. and moved to Krakow to practice. His first novel, *The Astronauts,* was published in 1951. Lem continued writing to supplement his income, producing such books as *The Magellen Nebula* (1955), *Eden* (1959), *The Investigation* (1959), *Memoirs Found in a Bathtub* (1961), *Solaris* (1961). In the 1960's, Lem's work began to be translated in Europe and the United States. Later works such as *Tales of Pirx the Pilot* (1968) and *His Master's Voice* (1968) garnered him an invitation to become an honorary member of the Science Fiction Writers Association in 1973. The appearance of his critique of American science fiction that year, *Fantastyka i Futurologia,* so angered SFWA members that the offer was quickly rescinded. His later works include *The Cyberiad* (1974), *Chains of Chance* (1978), *Golem XN* (1981), and *More Tales of Pirx the Pilot* (1982).

Lem's style can be grim and philosophical, like in his classic novel *Solaris,* or fun and playful, like in this story from *The Cyberiad.* With great wit and humor, he demonstrates why the adage about watching what you wish for is still all-too-true.

ONE DAY TRURL the constructor put together a machine that could create anything starting with *n*. When it was ready, he tried it out, ordering it to make needles, then nankeens and negligees, which it did, then nail the lot to narghiles filled with nepenthe and numerous other narcotics. The machine carried out his instructions to the letter. Still not completely sure of its ability, he had it produce, one after the other, nimbuses, noodles, nuclei, neutrons, naphtha, noses, nymphs, naiads, and natrium. This last it could not do, and Trurl, considerably irritated, demanded an explanation.

"Never heard of it," said the machine.

"What? But it's only sodium. You know, the metal, the element..."

"Sodium starts with an *s*, and I work only in *n*."

"But in Latin it's *natrium.*"

"Look, old boy," said the machine, "if I could do everything starting with *n* in every possible language, I'd be a Machine That Could Do Everything in the Whole Alphabet, since any item you care to mention undoubtedly starts with *n* in one foreign language or another. It's not that easy. I can't go beyond what you programmed. So no sodium."

"Very well," said Trurl and ordered it to make Night, which it made at once—small perhaps, but perfectly nocturnal. Only then did Trurl invite over his friend Klapaucius the constructor, and introduced him to the machine, praising its extraordinary skill at such length, that Klapaucius grew annoyed and inquired whether he too might not test the machine.

"Be my guest," said Trurl. "But it has to start with *n.*"

"*N?*" said Klapaucius. "All right, let it make Nature."

The machine whined, and in a trice Trurl's front yard was packed with naturalists. They argued, each publishing heavy volumes, which the others tore to pieces; in the distance one could see flaming pyres, on which martyrs to Nature were sizzling; there was thunder, and strange mushroom-shaped columns of smoke rose up; everyone talked at once, no one listened, and there were all sorts of memoranda, appeals, subpoenas and other documents, while off to the side sat a few old men, feverishly scribbling on scraps of paper.

"Not bad, eh?" said Trurl with pride. "Nature to a T, admit it!"

But Klapaucius wasn't satisfied.

"What, that mob? Surely you're not going to tell me that's Nature?"

"Then give the machine something else," snapped Trurl. "Whatever you like." For a moment Klapaucius was at a loss for what to ask. But after a little thought he declared that he would put two more tasks to the machine; if it could fulfill them, he would admit that it was all Trurl said it was. Trurl agreed to this, whereupon Klapaucius requested Negative.

"Negative?!" cried Trurl. "What on earth is Negative?"

"The opposite of positive, of course," Klapaucius coolly replied. "Negative attitudes, the negative of a picture, for example. Now don't try to pretend you never heard of Negative. All right, machine, get to work!"

The machine, however, had already begun. First it manufactured antiprotons, then antielectrons, antineutrons, antineutrinos, and labored on, until from out of all this antimatter an antiworld took shape, glowing like a ghostly cloud above their heads.

"H'm," muttered Klapaucius, displeased. "That's supposed to be Negative? Well...let's say it is, for the sake of peace....But now here's the third command: Machine, do Nothing!"

The machine sat still. Klapaucius rubbed his hands in triumph, but Trurl said:

"Well, what did you expect? You asked it to do nothing, and it's doing nothing."

"Correction: I asked it to do Nothing, but it's doing nothing."

"Nothing is nothing!"

"Come, come. It was supposed to do Nothing, but it hasn't done anything, and therefore I've won. For Nothing, my dear and clever colleague, is not your run-of-the-mill nothing, the result of idleness and inactivity, but dynamic, aggressive Nothingness, that is to say, perfect, unique, ubiquitous, in other words Nonexistence, ultimate and supreme, in its very own nonperson!"

"You're confusing the machine!" cried Trurl. But suddenly its metallic voice rang out:

"Really, how can you two bicker at a time like this? Oh yes, I know what Nothing is, and Nothingness, Nonexistence, Nonentity, Negation, Nullity and Nihility, since all these come under the heading of *n*, *n* as in Nil. Look then upon your world for the last time, gentlemen! Soon it shall no longer be..."

The constructors froze, forgetting their quarrel, for the machine was in actual fact doing Nothing, and it did it in this fashion: one by one, various things were removed from the world, and the things, thus removed, ceased to exist, as if they had never been. The machine had already disposed of nolars, nightzebs, nocs, necs, nallyrakers, neotremes and nonmalrigers. At moments, though, it seemed that instead of reducing, diminishing and subtracting, the machine was increasing, enhancing and adding, since it liquidated, in turn: nonconformists, nonentities, nonsense, nonsupport, nearsightedness, narrowmindedness, naughtiness, neglect, nausea, necrophilia and nepotism. But after a while the world very definitely began to thin out around Trurl and Klapaucius.

"Omigosh!" said Trurl. "If only nothing bad comes out of all this..."

"Don't worry," said Klapaucius. "You can see it's not producing Universal Nothingness, but only causing the absence of whatever starts with *n*. Which is really nothing in the way of nothing, and nothing is what your machine, dear Trurl, is worth!"

"Do not be deceived," replied the machine. "I've begun, it's true, with everything in *n,* but only out of familiarity. To create however is one thing, to destroy, another thing entirely. I can blot out the world for the simple reason that I'm able to do anything and everything—and everything means everything—in *n,* and consequently Nothingness is child's play for me. In less than a minute now you will cease to have existence, along with everything else, so tell me now, Klapaucius, and quickly, that I am really and truly everything I was programmed to be, before it is too late."

"But—" Klapaucius was about to protest, but noticed, just then, that a number of things were indeed disappearing, and not merely those that started with *n.* The constructors were no longer surrounded by the gruncheons, the targalisks, the shupops, the calinatifacts, the thists, worches and pritons.

"Stop! I take it all back! Desist! Whoa! Don't do Nothing!!" screamed Klapaucius. But before the machine could come to a full stop, all the brashations, plusters, laries and zits had vanished away. Now the machine stood motionless. The world was a dreadful sight. The sky had particularly suffered: there were only a few, isolated points of light in the heavens—no trace of the glorious worches and zits that had, till now, graced the horizon!

"Great Gauss!" cried Klapaucius. "And where are the gruncheons? Where my dear, favorite pritons? Where now the gentle zits?!"

"They no longer are, nor ever will exist again," the machine said calmly. "I executed, or rather only began to execute, your order..."

"I tell you to do Nothing, and you...you..."

"Klapaucius, don't pretend to be a greater idiot than you are," said the machine. "Had I made Nothing outright, in one fell swoop, everything would have ceased to exist, and that includes Trurl, the sky, the Universe, and you—and even myself. In which case who could say and to whom could it be said that the order was carried out and I am an efficient and capable machine? And if no one could say it to no one, in what way then could I, who also would not be, be vindicated?"

"Yes, fine, let's drop the subject," said Klapaucius. "I have nothing more to ask of you, only please, dear machine, please return the zits, for without them life loses all its charm..."

"But I can't, they're in z," said the machine. "Of course, I can restore nonsense, narrowmindedness, nausea, necrophilia, neuralgia, nefariousness and noxiousness. As for the other letters, however, I can't help you."

"I want my zits!" bellowed Klapaucius.

"Sorry, no zits," said the machine. "Take a good look at this world, how riddled it is with huge, gaping holes, how full of Nothingness, the Nothingness that fills the bottomless void between the stars, how everything about us has become lined with it, how it darkly lurks behind each shred of matter. This is your work, envious one! And I hardly think the future generations will bless you for it..."

"Perhaps...they won't find out, perhaps they won't notice," groaned the pale Klapaucius, gazing up incredulously at the black emptiness of space and not daring to look his colleague, Trurl, in the eye. Leaving him beside the machine that could do everything in *n*, Klapaucius skulked home—and to this day the world has remained honeycombed with nothingness, exactly as it was when halted in the course of its liquidation. And as all subsequent attempts to build a machine on any other letter met with failure, it is to be feared that never again will we have such marvelous phenomena as the worches and the zits—no, never again.

Acknowledgements

Permission to reprint the following stories is gratefully acknowledged to the following:

ISAAC ASIMOV for "Nightfall." Originally presented in *Astounding* magazine. Copyright © 1941 by Street and Smith, Inc. Copyright renewed 1968, by Isaac Asimov. Reprinted by permission of the author.

ROBERT BLOCH for "Yours Truly, Jack the Ripper." Originally presented in *Weird Tales* magazine. Reprinted version from *Such Stuff as Screams are Made Of.* Copyright © 1971, 1977 by Robert Bloch. Reprinted by permission of the author.

DON COGDON ASSOCIATES for "The Veldt" by Ray Bradbury. From *The Illustrated Man.* Copyright © 1950, renewed 1977 by Ray Bradbury. Reprinted by permission of Don Cogdon Associates, Inc.

THE CONTINUUM PUBLISHING COMPANY for "How the World Was Saved" by Stanislaw Lem, translated by Michael Kandel. English translation Copyright © 1974 by The Continuum Publishing Company. Reprinted by permission of the publishing company.

FRITZ LEIBER and RICHARD CURTIS ASSOCIATES, INC., for "The Girl With the Hungry Eyes." Copyright © 1949 by Avon Books. Published with the cooperation of the author and his agents.

LARRY NIVEN and SPECTRUM LITERARY AGENCY for "Relic of Empire." Originally presented in *If* magazine. Copyright © 1966 by Galaxy Publishing Corporation. Reprinted by permission of the author and his agents.

THE PIMLICO AGENCY, INC. for "The Chimney" by Ramsey Campbell. From *Whispers I,* edited by Stuart David Schiff. Copyright © 1977 by Stuart David Schiff. "The Dead Line" by Dennis Etchison. Originally presented in *Whispers* #13-14. Copyright © 1979 by Stuart David Schiff. "The Man Who Lost The Sea" by Theodore Sturgeon. From *The Magazine of Fantasy and Science Fiction.* Copyright © 1956 by The Mercury Press. Copyright renewed 1980 by Theodore Sturgeon. Reprinted by permission of the authors and The Pimlico Agency.

SCOTT MEREDITH LITERARY AGENCY for "The Sentinel" by Arthur C. Clarke. From *The Avon Science Fiction and Fantasy Reader.* Copyright © 1951 by Avon Periodicals, Inc. Copyright renewed 1953, 1983 by Arthur C.

Index to Volumes I-VI

A cumulative index to authors and stories